I0654931

# TRY HARDER

by

PETER SANKEY

ISBN 978-0-9919087-2-1

This is a work of fiction. Names, characters, places and incidents either are the product of the author's imagination or are used fictitiously. Any resemblance to actual persons, living or dead, events, or locales is entirely coincidental.

# Acknowledgements

Without the help and encouragement of Jerome Simpson, I never would have finished this book. Big thanks also to Leslie MacLeod for her invaluable assistance with copy editing. I'm also grateful to my wife and parents for their eternal love and support. Words can't express how much I appreciate it.

# June 26

Beyond the gates of the Mimico Correctional Centre, Buff was getting his first taste of fresh air as a free man. His real name was Bryan Burley, but nobody called him that outside of a courtroom.

Wearing a black suit and tie, he looked more like a banker than an ex-con. Not a thread was out of place, except for a big thick crease running right through the middle of it. That's what happens when you stuff a three-thousand-dollar British bespoke suit in a storage locker for eighteen months.

Buff had been convicted on a single charge of breaking and entering. Up until then his record was as clean as a preacher's sheets. He'd been connected to over a dozen scams and confidence schemes over the years, but since authorities only ever had flimsy circumstantial evidence, Buff was never charged with anything.

He was truly an excellent thief. Methodical and organized, he was responsible for hundreds of successful robberies. He never stole from anyone who couldn't afford it, rarely carried a gun, and left no trace. Among other thieves, his skills were legendary, particularly in the art of safe-cracking.

Two years earlier, his tenacity had gotten the best of him, and police caught him outside a jewellery store in Richmond Hill. He'd been behind bars ever since. He never should have served more than a few months, but since he was carrying an acetylene torch when he was caught, the police considered him "armed." As a result, the tenacious prosecutor pursued a tough prison sentence, and got it.

That was all behind him now. He was committed to changing his life. Things were going to be different. He was closer to forty than he'd like to admit, but he still had plenty of life left in him. He was smart. He still had his looks and his health. His body was in great shape, other than a little grey hair. If the lights were dim enough, someone could mistake him for a man ten years younger. For the first time since those handcuffs snapped down on his wrists, Buff felt confident about the future. This incarceration was just going to be a little setback.

Buff saw his sister waiting on the other side of the parking lot to pick him up. Her name was Emily, and she was a few years younger than him. Smart and hard-working, she carried a look of perpetual exhaustion. She was a law-abiding citizen who'd never even received a parking ticket, which put a strain on the relationship with her convict brother. Life had been tough for her. Emily worked hard for everything she had and she resented Buff for trying to skate by without paying his dues. Yet, Emily had faith that Buff could reform. Since she was the only family member still willing to speak with him, he was going to need Emily's help if he was serious about sorting out his life.

He tried smoothing out the crease in his jacket with the side of his hand. It was a futile move. He cursed the damn prison guards. They couldn't even bother to use a coat hanger.

As he walked towards his sister's decade-old Nissan Sentra, a sleek black limousine pulled into the parking lot. Buff watched it drive towards him, shimmering in the bright sun.

He let out a deep sigh. He knew exactly who the limousine belonged to, and it wasn't someone he was anxious to reconnect with. As it came to a stop, one of the tinted windows rolled down, and a rat-faced French Canadian named Roche popped his head out. He had a pencil-thin moustache, crooked yellow teeth and a cigarette dangling out of the corner of his mouth.

"Bonjour Buff," he squealed, with a stilted accent. "Is good to see you again. You dress nice just for to see me?"

"It's the only clean thing I had," replied Buff, forcing a smile. "It's nice to see you too, Roche." He was lying, of course. If he never saw Roche again, it still would have been too soon. He was nothing but a two-bit henchman for the French-Canadian mob, exactly the sort of person Buff was looking to avoid.

Roche opened his door and motioned for Buff to get inside.

"You come with me," said Roche. "I buy you a drink. Please. We have a talk."

"Thanks, but I've already got a ride," said Buff, pointing towards his sister.

"Jacques want to talk you."

"Tell him to use a phone."

"No, Jacques want to see you."

"He had eighteen months to come and see me. Visiting hours are over."

The conversation was starting to get heated. Roche paused for a moment. He knew he'd be in trouble if he went back to the boss without Buff. It was time to try a new tactic.

Roche pulled the cigarette out from between his teeth and smiled. "We miss you, Buff. The family is very happy with you. You stay quiet. You say no names. We want to show a thank you. We are very... what is the word?"

"Grateful."

"Oui, c'est ça! We are grateful. Jacques is grateful. He have a job for you. A big job. You are the best at the robbing the vault. You come with me."

Buff knelt down so that he was seeing eye-to-eye with Roche. In a calm, quiet voice he replied, "I won't. You tell Jacques that I appreciate the offer, but I'm out. I've moved on. So, thank you very much, but the answer is no."

Roche took a long drag off his cigarette as Buff stood back up.

"I understand. You just got out of jail, and you want to have some fun. You're not ready to talk business yet. That make sense. You think about it for couple of days, then you come down. You see us. You talk to Jacques."

"Thank you, but no."

Roche tried giving the most charming smile he could. "À bientôt, Buff," he said, and then rolled his window back up.

Buff watched as the limousine drove out of the parking lot and sped away. He hoped he wouldn't have to deal with that scumbag again.

Emily was leaning against her car with her arms crossed, looking more like a disappointed mother than a baby sister. When Buff walked over to her, there was no hug, no handshake, not even a nod.

"Was that a friend of yours?" asked Emily.

"More like a fan," replied Buff with a smirk. His sister did not look amused, so he dropped his grin. "He was a mistake from my past. I told him I was retired. You won't be seeing him anymore."

She rolled her eyes in disbelief.

"Whatever," she snorted dismissively, looking him up and down. "Nice suit."

"It was a rental."

Emily climbed into her car, reached over and unlocked the passenger side door. Buff opened it and got in. The car sputtered to life and drove away.

"If you're hungry, we can stop and pick up a burger from Harvey's on the way home. I don't have anything to eat in my apartment."

Buff shook his head. "No, thanks."

It was a twenty-minute drive back to Emily's apartment, and that was the only time they spoke the entire trip.

***

Emily lived in a modest one-bedroom apartment on Mutual Street. She lived alone, other than her six-year old pug Chang. The place was barely big enough for the two of them, and now Buff was moving in. It was sparsely furnished, but thoroughly clean and organized.

While his sister prepared coffee in the kitchen, Buff waited in the living room. There was a little TV in one corner, a small table and chairs in the other, and a single bookshelf lined with a dozen books about art. The walls were decorated with some classical art prints and a black-and-white poster of the Paris skyline. In the middle of the room was a futon that had been pulled out. Sheets, a pillow and an old blue comforter sat neatly folded on the corner. This was Buff's new bed, and it didn't look any more comfortable than the cot he had in prison.

Chang trotted over and nuzzled his snout into Buff's leg. It started wagging its little tail in appreciation as Buff gently scratched behind its ears. He couldn't believe how much that little dog had grown in two years. It looked up at him without judgment, and Buff smiled.

His clothes were now covered in dog hair. He carefully took off his jacket and draped it over the back of a chair. He started to unfold his new bedsheets when Emily walked in carrying two mugs.

"I don't have any milk," she said, handing Buff a cup. "There's sugar in the kitchen if you want."

"No, no. Thank you. Always bet on black."

Emily looked at him blankly for a moment. He took a sip of his coffee.

"Mmm, that's great."

It wasn't.

They sat down at the table in the corner, sharing silence for several minutes. Emily stared into her coffee, trying to avoid looking at her brother.

Buff spoke first. "This is a great place you've got here, Em. Right downtown, too. You've got a great view of the city."

She said nothing, and instead leaned over to pet Chang's neck.

"I want you to know how much I appreciate you letting me stay here. And for finding me a job, too. I can't thank you enough."

Chang rolled over onto his back, and she rubbed his belly.

"I promise you won't even know I'm here. I'll be out of here in a week. Two weeks at the most. As soon as I can afford it."

No response. Buff let out a deep sigh.

"Until I get my own place, though, I was hoping we could talk to each other."

Emily looked up and rolled her eyes.

"Look, Bryan, I'm willing to help you, but I haven't forgiven you yet. What you did to this family..."

The words got caught in her throat, and she took a breath.

"Forget it. No more lectures. And no more lies, either. Who was that man in the limousine?"

"In the parking lot?"

"Did you meet with more than one man in a limousine today?"

"He was nobody. Forget about him."

"What did he want to talk to you about?"

"Nothing. He was asking for directions."

"Bryan, either you tell me the truth about what's going on or I'll kick you out onto the street."

"Emily, please, don't worry about it."

She pounded her fists against the table, spilling her coffee. Chang sprang to his feet and scurried out of the room.

"Who was he?"

Buff slumped down into his chair.

"His name was Roche. He works for the Montagne family. We used to pull jobs together. He said he had a new one for me."

Emily let out a sigh of disgust, but Buff pressed on, calm and firm.

"I didn't know he was going to be there. I hadn't spoken to him in years. He showed up out of the blue, offered me a job, and I said no. I told him to leave me alone, that I never wanted to speak to him again. I'm done with that world. I don't want to be a thief anymore."

He waited for a reaction, but she just stared at him.

"Well?"

"Well what?"

"Aren't you going to say anything?"

"What do you want me to say, Bryan? I've heard you make these promises before. I'm sorry that I have trouble believing you, but you've lied to me too often. Not just me, either. Nobody trusts you. Did you know mom didn't even want me talking to you? She'd lose it if she knew I was letting you stay here."

"When have you ever listened to mom?"

"Dammit, listen to me! This isn't a joke. I stuck my neck out getting you a job at the factory. Don't make me regret it. I don't want you associating with any of those people again. I don't want you anywhere near that old lifestyle. Not if you expect any help from me."

Buff grabbed his sister's hand.

"Emily, I've changed."

She pulled away and stood up from the table.

"Prove it."

She walked away, went into the bedroom and shut the door behind her. Buff sipped his coffee and considered what his sister said.

He reached into his pants pocket and pulled out a crumpled photocopy. It had his parole officer's phone number written on it. It was time to check in. He leaned over and grabbed the phone off the bookshelf.

# June 27

Polytainers Incorporated made thin, rigid plastic containers for dairy products like yogurt, sour cream, cottage cheese and margarine. They had a huge manufacturing plant on Norseman Street, which consisted of three buildings: Administration, Assemblage, and Distribution. Adjacent to the main factory were five giant silos, stuffed with tiny acrylic pellets. These little gobs of plastic were shot through vacuum tubes onto the assembly line, where they were melted down and squeezed into moulds. It was a fascinating process, but unfortunately the silos let out a deafening hiss at all hours of the day, and the surrounding area perpetually stank like burning garbage bags.

Emily had been working there for over three years, and had risen to the level of Assistant to the Weekday Floor Manager. It may not have been a prestigious position, but it gave her enough influence to get her ex-convict brother a low-level job in the Shipping Department.

It was in a small room at the far end of the largest building, and also the only place in the whole factory without any air conditioning. Still, Buff was determined to make this work. He arrived promptly, fifteen minutes before his shift was supposed to start. He wore the regulation white lab coat and safety glasses, and had his hair neatly tucked under a hairnet.

His workstation was at the very end of the assembly line. A huge cardboard box full of empty cream cheese containers would come chugging down the metal rollers, and then stop abruptly right in front of Buff. It was his job to fill the boxes with packing foam. He used a plastic hose that snaked down from the ceiling, which released a torrent of Styrofoam peanuts when the nozzle was triggered. Once the box was full, he sealed it with a tape-gun, slapped the green button, and it slid down the line to the Distribution Department. A few moments would pass, and then the next box came barrelling in. Foam, tape-gun, button, repeat.

He checked his watch. He was forty minutes into his nine-hour shift.

He sighed as a fresh box of plastic containers slid down the assembly line. Buff aimed the hose towards it, pressed the trigger, and filled the box. A few stray foam peanuts missed and bounced across the factory floor.

Buff was sealing the box with packing tape when he saw someone walking towards him. It was Brent Patterson, his fat, bald little goblin of a manager. He had a face that looked pushed in, and horrible oily skin. Buff let out a sigh.

"May I speak to you a moment?" asked Brent, wheezing. He wasn't used to walking much. He usually never left his office. With a new man on the floor today, though, he was determined to throw on his white coat and hard hat, and make sure the job was being done properly.

Buff forced a smile. "Of course," he replied.

Brent pulled him aside and took off his hard hat. "How are things going?"

"Pretty good. I think I've got the hang of it." Buff was laying the charm on thick. Of course he had the hang of this brain-dead job. A monkey could do it. He couldn't understand why the company hadn't replaced the position with an automated machine.

Buff reached out to shake Brent's hand. "I want to thank you again for this opportunity, Mr. Patterson. I won't let you down. I'm a very hard worker."

"Of course. I'm sure you'll make a fine addition to our team. Any reservations I had with your... uh, background, well, they've been addressed with our surveillance cameras." He leaned back and pointed towards one of the newly installed security cameras above the workstation. He gave Buff a slimy, malicious grin, as though he were trying to publicly embarrass him. A humiliated Buff tried to smile through gritted teeth.

"You have nothing to worry about there," he said.

"Oh, I'm sure," Brent cooed. "I just have a few concerns about your packing process. I noticed that you've been depressing the trigger for the Styrofoam peanut dispenser in excess of the recommended three seconds. As a result, there is a surplus of unused styrofoam peanuts all over this floor."

"Yeah, sorry about that. I'm still learning the machine."

"Were you given a training session on this equipment?"

"Oh, yes. It was very thorough."

"I see. Now, I'm confused. This waste wasn't intentional, was it?"

"What? No, sir, of course not."

"I know that, Bryan. It was rhetorical. I'm trying to make a point. Last year, this company lost over twenty-five thousand dollars on wasted protective packing. That's somebody's salary, my friend. That's why I take this issue so seriously. I'm not here to single you out. I'm trying to nip this problem in the bud, to break the routine before it becomes a bad habit. Does that make sense?"

"Absolutely, sir. Very well put. A great analogy."

"Thank you. Now, I'm personally going to give you another ten-minute training session with this machine. After that, I don't want to see anymore foam peanuts on the floor."

"Sure thing. No problem."

"I mean it. I'll dock your pay a nickel for every foam peanut I find."

"You won't find any."

"Good." He snatched the plastic hose out of Buff's hand and shoved his hard hat into the new employee's arms. Brent began going through the entire packing process, being as patronizing as possible. "Now, this nozzle here is an airtight seal which regulates the flow of air through the dispensing tube. By depressing the styrofoam..."

The factory speakers squawked to life in a voice as garbled as an old NASA transmission. "Would Mr. Burley please report to Mr. Fred Patterson's office? Mr. Burley, report to Mr. Fred Patterson's office. Immediately."

Buff smiled wide. Saved by the bell. He turned to his manager and handed him back his hardhat.

"Sorry about that, sir," he said with a grin. "Duty calls."

***

Fred Patterson was Brent's father. He was taller, thinner, and better groomed, but he shared many of same unlikable qualities as his son, namely, a disdainful, suspicious attitude towards their newest employee. Unfortunately, Fred was the owner of the company, so his opinion mattered. He ran a tight ship, and often fired people for spurious reasons.

His office was on the top floor of the Administration building. Buff had to stop twice and ask for directions on how get there. After he found the door with the shiniest bronze nameplate, he knocked on it and let himself in.

Like everything else in the factory, it was clean and sparse. Just a single pine desk in one corner, with a comfortable leather chair on either side. A small wooden cross hung alone on the far wall. Mr. Patterson was behind his desk, talking to a tall man in a grey business suit.

Right away, Buff knew this was no business meeting. That man had to be a federal officer, or worse.

"Mr. Burley!" exclaimed Mr. Patterson, walking around his desk. He grabbed Buff's arm and pulled him into the office. "Please, sit down."

Buff slid down into one of the chairs. He eyed the tall man.

Nice suit, he thought. Definitely a federal officer. He might even be American.

Mr. Patterson went back around his desk and sat down. The American leaned against the edge. They both stared down at Buff.

"Is everything okay, Mr. Patterson?" he asked.

The company owner folded his hands together. "Well, Bryan," he started, softly. "May I call you Bryan?"

"I prefer Buff, but you can call me whatever you want."

"Very well, Bryan. I'm a God-fearing Christian. Which means I'm very forgiving. I was willing to overlook your felonious past based on Emily's good word. She's a great worker. One of my most trustworthy employees, too. Frankly, I find it baffling that you two could be related."

Buff leaned forward, confused.

"I don't understand. Did I do something wrong?"

Mr. Patterson motioned over towards the American. "This is Agent Johnson. He works with the government of the United States. He'd like to have a few words with you."

Buff stood up from his chair, outraged.

"I beg your pardon? What is this?"

Agent Johnson stepped forward to introduce himself. "Good afternoon, Mr. Burley," he said with a big, toothy grin. He reached out his hand towards Buff, who declined to shake it.

"It's a quarter to ten in the morning," he snorted. "Who are you? What's going on here?"

Mr. Patterson cleared his throat. "Please sit down, Bryan."

Buff stared at him incredulously.

"SIT!" he screamed.

Buff crossed his arms and stood in defiance.

Mr. Patterson sat up and threw his arms in the air.

"You have to admit," he said with a bitter voice, "it looks rather suspicious when federal officers from another country come knocking on my door forty minutes into your first shift. I'm not sure if you have a future with this company, son."

"Let's relax a second here," said Agent Johnson, putting a hand on Mr. Patterson's arm to calm him down. "It's nothing like that at all, sir. I'm just hoping Mr. Burley here will be able to use some of his past connections to assist us. He hasn't been accused of anything illicit. Yet."

"Still, it doesn't smell right to me," said Mr. Patterson, clucking his tongue. "I believe in second chances, but never a third. Understand?" He poked a finger towards Buff.

Johnson rubbed his forehead. His day was long enough already, he thought, and this Patterson guy wasn't helping make it any shorter. He turned towards the company owner and motioned to the door.

"Could you please excuse us for a moment, Mr. Patterson?"

The company owner's mouth dropped open in shock.

"What? This is my office! You can't ask me to leave!"

"Please. It'll only be for a few minutes."

Mr. Patterson threw his arms in the air a second time. Before he stormed out of the room, he swung around and waved a finger in Buff's face.

"This is coming out of your personal time bank. You go one minute over your lunch break, and you're staying late to make up for it. Now, if you'll excuse me, I'm going to call your parole officer."

He slammed the door behind him.

Johnson leaned back against the desk, exhaling deeply. He looked tired and weathered, like he'd been doing this job for far too long. His face was a relief map of scars. He had bags under his eyes and stubble on his chin.

Buff sunk back down into his chair. He looked up at the American.

"So, you want my help, huh?"

Johnson nodded.

"Well, you probably just got me fired, so it seems like the least I could do," Buff said, pouring the sarcasm on thick. Johnson grimaced and rubbed the back of his neck. That really wasn't his intention.

"Yes, I'm sorry about that. I'll speak with Mr. Patterson, and your parole officer, when I'm finished here. Smooth everything over. I'm going to try to get you the rest of the day off, too."

"My hero."

"Mr. Burley, my name is..."

"Call me Buff."

"Mr. Buff, my..."

"Just Buff."

"Buff?"

"Buff. "

"Why Buff?"

"Because I'm tough."

"Fair enough. Well, Buff, my name is Ronald Johnson. I'm with the

Federal Bureau of Investigations."

"You're out of your jurisdiction."

"That's true. We're hoping you'll volunteer to help with our situation. There's a good man's life at stake."

"I know. Mine."

"Please, just hear me out. We just want to ask you a few questions. It has come to the attention of my department that you recently spoke to a man with known connections to the Montagne family."

"I don't know what you're talking about."

Johnson exploded in rage, kicking the desk with his foot. Buff didn't flinch.

"Dammit, I don't have time for this! We know about the offer from Roche. We want you to take it. You have to call him immediately and tell him you'll do it."

"Uh..." Buff was dumbfounded. He couldn't find the words.

"Call your contact and tell him you'll do the job. If you comply, we'll completely erase your criminal record, and you'll be paid one hundred thousand American dollars, tax free."

"What are you talking about? I'm on parole!" Buff scoffed, shaking his head at how ridiculous Johnson's suggestion was. "Besides, I already said no. I don't even know what the job was! I want to get out of that world. Out and clean. Too legit to quit."

Johnson laughed. "Out and clean? Are you kidding? I've seen your record, Buff. You've never been clean for more than a few weeks. Safe-cracking is the only thing you're good at. And this time, you'd be doing it for the benefit of one of your government's strongest allies. That's got to count for something. Now do us both a favour, call up your contact and tell him you've reconsidered."

Buff had heard enough of this. He stood up. "I think I'm going to go now, Agent Johnson. You're eating into my overtime."

He tried storming out of the office, but Johnson stood between him and the door.

"Do you really think that's a good idea, Mr. Burley? You were only convicted once, but we can connect you to dozens and dozens of other scams and cons, including, if I'm not mistaken, one in Rochester, New York. Remember that one? Did you visit the Susan B. Anthony House while you were there?"

"I've never left the country. I don't even have a passport."

"Sure, Buff, sure. You know, we might not be able to nail you up here, but I've got some really close friends in the RCMP. We could easily have you dragged down south of the border, where I know some judges who are a lot more open-minded about what can be considered evidence."

Johnson stepped back and sat down on the desk, crossing his arms confidently. "That's the hard way," he said. "You sit back down and listen to what I have to say, that's the easy way. It's your call. Buff."

Buff turned away from the door and sat back down in the chair. He spent the next twenty minutes listening to what Agent Johnson had to say.

***

Most of the French Canadians living in Toronto kept to a small neighbourhood in the city's east end, known locally as "Little Montreal." It was the best place to get good poutine and cheap smokes. The smell of freshly baked bagels persistently filled the air. Flags bearing the Montreal Canadiens logo hung from the rooftops, and there was a fleur-de-lis in every window.

The Jean Béliveau Arena was located in the heart of Little Montreal. It resided right across the street from the St. Gabriel Lalemant church, and both could be considered places of worship. It was a modest, four-thousand seat hockey rink, used by junior and amateur leagues. It was also fully owned and operated by the French-Canadian mob.

Buff had taken off his white lab coat, and arrived at the arena in his sleek black suit. When he walked into the front lobby, Roche was already there, waiting for him under a giant black-and-white portrait of "Le Gros Bill" Béliveau. He saw Buff and snapped his fingers.

"Buff, mon ami," he said, with an air of superiority. "You miss me? You come back here for to see me?"

"You know why I'm here," Buff snapped.

Roche smiled, smugly. "Bien sûr, I know why you are here, Buff. Jacques is waiting. Follow me."

He led him over to the elevator and took him up to the top floor. That's where Jacques' office was. It was bigger than most convenience stores, and looked more like a set from *The Godfather* than a place of business. The walls were wood-panelled and the floor was carpeted with tufted nylon, inlaid with a subtle mahogany pattern. In the corner, a shelf of leather-bound French books sat next to an impressive stereo and a well-stocked liquor cabinet. The other side of the room was lined with huge windows that looked down onto the ice rink. Jacques' desk sat in the middle of the room.

Roche led Buff into the office, and then retreated back out to the hallway, closing the door behind him. Jacques was already there, standing by the window. He was looking down at the ice as the local junior team ran practice drills and took shots at an empty net.

Even at age 74, Jacques was an imposing figure, befitting the head of the Montagne crime family. He was prim, well-groomed and perfectly manicured, looking like an investment banker about to woo an investor. An expensive custom Italian suit hung from his chiselled six-and-a-half-foot frame. A sparkling gold Cartier watch was draped around his wrist. His skin was flawlessly smooth, except for a small scar just beneath his chin. His hair was mostly grey, slicked back and freshly styled. He seemed gently conniving, as though he were always sizing you up, regardless of the situation.

He turned to Buff and smiled.

"Buff, my friend," he said, shaking hands. He pulled him in and gave him a hearty slap on the back. "Please, have a seat."

Buff sat down in a leather chair that was the same colour as the books on Jacques' shelves. The Frenchman was nothing if not coordinated.

"Nice place," said Buff.

"Oh, merci," said Jacques warmly. "I really love it here. It's great. I get to be closer to the game I love." His accent had gotten better since Buff had last seen him, but there was still a hint of that French-Canadian twang.

He turned back to the window. He saw one of the big, muscled players below bodycheck a hotshot rookie into the boards. "Do you like hockey?"

"I like ice."

"I love hockey. As a boy, I would watch every game with my father. We had a tiny little television with no colour. The reception it got was very bad. You could barely make out a picture! But those are some of my best memories. It was the only real time I got to spend with him. He was a big fan of the Montreal Canadiens. He never missed a game. His favourite player was Maurice Richard. He was even at the Forum for game five of the finals against Boston in '58. Remember? Where the Rocket scored the game-winning goal in overtime? That night was the happiest I ever saw my father."

As Jacques gave his heartfelt speech, a man in the bleachers was watching him. He was trying to look inconspicuous, wearing a baseball hat and a purple windbreaker with a Toronto Raptors logo on it. He was an officer with the Canada Revenue Agency. They did routine surveillance on lots of people they suspected of falsifying income, and Jacques' mob ties put a huge target on his back. The CRA had been trailing him for eight months and hadn't turned up anything. Of course, they had no warrant, which meant they also had no bugs, no tapped phones, no inside men, nothing. Just a single agent, looking through binoculars into Jacques' office, trying to read the Frenchman's lips.

"Suspect visited by unknown man at 2:15 P.M.," the agent noted, speaking into a microphone hidden in the cuff of his coat. "Age: mid-thirties, wrinkled suit. Appears to be getting the Montreal Canadiens loyalty speech."

"Being a Montreal fan, you know what my father hated?" continued Jacques. "The Toronto Maple Leafs. He despised them. He wouldn't even say their name. And the only thing he hated more than the Toronto Maple Leafs were their fans. Not me, though. I love the fans in Toronto. They're so vocal, so passionate, so... what's the word? Fantastical? No, no."

Jacques stumbled for the word in an utterly rehearsed fashion. He was no great actor.

"Um... fanatical!" he exclaimed, snapping his fingers. "That's it! They're fanatical! The Maple Leafs haven't won the Stanley Cup in over four decades, and they still sell out every game. It doesn't matter how many times they lose or how badly they play, the fans remain faithful. I respect that kind of loyalty."

Jacques looked Buff squarely in the eyes, as though his gaze could bore a hole through his skull. He brought a finger up to his lips, walked over to his stereo and pressed play. The soothing sounds of Gilles Vigneault's "Mon Pays" filled the air.

*Mon pays, ce n'est pas un pays, c'est l'hiver.*

*Mon jardin, ce n'est pas un jardin, c'est la pleine.*

Jacques slowly turned up the volume. He strolled back over to the windows and pulled the curtains shut.

The CRA agent's view was blocked. He threw his binoculars down in frustration and kicked the chair in front of him.

"Dammit!" he muttered under his breath. He brought the hidden microphone back up to his mouth and spoke into it. "Suspect obstructed view of office at 2:17 P.M. We lost him. Surveillance on standby."

*Mon chemin, ce n'est pas un chemin, c'est la neige.*

*Mon pays, ce n'est pas un pays, c'est l'hiver.*

Jacques turned back to Buff and motioned over to his liquor cabinet.

"Do you want a drink?" he offered.

"No, thank you."

"Would you like something to eat? A cigar?"

"No."

"Can I get you anything? Anything at all?"

"You can get to the point. You know why I'm here."

"Hey, my friend. Come on. You are my guest here. You helped me. I owe you a favour."

Buff looked at him and cocked an eyebrow.

"Eighteen months," he said. "Both you and that piece of shit lawyer told me three. At the most. It ruined me. I'm starting again from scratch."

"From scratch?" asked Jacques, puzzled. "You didn't save anything?"

"My ex ran off with whatever the cops didn't take."

Jacques winched. "Mon Dieu!" He thought for a moment, and then asked, "Elizabeth?"

"Anastasia."

"The brunette?"

"Blond. From a bottle."

The Frenchman chuckled.

*Mon refrain, ce n'est pas un refrain, c'est rafale.*

*Ma maison, ce n'est pas ma maison, c'est froidure.*

He leaned in closer, dropping his voice to just above a whisper. Buff had to struggle to hear every word. "Buff, I cannot express the family's gratitude, and my own gratitude, for keeping quiet and not naming names these past two years. We know the offers were on the table. We will take care of you during this time. We will get you money, we will get you a place to stay, we will get you work."

"That's why I'm here."

"I have an offer for you. I need you to break into a safe."

"What's the take?"

"The safe is in a law office in the west end. Inside the safe is an important piece of evidence that you need to bring back to me."

"What is the take?"

"The job needs to be pulled soon. I need that file back by Monday morning."

"What's... the... take?"

"$150,000, and anything else you find in the building is yours to keep, minus the family's thirty percent, of course."

Buff stood up from his chair.

"Thank you, sir. I appreciate the offer, but the answer is no."

"Buff, my friend, please..." started Jacques.

"I'm broke, but I'm not desperate. 150K is a first-timer's rate. I'd need double that to pull a decent team together. And I don't work with decent teams. I work with excellent ones. So, politely, no thank you."

Jacques put his hand on Buff's shoulder and forced him back down into the chair. "Let me ameliorate my offer. Working in that same law office is one Harry Bockner."

Buff's eyes lit up like a slot machine that hit jackpot. If he lived a thousand years, he'd never forget that name. Harry Bockner was the lawyer who represented the jewellery store he was caught robbing. He's the piece of shit that was responsible for bumping his three-month sentence up to almost two years.

"The same Bockner who..." asked Buff, his voice trailing off.

"The very same one."

Buff's mind reeled at the possibilities. He was not a vengeful man, but he was convinced that what Bockner had done to him was wrong. He could ruin the man's career. Plant drugs in his office and make an anonymous phone call to the police. Put a virus on his computer. Hide rotting seafood under his desk.

"Isn't revenge worth a little pay cut?" asked Jacques.

Buff was quietly pensive for several moments.

"I'll go as low as $250,000," he said.

"That's higher than I was expecting."

"That's too bad. A job like this needs a team of five or six, at least. All those people need to be paid. You've given me a tight deadline and almost no time to prep. Given the circumstances, I'd say you're getting a bargain."

"Fine. $250,000, but the family gets thirty-five percent of anything else you find in there."

Buff was satisfied with the deal. He stuck out his hand for Jacques to shake.

"There's just one more thing," Jacques said, hesitantly. "It's a favour I have to ask, on behalf of the family. It's about one of our own. We need you to take him on the job with you."

"No way. I can't do that. I don't work with anyone I can't vouch for personally. That's always been the deal."

"He's a small-time thief. We call him Fou. We'd like you take him with you, and we'd like it if he didn't come back."

Buff paused for a moment, stunned. This wasn't the kind of job he expected.

"You mean..."

"Exactly," continued the Frenchman. "We need Fou to go away. Forever. He is a little man, but he has very powerful friends. That's why we cannot use the normal channels when dealing with a problem like this. I hope you'll understand."

"Oh, I understand, alright. I understand my price just went up. $300,000, paid upfront."

"Buff, my friend..." Jacques cooed.

"No more negotiating. I'll have to hire another specialist to take care of your little 'favour.' Either you pay what I want now or I walk."

"Fine," the Frenchman said with a pout. "$300,000."

This time Jacques stuck his hand out, and Buff shook it.

"Good. Now, tell me more about this law office..."

***

An hour later, Roche was ushering Buff out the front of the building. The slimy goon pulled an envelope full of cash out of his breast pocket. Buff snatched it out of his hands.

"Did he give you the Montreal Canadiens loyalty speech?" asked Roche.

Buff ignored him and walked away. It was almost time to check in with his parole officer.

"À bientôt, Buff," chortled Roche.

# June 28

That morning, Buff waited until his sister left, and then called in sick to work. He grabbed the most masculine T-shirt he could find from her closet and threw it on. After spending twenty minutes gently tidying up her apartment, hoping it would help him get on her good side, he left.

He took a bus north up Highway 10 for an hour and half to the small town of Primose. He was dropped off at a greasy diner named Super Burger. It was a venerable place with a funky orange and brown decor, and wall-to-wall glass. There was an old TTC streetcar sitting out front, which was used as a dining room.

It was a familiar place to Buff. There was a man he consulted with before every big job, and Super Burger was where he always found him.

Buff ordered the cheeseburger combo with onion rings and a bottle of water. He grabbed a booth in the corner and started eating. The burger was delicious.

Less than ten minutes later, an old bald man walking with a cane came into the diner. He was wearing a loud Hawaiian shirt. Buff watched him hobble up to the front counter and ask for a burger and a pop.

"That will be six twenty-five," said the girl taking his order, smiling.

The old man reached into his pants pocket. A pile of crumpled American bills tumbled out onto the counter.

"D'ya take American money?" he asked, speaking with a strong, distinct Newfoundland accent.

"Well, we don't normally..."

He immediately interrupted her. "Huh?" He adjusted the hearing aid buried deep in his ear. "Sorry 'bout that, b'y. Had the thing three weeks and already the arse fell out of 'er. What'd ya say, me ducky?"

"We don't normally accept American money," she repeated, emphasizing every word.

"Oh," he said, looking despondent. "I'm sorry, me dear, but this is alls I got. I been down in the States gettin' hip surgery." He droned on for what felt like ages, detailing every inane part of his trip. The girl grew more exasperated with every anecdote. She looked past the old man and saw a lineup forming behind him, growing longer with every minute this coot wasted. She was hitting her breaking point.

"You know what?" she said, sharply. "It's fine. You can pay with your American money. Six twenty-five, please."

"Come on, hurry up, man!" shouted a voice from the back of the line.

"Me girlie, d'ya mind if I change some of this for Canadian money, too?" asked the old man.

"Fine, whatever," she said impatiently. "Just make it quick. There are other people waiting to order."

The old man smiled. His trap had been carefully set, and the young server had fallen right into it. Over the next minute, Buff watched him pull over thirty dollars out of her with a simple short counting and change-raising scheme. That's why the old man had insisted on using American cash; it's an easier con to pull when every denomination looks the same.

Buff was impressed. The old man still had some skills.

His name was Marcus, and he was the reason Buff was here. Marcus had been his mentor a decade earlier, introducing him to the art of safe-cracking. He was originally a fisherman on the east coast, but took up thievery after his boat sank in a rough storm. He used the few unsavoury connections he had, learned the trade, and quickly gained notoriety among the criminal underworld for his brazen robberies. By the time Buff met him, he was one of the best cat burglars in the country.

He was in his sixties now. His best days were long behind him. Time had waged a vicious war against his features, and mostly won. He had wrinkles, liver spots and a round potbelly. The cane and the hearing aid were new since the last time Buff had seen him.

"Take care, ducky," he said to the server, and then got his lunch and shuffled off towards the dining room.

Buff got up and stopped him. Marcus recognized him immediately.

"Oh my Lard, Buff!" he exclaimed, radiating delight. They shared a warm hug.

"How's ya gettin' on, ya little frigger? When'd ya get out? Is that a girls shirt ya wearin', b'y?"

"Nice to see you again, Marcus. When did you start walking with a cane?"

"Oh, b'y, these are just for the sympathy, me cocky."

Buff chuckled, and they both sat down in the booth. Marcus threw his cane to one side and took out his fake hearing aid.

"That was a nice change raise, by the way. I counted thirty-one. What did you really score?"

"Thirty-eight."

"Hmm, not bad."

"Well, b'y, I saw 'er here some days ago, and I think she's new. She looks stunned as me arse, so I had to give 'er a go, eh?"

Marcus smiled widely, but Buff just cocked an eyebrow and gave him a stern look.

"Short counting a fifteen-year-old?" he asked, with a hint of sanctimony.

The old man looked down at his feet.

"Eh, ya right, b'y," he said, regretfully. "I am ashamed. It's embarrassin', but I had no choice, me b'y. I need the money. I'm so broke I'm eatin' the putty out of the windows."

"Broke?" asked Buff, incredulous. "That's impossible. You're a pro, probably the best in the business. You taught me everything I know. How can you be broke? Are you an alcoholic? Is it gambling debts? Drugs? Women? Men?"

Marcus smirked and shot him a dirty look. "Dammit, Buff, me child! I'm no addicted to anything! Respect ya elders, b'y, ors I gives you a crack. Lard t'underin' jumpin'! I just can't find me a decent score, b'y. That's all. You know, there ain't much call for a specialist like us no more, b'y. Most of the safes ya can buy today, why, any scut jinker with longers for arms could tear them apart with a power tool or a couple of clouts from a sledge. Wouldn't take ya more than five minutes."

"I don't understand. What happened?"

"Oh, b'y, this economy's hit everyone hard, even us thieves. It's all 'cause of them damn Chinese, floodin' the market full of cheap safes. They been doin' it for years now, b'y. Shit-picky safes made of plastic and rotten metal that couldn't keep a cod chinched, b'y. No word of a lie."

Marcus threw a couple of French fries into his mouth.

"Mmm, good prog!" he said. He swallowed, and then continued, "So, anyways, all the safe manufacturers in North America got screwed right in the stern. The only way any of 'ems could stay in business was to make cheaper safes with shabby, bargain-bin metals. Some of the old sqaubby builders retired, and most of those that didn't, went tits up. I think there's nare but two or three companies out there still makin' proper quality safes."

"What about a company called 'Strongbox'?" asked Buff. "Are they one of the good ones?"

Marcus stopped in mid-bite, stunned. "A Strongbox?" he balked, sounding just slightly intimidated. "Lard t'underin' b'y, have ya gone right out of 'er? Thems ain't no wall safes for granny's pearly bobbillies."

"What do you mean?"

"Them safes they build is not a bad bit nice, b'y. They's a nice piece of stuff. Strongbox means strong as an ox. They only makes giant custom vaults, and they're the least accessible commercially-available safes money can buy."

"Have you ever cracked one?"

"Nah, b'y. I ain't never even seen one."

Buff pulled a worn photocopy out of his pocket and laid it on the table, smoothing out the creases with his hand. It was the blueprints to a huge Strongbox vault, which was almost the size of his sister's apartment. Marcus gasped.

"Yar some ticket, b'y," he said. "What are ya gettin' on with?"

"I've got a big score with a juicy take," said Buff, coyly. "I'm trying to put a crew together. The job's in four days."

Marcus didn't hesitate. "I'm in, b'y. The ol' dog for the hard road, best kind." He pulled the vault plans closer and examined them. "Lemme takes a gock at these and sees if we can figger this out, me chummy."

He looked over the detailed diagram, tracing the safe's outline with his finger. They were complicated and densely technical, more akin to blueprints for a space shuttle than a simple safe.

"Well, b'y, I tells ya, she's a bit of a cramp-hand," the old man said, taking a sip of his drink. "This won't be easy by a bit. She's a beast, b'y. The whole thing's got tremor-sensors all over 'er."

"What?"

"Tremor-sensors. Little things that go off if ya tickle the safe's arse. They're all connected to three backup servers and the alarm system for the buildin'. Unless ya gots an access code, b'y, yar only chance of gettin' in, if the good Lard please, is with a level-seven cracker. A competent electronics man would help the cause, too."

Buff thought about it for a moment. There weren't too many people he knew that fit that description, and he hadn't spoken to the few he did in over two years.

"What about R and D?"

Marcus sighed dramatically. "They parted ways," he said with a shrug. "Love's fickle, b'y, especially when yar young, me mate. Doug's gone straight and gots a real job, but Rebecca's still in the game. Although I think she now goes by the name Beka Byte."

***

Like the rest of her generation, Beka had never known a world without the internet. Computers were always ubiquitous in her life. She learned to type around the same time she learned to walk. However, she had an aptitude for understanding complex networks that was unique, even amongst her peers. In high school, while all her friends were texting and updating their MySpace pages, she was hacking H cards to get free satellite TV channels.

Her first big splash in the hacking community came a few years later, when she successfully cracked a notoriously inaccessible server. Located at the University of Toronto, it was referred to as RDRR, a reference to an episode of *The Simpsons* that aired before Beka was born. Since then, her services had always been in demand, despite her reputation for being snarky and opinionated.

That afternoon, she had planned on meeting up with her new boyfriend. She was going to surprise him at work with some donuts.

They'd only been out on a couple of dates, and she still wasn't sure how she felt about him. He was nice enough, had a job, and looked decent, but she wasn't feeling the sort of overwhelming excitement she had with her last boyfriend.

Regardless, she was still willing to give the new kid a shot. She had prettied herself up in her own unique style. Her hair was cut short and dyed bright blue, and then put up in little pigtails and clipped off with plastic Hello Kitty hairpins. Her baggy T-shirt was the same shade of blue as her hair. It featured a picture of Ryuk, the shinigami death god from the popular Japanese manga series *Death Note*. She wore big, heavy military boots and a plaid skirt. There was a silver skull on a chain around her neck. She never wore makeup.

The new boyfriend's name was Paul, and Beka hoped he appreciated the amount of work she put into this outfit. Normally she just wore jeans and a T-shirt.

Paul worked right downtown, at the TechMart on the corner of Yonge and Dundas. It was one of those giant franchise electronics stores, the kind where all the employees had to wear bright red collared shirts.

Beka hated places like this. These retail chains always put their own profits ahead of their customers. They would resell defective items, try to sneak unexpected charges into sales, and align themselves with opportunistic, predatory financial companies. What really offended her, though, was their lack of technical proficiency. TechMart infamously had the worst tech support, anywhere, bar none.

She walked in, and immediately felt uneasy about the sheer enormity of the place. It was like something out of a Daniel Clowes comic, intended to illustrate the emptiness of contemporary culture, only it was real and even emptier than could ever be imagined. Huge display tables were stacked with expensive phones, cameras and music players. Shelves stretched back as far the eye could see, each lined with rows and rows of LCD televisions in a range of sizes. Every screen was displaying an episode of *The Big Bang Theory*. With motion smoothing, noise reduction, added sharpness, and every other redundant "enhancement" feature cranked to the maximum setting, the pictures looked garish and overly bright. It hurt Beka's eyes, and reminded her how much she disliked these big box stores.

She saw Paul working at the customer service desk. He was a handsome, clean-cut young man with short brown hair. He looked incredibly bored.

She walked right up to his desk, beaming.

"Hey Paul!" she exclaimed.

Paul looked up, shocked.

"Oh, hi Beka," he said, feigning enthusiasm. He was clearly uncomfortable being seen in his silly TechMart uniform. "What are you doing here?"

"Oh, you know. I was just in the area, picking up a box of Timbits. I thought you might want some company."

"Cool."

She opened the box of doughy treats and offered him some. He plucked out two chocolate ones, tossed them into his mouth and gave a nod of thanks.

Beka looked over at one of the TV screens. She saw actor Jim Parson's character Sheldon stumble over a couch like a buffoon, and then deliver his trademarked catchphrase. A cacophony of fake, hollow laughter spewed out of the speakers.

She turned back to Paul and rolled her eyes.

"Who's the idiot that decided to put that on all the TVs?" she asked, jokingly.

"I am," answered Paul, sounding wounded.

Beka winced. She paused a moment to pull her foot out of her mouth.

"Sorry," she said sheepishly. "You couldn't find something better to put on? Like a documentary about tigers, maybe, or *Avatar*?"

"Ugh, no," he said, disgusted. "They had *Avatar* on a loop for eighteen months. Every day, every night, always *Avatar*. I heard one of the discs was so worn they had to use pliers to pull it out of the Blu-Ray player.

We are never playing *Avatar* again, as long as I have any say in it."

"That's cool. I get that. But can't you play something that's actually entertaining? Why do you have to play this stupid show?"

Paul looked at her like she was from another planet.

"You don't like *Big Bang Theory*?" he asked, incredulous.

Beka's eyes bugged out. Paul had inadvertently just poured gasoline onto her simmering fire.

"Like it?" she howled, indignant. "I hate it! It's awful. It's like a nerd minstrel show. It's exactly what people who aren't geeks think geeks are like, and it gives them licence to laugh at us."

She wasn't convincing him. She tried breaking down her argument further.

"Look, they're supposed to be a bunch of scientists, right? Real scientists are the complete opposite of the stereotypes on the show. People with jobs like that spend their time working in a lab and doing research, not visiting the comic book shop every Wednesday. The guys on that show are more like geeks who write blogs and make iPhone games. You know, laid-back jobs that would give you the time to mod an RTS or properly subtitle an imported anime. Am I right?"

"I don't know, Beka," he said with resignation, not wanting to fight. "I don't think you're supposed to take it that seriously. It's just a sitcom, and I think it's funny."

"That's because the laugh track is telling you it's supposed to be funny," she said, raising her voice, "but it's not. It's just dumb, endless references. I hate that kind of 'comedy.' It's boring and lazy. Oh, and the way the show treats women..."

"Excuse me," said a soft woman's voice, coming from behind Beka.

She turned around. There stood an old woman with curly grey hair and a turquoise dress, holding an ancient laptop under her arm. Beka had been so consumed with her own rant that she failed to notice this lady walk up to the customer service desk.

She stepped aside, and the woman handed her busted computer to Paul. Beka immediately recognized it as an old Fujitsu E Series Lifebook. She knew it had to be at least six years old, which in computer terms made the thing an antique.

The old lady proceeded to explain how her email was no longer working, and that strange error messages kept popping up at random intervals. She had great difficulty trying to explain her problem, struggling to find the right terms to describe what she'd seen. The words "thingy" and "whatchamacallit" came up more than once.

"I don't understand it," she pleaded. "I don't do any of the downloads. I just need my email to work. It's how I talk to my grandchildren."

Paul listened patiently, diligently entering every detail in his computer.

"It sounds like a simple malware issue," said Beka.

Paul shot her a dirty look. This was his job. She turned away, rolling her eyes.

He turned back to the old woman and smiled.

"Mal-ware?" she asked, unsure.

"She's right," he said. "It does sound like a malware or virus problem. We can fix that for you, ma'am." He turned back to his keyboard and tapped on a few more keys. "Okay, ma'am, with parts and labour, your total with tax comes to $198.85. You'll be able to pick your laptop up in three days."

Beka scoffed. She couldn't help herself.

"Three days?" she hooted, scornfully. "Are you on meth? That's insane!"

Paul looked like his head was going to explode. He turned bright red and his cheek began twitching just beneath his left eye.

"Beka, what are you doing?"

"Come on, Paul. That's unfair and you know it." She bent down and spoke to the old woman directly. "Miss, I'd be happy to get your email working for you again. I'll do a better job than anyone here at TechMart, I'll only charge you fifty bucks, and you can have your computer back in an hour."

The old woman smiled wider than a fat man at Thanksgiving.

"Young lady, you've got yourself a deal!"

The two of them shook hands.

Paul shook his head in disbelief. He was stunned. He saw his manager walking towards them with a scowl on her face.

"Um, Beka?" he said nervously. "I think I'm going to have to ask you to leave the store."

"That's fine," she said flippantly. "The food court's a Wi-Fi hotspot. We can fix it there." The two women strolled out the front door together, but before she left, Beka turned back to Paul.

"I don't think we should see each other anymore," she yelled.

***

Marcus took another huge bite out of his hamburger. A little grease dribbled down his chin and fell onto the vault blueprints. The old man quickly wiped his mouth with a napkin.

"Well, b'y, ya'd better hope Beka agrees to jig yar squid," he said, his mouth still half full. "If she ain't, b'y, I lows yar gonna get a trimmin' there the once. Ya can't nare touch one of them Strongboxes 'til the whole damn thing's disconnected from the network, chum."

Buff was not dissuaded. "Can it be done?" he asked, flatly.

"Well, she ain't no can of dickie birds, but we can crack 'er, sure as there's shit in a cat, b'y. Anything's possible. But we're just gettin' warmed up, me cocky. Takin' the network out just lets us touch the vault. Openin' 'er up is a whole other bucket of fish."

"What kind of timeline are we looking at?"

"Well, b'y, ya've got three four-inch plates of steel on all sides, with two glass relockers and a thermal relocker between 'em. With thems alone, ya'd be lookin' at four hours of drillin' time at the minimum, maybe three if ya uses a diamond tip."

"Four hours. That's doable."

"Things ain't that easy, b'y. The whole damn thing is encased in solid ballistic armour, b'y, thicker and stronger than a schooner's crew. Ya'd need a damn Tommyhawk missile shot at point blank range to makes a dent in the stuff. So, me ol' trout, ya want this nut to crack, yar gonna need the best munitions money can gets ya."

"An explosives man, eh?" Buff thought aloud. "Is Scoots still in the game?"

"Lard love a duck," scoffed Marcus. "I ain't workin' with that low squint, b'y. He's nice enough to throw rocks at. He's got more lip than a rubber boot, full of shit and up a quart."

"Okay, okay. What about Big Frank?"

Marcus cocked a wary eyebrow. "Big Frank? Ya sure 'bout that, b'y? I heard he went vigilante."

"He's still got to eat," retorted Buff.

"Ya think you can keep a leash on that mad dog?"

Buff smiled.

"Don't worry. He owes me a favour."

***

Big Frank drove a big car. It was a heavy, brawny 1973 Lincoln Continental, black as the bottom of a coal mine, with an engine that'd been completely overhauled. It suited him perfectly.

As it chugged south along Islington Avenue, it sounded like a Formula One race car dragging a steam train behind it.

He pulled into the parking lot of a busy Tim Hortons. Right away he noticed the two undercover police officers sitting in a parked car. They had military-style crew cuts, while their vehicle had no hubcaps on the wheels, to accommodate the special tires cops use. Big Frank chuckled to himself. He could spot these clowns a mile away.

Not that they needed to hide, as there were four normal police cruisers parked in the same lot. Big Frank pulled his massive car into an empty space beside one. For a moment, he considered slamming his driver's side door into it, but decided against it.

He got out, locked his doors and marched towards the bustling donut shop. He was a huge, muscled hulk of a man, as big as a bodybuilder wearing shoulder pads. His hair was jet black and slicked back. He had a deep, jagged scar stretching prominently across the left side of his pockmarked face. He wore a long dark trench coat that fluttered in the wind behind him like a superhero's cape.

One of the undercover cops turned to the other.

"That's our boy," he said. "Asshole must have a huge pair of big brass ones to try and pull a deal here."

The two men were both members of the city's elite Guns and Gangs division, and they'd been working on this case for months. Once they put this menace behind bars, they'd be lauded as heroes.

They watched Big Frank stride through the door into Tim Hortons.

Inside, the shop was teeming with patrons. Every table was occupied. There was a line of six people waiting to order. The two young servers behind the counter were hustling to keep up.

The place was swarming with cops. Over a dozen uniformed police officers were sitting around drinking coffee, most with a donut in their hand. Some noticed Big Frank as he walked in, but no one gave him a second glance.

He saw the two men he came to meet on the other side of the shop, sitting in a booth. They were both mean-looking thugs who seemed about 20 years old, maybe younger. They wore baggy clothes, sideways baseball caps, and neck tattoos. Both had three links of chain, painted bright purple, hanging from their belt buckles, signifying their allegiance to a notorious street gang known as the "Etobicoke Slingers." They looked nervous.

As soon as they spotted him, they jumped up from their seats and gave Big Frank a nod. As casually as they could, they both sauntered over to the men's restroom and went inside. Big Frank rolled his eyes and followed them.

The washroom in Tim Hortons was the cleanest place in the whole shop. It was small -- only two stalls and a urinal. The tan and maroon ceramic tiles on the walls and floor were freshly scrubbed, smelling like lemon and pine. There was a metal grate in the ceiling, filtering foul odours out of the air.

Big Frank quickly ensured all the stalls were empty, and then locked the door behind them.

Right away, one of the thugs stood up to him and got in his face. Now that the police couldn't see them, he began posturing like a hardened street tough.

"What's your problem, old man?" he shouted, his gold tooth glinting under the fluorescent lights. "Who pulls a drop at a fucking donut shop, huh? Did you see all the cops out there? You trying to get us busted? Is that it? You dick around with me, I'll smash your face in, you old fuck." He tried to look threatening, but Big Frank was unfazed.

The other thug grabbed the first by the arm. "Chill, man, it's cool," he said reassuringly. He didn't appreciate the tension his partner was bringing to the situation. Finding people in this city who were willing to sell black market firearms, especially assault rifles, was impossible. If this Big Frank guy got offended and stormed out, it would take them weeks to find another source for weapons.

"Big Frank checks out," he said, calmly. "T.J. vouched for him. Be cool."

The gold-toothed thug stuck out a finger and poked it into Big Frank's chest, hard.

"Watch yourself, grandpa," he said gravely, giving the most intimidating mean mug he could.

Big Frank didn't flinch.

The other thug grabbed the first by the elbow. "Come on, man," he said in a nervous rush. "Let's just do this and go."

He reached into his coat pocket and pulled out an envelope. It was wrapped in a rubber band, bursting with hundred-dollar bills. He stuffed it into Big Frank's hand, who took a moment to thumb through the money.

"It's all there, old man," said the thug with the gold tooth. "Now quit dicking us around. You got our Russian automatics, or do I have to spend the afternoon carving you into little pieces?"

Big Frank smiled.

He flicked his wrist, and a metal tube the size of pen flew out of his right jacket sleeve and into his hand. In a flash, the tube made a clang and extended out into a long, heavy rod.

He smashed it into the thug's shin, cracking the bone.

In one swift motion, Big Frank threw his free hand up over the thug's mouth, muffling the scream.

He swung his other arm around, bashing the other punk in the neck before he could react. The young man gagged, spat out blood and turned white. He collapsed onto the floor, unconscious.

Big Frank spun back around to face the thug with the gold tooth and bad attitude. The goon was squirming helplessly under Big Frank's kung-fu grip.

The hulking vigilante raised the metal baton over his head. The thug's eyes went wide, pleading for mercy. Big Frank had none in him.

He brought the club down as hard as he could, smashing it against the young man's skull. The blow was hard enough to knock the thug out instantly and dislodge that gold tooth, sending it clattering along the tiled floor.

Big Frank released his grip on the goon, and let the young man's body flop onto the ground.

He checked his watch. It had taken him seventeen seconds to incapacitate them both. That was slower than usual.

Big Frank never had any intention of selling weapons to these punks. He was indeed a soldier of fortune, but one with a conscience. In the years since he lost his wife, he'd dedicated himself to ridding his city's streets from scum like these two goons.

Outside in the parking lot, the two undercover officers began to worry. Through their windshield, they could see right into the Tim Hortons. They'd watched their suspect walk into the washroom with two suspicious men. Considering how much money had been spent on trailing this guy, they were understandably nervous when he was out of sight.

"Should we go in after him?" asked the smaller one, anxious.

"Christ, Jimmy, would you relax?" said the other, frustrated. "They've been in there for one minute. We've got fifty guys inside. We're covered. He's not going anywhere. Let him commit a crime first, okay?"

Seconds later, they saw every cop inside the donut shop jump up out of their seats and charge towards the washroom door.

The two undercover officers threw open their car doors and jumped out.

"I told you, dammit! I told you!" the small officer screamed.

They scrambled through the parking lot, guns drawn and badges exposed. Bursting through the front doors, they pushed their way through a crowd of officers and into the washroom.

The thugs were on the floor, bound and gagged with duct tape and zip-ties. They were both unconscious, with blood gushing out their noses and pooling beneath them. Just in front of them sat their envelope of money, minus a few hundred dollars. The word "EVIDENCE" was scrawled on it in big black marker.

Big Frank was nowhere to be seen.

"Shit!" yelled the undercover officer, pounding his fist against the wall.

He instantly turned and ran back out of the building, charging through a bustling crowd of cops and curious onlookers.

"Move! Move! Now!" he screamed.

He shot out the door and into the parking lot, but it was too late. Big Frank's big black car was already long gone.

***

There was nothing left on Marcus's plate but a few fries and some greasy crumbs. He dipped one of the fries into a dollop of ketchup and tossed it into his mouth.

"Buff, this ain't no water haul, eh?" he asked, concerned. "Ya sure ya nare shuffin' more in yar gob than ya can chew, me b'y?"

"What do you mean?" asked Buff, confused.

"What I mean, me cocky, is that no cracky with a Strongbox is keepin' 'er in the garage under a tarp. Ya mind me now, b'y? These kind of things is for the government or the corporate world, for trade secrets, and gems, and bars of gold and the like. Unless the house yar plannin' on robbin' belongs to the Sultan of Brunei, I'd whack a guess and say yar lootin' an office, eh chum?"

"You're right."

"Give the goose a cracker! I's always right, b'y, but lootin' a business ain't the same tune as lootin' some ol' cod's nish house. I needs details, me cocky."

"I can lay out the basics. The target is a law office on the west side of town. What we're looking for is on the eighth floor, inside one of these Strongbox vaults."

"Well, b'y, now yar not just dealin' with a Strongbox, eh? An office buildin' gets ya a whole new box of snakes to deal with. Ya gots yer cameras and alarms, security guards, employees workin' late. The whole buildin' needs clearin', 'cause the drill ya needs to punch through that Strongbox is louder than a bucket of maul-mouth screechers in the middle of Sunday service. Now, that's a lot of spray on the rocks, b'y. Lots of variables to think 'bout. Goin' to need a big team to make sure she's spot on and runs clean."

"I know. We'll need muscle, probably two of them, maybe three. A hardware man, too, and a couple of drivers. I was thinking a team of nine, maybe ten."

Marcus chuckled. "There's usually eleven of them in the movies."

"You're not the first person to compare me with George Clooney."

The old man snorted and gobbled down another French fry. "There's another thing to consider, b'y. That drill we be using is heavier than yar date to the prom. She won't fit in the back of no cube van, me chum."

"We need to find a driver who can handle a big rig, then. Preferably someone with their own truck."

"Well, praise be to the Lard that yous are mates with a proper bud like meself, b'y. I thinks I may know a bird what can help us with that."

# June 29

That morning, Buff snuck out of the apartment before his sister woke up. He'd been avoiding her for two days now. He wasn't ready to answer the barrage of legitimate questions she was bound to ask him. Truthfully, he didn't want to look her in the face and lie to her.

Marcus picked him up from a dingy coffee shop around the corner from Emily's place. He drove an ugly brown minivan, the kind parents warn their kids to avoid when they talk about "stranger danger." It stunk worse than a men's locker room.

"Good mornin'," greeted Marcus, warmly. "Get aboard."

Buff climbed into the passenger's seat. He almost made a joke about the horrible smell, but noticed a sleeping bag and a pile of clothes in the back seat. Marcus had obviously been living in his van. He suddenly felt immeasurable pity for his former mentor. He knew things had been rough for him, but never once considered that the old man might be homeless.

"Thanks for the ride," said Buff.

"Eh, b'y, can ya jigger me some coin for gas? I's a wee bit short."

"No problem."

"Thanks, me chum."

They left the city's downtown core, and drove twenty minutes away to the Ontario Food Terminal, just off the Queensway. The forty-acre facility was the main distribution centre for produce in the city. Fruits and vegetables were shipped here from farms across the province, and around the world, and then local grocers would haggle with sellers over prices. Almost all of Toronto's fresh food passed through the terminal, and it was the main market for establishing produce prices in the region.

Marcus had a contact there he thought could prove useful. His niece, a foul-mouthed middle-aged woman whose friends had nicknamed "Surly Shirley," owned a small shipping company with an office at the terminal. The two of them had remained in contact through email over the years, due in large part to their shared affection for breaking the law.

Shirley's office wasn't much more than a trailer in a fenced-off area of the parking lot. Inside, it was meticulous and sparse, with nothing but a map of southern Ontario, a couple of filing cabinets, and a small desk with a computer and telephone sitting on it.

Buff and Marcus walked in and found Shirley sitting alone, doing paperwork. She looked up, and when she saw Marcus she leapt up out of her chair.

"Holy shit!" she exclaimed, excited. Her voice was deep and hoarse, as though she gargled with sand each morning. "Uncle Marcus, you fat son of a bitch! How the hell are you? Come here, cocksucker!" She ran towards him, threw her arms around him and gave him a giant bear hug.

Immediately Buff could sense that Shirley was one of a kind. She was as short as a fifth grader, but as tough as the sixth graders who picked on them. She had the dainty physique of a ballerina, but could be as crude and vulgar as a morning radio shock jock. She was a simple, modest woman who never wore makeup, and was rarely seen in anything but jeans and a hooded sweatshirt. Her long dark hair was pulled back tightly into a ponytail.

"Easy there, Shirley me love," Marcus laughed. He pulled Shirley off and looked her up and down. "Lard God me child, some good to see ya. Why, ya look fit as a fed dog. Hows ya gettin' on?"

"Shit, you know, good as always," she said cheerfully. "Business is good, life is good, same old shit. What have you been doing, you old prick? You know, you still owe me two hundred fucking dollars."

"Did ya nare get the cheque I mailed ya?"

"Yeah. It fucking bounced."

"Go on with ya! Sorry if I gots ya some vexed, ducky. I gets ya back, proper thing."

"Uh huh," she snorted with disbelief. She put her arms on her hips and looked over to Buff. "Who's this fucking guy? You're not trying to set me up, are you? I've already got a fucking boyfriend, you know."

"This young fella's me chummy," Marcus said, throwing his arm around Buff's shoulder. "Goes by the name of Buff, and I knows him for thirteen years, me love. The b'y may look like he's been hauled through a knothole, but this figger's a hard case with a heart of gold. And brains like an astronaut, to boot!"

"Jesus, sounds like you're the one fucking dating him." She reached out and shook Buff's hand. "Nice to meet you."

"The pleasure's all mine," said Buff. "It's great to finally meet you. Your uncle's said such wonderful things about you." That was a lie. Marcus had never mentioned her before.

"He loves to talk," said Shirley with a girlish giggle, "that's for fucking sure, but it's usually only about his damn self. Sorry, your name was Biff?"

"Buff."

"Buff? Really? That's a stupid fucking name."

"It was my grandmother's."

Shirley laughed. "Oh, I like this guy, Uncle M. He's fucking funny." She gave him a wink.

"Eh, easy there, love," said Marcus. "Ya can ballyrag the poor b'y bumbuy, not now, ducky."

"So, you're not here to get me paid, and you're not here to get me fucking laid. What the fuck are you doing here? Cheap fruit?"

"There's a wee piece of stuff we needs to jaw with ya about, love. We's plannin' a job, something big, and we needs a driver with a big truck."

Shirley didn't seem fazed by the proposition. This was a woman who'd spent her share of time on the wrong side of the law. She only took a moment to think about it before answering.

"When?" she asked.

"Two days," said Buff.

"Fucking Canada Day? Perfect. This place will be closed. What kind of fucking timeframe are you bastards thinking?"

"Overnight. Five hours, hopefully less."

There was a pause as Shirley thought about it some more. Her shipping business was doing well, so she really didn't need the money, but a part of her missed the rush of pulling a big score. She'd do it for sport.

"Why the fuck not? I'm in."

Marcus threw his fist into the air and cheered. He went to give Shirley another hug, but she stopped him.

"My rate's ten grand for the night," she said, with deadly seriousness, "and my truck's fucking fifteen. Cash upfront."

"Don't you want some details first?" Buff asked, confused.

"Fuck no! I don't want to know a goddamn thing. Keep me at an arm's fucking length, boys, understand? I'm just a fucking driver. No fucking guns, no fucking masks, no fucking hostages. Deal?"

"Bless yer heart, girlie," said Marcus with a smile. "Y'always were an angel. Shirley, me ducky, ya'll hear no blearin' from neither of us. We's all pros here, straight as lops on the pond. No guns, no masks, none of that, me love."

"This is no smash and grab," confirmed Buff. "It's a surgical strike. No one gets hurt, everyone walks away richer." He held his hand out to Shirley.

"Then it's a fucking deal!" she shouted, shaking Buff's hand, and then her uncle's.

"There's one more thing we needs yar help with, ducky," said Marcus.

"If it doesn't have to do with being the fucking driver, it'll cost extra."

"Just two or three names, me love. We needs some more muscle for the team, directly."

"Oh, shit, that's no problem. I know a couple of tough fucks from up north. I've worked with them before. They're not the smartest fucking kids in the class, but they're perfect for moving a piano, or busting some asshole's jaw."

"Sounds exactly like what we're looking for," said Buff.

Shirley grabbed the phone off her desk and gave the Fodder brothers a call.

***

Wellington County was an incredible stretch of southern Ontario, with some of the most beautiful farmland in the country. It was full of rolling hills dotted with healthy cows grazing, fields lined with budding crops of corn, and orchards stocked with bountiful apple trees. These farms were idyllic and family-owned, a reflection of man's delicate balance with nature.

The land owned by the Fodder family was definitely not one of those farms. It was just a single farmhouse, sitting on a dozen acres of untended land. Everything was rundown and decrepit, the perfect setting for a low-budget horror movie. The grass looked as though it hadn't been cut in six months. There were rusted shells of old cars resting on cinder blocks in the field. Stacks of rotted lumber and old newspapers were piled up outside the house. Dozens and dozens of empty beer bottles were strewn about everywhere.

Some three hundred yards away, a cop was checking the place out through binoculars, and was disgusted by what he saw. He was following up on an anonymous tip, claiming the brothers were growing marijuana. He'd been unable to secure a search warrant, so he decided to try some simple surveillance from a hilltop overlooking their farm. One look at their home and the officer was confident they were guilty.

As a member of the Ontario Provincial Police, he'd seen plenty of flophouses over the years, but never one that looked so deliberately ramshackle. The place looked like a rowdy frat house. He couldn't believe people lived there, but then again, the Fodder brothers barely qualified as people.

He watched the house for over two hours, but hadn't seen any illegal activity. He was about to leave when he saw the two brothers, Kane and Dwayne Fodder, stumble out their front door, both drunk as a coal miner on payday. They were huge, hulking men, like Neanderthals in lumberjack shirts. They were hicks and hillbillies, no doubt, but they were in fantastic shape. They looked like the kind of guys who participated in those "World's Strongest Man" competitions where men pull transport trucks with one arm. Kane was older and taller, with a crooked nose and lustrous blond mullet. Dwayne was fatter and hairier, had a wild bushy beard, and was never seen without his Toronto Maple Leafs cap on.

"I've got dibs on driving first," said Dwayne.

"Take off," Kane replied, playfully punching his brother in the shoulder. "You're too tanked to drive, you knob."

The officer watched them shamble back behind the house and out of view. He started to get excited. Maybe he wouldn't need a warrant after all. If he could bust these two yokels for drunk driving, he'd be able to put them behind bars, if only for a few months.

He heard the sound of a motor roaring to life. It made a thunderous noise, far louder than a car's engine should make.

A moment later, a giant yellow excavator came charging around the corner with Kane at the controls. The two idiots had tied an old couch to the earthmover's scoop with duct tape and ratchet straps, and Dwayne was riding it. The machine was like a huge carnival ride built by rednecks. As the excavator tore through the field, Kane swung its arm back and forth wildly. Dwayne was laughing and screaming, holding on for dear life but having a great time.

"Whoa! Not so fast, eh?" he shouted. "You're going to make me puke!"

Kane's cellphone began to ring. It was Surly Shirley calling. He reached down to answer it, slamming on the brakes.

The machine came to a sudden, screeching halt. Dwayne was thrown off the couch, flew through the air and landed in a muddy puddle with a painful thud. Kane began laughing maniacally.

Surly Shirley could hear the commotion on her end of the phone.

"Hello? Dwayne? Kane?" she shouted, confused. "What the fuck is going on over there?"

"Hang on a sec there, Shirley. Dwayne just got hosed."

Kane put the phone down, jumped off the excavator and ran to his brother's side.

"That was some nice air you got there, bud," he said. "Real beauty, eh?"

"You did that on purpose, you goof!" shouted Dwayne, rubbing his forehead. "That really hurt. I think I broke my ass. I told you we should have put a seat belt in 'er."

Kane helped his brother get back onto to his feet.

"My turn to drive now, eh?" insisted Dwayne.

"Later. Surly's on the phone. I think she's got a job for us."

Disappointed and despondent, the police officer threw his binoculars onto the passenger seat and started up his car. As long as the Fodders stayed on their own property, he couldn't touch them. Not that it mattered. Seeing how they spent their free time, he doubted whether those two idiots could grow anything on their farm. They looked too dumb to grow mould on stale bread.

The cop drove away, empty-handed.

***

Doug was at the tail end of his twenties, but never outgrew his awkward phase. He was a gangly nerd, but he embraced it. His niche was horror movies, and he lived every day like it was Halloween. His left arm was covered in tattoos of the Creature from the Black Lagoon and Boris Karloff as Frankenstein's monster, while on his right was Freddy Krueger and Bruce Campbell's character from the *Evil Dead* movies. He wore a black T-shirt emblazoned with the poster from *Creepshow*. His hair was dyed jet black, cropped short and slicked back.

He found himself in what looked to be a clean, brightly lit medical laboratory. There was a metal autopsy table in the centre of the room, and in the corner was a desk with a microscope on it. The walls were tiled with polished white ceramic. The shelves were lined with beakers and test tubes, some filled with a glowing green liquid. An array of expensive-looking equipment filled the room. It looked like a real science lab, even if it didn't exactly feel like one.

Doug used his shirt to wipe away the smudges from his thick, square-frame glasses, and turned to the autopsy table to resume his work. There was an enormous alien monster splayed out in front of him. The awful beast was the size of a refrigerator. It had the head of a snarling dog, three powerful arms with jagged claws, sharp fins along its spine, and a long, twitching lizard tail. It was pink and flesh-coloured, coated with a glaze of gelatinous ooze. The thing sat idle, with eight big black air tubes snaking out from its belly.

Doug grabbed a jar of fake blood from his toolkit, and went back to smearing it all over the creature's mouth and teeth. He was on a film set, and the monster was just an animatronic prop – a very expensive prop that a team of artists spent three weeks building. It was a crucial element of the next scene, so it had to look perfect.

The film was a prequel to *Re-Animator*, Stuart Gordon's mischievously gory 1985 splatter-horror cult-classic. It was one of Doug's favourites. Unfortunately, this new movie represented everything he hated about the current state of horror films. Everything was a sequel, prequel, reboot or, worst of all, a remake. It was being directed by some pretentious hack with no interest in the genre, whose only previous experience was a car commercial. It wasn't written so much as it was developed around a soundtrack. None of the cast or crew from the original film were consulted or given creative input. Most disheartening of all, the studio was insistent that all of the special effects be done with computer graphics.

Doug worked in practical effects, which were special effects that were produced on-set, without computer-generated imagery. He knew less about computers than the average grandmother. He worked with his hands, and his specialty was electronics: circuit boards, pneumatics, and wireless telemetry systems. It was his passion, what he'd wanted to do his whole life. He grew up poring over the pages of *Fangoria* magazine, idolizing people like Rick Baker, Stan Winston, and Rob Bottin.

One of the film's producers saw Doug's demo reel on YouTube and convinced the director and studio that he should be brought onto the production. Normally the talented young artist would turn down a job that went against his artistic principles, but times were tough. Work was getting harder to find every year, as more and more films relied on computer graphics. Integrity dissipates quickly when you've got to eat.

A few years earlier, things had gotten so desperate for Doug that he was forced to look outside of the film industry, and offer his services to the criminal underworld. It wasn't much of a leap. In fact, he found most of the "criminals" he dealt with to be a lot more honest than your average film producer.

His technical skills made him adept at unlocking doors and disabling alarm systems. He found himself a partner, and they spent the better part of two years breaking into buildings for a substantial fee.

That's not who Doug was anymore, though. He'd broken up with his old partner several months ago, and had dedicated himself to living on the straight and narrow. If that meant swallowing his pride and working on a crass straight-to-video prequel, so be it.

The film set was bustling. People were buzzing about in all directions, each with their own important task. Burly grips were setting up lights, gaffers were running electrical cables, technicians were mounting a matte box to the camera's lens, and set decorators were adding the final touches to the lab. Doug was oblivious to all of it, concentrating on his work.

Satisfied with the gore on the monster's jaws, he set the jar of fake blood aside. His monster looked pretty, but now it was time to test the beast. He grabbed the animatronic's control panel and fiddled with some buttons and switches. It was supposed to send compressed air shooting through the tubes inside the creature's belly, making the awful thing thrash wildly. Unfortunately, the rubber monster just sat there, lifeless and impotent, hissing like a deflating balloon.

There had to be a tear somewhere along the hose. Doug started looking for it, ready to patch the hole with electrical tape. He was so focused that he didn't notice Buff walk up behind him.

"That thing looks like my ex," he said with a wry smile.

Doug reacted the way a dog does when its owner comes home. "Buff, dude!" he exclaimed, giving his old friend a big brotherly hug. "Damn, it's great to see you again. It's been, what, like two years? How've you been, man? I heard you got pinched."

"I just got out."

"Hey, that's awesome, dude. Welcome back to the world. We need to go get a beer and catch up, soon." He started looking around, furtively. "But, dude, uh, you can't be here right now. This is a closed set. If somebody catches you here, they'll call the cops. For real."

Buff laughed. "It's okay," he said, calmly. "I know the production manager. He owes me a favour."

"She," snapped Doug, correcting him.

Buff couldn't take his eyes off the disgusting monster. "That's really impressive, Doug. Did you make this yourself?"

"Well, there was a team that designed and sculpted it, but the internal mechanics and electronics are all me."

"That's incredible. This thing looks great."

"Thanks, dude. We put a lot of work into it. I haven't slept in a couple days, and you don't want to know how much this bastard costs. Want to see something cool? Check this out."

Doug flicked a button on the control panel, and the creature's tail thrashed back and forth wildly. Doug pressed another button, and the tail split apart and opened up like a flower, spurting out streams of fake blood.

Buff jumped back, startled. He found this sort of thing distasteful and unpleasant, but appreciated the craftsmanship Doug put into it. The enthusiasm on the young man's face was undeniable. As Doug watched the ghastly beast come to life, he was beaming with pride and excitement, like a parent at a preschool Christmas recital.

"Isn't that awesome?"

"It's great, Doug. What is it supposed to be?"

"It's an alien."

"I thought *Re-Animator* was about zombies."

"Ugh, I know. Dude, don't get me started. This movie is going to be terrible."

"Okay, sorry. The monster looks great, though. Very convincing, very scary. The work that must have gone into making that is really impressive. You always were great at that kind of thing."

"Hey, thanks, dude. Seriously, though, you need to get out of here. They're hardcore about unauthorized people on set. I can't imagine how you even got in here in the first place."

"I need a good electronics man, Doug. I need you. I'm planning a job."

"No way, dude. I'm out."

"I heard. I tried that too, and it didn't last two days. How long have you been legit now?"

"Almost eight months."

"How has it been?"

"You know, not bad. All my effort goes into my art now. It's more stress and a lot less money, but I'm doing what I love, and I'm not looking over my shoulder every time I leave the house. I mean it, Buff. I'm out."

Buff took a long, hard look into Doug's eyes, and saw that there was no changing the young man's mind. He'd built a new life for himself within the confines of the law, and he did it by following his passion. It made Buff a little jealous. It was exactly the sort of life he'd envisioned for himself upon leaving prison, but failed to achieve.

He smiled and patted Doug on the shoulder. Seeing him at work, he didn't even want to change the young man's mind. Buff knew he was a bad man, but not bad enough to lure a good man off the right path. He was happy for him.

"You're right," said Buff. "I'm sorry. It was great to see you again. Call me sometime and we'll catch up."

"Sure thing," Doug said, relieved. "Real soon, dude. Sorry I can't help."

"No, it's okay. I'm happy for you. I'll let you get back to work. I'll talk to you soon."

Buff started walking away when a dozen people suddenly swarmed the set and stood around the autopsy table. It was the director and his entourage of assistants, all wearing headsets like air traffic controllers.

He was a young man, barely older than Doug, with a scruffy beard and flannel shirt. Most of his dark, shaggy hair was tucked beneath a black baseball cap, emblazoned with an Arri logo. He looked like a film student, not a full-fledged director. He strode onto set like a celebrity at an exclusive club, dragging an unearned sense of entitlement with him.

He stopped in front of Buff and looked him up and down.

"This is a closed set," he said with condescension.

"I'm with the studio," Buff answered, dryly. "We've met before."

The director's demeanour changed instantly, and he became a snivelling, sycophantic yes-man. He grabbed Buff's hand and shook it.

"Of course!" he said, fawning. "Great to see you again. You look fantastic! Can I get you a latte?" Without waiting for an answer, he turned to one of his female assistants. "Get this man a latte, right away."

"Copy that," said the young woman as she dashed away.

Doug flashed Buff an incredulous look.

"This movie's going to be great," the director continued, turning back to a smirking Buff. "Really fantastic. You're going to be really impressed. Every penny will be on screen."

"We'll see," said Buff.

There was a long, awkward pause before the director responded.

"Alright," he said with a hesitant nod. He looked to Doug. "So, how's our alien queen looking?"

"Camera ready and standing by," said Doug, confidently. "I just put the finishing touches on the teeth, we fixed the articulation in the arms, and the tail has been tested. I think we're ready to go."

"That's great. Can I see it move?"

"No problem."

Doug took the control panel, grabbed the joystick and pushed a few buttons. The monster's jaw began to snarl and gnash its teeth. The arms reached out, swiping their claws back and forth. The tail shook, and just as Buff had seen before, it split apart and spat out gobs of fake gore.

The creature moved convincingly, even up close. Doug swelled with pride. It would look even better through a camera lens once properly lit.

The young woman ran up beside Buff and handed him a latte.

"Great work, Doug," the director said, patting him on the shoulder. "That's fantastic. Can we get some movement on the fingers?"

"Uh, maybe, yeah," Doug mumbled.

He flicked a dial on his control panel, and the left arm rose up. Two of the fingers wiggled in a jarring, robotic way. It didn't look good.

"Is that it?" the director asked.

"That's as good as it's going to get. There are no pivot points in the extremities."

"Hmm, that could be a problem. There have been a few script changes."

"Changes?"

"Yeah. The scene needed a little punch, you know? Something to make it extreme. Memorable. Fantastic. Is there any way you can get the alien queen to stand up and give the finger?" The director acted out the movement he was looking for.

Doug was stunned and confused. He really hoped the man was joking.

"Give the finger?" he asked. "Like, the middle finger?"

"Yeah! Flip him the bird, you know? It's cool. It's way to get a 'fuck you' in there while keeping it PG-13."

"Huh. Well, uh, no. No, I can't do that. Of course I can't do that."

The director crossed his arms, dramatically. "And why not, exactly?"

"We're not prepared for that. We didn't plan for that. The thing's bolted to the table. We designed it around the script we were given. It took weeks to build." Doug was talking faster and faster, his emotions getting the better of him. His voice started to crack. "This was approved a month ago. You can't change it now!"

The director was ambivalent to his pleas. He smiled and took a sip of his coffee, waving his hand in the air. "It's okay," he said. "We'll just do it with CGI. Don't worry, though. The puppet won't go to waste. We can still use it for lighting reference. We'll replace it in post. It'll look better, anyway."

Doug was crushed, but kept a brave face.

"So," the director continued, clapping his hands to get everyone's attention, "Let's get this lit for some wide plates, then move in close and let the puppet do its thing, then get the reverse angle from the other side of table. Fantastic. Sound good?"

The various assistants around him nodded, answering in unison, "Copy that." They all scattered away in various directions, like dancers when the lights go down after a big number. The director walked over to the craft services table.

Buff and Doug were left alone with the expensive prop that no audience would ever see. Doug's shoulders drooped down and he hung his head like Charlie Brown did when he was sad.

Buff took a sip of his latte, looking away. He felt terrible for his friend.

"What's the take?" asked Doug.

The question caught Buff off guard. "Doug, look, you've got a good thing here. I can't ask you to do anything..."

"How much? What am I walking away with?" He was adamant and forceful.

Buff took a deep breath. He wouldn't push. He'd let Doug make his own decision. "Name your price."

"I don't want a contract. I want a percentage."

"It's not really that kind of job, Doug."

"Dude, do you want an electronics man or not? If I do this, I want to be able to walk away with enough to turn down crap movies like this."

"How much will that take?"

"Fifteen percent."

"The target's not a bank, Doug. It's an info grab. Give me a number."

"Two hundred grand."

Buff scoffed. "Fifty."

"One hundred grand."

"Fifty. Maybe."

"When?"

"July first."

Doug inhaled deeply, thinking it over. "Dangerous?"

"I hope not."

"Okay, man. I'll do it." He pulled a business card out of his pocket and handed it to Buff. "Call me later with details. I've got to get back to work."

Buff grinned. "Thanks Doug. Really."

Doug smiled and waved him off, turning his attention back to re-filling the hideous monster-puppet with fake blood.

A twinge of guilt gnawed at the back of Buff's head as he walked off the set and out of the studio. He had mixed feelings about what he was asking of his friend. He knew getting Doug back into crime was a bad thing, but the young man was the best at what he did. The team needed him.

Out in the parking lot, Buff saw the Fodder brothers' pick-up truck waiting for him. It was badly beaten, covered in mud and horribly rusted. It was once bright yellow, but had long since faded to pale, bland beige. Kane sat behind the wheel, Dwayne was in the passenger seat, and Marcus waited in the back seat.

Buff opened the side door and climbed in.

"He's in," he said.

Marcus laughed and slapped his knee. "Eh, b'y, ya gots a way with the words, convincin' peoples and the like. Ya could sell a bucket of ice to the Eskimos, me chum. Did ya tells him 'bout Beka?"

"He didn't ask."

Marcus stared at Buff, dumbfounded. He did not look amused.

"Don't make me douse ya on the head, b'y. They need to know they're workin' together, cocky. What do ya think will happen when they see each other at the meetin' tomorrow?"

Buff looked out the window, waving Marcus' question away. "We'll cross that bridge when we get to it."

Marcus shook his head and threw his arms up in defeat. He was in no mood for an argument.

Kane started up the truck and sped away. They pulled out of the studio parking lot and headed towards the highway.

"So then, b'y, we got us an electronics man. We all good to go then, best kind?"

"No," Buff answered, sternly. "Not yet. We still need another driver. A getaway man."

"I thought ya called Bishop?"

"Bishop joined the army. He's in Afghanistan."

"No foolin'? Count me stunned, chummy. Lard bless the young fella's cotton socks, me b'y. Thems the real heroes, eh?"

"Got to support the troops," said Dwayne.

"Do you know anybody else we could call?" Buff asked Marcus.

"No, b'y," he answered. "Ya gots me stumped as skiff in the ballycater. Getaway drivers got a short life on the shelf, eh? Price of gas and all. Why not get one of these charmin' b'ys to do it?"

"No. We need them for muscle."

"We've got a bud in the city you could call, eh?" Dwayne said. "He's a beauty of a driver."

"Really?" asked Marcus, skeptically. "Who's that now?"

"You wouldn't know him. I don't even know what his real name is, but he's, like, unstoppable behind the wheel. He delivers pizza."

***

The baby-faced young man thrust two boxes of pizza into Buff's arms.

"The name's N-Dig," he said, fishing a set of car keys out of his pocket.

"N-Dig?" Buff asked, unsure.

"Yeah, bro. N-Dig, or N-Dog, or N-Diggity. Short for 'indignant,' see?"

"Hmm, interesting. That's not a very common name."

"Funny coming from a guy named Buff."

Buff laughed. "Fair enough."

"Is that name short for something?"

"No."

N-Dig took the pizzas back and tucked them under his arm. He was young, strong, and swaggered like a rock star, with baggy pants, dreadlocks and a long gold chain. He claimed to be 25, but he looked much younger than that.

He puffed out his chest, trying to look tough, but it wouldn't work on Buff. For one thing, N-Dig was significantly shorter. Secondly, he was wearing a bright orange jacket with a cartoon pizza on the back, which made it hard to take him seriously.

"The Fodders told me I should hear what you've got to say," he said, in a voice deep enough to attract snakes.

"I have a job offer for you," Buff said, flatly.

"I've got a job, bro."

"This one's five grand for one night."

"How do you know the Fodders?"

"Long story. Friend of a friend."

"Friend of a cop?"

"Well, I have a parole officer. Does he count?"

N-Dig smirked. "My car's over there."

They two of them walked through the parking lot to a rusty old Ford Focus with a huge photo of a pizza slice pasted onto the hood. Buff walked around to the passenger side, but N-Dig waved him into the back seat.

"Pizza sits up front, bro," he said.

N-Dig worked as a driver for the Big Puck Pizza location on the corner of Dundas and Church Streets. His route covered both the extremely wealthy in the glass towers of Bay Street, and the desperately poor in the slums on Sherbourne Street. It was the pizza chain's most popular location in the whole city, by a wide margin. Some nights, it would make more money than most other pizza places earn in a week. In fact, Big Puck's profits were so big that it got the local police department's attention.

Across the street from Buff, a police cruiser sat parked at a gas station. In it, two officers with the local drug squad were watching the pizza shop. They had no proof of wrongdoing, only suspicions, and were just starting their investigation.

As N-Dig's car tore out of the parking lot, one cop turned to the other.

"Our driver's got a friend with him tonight," he said.

"Follow them," the other officer ordered. "Be discreet about it."

The police car pulled out of the gas station and drove east along Dundas Street, trailing several car lengths behind N-Dig's worn-out vehicle.

It was dusk, and the last orange gasp of daylight was fading away behind the city's tall metal skyscrapers. The neon storefront signs and hanging streetlights began twinkling to life. The air was the warmest it had been in months. People were dressed in their best outfits, sauntering along the sidewalks, talking and laughing, on their way to a restaurant, a night club, or a show at the theatre. It was a beautiful summer night.

The engine beneath the hood of the Ford Focus was in desperate need of a tune up. It was indescribably loud and noisy. It made a cacophonous mix of grinding, squealing, and rumbling as it thundered down the street, like a washing machine full of rocks. Yet, the car still managed to dart through traffic fast and smoothly.

The inside of N-Dig's car was filthy. Empty cans of pop, old napkins and other assorted garbage were strewn all over the floor. It reeked of stale marijuana smoke.

N-Dig drove with only one hand on the wheel, while he draped the other arm over his precious pizzas. The young driver had the latest Kanye West song blaring on the car stereo with the bass cranked, and the whole vehicle shook and vibrated every few seconds as the beat pounded relentlessly. He bobbed his head along with the music.

Buff could feel himself getting a headache. He began rubbing his temples.

"Too loud, bro?" asked N-Dig.

Buff nodded, emphatically.

"Sorry," N-Dig said, turning the music down slightly. It was still too loud, but at least now Buff wouldn't have to shout to be heard.

"Mind if I open a window?" he asked. "It smells like Willie Nelson's tour bus in here."

"You want some? Best prices in town."

"No, no, thanks. I'm good," Buff said, as though he'd just been offered something from inside a toilet bowl. "Wait, are you a drug dealer? I thought you were a driver."

N-Dig let out a booming laugh.

"I'm both, bro. Why do you think I deliver pizza?"

"I don't get the connection."

"Money, bro. It's business. Almost every place I deliver to is looking for weed. I mean, seriously bro, the only people that eat Big Puck's pizza are kids' birthday parties and stoners. Nobody orders it for a first date, you know? I just wait for them to ask and provide. I'm no pusher, bro. Believe."

Buff sunk back into his seat. He had serious doubts that N-Dig was the right man for the job. He didn't have anything against pot smokers. To him, it wasn't any different from drinking a few beers. However, he took his work very seriously, and didn't like the idea of his getaway driver being impaired on anything.

"Look," said Buff, his voice getting stern and serious, "I need a wheelman. I need a driver. If we're going to work together, I need you clear-headed and sober."

N-Dig seethed. He hated being told what to do.

"Easy, bro, easy," he replied with a smile, drawing out every syllable. "Just chill, man. I'm the best driver in the city, bro. Thirty minutes or less.

Every time. I'm like Vin 'Fast and Furious' Diesel behind the wheel, man. For real. Setting land speed records. Ran the Kessel Run in less than twelve parsecs, bro." He started laughing gregariously.

Buff didn't.

He still wasn't convinced. N-Dig just wasn't the kind of driver they were looking for. It stung, because this was the first snag he'd hit so far in putting his team together. He had less than 48 hours to find another driver and didn't know anyone he could call.

"I just don't think this is going to work," he said.

"You don't think I can drive?" N-Dig asked, offended.

Without waiting for a response, he slammed his foot down on the gas pedal. The engine growled like a caged lion, the tires squealed, and the car blasted forward like a shot from a cannon. It charged towards an empty intersection. The traffic light hanging above was red, but N-Dig recklessly sped his vehicle right through it.

The cops following him noticed. The red and blue lights on their cruiser began flashing, and the siren began to wail. They tore off down the street, chasing after the rusty old Ford Focus.

N-Dig saw them in his rearview mirror. He took a quick scan of the road ahead of him, and then gripped the steering wheel tightly with both hands.

"Hold on," he said.

Suddenly, the car swerved sharply to the left into the next lane, right into the path of an oncoming streetcar!

The massive metal tram shuddered and screeched as the driver slammed on the brakes. Its horn was blaring like a screaming newborn. Sparks shot out from the tracks beneath it. The last wheel became derailed, and the enormous weight of the streetcar dug into the concrete. It lurched to an abrupt stop.

N-Dig swerved the car the left again, inching between the streetcar and two parked delivery trucks. Buff was screaming the whole time.

The police cruiser was forced to stop suddenly. The tires made a terrible noise as they skidded to a halt, narrowly avoiding the derailed tram.

N-Dig stepped on the gas, and both he and Buff were thrust back into their seats. The car sped down the street, moving so fast the frame was shaking. It darted from one lane to another, weaving in and out of traffic like a breeze through the leaves.

He came up to Ontario Street and made a hard left.

"No!" shouted Buff, slamming his hand against the back of N-Dig's seat. "This is a one-way street! Wrong way! Wrong way!"

The driver ignored him. He kept tearing down the dark side street at dangerous speeds. Luckily, there was no oncoming traffic. The car was going faster and faster, gaining momentum as it approached the next intersection.

Suddenly, N-Dig grabbed the gearshift and slammed it into neutral. As the engine's rattle dissipated, he ripped the key from the ignition. All of the car's lights went dark.

He pumped the brakes and drifted into a deep, empty driveway in between two townhouses. The car crawled to a stop, and within seconds was silent. It was shrouded in shadow and couldn't be seen from the road.

Buff was in a panic, sweating profusely.

"What the hell are you doing?" he asked, apoplectic.

"Get down," N-Dig said with a whisper, ducking his head behind the passenger seat. Buff threw himself against the floor.

They could hear police sirens get louder as they approached, peak as they sailed by, then fade off into the distance.

N-Dig reached into the glove compartment and pulled out two new licence plates and a torque wrench. He jumped out of the car and got to work. In under a minute and without making a sound, he'd replaced the plates on the front and rear of his vehicle and tore the pizza decal off his hood.

After climbing back into the car, N-Dig threw a clean napkin at Buff.

"Towel off," he said with a laugh.

Buff took it and wiped his brow. His heart was racing. He'd forgotten what it felt like to be chased by the police.

"What good is changing the plates going to do?" he asked. "They know where you work. They'll track you down."

"You kidding me, bro?" N-Dig asked with a cocked eyebrow. "I told you I'm the best, man. My shift's over. I'm not going back to Big Puck's tonight."

Buff's eyes went wide. He couldn't believe how careless this kid was. "All they have to do is ask the manager who was making deliveries tonight!"

N-Dig laughed. "Mitch? Bro, I'm his best driver. I put his kids through college. He's not giving me up. He never has. You think this is the first time I've ever had to ditch the cops, man?"

"I do my best not to get noticed in the first place."

"Listen to me, bro," N-Dig said, deadly serious. "You wanted to see skills. I showed you skills. I'm the best driver in the city, I'm telling you. Believe."

There was a long pause. Buff sighed deeply and shook his head. The kid was reckless, but he couldn't deny that he'd make a great wheelman, as long as he kept his head straight.

"Okay," he said, hesitantly. "You're in, if you want it. Five grand for one night, paid after the job. You show up high, you leave without the money."

"Relax, bro. I'm good."

"I'm serious."

N-Dig gritted his teeth. He hated being talked down to, and he really hated being told what to do. He took a deep breath, and looked right into Buff's eyes.

"Chill, bro. I heard you. I get it. It's all good. Just count me in."

"Good. Welcome aboard."

N-Dig reached over and shook Buff's hand.

He gave a big grin and a thumb-up, and then shoved the key back into the ignition, starting the car. "We need to go. These pizzas have to be at Eastern and Carlaw in seventeen minutes."

The vehicle pulled out of the driveway and drove back down Ontario Street, this time travelling in the appropriate direction. N-Dig drove with caution, obeying every traffic law and giving a wide berth to other drivers on the road, and still made his delivery with five minutes to spare. Nobody knew this city's streets better than him.

***

Buff returned late to Emily's apartment. He hoped to avoid seeing his sister, but when he walked through the front door, she was sitting in the living room, waiting for him. Her arms were crossed and she wore a scowl on her face. She looked like a stern parent waiting up for a teenager who'd stayed out past curfew. Chang sat in her lap, panting loudly.

Buff stood on the other side of the room, speechless. There was a tense, awkward silence hanging in the room.

The adorably chubby pug leapt up when he saw Buff. He anxiously waddled over to the ex-con and nuzzled his leg. It was heartening for Buff to know that no matter what, he couldn't disappoint that little guy.

"Where were you?" asked Emily, tapping her foot.

"Just meeting up with some friends," Buff answered, his voice lilting.

Emily scoffed. "What kind of friends?"

"Old ones."

"I bet. What are you up to, Bryan?"

Buff bent down and scratched Chang under his chin. He was stalling for time. The dog began wagging its tail.

"Well?" she yelled, indignant.

"Nothing!" said Buff, shrugging. "I've been seeing the city, smelling the fresh air, thumbing through magazines at bookstores. Normal stuff. It can be pretty exciting after two years in jail."

"I'm not mom, Bryan. Don't make me feel bad for being suspicious.

That doesn't work on me. I know something's going on. I know you haven't been back to work since your first day."

"Mr. Patterson gave me a week off. He said I was a great worker."

"Really? He said that?"

"Well, he might have been talking about you. But he did give me a week off!"

Emily buried her head in her hands and growled loudly. It scared poor Chang out of the room. Buff hadn't seen his sister this frustrated in years.

She got up from her chair so she could look her brother in the eye. She cleared her throat, taking a moment to compose herself before continuing. "Look, Bryan, I'm just trying to help. I want to help. But I need you to be honest with me. I told you I didn't want you involved in anything illegal."

"I'm not, Emily. I swear."

"Then what have you been doing? Honestly. Where are you going? Who are you seeing?"

Buff could feel his throat tighten. He looked at his sister a moment, and contemplated telling her everything. She wouldn't understand. She couldn't possibly, and the truth was so complicated at this point that it's doubtful she'd even believe him.

He shrugged again.

"It's nothing you have to worry about, Em," he said, pleading. "Trust me. Please."

"Well, that's the problem, isn't it?" she asked, putting her hands on her hips. "I just can't anymore. I tried, Bryan." She paused and took a deep breath. "I want you out of this apartment by the end of the week."

Buff thought about arguing, but she was wearing a look on her face that let him know she meant business. He looked down at the floor, ashamed of himself for letting his sister down.

"Okay," he said with a nod.

Emily said nothing. She looked at Buff a moment, shook her head and walked away. She went into her bedroom and shut the door behind her.

Buff walked over to the bookshelf and grabbed the phone. He was two hours overdue for checking in with his parole officer. He braced himself for another scolding as he dialled the number.

# June 30

Since the early 1980s, every child who lived in or around Toronto has had a birthday party at the Organ Grinder. Just south of Front Street and housed in a renovated warehouse, it was an idiosyncratic place that was more playground than restaurant. It predated the rise of children's eat-and-play chains like Chuck E. Cheese, but did it with far more charm. For one thing, instead of being designed around a colourful cartoon rat, it seemed as though it had been decorated by a flea market P. T. Barnum. Between the stuffed moose head that whistled every six minutes and the eleven-foot-long alligator that wore sunglasses and a straw hat, the place surely set a record somewhere for the amount of zany, crazy stuff mounted on the walls.

The restaurant's main attraction, however, was the mighty Wurlitzer, an enormous theatre organ the size of a small bus that sat in the middle of the main dining area. Thousands of feet of brass and copper pipes snaked throughout the restaurant, from pencil-sized or piccolo, to ones big and thick enough to produce thunderous bass notes that would shake the tables. Mixed amongst the pipes were dozens of fascinating instruments, ranging from drums and cymbals, to xylophones, all playing along with the organ's music, as if by magic. A single piano player, who sat on a throne in front of the incredible instrument, controlled them all. When the music peaked, it recalled the wondrous, timeless sounds of old boardwalks and carnivals. Best of all, the piano player would take requests.

Not only was the Organ Grinder a restaurant that tested the sonic tolerance of its patrons, but there were also enough flashing, blinking, strobing lights inside to give an epileptic nightmares for years. It was lit up like the Las Vegas strip, all throbbing neon and multicoloured bulbs, and all of it dancing and twinkling in time with the music. Hanging above it all was a giant mirrored disco ball more than ten feet wide. It was a garish extravagance, the kind that could only be found in the most populous city in the country.

The restaurant was filled with a wide range of arcade video games, varying from classics like *Pac-Man* and *Asteroids* to more recent hits like *Dance Dance Revolution* and *Dead Heat Racing*. In addition, there were rows of old pinball machines, love testers, strength testers, and fortune telling machines, all in perfect working order. For the young and young-at-heart who are easily distracted and have a pocket full of quarters, this was easily the best way to spend a Saturday night.

The Organ Grinder served pizza, spaghetti, hamburgers and hotdogs, the kind of mediocre food that played to the appetites of eight-year-olds. As the poor cooks who worked there learned, no one cares what they're eating when seated next to an imposing, oversized organ blaring the theme song from *The Addams Family*. The food wasn't bad; it was just bland, uninspired and cheap.

It would be hard to imagine a business meeting taking place here, amidst booster seats and skeeball, but the Organ Grinder did have a private room at the back of the restaurant. Buff had rented it out for the evening, and this was where he was going to lay out his plan for the heist.

When he arrived, the place was congested, crammed full of swarms of sticky toddlers and noisy adolescents. Weekends were always busy, but given that the following day was a national holiday, the restaurant would be especially hectic tonight.

It was perfect. Buff knew people would be too distracted by their own kids to pay any attention to his ragtag clan. They'd be hiding in plain sight.

Buff brushed off his shoulder and adjusted his shirt collar. He was wearing his expensive suit again, although this time it was freshly pressed. He looked rich and important, two attributes not normally associated with patrons of the Organ Grinder.

"I'm sorry, sir," the hostess at the front said to him, "but I'm afraid your table isn't quite ready yet. It will only be a few more minutes."

He shrugged. Two seven-year-old boys with plastic toy pistols ran past him, bumping the back of his knees. The hostess cringed.

"It's a madhouse in here tonight," she sighed, apologetic. "I'm really sorry. Kids, right?"

"It's not a problem," said Buff with a warm smile. "I'm sure the sugar and video games will calm them down."

The hostess laughed nervously.

"This place serves alcohol, right?" Buff asked.

"Of course, sir," the hostess replied, relaxing slightly. "The bar's right over there. The first drink is on the house. I think some members of your party have already arrived. We'll call for you when your table is ready."

"Thanks," he said, loosening his tie. He gave the young woman a nod and wandered over to the bar.

He grabbed a stool beside a pair of weary middle-aged fathers with loud shirts, each nursing a bottle of beer.

Looking around, he noticed Big Frank and Beka sitting next to each other at the other end of the bar. They weren't talking.

Big Frank was freshly shaved, and wore his signature long black trench coat. He held a glass of rye whisky, and stared off into the distance, vacant and blank, like a machine that had been turned off.

Beka's attention was focused squarely on her phone, as she furiously texted her friends. Her fingers danced across the tiny touch-screen with astounding speed. She had her bright blue hair pulled back into a pony tail. She wore a pair of unblemished black and pink Converse sneakers, along with some ragged jeans and a Sunnydale High School T-shirt.

Across the room, Buff saw N-Dig and the Fodder brothers playing *Cruis'n Exotica,* racing each other around the Las Vegas track. They were boisterous and cheerfully competitive, laughing and hollering like the other children in the restaurant.

The Fodders were both wearing brand new Toronto Maple Leafs jerseys.They'd just purchased them earlier in the afternoon, after an eventful trip to the Hockey Hall of Fame. Both brothers were already very drunk.

N-Dig had a pair of extravagant gold chains around his neck, hanging over a big, baggy, green golf shirt. A pristine green baseball cap sat askew on his head. He was losing badly in his race against the brothers, lagging behind Dwayne's Jeep Wrangler.

As they came up around a tight hairpin turn, N-Dig leaned over, grabbed Dwayne's steering wheel and pulled it in the opposite direction.

"Hey, you goof!" shouted Dwayne, spilling warm beer all over his lap. N-Dig laughed derisively as they struggled over the wheel. On screen, the Jeep smashed into a wall and flipped over. N-Dig's Plymouth Prowler flew past him and sped off into second place.

Dwayne gave N-Dig two sharp punches in the shoulder. They fought playfully.

Around the restaurant, a few people were starting to notice the commotion.

Kane jumped up and stood between his brother and his friend, holding them apart.

"Knock it off!" he said sternly, like an angry father. "Do it now, boys. You're scaring the women and children, eh?"

Buff walked over, quickly and calmly, to provide some backup. He gave Kane an appreciative pat on the back.

"This is why I can't take you guys some place classy, like Red Lobster," he said with a smile. "Let's keep things clean and PG, okay? This is a family restaurant. If you get kicked out, you don't get paid."

Kane and Dwayne nodded like scolded children. N-Dig brushed him off, focusing on the race as his Prowler zoomed past the finish line. The words "FIRST PLACE" flashed across the screen.

"I won!" he shouted, pumping his fist in the air. He was ignoring the others on purpose. It was a defense mechanism he'd developed to mask his seething anger. He hated being told what to do.

Buff looked to the Fodders for support, but they just shrugged.

Before he could say anything, someone tugged the back of his arm.

He spun around and saw Marcus, wearing a suit and tie, holding two cold bottles of beer in his hands. The old man had the radiant smile of a lottery winner.

"Eh there, b'y!" he exclaimed. "Have a nish cold bit of the sweet sauce, me cracky. What are ya at?"

Buff grabbed the beer from Marcus's hand. The old man held up his own bottle. They clinked the necks and each took a swig.

"Is everyone here?" asked Buff.

"No, b'y. I ain't seen Shirley around here yet. Doug's not here neither, and there's something tellin' me ya still have not told him 'bout Beka."

Buff shrugged his shoulders and smirked. Marcus was not amused.

"This ain't a laugh, me cocky!" he shouted, stamping his foot. "Lard t'underin', ya can't be keepin' a man in the dark in regards to his ol' squeezy-duck, b'y! Doug's not gonna be happy to see an ex-girlfriend on the team, that's for sure and all."

"Marcus, relax," Buff said calmly, putting a hand on the old man's shoulder. "They're both professionals. This is just another job. There's nothing to worry about."

"Says you, b'y," Marcus scoffed. "This is all on yar shoulders, chum. I'm on the record now as sayin' ya should of tolds him."

"Fine." Buff shook his head and took another drink of his beer.

"Speakin' of things ya should of tolds, can I have a word with ya 'bout this fella here?" Marcus pointed out towards N-Dig. "The one there with all them gold chains on him, lookin' like Mr. T 'bout twenty-five years too late, b'y. Y'know, the b'y ya hired to be our driver, me chum."

"I've seen him behind the wheel, Marcus. He's good. Trust me."

"Eh b'y, ya done plain sure that he ain't part of no street gang?"

"What?"

"Is he a hoodlum, ya know? A goon, a thug. Be sure he's got no part in some gang, b'y. Big Frank don't look kindly on them types, me cocky."

"Oh, please. Calm down, Marcus, the kid's fine. He's not Scarface, he's just some pothead who delivers pizzas."

"Ya sure 'bout that, b'y? Me, I ain't. See, I can vouch for all these people here. I've worked with 'em before and looked into their past. Shirley's willin' to give the good word on the Fodder brothers, and I trust 'er. If she says they're good, then they are, b'y. But this driver fella with the silly name..."

"N-Dig."

"Sounds like the name of a damn multivitamin. We know nothing 'bout him, and the good word of two drunk, colliwoggin' hillbillies ain't near enough to convince me he's the best man for the job, me chummy. I don't like him."

"Do you think I just picked his name out of a hat? I told you I've seen him drive. The Fodders have worked with him before. What more do you want?" He held out his arms, exasperated.

Marcus sighed deeply. The two men stared at each for a tense moment, neither willing to back down. Their argument was stalled.

"Are you okay?" asked Buff, leaning closer to Marcus. "I've never seen you this jumpy before a job. What's gotten into you?"

"I bet it's a big fat cock!" shouted Surly Shirley as she pushed her way in between them, holding a drink. She raised it into the air.

"Drink up, you sour-faced bastards!"

She tilted her head, threw her pint back and downed the entire glass. Buff and Marcus lifted their drinks and did the same. They all ignored the dirty looks they were getting from parents horrified by Shirley's language.

Buff glanced down at what Shirley was wearing, and was stunned. She looked like a completely different person from the woman he'd met the day before. Now, she was dolled up like a married woman out for an anniversary dinner. She'd traded her sloppy overalls for an elegant black dress. Her hair was styled. She didn't wear makeup, but she was sporting some sparkling jewellery. She was looked beautiful.

Marcus threw his arm around her. "Some good to see ya, me child," he said. "Ya looks all made up like a stick of gum."

"Hi Shirley," Buff said, smiling. "Thanks for coming."

"I couldn't pass up a free dinner at a fancy fucking place like this," she said sarcastically. "It's louder than a fucking Motorhead concert in here. I hope you got a great fucking group rate."

"They've got the best spaghetti in town."

"I fucking bet. I need another fucking drink. Marcus, can I talk to you for a second?"

Without waiting for an answer, she grabbed the old man by the elbow and pulled him out of earshot from Buff. She didn't let go until they were beside the front bar.

"What is it, me girlie?" he asked, shaking his arm free of her grip.

She dropped her genial attitude and crossed her arms. She looked angrier than a hungry bear. Marcus stopped smiling.

"Are you out of your fucking mind?" she demanded, calmly and quietly. She knew better than to make a scene in a public place. "What the hell is wrong with you? What the fuck is that asshole doing on the team?"

Marcus was genuinely confused. "Who?"

"Who?! Big fucking Frank, the fucking psychopath homicidal butcher, that's who!"

She pointed over towards him. He was sitting in a chair beside Beka, his hands neatly folded in his lap. He seemed to be staring blankly into space.

"Just fucking look at him! He's zoned out like some fucking crazy junkie zombie! His head's not right, Marcus. His shit's fucked up."

At that moment, Big Frank got up from his chair, and it became apparent what he'd been staring at. Someone had just finished playing *Lethal Enforcers*, and now that the machine was free, Big Frank walked right up to it. He plunked down his quarter, picked up the plastic pink handgun, and started playing.

Marcus breathed a sigh of relief. Shirley's "I told you so" would have to be postponed.

"No, sorry, me love," he said, "but yar off it. The poor b'y is harmless."

"No, he's fucking not!" she cried, grabbing the old man by the shoulders. "He's a fucking savage! You know, I heard one time he threw some fucking gangster piece of shit into the polar bear tank at the zoo because he owed him forty fucking dollars!"

Marcus shook his head. He knew all about the incident, although the version he heard involved the tiger's cage. Either way, he feared Shirley was right, but he couldn't risk showing any doubt in Buff's judgment. He'd seen how quickly crews fall apart once they start second-guessing each other.

"Where is ya hearin' these tales of whimsy?" he said, wearing the poker-faced grin of a used car salesman. "Sounds like something out of one of them Schwarzen-fella movies, love. I ain't heard a fish story like that in all me time. Things are squared away, me girlie, it's all good. Big Frankie there has worked with ol' Buff before. He owes him a favour, in fact."

Shirley put her hands on her hips. "Not fucking good enough," she said, steaming. "He's a fucking madman. I don't want to work with him."

"I sympathize with ya, me love," Marcus replied, resigned. "No foolin' and all. But we needs him, girlie. Needs him. He's our munitions man, duckie, and we needs his explosives to get into the safe, see? He's the only fella in town with 'em. So Big Frank there is on the job, lass, and that's the end of 'er."

He paused to take a breath, and Shirley scrunched her face in discontent. "Now, love, he ain't the muscle on this job, right? He ain't bringin' no gun with him. There ain't no guns on this job, love."

"There better fucking not be," she said, emphatic. "We had a fucking deal, Marcus. No guns, no masks, no hostages. Nobody gets hurt. Those are my fucking rules. I see a fucking gun, I walk."

"That's fine, me girlie. Not a problem," he answered, waving his hand.

"I'm serious, Marcus."

"I don't doubt that y'are, love."

"And my fucking price went up. An extra three grand."

"Shirley!" he exclaimed, shocked.

"Consider it my 'dealing with your bullshit' tax."

Marcus shook his head and smiled. "Ya know this is comin' right out of my pocket, ya damned biniky angishore!"

"I fucking hope so."

"Fine. Take me hard earned money. Take the fillings out of me teeth while y'are at 'er, me duckie! But I still loves ya."

"Whatever." Shirley rolled her eyes. "You keep that fucking Big Frank freak away from me. He creeps me the fuck out, and I work with weird-ass sex offender truck drivers every fucking day."

Marcus laughed. "Relax, girlie. Have another drink. Make 'er a double."

The old man pulled his foul-mouthed friend over to the bar.

He spent the next few minutes trying to placate her with drinks, with moderate success.

Meanwhile, Buff stood near the restaurant's front door, waiting to meet Doug as he walked in. He was hoping to catch their electronics man before he noticed Beka was there too. He knew Marcus was right; the young man should have been told that his ex-partner had also been recruited to the team. Since Doug was such an affable guy, Buff had never really considered that he might have some reservations working with her.

In truth, there was no way to know how he'd react, and that fact was slowly eroding Buff's confidence. Doug could decide to bail on the job, and then the whole plan would fall apart. He couldn't pull this off without the young man's expertise.

Buff cursed himself for not dealing with this sooner.

He rubbed his forehead, trying to think positive thoughts.

When Doug finally did arrive, Buff didn't have a chance to say a word. The young man immediately saw Beka's bright blue hair from across the crowded room. His mouth dropped and he froze. Buff tried reading his expression, but couldn't discern anything beyond utter shock.

Moving quickly, Buff grabbed him by the arm and pulled him aside.

"Hey, Doug!" he asked, nonchalant. "Did you find the place okay?"

"What the hell is she doing here?" Doug demanded.

"Who?"

Doug punched Buff in the shoulder. "Not cool, dude. Not cool. You know damn well who I'm talking about. Why is Rebecca here?"

"Look, I'm sorry," Buff said, sincerely. "I really am. I know you guys split up, but I didn't have a choice. We needed a good cracker, and she's the best."

The young man's eyes fell to the floor. His shoulders slumped and he started shaking his head. "You don't understand, Buff," he said. "I don't think I can do this. I need to go."

He turned to leave, but Buff threw up his arm, blocking him in.

"No, no, no," Buff stammered, insistent. "We need you, Doug. I wouldn't trust anyone else with this job. It's too important. Please don't leave. Please. I'll pay double. I'll pay whatever you want."

"It's not about the money, Buff."

"Good, because I probably couldn't afford to pay you double." He smiled, pausing for a laugh.

"Dammit, Buff!" Doug snapped. "This isn't a joke! I'm serious."

Buff was taken aback. He knew Doug would be upset, but he didn't expect this kind of adamant anger. The girl must have really hurt him.

"You're right. I'm sorry. Really sorry. Honestly. What happened between you two, anyway?"

The young man let out a deep sigh. "What do you think, dude? She didn't want to stop breaking into places. I got a gig building an animatronic talking kitten for a cat food commercial, so we had to turn down a couple of high-profile scores. She got all pissed about it. Anyway, we got in this big fight, and... Man, I just couldn't take it anymore. You know how she is, right? She's got an opinion on every little thing, you know? Every damn day, dude. So I left."

"That's it? You two were so close."

"Well, you know, for every hot chick out there, there's a dude who's sick of dealing with her bullshit."

Buff held up his hands, motioning for Doug to quiet down. "Come on now, that's harsh," he said calmly. "She's an adult. Every breakup hurts, but it couldn't have been bad enough that you have to hide from her."

"No, man, I left. No note, no phone call. I haven't seen her since, dude."

"What?" shouted Buff, stunned. "Ah, Doug, no. No. That's bad."

"Hey, fuck you, man," Doug barked, defiant. "You weren't there. Don't judge me, dude. I tried, okay? I can't talk to her. I won't. If she sees me here she'll probably kill me. Does she know I'm coming?"

"I didn't tell you, did I?"

"Ah, Jesus, Buff. This is bad. Dude, you should have told me, man."

"I know, I know. I'm sorry. I didn't think it would be that big of a deal. You were both together for so long... I have trouble picturing the two of you apart."

Doug looked down at his sloppy T-shirt. On it was a faded picture of Bettie Page in a bikini, as well as a noticeable mustard stain.

"You should have told me," he muttered. "I would have at least worn a cleaner shirt. Probably gotten a haircut, too."

Buff's head was starting to hurt. He saw that Doug was ready to leave. The young man took another frightened, wistful look at Beka, and then shook his head.

"I'm sorry, Buff," he said, keeping his eyes to the ground. "I can't do this. I have to go."

He turned to leave, but Buff jumped in front of him.

"No! Please!" he pleaded. "You have to stay. You won't have to talk to her."

"Uh oh," said Doug, looking past Buff. The colour drained from the young man's face. "Too late."

Beka had seen them from across the room, and was storming through the restaurant towards them. She looked at Doug with a fiery vengeance in her eyes, a scorned woman with sharpened nails.

"Here we go," he said, wincing like a child before a vaccination.

The tiny girl marched right up to her ex-boyfriend, reared her arm back, and slugged him right between the eyes.

Doug was knocked backwards. A spurt of blood shot out his nose.

Instantly, the entirety of the Organ Grinder erupted into chaos. Kids began crying and mothers began screaming. Shocked waiters dropped their trays. The restaurant was a blusterous fury of activity and panic.

"You scruffy son of a bitch!" Beka screamed. "I hate you!"

Buff jumped in between them, and spread his arms to push them apart.

"Take this outside," he growled. "Now."

Doug and Beka glared at each other with teeth gritted, both boiling with rage.

"Now!"

They jumped, startled by the ferocity in Buff's voice. Marcus quickly walked up behind them and gently pushed them out the front door.

Buff immediately went into damage control. He ran from table to table, apologizing profusely and handing out twenty-dollar bills to patrons, bartenders, and wait staff. He thought that with a few hundred bucks, he might be able to smooth over the outburst.

It wasn't enough.

***

Right next door to the Organ Grinder was the Olde Spaghetti Factory. It was a similar family-friendly restaurant, but without the arcade games and tacky decor. The place featured a lot of Venetian architecture, and was decorated to look like ancient Italy. Near the entrance was a large pool reminiscent of Rome's Trevi Fountain. As the name would suggest, they served mostly pasta, in portions normally reserved for animals that eat from troughs. The Olde Spaghetti Factory didn't have a Wurlitzer organ, but it did have an old man softly playing an accordion in the corner, limitless servings of garlic bread, and a private meeting room in the back of the restaurant that was available on short notice.

Beka and Doug sat on opposite ends of the long dining table in the centre of the room. They were both still stewing with rage. Her hair was ruffled and mussed. He had a wadded up bit of tissue stuffed up his bleeding nostril. It had been a vicious fight outside the restaurant, with Beka managing to get in some damaging blows to Doug's face, an elbow to his stomach, and a couple kicks to his groin. The Fodder brothers eventually had to come in and break them up.

After they'd calmed down, Buff was able to get them to sit down and talk business. He needed them both on the team, and was willing to do whatever was necessary to make them stay. He made a convincing case, emphasizing the lucrative nature of the job he was planning, and offering an additional $6000 each, on top of their original fees.

There was some debate back and forth, but eventually Doug and Beka were willing to put aside their differences. They would pull this job for Buff, but only so long as they didn't have to speak to (and whenever possible, look at) each other. They shook hands, which did little to diffuse the tension between them.

Eventually, Buff was able to herd the rest of the team into the new meeting room and get them to sit around the giant table. A perky young waitress brought in menus and three large platters of warm, gooey garlic bread. Dwayne immediately dove into the one in front of him, grabbing a piece with each hand and stuffing them into his mouth.

As everyone looked over the dinner specials, Buff noticed that people were eyeing one another warily. Surly Shirley was giving Big Frank stern looks. Big Frank and Marcus were both sizing up N-Dig. N-Dig glowered at Kane, who gazed disapprovingly at Beka and Doug, who were glaring at each other like coiled snakes ready to strike. An uneasy feeling of bitterness hung over the room, but like a bad smell, everyone tried pretending it wasn't there.

Buff rubbed the back of his neck. He was having a terrible night. Not only was everyone simmering and miserable, but the dinner was costing him a fortune. Almost everyone's price had gone up, and the Olde Spaghetti Factory's private room cost twice as much to rent as the Organ Grinder's, who had refused to refund his original $80 deposit.

"This place is really nice," said Kane, admiring the marble columns and gold trim decorating the meeting room. It was the fanciest place he'd been since his aunt's funeral.

"Why the fuck didn't we just eat here first?" Shirley asked the group. Everyone except Buff got a good laugh.

Dwayne licked the cheese grease off his fingers.

N-Dig was looking over his menu in great detail, studying it like a scholar scouring an ancient papyrus scroll. He seemed fascinated by it.

"I want to try their pizza," he said, to no one in particular. "It says here 'best in the city.' I seriously doubt that, bro, you know?"

The waitress returned with a round of drinks. Buff grabbed his rye and ginger with both hands and drank it down like a man dying of thirst. He felt the ends of his frayed nerves slowly soothe over.

After taking everyone's order, the waitress left the room. Buff stood up, walked over to the door and closed it.

He held his arms out to silence the room, and everyone turned their attention to him. Now that people had a little alcohol and cheesy garlic bread in their system, the atmosphere in the room was more relaxed.

"I want to thank you all for coming," he said, clasping his hands together, "and apologize for all the... let's say, 'confusion' there's been this evening. It was all a simple matter of miscommunication, I assure you."

There was a low murmur as people began whispering with each other. Buff raised his voice to speak above them. "I take full responsibility. It was my fault, but everything has been talked through and dealt with, so there's no need to go over it again. We've all agreed to work together and be professional. This job is going to make us all a lot of money, enough to make it worth putting aside whatever differences we may have."

The group was sitting in rapt attention. Buff had finally brought them all together. For the first time in hours, he was optimistic about the job's success.

He cleared his throat. "I think everyone here has met, so there's no need for introductions. Now, if there are no more surprises, I think we can get down to business."

There was a knock at the door.

Buff opened it, and in walked a short man who looked like he managed a sleazy strip club. He wore a loud purple shirt with a wide collar and the top three buttons undone, two gold chains around his neck, three gold rings on each hand, bright white slacks and alligator skin shoes. He was bald, and held a toothpick between his teeth, which he twiddled back and forth with his tongue. He smelled like an Italian nightclub: an obnoxious mix of body sprays, aftershaves and colognes that would sting the eyes of anyone who dared get close.

"I'm looking for a man named Buff," he said. His accent was faint, but distinct. Buff couldn't place it, but guessed it was likely French.

"Jacques sent me," he continued. "The name's Fou."

He looked out at a sea of puzzled faces. Nobody had ever seen this guy before.

Buff's shoulders slumped down. He knew exactly who this man was, and dreaded the questions his arrival would prompt.

He reached out and shook Fou's hand.

"Great to meet you, Fou."

"Sorry I'm late. Thought we were meeting next door. They told me to try here."

"Yeah, there was a little confusion. I'm sorry about that."

He turned to the rest of the group, preparing to introduce Fou. No one seemed excited to meet yet another addition to the team. Marcus looked especially angry, turning red with rage.

"Everyone, this is Fou," Buff said, gesturing like one of the models introducing a prize on *The Price is Right.* He then went around the table and gave everyone's name. There were a lot of vacant stares and confused expressions.

"Wait, your name is Fou?" asked Beka, doubtful. "Like *To Wong Foo*?"

"Are you the guy Dave Grohl's been fighting?" Doug said, making himself giggle.

"He's going to be joining the team," Buff said. "Please avoid talking to him."

A smattering of confused whispers emanated from the crowd.

"What d'ya mean this figger's joinin' the team, b'y?" Marcus shouted, barely restraining his fury. "Just exactly what pray tell is this fellar doing for us, me chum?"

"He's our inside man," snapped Buff, and then shot the old man a look that would make a trained dog cower in fear. The room went silent.

Marcus clenched his fists and bit his lip. He instantly understood that this was a conversation to have in private.

Buff leaned over to Fou and pointed to a free chair at the end of the table. "You can take a seat over there and keep quiet."

Before the sharply dressed bald man could sit down, Marcus had jumped up out of his chair and was at Buff's side, tugging his arm.

"Eh b'y, d'ya mind if I has a word with ya out in the hall?" he whispered.

Buff didn't get a chance to answer. The old man rushed him out the door, shoving past the poor waitress who'd come to take their dinner orders. Marcus managed to push him all the way out to the main hallway before Buff shook off his grip and threw up his arms.

"Hey!" he shouted, bucking his old friend backwards. "Take it easy, Marcus. What's wrong with you?"

"Wrong with me, b'y?" Marcus answered, incredulous. "Lard t'underin', don't ya blear at me like I were ya mother, ya damn shit-picky chucklehead! The hell's wrong with you and all, me cocky?! Just who the hell is this damn Fou fella, eh? Ya didn't talk to me 'bout any Fou. Did ya do a thorough background search on him? 'Cause I sure can nare vouch for him. And I don't like workin' with fellas what I can nare vouch for directly, b'y. Did we not just talk 'bout this very thing twenty minutes ago, Buffy b'y?!"

"Calm down, Marcus."

"And what's all this bullshit yar flicking 'bout him being an 'inside man.' This ain't no inside job. An inside man sells ya the codes to gets into the vault, so that's ya don't have to hire three other people to break into 'er, me chum. An inside man don't join the team in plannin' the damn heist, b'y!"

"Keep your voice down!"

"Buff, mate, in the thirteen years I has known ya, ain't once that I seen ya act this recklessly. Keepin' secrets and hirin' random fellars that ya ain't know where they longs at? That's not like ya, b'y. Yar not thinkin' properly, me cocky. If this were any other scut but yourself, b'y, I would've walked away from this job already."

With nothing left to say, he crossed his arms and looked at his friend, expectantly. "Any of this cuttin' through, b'y, or is ya deaf as a cod?"

Buff closed his eyes and pinched the top of his nose, sighing loudly.

"You're right," he said, holding his arms up defensively, "but let me explain. Not here. Outside."

***

It was a warm night, and there were plenty of people milling about in front of the restaurant. The two men took their conversation to the parking lot across the street. It was the only place Buff was confident they could speak privately, as long as they kept moving. He led Marcus down a long aisle of cars, waiting until the very end before he finally spoke.

"Promise me you won't throw a tantrum," Buff said.

"Enough with the games, me son," Marcus replied sternly, crossing his arms. "Just say what ya gots to say."

"Do you know who Jacques Montagne is?"

"Eh. I think so, b'y. Part of the French mafia, ain't he?"

"Exactly. He's the boss."

"Damn frogs. I hates them francophones. They're assholes, and ya cannot trust 'em. Don't tell me ya gots yar stern tangled up in their trawler's net again, b'y."

"They came after me, Marcus. They kept hounding me from the second I walked out of prison, trying to get me to pull a job for them. This job."

Marcus couldn't believe his ears. He shook his head in disbelief. "Y'agreed to do it, didn't ya? Yar stunned as me arse! I always told ya to stay away from them types, b'y. They'll just ballyrag ya until the ends of the Earth. Ain't they the ones that got ya pinched in the first place, b'y?"

"Actually, Marcus, that was the cops."

"Oh, well then, my mistake," Marcus replied, sarcastically. "Buff, me chum, yar either the dumbest smart-ass I ever met, or the smartest dumb-ass. It were their job you were pullin', b'y, so they share in the blame when ya gets caught. I don't know why ya never once dropped a dime on them French skitters, b'y. Ya don't owe them nothing. Ya could've got out of jail plenty earlier if y'ad given the cops a few names, eh b'y?"

"I am not a snitch, Marcus."

The old man rolled his eyes.

"Besides," Buff continued, "I turned the job down. I said no. Repeatedly. I didn't want anything to do with them."

"Then why is we talkin' 'bout 'em, b'y?"

"Well, the next day I got a visit from the FBI."

Marcus looked baffled. He'd heard what Buff had said, but the words wouldn't register in his brain. It was too preposterous.

"Huh?" he uttered, cocking his head. "What is ya sayin', b'y? I don't get 'er."

"Some agent from the FBI showed up at my work. He made me an offer. He told me if I took the job from the Montagne family, they'd pay me a hundred grand."

The old man's jaw went slack. He was shocked and speechless.

"W-w-wha..." he stammered, still searching for words. "Buff, b'y, I... I don't understand." His confusion morphed into anger as he began putting the pieces together inside his head. "Is ya workin' with the cops now? Ya just says you were no snitch, b'y!"

"I'm not working with the cops, Marcus, and I am not a snitch. They just wanted me to agree to do the job. He also said they'd clear my record..."

Marcus groaned. "Oh, that ol' chestnut. They always say that. It's a myth, b'y. It cannot be done, me chummy."

"I had to. They had me over a barrel. They said if I didn't take the job, that they would nail me for the Rochester heist."

"Rochester!? B'y, that was seven years ago! They gots nothing on ya! They got no jurisdiction in this country, b'y!" He leaned against one of the parked cars and buried his head in his hands. "Oh, me sweet Lard, Buff, what has ya done? All of this for a hundred grand. Damn, b'y! That ain't gonna be near enough to pay everyone, me son."

"No tantrums, Marcus. You promised."

The old man couldn't even look at Buff.

"There's plenty of cash to go around, Marcus. We're still being paid by the Montagne family. This is still a job for the French mob. The FBI just gave me an extra hundred grand to ensure I took the job."

"This sounds like a load of horseshit, son," the old man said, shaking his head. "It don't make a lick of sense. Why would they want ya breakin' into places once yar fresh out of the clink? This must be a set-up, b'y. Did ya sign anything? Is there a record of this? Ya know, anything on paper?"

Buff reached out and put his hand on Marcus' shoulder.

"You don't understand. There's more."

"More?!" he shouted, shaking off Buff's hand. "Lard t'underin' Jesus, Buff! More? The mob and the FBI weren't enough for ya?" He was spitting out words, his voice quivering with anger. He shook his arms in from of him. "Forget 'er, b'y. I don't wanna hear it. I'm done, me chum. Yar on yar own."

He turned to walk away, but Buff grabbed him by the arm and pulled him back.

"Please, Marcus," he pleaded. "Please hear me out. I'm trying to explain."

"Ya haven't explained nothing yet!" Marcus yelled back. "Tell me who the hell this Fou fella is, b'y, or I'm leavin'."

Marcus was fuming, eyes bulging and panting heavily. Buff knew that his mentor was sincere about walking away from the job. He'd have to swallow his pride and come clean about everything if he hoped to win him back over.

"Look, he's one of Jacques' men. Bringing him along was one of the conditions of taking the job. He wants... he wants me to kill him."

The old man's jaw went slack. He took a shaky step backwards.

"I'm not going to do it," Buff was quick to add. "He's an FBI agent, working undercover."

Marcus threw his head back, letting out a loud, long grunt of frustration.

"Ah, no! No, Buff, no! How could ya?"

"It's fine, Marcus. They just want to get their man out of the field, that's all. In return, they've agreed to look the other way. They can't do anything to keep the local cops off our back, though, but if we just follow the plan, that won't be an issue."

"Dammit, me boy! Ya jus'... ya can't... aw, Lard Jesus."

He shook his head. He couldn't help himself, and started laughing heartily. His body shook and his face went red.

"This is too much, b'y," he said through a chuckle, wiping away a tear. "I can't take 'er. I can't even believe 'er. She's too complicated. Ya got too many sailors on deck, b'y. This can't work."

"It can work, Marcus. Please."

Buff was begging like a child whining for candy. The old man was starting to take pity on him.

"Does ol' Jacques know that Fou fella's with the FBI? Is that why he wants him dead?"

"No, no. I don't think so. I think he just doesn't like him."

"And this heist, the vault and all of that... is there anything there? Is it all just a cover?"

"Oh, it's real. That law firm's got some evidence they've been holding to use against the Montagnes. They're willing to pay big for it."

Marcus put his arm on Buff's shoulder.

"Ya should of told me 'bout all this, b'y," he said, softly. "Ya told me this were a simple data grab, a smash and go. I don't think this'll work out, me chum. I really don't. There's too many variables."

"It's okay. Really. I've got it all planned out, down to every last detail. Trust me."

"If that's what ya want, b'y. I'll stick with ya, me son, but I think this is our last job together. After this, I don't think we'll be working together no more."

"After this, if we play our cards right, we won't have to."

***

When the two men returned to the restaurant's private meeting room, the group was well into their third round of drinks. Their meals had already arrived, so everyone was digging into enormous, steaming plates of pasta. There was more food on the table than at a Thanksgiving banquet.

It definitely lightened the mood in the room. Everyone was warm and friendly as they all ate, drank, and laughed together loudly. Both Fodder brothers already had pasta sauce stains all over their brand new hockey jerseys.

Buff grabbed a fork and tapped the side of his drinking glass with it. The group went quiet, turning their attention to him.

"Sorry about the delay," he said. "Now we can get down to business. Those of you still sober, pay attention. You'll have to explain it to the others later."

Buff reached into his pocket and pulled out an envelope. Inside it were a handful of printouts, which included blueprints for a Strongbox vault, floor plans and photos of a modest, eight-storey office building, as well as pages and pages of hand-written notes. He pulled out one of the pictures of the building and held it up, and then circulated the rest of the printouts around the table.

"This is our target," he said, pointing to the photograph. "The law offices of Bennett, Olsen, Nygärd, Jørgensen, and Holm."

"Fucking lawyers!" Shirley squealed with a laugh. "I hate those cocksuckers. I'm in if it means we get to fuck those assholes over."

Both the Fodder brothers and N-Dig cheered her. They all clinked their glasses and took another drink.

"Okay, everybody, settle down," said Buff.

"Sound like a bunch of fucking Swedes," Shirley added.

"They're Norwegian, actually," said Fou.

"Shut up, Fou," Buff shouted, annoyed. "Just sit there and be quiet." He paused to take a breath before continuing in a calmer voice. "The law office we're targeting is in the west end of the city, on Matheson Boulevard. There's a map on one of the sheets being passed around."

Beka had already pulled out her 10-inch tablet computer and was examining the firm's website, and their location on Google Street View.

"They will be closed tomorrow for Canada Day," he continued, "and that's when we're going to hit it. You'll see from the pictures that it's in an industrial park, and fairly isolated. There's a big warehouse beside it, but it's been vacant for months, and a few office towers on the other side, mainly insurance brokers and realtors, so they'll be closed tomorrow, too. We shouldn't have to worry much about being seen."

"That's a sweet spot, bro," N-Dig said, looking over the map. "For real. No bottlenecks, lots of exit points. You've got highways on either side for a quick getaway, in any direction. This is no problem, I'm telling you."

"I know," Buff answered. "The nearest police station is eleven kilometres away, too, so they'll have a six-minute response time, at best. Hopefully, though, it doesn't come to that. There's a private company that handles the building's security, and they only have one guard scheduled to work tomorrow night. He's at the front desk."

Around the table, everyone was nodding appreciatively. Buff appeared to have done his research quite well.

"When we go in, we go in two teams," he continued. "Marcus, Kane, Doug, and Beka are in N-Dig's car. You guys approach from the front. He waits in the parking lot while the other four go in through the main door."

"I thought you said there was a guard at the front desk," Doug said.

"I'll take care of that goof," Kane chuckled.

"No!" Buff shouted. "No, no. Absolutely not. No punching, no shooting, no violence. We're professionals. You leave the guard to Marcus. We have a plan to deal with him. Right, Marcus?"

"Sure thing, b'y," the old man answered, barely paying attention.

Kane held up his hands and shrugged in defeat.

"No violence? No problem," he said.

Buff nodded to Shirley, who smiled.

"Moving on," Buff continued. "The building itself is armed with infrared motion and smoke detectors. They're all routed through a server room on the second floor. We need Doug to get into the room, and Beka to disable the alarms."

"Is it a mortise lock?" asked Doug.

"Yeah. Yale 8800 series, with reversible latch-bolt and a double-cylinder intruder lock. All the information is on one of those sheets I passed around. Best of all, the lock's completely inaccessible until you swipe the proximity card reader with a key tag... which we won't have."

"No problem, dude," Doug replied with a smile.

Beka rolled her eyes derisively. She knew her ex-partner was trying to show off. She could play that game just as well as he could.

"Are we looking at the usual DVAC line and GSM transmitter?" she asked with a smirk.

"Exactly. There's even a radio connected to the control panel in case the telephone line is cut... which we'll have to do regardless, by the way. Like I said, it's all on those sheets I handed out."

She smiled wide. "I wouldn't be surprised if they had a backup wireless transmitter, too. I've seen it before. I'll cut all network connections, and set a feedback loop for anyone monitoring the system. It's very easy."

Doug snorted and furrowed his brow. He knew that Beka was trying to undermine him, and it made his skin crawl.

"You know, I have a cell phone blocker that I made which would block any outgoing calls," he said.

"Make sure he tests it first," Beka scoffed.

"That was one time!" Doug yelled, pointing his finger at Beka. "You know it works, Rebecca! You've seen it! Don't be such a bitch."

"Stop being such a dick!" she screamed, jumping to her feet.

"Enough!" Buff cried, in a commanding voice. "Everyone sit down! What did I just say about being 'professional'?"

With her arms crossed and her face tight, Beka slunk back down into her chair while exchanging dirty looks with Doug.

Buff took another deep breath before continuing.

"Moving on. With the alarms down, we can open the shipping dock at the back of the building. That's how we get Shirley's truck in, with all the gear and the rest of team. Are we all good so far?"

There was a murmur of recognition. Most heads around the dining table nodded in acknowledgment. Buff cleared his throat.

"Once the alarm's disabled and the truck's inside, we need everybody to help get the drill and the rest of the gear into the service elevator and up to the top floor. When we get it to the vault room, then Big Frank and the Fodders check every floor, make sure we don't have any unwanted guests. Understood?"

They all did.

"Good. Now, floors three, four, and five are all the associate offices. There shouldn't be anyone there, but I'd still like you guys to search them anyway. Is that okay?"

"No problem, bud," Dwayne said.

Kane gave him a big thumbs-up, while Big Frank nodded his agreement.

"Thank you," said Buff.

"I can help with that," Fou said, meekly.

"Dammit, Fou!" Buff shouted with fury. "I told you to keep your mouth shut. I'm not going to warn you again."

No one said anything, but they all looked at each other with concern. They didn't understand Buff's relationship to Fou, but the interactions between them were both puzzling and worrisome.

In truth, all Fou wanted to do was help. He'd always found that collaborating on a project was they best way to ingratiate himself with a gang of criminals. However, Buff was going to do everything in his power to keep the undercover officer at an arm's length from the others. Fou may have been part of the team, but he was still a cop.

Buff pointed down to the building's blueprints and carried on. "Now, the sixth floor is accounting. Those offices need to be checked, too. The seventh floor is the executive suites. They're under renovation right now, so they should all be empty, but we'll search them too, just to be sure.

"The eighth floor is the top floor, and that's where our prize is: the vault room. This is where things get tricky. The vault room is locked with an electronic swipe card and a six-digit code that changes daily."

"If it's an RFID system, man, then it should only take me a few minutes to open it," Doug said, beaming.

Again, Beka rolled her eyes. Buff noticed, but ignored it.

"Once we get to the vault," he continued, "it's all hands on deck. It's a Strongbox safe, and those damn things are built like Fort Knox. It's coated in ballistic armor, covered in tremor sensors, and connected to three separate backup servers. It's easier to get into Harvard than it is to get into a Strongbox."

"He's not lyin', me chums," Marcus said, playing with the ice in his empty glass. "I heard lots of stories 'bout these things, and they's a cramp-hand beast, no foolin'."

"The specs for the vault are on one of the sheets being passed around. I suggest you all take a look at them, especially those of you who'll be working on it. Doug will bypass all the sensors, and then we'll need Beka to crack the network. Once she's severed the connection to the servers, Big Frank will use explosives to get through the vault's outer shell."

"Hold on. Fucking explosives?" Shirley asked loudly. "Don't you think that kind of shit might attract some fucking attention?"

"We've planned for that. Don't worry."

Shirley responded with a skeptical sneer. Marcus put his hand on her shoulder, reassuring her that they were, in fact, well prepared to deal with the noise. It wasn't an answer, but it was enough to placate her.

"After that," Buff went on, "Marcus and I will drill down to the tumblers and crack the safe. All told, we're looking at between four to six hours."

"Bro, how much do you honestly expect to get from a bunch of suits and desk jockeys?" N-Dig asked.

"This is a data grab," Buff replied. "That's why everyone's getting a flat rate instead of a percentage. If we find anything else valuable in the building, we'll split it evenly, but I wouldn't hold your breath."

He anxiously looked down at his watch and sighed. This meeting should have been over already.

"Any other questions?"

There were lots of questions. Everyone had something to ask. Shirley wanted to know if the shipping entrance was a ramp or a dock. N-Dig wondered where they would meet afterwards if they had to make a quick getaway. Doug asked about the building's electrical systems. Beka had endless questions about the alarms and computer network, to which Buff kept referring her to the detailed sheets he'd handed out. Fou had his arm raised high, waving it like an anxious student, but Buff just ignored him. The group talked for well over an hour, going over every single detail. Only Big Frank had nothing to ask.

When every last element had been explained and exhausted, and everyone was satisfied and comfortable with the plan, Buff stood up and reopened the meeting room's doors. He called the waitress in and ordered another round of drinks.

The evening ended with everyone in a good mood. The pall that hung over the proceedings earlier in the night had been lifted, replaced with a more genial and cooperative attitude. People seemed happy, maybe a little drunk, and largely confident with the heist as planned. The Fodders told a few dirty jokes, and N-Dig told a hilarious story about delivering pizza to Charlie Sheen's hotel room. Everyone was laughing and toasting their drinks.

One thing Buff did note, however, was that Marcus seemed to be conspicuously quiet. He wasn't telling jokes and he wasn't mingling with the others. He simply sat in his chair, slowly picking at his leftover spaghetti.

Eventually, people tired and began trickling out of the restaurant. Twenty minutes later, after the bill had been paid and everyone had gone home, Marcus and Buff were left alone at the bar. They were each nursing a tall glass of ice water.

"I think that went well," Buff mused.

"Mm-hmm," Marcus replied, distant and bored, staring at the swirling water in his glass.

The two men sat in silence for some time. There was still some tension between them, something that had never existed in the years they'd been friends.

"Hey," Buff said, softly nudging his mentor, "uh, I, um, I don't really have a place to stay tonight."

"There's a Holiday Inn down the street, b'y. I got to be hoistin' me sail and headin' on out, I thinks." Marcus took one last drink of water and set his glass down on the bar. Not once did he make eye contact with his old friend. "See ya soon, b'y."

He stood up and walked out of the restaurant. Buff's shoulders slumped down as he felt the horrible mass of all the pressures weighing on him. He was broke, needed a shower, his head ached, and he didn't know where he'd be sleeping tonight. He hadn't felt this low since he was first thrown in jail.

Buff went outside, hanging his head and shuffling his feet. His stomach was in knots; a terrible twisted feeling that grew stronger and more painful with every step.

He took a deep breath and reached into his pocket. He pulled out a brand new pack of cigarettes, slid one out and lit it. It was his first since having quit over two years ago.

It was an awful burning feeling, but he choked it down. For a reason he couldn't explain, some part of his brain was craving that hollow, ashen taste in his mouth. The pain in his gut began to relent. He coughed a few times, and then brought the cigarette back to his lips again. He inhaled deeply, savoured the taste, and exhaled an ugly cloud of pungent smoke. After a moment, it was as though he'd never quit at all.

His scanned the streets around him, looking for a payphone. He had missed the appointed time to check in with his parole officer for the second night in a row. He was going to have to be especially charming if he were going to smooth things over.

# July 1
# 6:30pm

Canada Day is a national holiday, celebrated every year on the first of July. It's often called "Canada's birthday" as it recognizes Canadian Confederation, the day in 1867 when four colonies joined to form a single country within the British Empire. Most communities organize parades, concerts, barbeques, and after sunset, a fireworks display. However, there is no real "traditional" way to celebrate the holiday. Like the country itself, Canada Day lacks a true identity. The only constant is that everybody gets a day off.

There was almost nobody working in the law offices of Bennett, Olsen, Nygärd, Jørgensen, and Holm that day. Their building was spectacularly ordinary, a dull and boring structure with all the beauty of a backyard shed. An uninspiring concrete hulk, it was little more than a giant, flat, grey cube, lined along one side with windows that wouldn't open. There were no ledges or awnings, just a monolithic slab of rock and glass. It looked like it was built to protect people from nuclear fallout. Depressing, utilitarian buildings like this filled out all the industrial areas around Toronto. It was unfortunate, because if someone tried to build it downtown, this ugly eyesore would have every city councillor and amateur architect demanding it be demolished.

The office was flanked on either side by large, untended green hedges. Other than a small patch of grass, there was nothing in front of the building except a sprawling parking lot. A single lane led around the building to the rear shipping entrance.

There were two parked vehicles scattered around the lot. In the far corner was a small, well-used compact car. It was a brown Chevrolet Cavalier, and covered in dirt, dents and dings, as though tt were used in demolition derbies on the weekend.

The sports car right next to the front entrance, however, looked like it just drove out of the dealer's showroom. A shiny red BMW M5 with a 500-horsepower V8 engine, it had a top speed of 250 kilometres an hour, but the unblemished bumpers and pristine silver rims on the tires suggested that the car rarely went above 100. It had a vanity licence plate, which read "I WIN."

Other than those two cars, the property was empty.

The few buildings surrounding the office were noticeably vacant as well. On a statutory holiday like Canada Day, the industrial areas of the city are nearly deserted.

Inside the front doors, the office's main lobby was large, open and sparsely decorated. The ceiling was over twelve-feet high, the floors were polished granite, and there were leafy ferns in huge, five-foot-wide planters located in the corners. There was a hallway on the left that led to the building's three passenger elevators and service elevator, as well as doorways leading to two stairwells. On the wall beside the main door was a building directory listing the office of every lawyer and associate at the firm.

In the centre of the lobby was a large desk, carved from stone and accented with glass and wood. The law firm's name in bold silver letters hung on the wall behind the desk, next to a silver-framed original oil painting by Gunnar Berg.

There was a security guard sitting at the desk, a middle-aged man named Donald Thorp. He wore the standard uniform – a black shirt and pants, with a shiny security badge pinned to his chest. He didn't have any weapons, but he was provided with a flashlight. Not that he'd need more than his fists. He was in great shape, with only his receding hairline betraying his youthful appearance.

Donald wasn't exactly committed to his job. He'd held this same position as security guard for almost six years, and was still earning the same salary as when he began. He'd considered findng other work, but this was such an easy, low-stress job that he eventually decided quitting wasn't worth the bother.

He was an hour into his shift, and hadn't seen a single person. He wasn't expecting to see anyone all night, either. He settled back into his chair, propped his feet up on the desk, cracked open the latest Robert Ludlum thriller and started reading.

The only other person in the building was up on the sixth floor, where the accounting offices were. These offices were the ugliest, least hospitable spaces in the building. Dimly lit by fluorescent bulbs hanging overhead, it was a miserable labyrinth of tiny cubicles and endless corridors, all lined with dozens of identical filing cabinets. Rows of sad, cramped desks sat buried under heavy piles of paperwork.

None of the accountants were working that day, of course. People forced to work in that kind of environment treat national holidays like precious gifts, and never waste them. However, on this particular Canada Day, one of the smallest cubicles, way off in the far corner, was occupied.

Sitting in front of an ancient, beige computer screen was a man in his late fifties, typing away furiously on the keyboard. His suit jacket was neatly draped over the back of his chair. The designer white shirt he wore was wrinkled and stained with sweat. He'd undone the top three buttons and loosened his expensive silk tie. His eyes were red and weary, and his face wore the strains of great pressure. He looked like a college student who'd been cramming for a final exam.

The man's name was Harry Bockner, and he was one of the top lawyers at this firm. He wasn't used to working in an office this small. He had his own executive suite on the seventh floor, and he'd worked very hard to earn it.

He began his career as a young idealist, anxious to make the world a better place. However, the years since then, particularly his time at this office, had warped his ethics, and acquiring wealth became his driving goal. It affected him to the point that he found himself coming into the office on a holiday to embezzle thousands of dollars from his own law firm.

Not that he needed to steal money. He was already rich. Over his long career he'd earned a reputation as an excellent lawyer, vigorously defending his clients and mercilessly prosecuting those who acted against them. After a decade, however, he found his success in the courtroom wasn't translating to financial reward. A few frustrating meetings with the firm's accountants yielded nothing, so he started doing a little research on his own time. He spent months poring over the firm's myriad of business accounts spread through dozens of different banks. Around the time his hair started going grey, Harry found where his money was going. Buried away in a tiny bank in Norway, hidden in a dozen accounts under fake names, Harry discovered a secret slush fund worth millions.

He'd known for a long time that his law firm was controlled by the Norwegian-Canadian mob. You can only defend so many muscled enforcers named "Sven" before you start asking yourself questions. It didn't bother him for any moral reasons. He had no compunction about working for the guilty. If anything, he preferred the regular business they brought in. What really upset him was that they were stealing money he'd earned, and he felt he alone deserved it. So, he decided to steal as much of it back as he could.

That was six months ago. Now, he would sneak into his firm's accounting office every few weeks. Using only the most basic computer skills, Harry was able to siphon off a few thousand dollars and move it into a secret account he kept in a Jamaican bank branch. He was careful only to take a small, unnoticeable amount, and always created fraudulent contracts that could account for every missing dollar. The process only took a few minutes, after which Harry would spend a few more hours in the accounting office cooking the books and covering his tracks completely.

In that time, he'd squirreled away an impressive nest egg of almost sixty thousand dollars. The initial rush was exciting, but now that Harry knew he could get away with it, he wanted more. It wasn't enough that he could afford a flashy sports car. He wanted to be able to buy a fleet of them.

He finally came up with a plan he thought was foolproof. It was one big score that would leave Harry with enough to walk away from the law offices of Bennett, Olsen, Nygärd, Jørgensen, and Holm for good.

First, he would pool all of the slush fund money into one big account. Because it was a national holiday, the banks were closed today, and it would take 48 hours for the records to reflect the change. Harry would then bury all of the old secret accounts under a mountain of fraudulent transactions, so that if one of the Norwegian accountants took a cursory glance, no money would appear to be missing. Of course, the numbers wouldn't hold up to scrutiny, but if Harry was thorough enough, it would take months to unravel.

Secondly, he would pilfer that big account in a single raid, transfering all the money to an alias account in a bank in Jamaica. Harry would then break that account apart into a byzantine maze of splinter trusts. By that point, the money would be so thoroughly laundered that if anyone bothered to chase the paper trail that far, they'd need an army of forensic accountants to untangle the mess, and they would never find Harry. He planned on being on a secluded beach in the Caribbean, sipping drinks with paper umbrellas in them.

He leaned back in his chair and stretched. Exhausted, he rubbed his eyes and let out a big yawn. He'd been at for a while now, but had only transferred a fraction of the slush money. He still had quite a few hours of work ahead of him, and decided it was time to take a break.

Harry smiled to himself as he contemplated his new wealth. All told, he would walk out of the office today over half a million dollars richer. Not bad for a day's work.

Stealing from his employers left him with no feelings of guilt or remorse, only supreme satisfaction. He started to imagine the palatial mansion in the Caribbean he'd buy. He pictured a place with an enormous infinity pool, numerous hot tubs, and a 60" 3D TV in every room. The garage would have room for a dozen vehicles, at least. He definitely wanted to get one of those pretty new Ford Shelby GT500s, and wondered what colours they were available in.

Harry smiled. He was going to enjoy retirement.

***

Less than three kilometres from the law office was a small gas station that only sold diesel fuel. It remained open on Canada Day, but the owners could count the number of customers they had that day on one hand. This is where Buff and his group had decided to meet before the heist. They all gathered in a small corner of the parking lot, behind the dumpster.

A stone-cold sober N-Dig sat behind the wheel of his old Ford Focus. Remarkably, his rusty car looked like it was in worse shape than the last time Buff had seen it. However, the vehicle's interior had never been cleaner. The trash was removed, the seats were vacuumed, and it even smelled nice. The only noticeable odours were old air fresheners and stale pizza. For all his bravado, N-Dig was taking this job seriously. He had his dreadlocks tied back neatly behind his head, and he'd taken off his gold chains. He tapped his fingers against the steering wheel while he waited for a signal to go.

Beka sat in the passenger seat playing with her phone, intently focused on a consuming game of Tetris. She'd changed her hair colour from blue to bright purple, because she always dyed her hair before a big job. She wore a loose, black hooded sweatshirt, with a patch of Jack Skellington's face sewn onto the shoulder. She also had several pairs of surgical gloves stuffed into her pockets.

Both Doug and Kane sat in the back seat, waiting patiently. They were also wearing black hooded sweatshirts. Doug had all his tools and cables in a duffle bag on his lap. Kane kept a collapsible baton up his sleeve, as well as a hunting knife in a sheath around his ankle.

Next to N-Dig's sad old car, Surly Shirley had parked her big white truck. It was a sixteen-foot-long monster, with over eight hundred cubic feet of storage space. The words "PACIFIC COURIER" were professionally stencilled onto the side in bold, red letters. The huge vehicle sat atop six thick, beefy tires. Shirley sat in the cab of the truck, sipping on a Tim Hortons coffee that was now over forty-five minutes old.

There was hardly any empty space in the back of the truck. The huge industrial drill they were going to use to punch through the vault door took up most of it. The drill was a diamond-tipped MD-9000 by Baileigh Industrial, the most powerful magnetic drill that money could buy. It employed a process known as "thermal friction," where three 220-volt motors are used to get the bit turning more than 4000 rotations per minute, so that the drill isn't actually cutting the target, it's melting through it. It utilized a pressurized coolant system to control the excess heat, and a powerful electro-magnet to hold the drill at any angle. This giant piece of machinery was truly a beast, almost five feet wide, six feet long and weighing over 450 pounds. It was going to take everyone working together to get it up to the top floor of the law firm.

Dwayne, Big Frank, and Fou were all standing beside the truck. Dwayne was wearing the same kind of hooded sweatshirt as his brother. Big Frank wore the same trench coat he always did, which billowed out around him in the wind. Fou showed up in a suit and tie, like a super-spy on his way to a baccarat game. He really hadn't been paying attention at the previous night's meeting.

The three of them never talked with each other. Instead, they stared at their feet or off into space, waiting.

Buff gave them all a nod as he walked past them. He was also wearing the requisite black hooded sweatshirt.

He walked over to N-Dig's car and rapped on the rear door.

Kane rolled down the window and poked his head out.

"We ready to go, bud?" he asked.

"Almost," Buff answered. "Can I talk to you for a minute?"

"No problem, eh?"

"In private." Buff smiled and motioned away from the car.

Kane hesitated for a moment, confused. Buff had shown almost no interest in him or his brother since they were hired for the job. This would be the first time he'd spoken with either of the Fodder brothers privately.

"Oh, uh, okay, sure," Kane said, stepping out of the car.

Buff pulled the young man around behind the truck, where no one could hear them.

"I need to ask you for a favour," he said.

"Better not be a pay cut, eh?" Kane answered with a laugh.

"It's nothing big, but you can't tell Marcus. That's important."

"What do you want me to do?"

"Once you're inside and the security guard is taken care of, I need you to check the building directory in the front office for me. I need you to find out where Harry Bockner's office is. He's a lawyer at the firm."

"Okay, then what?"

"That's it."

"That's it?"

"That's it. Harry Bockner. Do you want to write it down?"

"No, no, I got it. Why's that such a big secret?"

"It's not," Buff said, rubbing the back of his neck. "Don't worry about it. Just don't tell Marcus. He thinks the job's too complicated already. This would just confuse him. He's a very old man."

Kane laughed.

"Okay, bud," he said, "I'll find him for you, but I'm not doing it for free, eh?"

Buff winced. Did no one understand the concept of a "favour"?

"How much?"

"Ten bucks. Cash." Kane looked at him with deadly seriousness. The young man held his hand out in front of him, palm facing up.

Buff smiled, reached into his pocket and pulled out a purple ten-dollar bill. He neatly folded it in two and placed it in Kane's hand.

Stuffing it into his pocket, Kane gave a smile of thanks and walked back to N-Dig's car.

Buff shook his head in disbelief. Those Fodder brothers were like walking cartoon characters. He was surprised no one had given them their own reality show yet.

He reached back into his pocket, pulling out a sheet of paper and a red pen. On the paper was a list of names and phone numbers he'd stolen from the law firm's security company. He read over them carefully.

Marcus suddenly snuck up behind him, clamping his hand down on Buff's shoulder. The old man was dressed in the same black hooded sweatshirt as everyone else.

"We ready for this thing, b'y?" he asked, enthusiastic.

"I have to call the guard first," Buff answered.

"Eh, chum, do ya even have the fella's number?"

"Relax," he said sharply, waving the list under Marcus's nose. "I've got it right here. You know better than to doubt me."

Marcus rolled his eyes, while Buff looked back at his precious list. A few seconds later, he found the number he wanted and circled it with his pen.

"Ya sure this thing'll work, b'y?"

"It's plan A. I have others."

Marcus shook his head and laughed. "Fine then! Give 'er a try, me chum, but this money's comin' out of yar end, b'y."

"Give me your phone."

The old man held out his cell phone, which Buff snatched up and immediately flipped on. He opened two programs on the phone, a caller identification blocker and a voice scrambler. Once they were up and running, he punched in the number he'd circled in red. He held the phone to his ear and listened to it ring.

It was answered promptly.

"Hello?" The voice on the other end was warm and jovial. It belonged to Donald, the security guard stationed at the front desk.

"Is this Donald Thorp?" Buff asked.

"Yes. Who is this?"

"Do you work at the law offices of Bennett, Olsen, Nygärd, Jørgensen, and Holm?"

There was a brief pause before Donald responded. "I'm not interested," he said curtly, and then hung up.

Buff was taken aback, and stood in shock for a moment while the dial tone hummed in his ear.

Marcus smirked. "I told ya so."

Buff held up his index finger, waving off Marcus's concerns.

He pressed the redial button. A few seconds later, Donald answered.

"Hello?"

"Don't hang up," Buff said, forcefully. "I am not a telemarketer, Mr. Thorp. I want to change your life."

"What? Who is this? What is this about?"

"This is an opportunity, Donald. This is free money."

Buff paused a moment to let Donald consider the thought. If he hung up a second time, then his plan wouldn't work. Luckily, the security guard was curious.

"Go on," he said, intrigued.

"I have just two questions for you. Do you like your job?"

"Ah geez, I don't know. I'm not particularly fond of it, but it's a good job..."

"How much would it cost to make you walk away from it?"

"Excuse me?"

"How much money would it take to make you quit? Hypothetically speaking, of course."

There was a prolonged silence on the other end of the phone. Either Donald was giving the question serious thought, or he was debating the veracity of the offer. Buff didn't have time to wait.

"Mr. Thorp?"

"Ah, well geez, you know, I'm making thirty grand a year now, so it would probably have to be better than that, depending on benefits..."

"No, no, Donald. This is not a job offer. It's a question. How much to make you leave your job right now? To just get up and walk out the front door?"

Another pause.

"Hypothetically?" Donald asked, hesitantly.

"Of course."

"I don't know. Maybe, uh, ten grand?"

"How about seven?"

"No, I think ten sounds right."

Buff closed his eyes and bit his lip. He wasn't happy with the price, but he couldn't fault the man for trying to earn a little extra. He probably would have done the same thing if their positions were reversed.

"Thank you, Mr. Thorp."

He quickly hung up the phone, without giving the security guard any further details. He tossed the phone back to Marcus and smiled.

"We're in."

# 7:00pm

Two vehicles turned off the main road and pulled into the parking lot for the law offices of Bennett, Olsen, Nygärd, Jørgensen, and Holm. One was N-Dig's old, rusty Ford Focus and the other was Surly Shirley's big, heavy moving truck. They drove them into position quickly and quietly.

N-Dig pulled his car right up next to the front doors and put it in park, but kept the engine running. From the driver's seat he could see right into the lobby.

Surly Shirley moved the truck around to the other side of the building, where the rear entrance was. It was a standard shipping dock, with a large retractable door and soft bumpers on either side. She lined up her back tires so they were parallel with the door, and then backed the truck up against it.

Buff was sitting next to her in the front cab. Clearly impressed with her driving, he let out a little wolf whistle.

"Nice parking," he cooed with a sly smile.

"Fuck yeah it was!" she cheered. "Now the rest is up to you, cocksucker."

Buff laughed. He'd never met anyone as blunt or profane as her, and he loved her for it. He hoped they'd stay friends after the heist.

He reached into his pocket and pulled out a small two-way radio. It was roughly the same size as a cell phone and built of rugged black plastic. There was a thick, stubby antenna poking out the top, beside a row of knobs and switches.

Everyone in the group had been given one of these eXRS two-way radios. They were more expensive than a normal walkie-talkie, but Doug claimed they were the best on the market. Unlike typical radios that relied on a single channel frequency, these continuously hopped between fifty different frequencies in a random sequence, providing up to 10 billion separate channels. In addition, they used voice-inversion technology that scrambled transmissions between people using the same channel. For those reasons, these radios were the most secure and private means of communication available commercially.

Buff flicked his on and fiddled with the knobs until it squawked to life. He held it up to his mouth and clicked the button labelled "TRANSMIT."

"Testing, testing. Over."

He waited a moment, and then his radio lit up and Doug's voice answered. The sound was crisp and clear, like he was right beside them.

"We hear you," he said, "but don't hold the radio so close to your mouth. You're distorting. And you don't need to say 'over,' either. Just look at the top. The green button lights up when somebody's transmitting."

He glanced down and saw that Doug was right.

"Oh," he uttered with a groan.

Shirley snickered.

"Thanks for the advice," Buff continued into the radio. "Turn the cell blocker on now."

Squeezed into the back seat of N-Dig's car, Doug didn't have much room to maneuver. Kane and Marcus were wedged in beside him. He tried elbowing them to one side, but they had nowhere to go. Doug was going to have to make do with the limited space he had.

He pulled his duffle bag up to his chest, unzipped it, and dug through it.

Eventually he found a small metal device the size of a shoebox, with a dial on the left side, and a single red button in the middle. He'd built it himself, modifying designs he found online and going through months and months of trial and error. Basically, it sent out a pulse that dropped all cell phone signals within a two-hundred-yard radius. It was highly illegal, but it did make going to a movie theatre a much more enjoyable experience.

Doug flicked the dial, crossed his fingers and pushed the red button. The box made a soft humming sound.

"Is she workin' there, b'y?" Marcus asked.

"I think so," Doug replied. "Check your phone."

Beka answered before anyone could comply. "I'm not getting a signal," she said, waving her phone above her. Kane checked his phone and found the same thing.

"It's working," Doug said into the radio.

"Good," Buff said. His answers were a little distorted. He was still holding the radio too close to his mouth. "Remember: nobody gets hurt, everybody gets paid. We'll see you on the inside. Go."

Everyone in the car took half a second to look at each other, and then set about getting down to work.

Kane handed everyone a balaclava, the kind of knit face mask worn by skiers and snowmobilers. They were tattered and well-worn, and the Fodder brothers had brought enough for everybody.

Marcus put his on without a second thought.

Doug looked down at his, dumbfounded.

"Hey man, why do you have all these?" he asked.

"Eh? Because me and my brother own, like, seven Ski-Doos, bud," Kane replied.

Doug gave a shrug, and reluctantly put it on. It was made of coarse wool, which was terribly uncomfortable to wear.

Beka held hers under her nose and gave a sniff. She shuddered and handed it back to Kane.

"That's okay," she said, sardonically. "I brought my own. Thanks, though."

She reached into her pocket and pulled out her own knit ski mask. It was black, with little cat ears on top of the head and tiny whiskers sewn onto the face. It was unspeakably cute. The sight of it gave Marcus a beaming grin.

"That's adorable, me love," he said.

She let out a comically coy giggle, held her hand up like a tiger's paw, and made a cat sound.

Marcus chortled, which was muffled by his mask. He leaned forward and put his hand on N-Dig's shoulder

"When we muck off into there, we needs ya to stay here, b'y," he said, ensuring he had the boy's full attention. "Watch that security guard. Watch him close, b'y. When he walks out that door, make sure the fella just goes to his car and leaves. Nothin' else, b'y. And don't douse yar engine 'til then, eh? Then, when the Rodney screecher's gone, give us a wee bamp on the horn. Simple look-out. Easy as a solo on the tickle, me b'y. Do y'understand?"

"No," N-Dig said, dryly. "For real, bro. I think I missed a lot of that. You used a whole bunch of words that don't make sense."

Beka began laughing.

"Don't worry about it, bro," N-Dig continued. "I've done this before. For real. I'll manage, bro. Believe."

Marcus inhaled deeply. N-Dig didn't exactly fill him with confidence, but he was the only getaway driver they had. He would have to do.

"Good enough," he said. "This is it, chums. Fair weather to ya and snow to yar heels. Let's go."

It only took an instant for Marcus, Beka, Doug and Kane to jump out of the car, march up to the front doors and burst through them into the law firm's main lobby.

They quickly surrounded the stone desk. Although unarmed, the four intruders looked incredibly intimidating, with their dark masks on and black hoods pulled up. They moved with choreographed precision, like a military unit infiltrating an enemy base.

Donald was taken completely by surprise. He didn't have time to react. He barely had time to pull his feet off the top of the desk, and nearly fell out of his chair. The look on his face was one of sheer terror.

Under the edge of the desk was a hidden button that tripped the silent alarm. Donald leaned forward to push it.

Kane took two swift strides toward the desk. With a flick of his wrist the collapsible baton fell from the inside of his sleeve into his hand. In a single, fluid motion he reared his arm back, making the baton extend to its full length and snap into place, and then he ferociously smashed it against the top of the desk.

It made a thunderous, violent crashing sound, causing the room to shake. Tiny bits of stone shot outwards in all directions. The impact left a sizable crack along the desk's smooth surface.

Donald jumped back in fear. He pushed himself back up against the wall, holding up his hands in surrender. Any traces of courage or bravery he had melted away.

"Please," he pleaded, overwhelmed, words falling from his mouth at a breakneck speed. "Please, don't hurt me, please! I won't stop you! I don't even like this job! Just don't hurt me, please! Please!"

Kane held the baton at his side while the other three intruders remained motionless. They stood around the security guard, looking dangerous and threatening. With their hands on their hips and their chests puffed out, they exuded a powerful menace.

After a beat, Marcus put his hand into his pocket and stepped up to the desk.

Donald cringed. He was sure the man was going to pull out a gun and shoot him. He tightly shut his eyes and winced.

Of course, it wasn't a weapon at all. It was a stack of twenty-dollar bills, tied with a bank wrap and totalling $1000. Marcus pulled it out and tossed it onto the desk.

Hearing no gunshot, Donald opened his eyes. Once he saw the

money, his whole body shifted, as he moved from fear to confusion. He cocked an eyebrow and tilted his head.

Marcus threw another stack of bills on the desk. Then another. One by one, he pulled out a total of ten bundles of cash and dropped them in front of the security guard. When he was done he flared his arms out, presenting it to him like a fancy waiter delivering the main course.

It took a while for Donald's mind to make sense of what was happening. When it finally clicked, his face lit up with a smile.

"Ten grand?" he asked anxiously.

Marcus gave him a nod.

Donald leaned forward, but stopped himself before touching the cash.

"You know, they have cameras everywhere in here," he said.

"No! Really?"Beka asked sarcastically, and then gave a derisive cackle. "Keep your pants on, Paul Blart. We've got it all taken care of. It will all be erased, including this stupid conversation."

With that, Donald pounced on the money like a cat catching a mouse. He gleefully stuffed it into his jacket one stack at a time, his face a vision of pure greedy ecstasy. He looked like Scrooge McDuck after he was stricken with "gold fever."

"Ya don't tell anyone 'bout this," Marcus said. He was speaking slowly and clearly, trying hard to mask his Newfoundland accent. "Anyone asks ya 'bout the money, ya say ya found 'er. Ya don't call the cops. Ya go straight home and keep yar mouth shut. We knows where ya live and how to find ya, chum."

Donald gave him a dismissive wave. He picked up the last wad of bills and held it under his nose, fluttering them like a deck of cards. He grinned like a goat in a garbage dump.

"Go," Marcus yelled. "Now."

Startled out of his stupor, Donald shoved the money into his pocket. He hadn't felt this good in months. He looked like a new man, enlivened and reinvigorated.

"Thank you!" he said, a big grin plastered across his face.

He gave a big, animated wave goodbye to the four intruders, but they didn't flinch. They followed him with their eyes as he picked up his book and skipped out through the front doors.

"That was surprisingly easy," Doug said, pulling off his mask.

Marcus held up his hand to silence the young man.

"Wait for the signal, b'y," he said.

Outside, N-Dig was watching an oblivious Donald parade to his car. The security guard was in high spirits, dancing and shaking like no one was looking. He strutted back to his Chevrolet Cavalier with a swagger, as if he were John Travolta in *Saturday Night Fever*.

He opened the driver's side door and climbed into the car. The old Chevrolet rumbled and wheezed as the engine sputtered to life. He threw it into drive, and tore out of the parking lot so fast he nearly travelled through time.

N-Dig lightly tapped the car horn twice and shut off the engine.

"He's gone," he said into the radio.

Once everyone in the lobby heard this, they took off their masks. Marcus got between them all and took command.

"Okay then, let's get to work!" he said, clapping his hands together. "Beka and Doug, get to the server room upstairs. Do yar thing, lassie, and do 'er quick. Directly. Kane, you come with me to the shippin' door. That drill we got weighs more than a trawler, b'y, and we gots to move 'er into the service elevator."

Everyone nodded in agreement. Beka and Doug turned and ran off towards the main stairwell. Marcus spun around in the opposite direction and began walking towards the shipping door.

He was halfway there when he noticed Kane wasn't following him.

The young man was over by the front doors, examining the building's office directory. He was running his finger down the list, as though he were looking for someone in particular.

"What the hell is ya doin' there, ya duff b'y?!" Marcus shouted. "We gots a schedule to keep! What are ya gockin' at that thing for?"

Kane ignored him completely. He scanned the list until he saw Harry Bockner's name, and made a mental note of the office number.

Confident that he had it memorized, he turned back and rejoined a fuming Marcus.

"If it were up to me, b'y, ya'd be off the team right the once for doin' that!" he bellowed, wagging his finger in Kane's face. "Ya hold me back like that again, ya little figger, and I gives ya a crack so hard there'll be no teeth left in yar head! Let's move!"

Kane had no reaction. It was easy to discount someone's criticism when you could barely understand them.

Outside in the parking lot, N-Dig peered into the lobby through the front doors. He watched as Marcus and Kane ran off towards the shipping doors. The spacious first floor was now vacant.

N-Dig settled back into his driver's seat, turning to face the road. Now his only job was to watch for cops or nosy passersby. He knew he was going to be here a few hours, so he got himself comfortable.

***

The building had two stairwells, but both of them were ugly and depressing, completely concrete and adorned with nothing but a metal railing. One was the emergency stairs, located on the building's east side. The doors leading into it were all tied to a closed-circuit alarm. The other was considered the "main" stairwell, and had no alarm. It was on the west side, next to the passenger elevators.

The latter were the stairs Doug and Beka ran up to get to the second floor, which was reserved for storage and maintenance.

They burst into a corridor lined with doors, most of which were just large closets. Each had a unique purpose: some just for paper and ink for printers, one just for pens and stationery, one for the custodial supplies, another with spare tables and chairs.

Since people rarely visited the second floor, it was sparsely decorated. Large patches of the walls were unpainted, with sizable gouges in the bare drywall. It was dimly lit by a few bare lightbulbs hanging from the ceiling.

There were two large rooms at the far end of the hall, one containing the building's dozen circuit breakers, the other holding all the computer servers and network routers. Two separate locks, one that used a swipe card and another that used an actual key, protected both rooms.

Getting through those locks was Doug's job. He sprinted down the hallway, and slid to a stop in front of the server room.

He got down on one knee facing the doorknob. Beneath it was a small grey panel, housing a physical lock and the card reader.

Doug leaned to one side and rummaged through his duffle bag. He pulled out a plastic device the size of an old Nintendo Game Boy. It was another homemade contraption, wrapped in duct tape except for a single green button protruding from the top. This machine worked with any reader that used an RFID system, using the scanner's latent memory against itself. It would search for the last passcode used on the reader, and then resend that same passcode back through the scanner's system, mimicking the last person to open the door.

Doug pushed the green button. His device hummed softly, and after a moment the door made the distinct clack of a lock sliding open. One down, one more to go.

Setting the device aside, he reached back into his bag and pulled out a lock-picking tool. It was specially designed for mortise locks. It looked like a can opener with a thin metal wire poking out the sharp end, and it fit neatly in one hand.

He slid the tool into the lock and twisted it clockwise. He could feel the tumblers falling into place, but it would take a few seconds before the lock opened.

All the while, Beka was looking over his shoulder, arms crossed and tapping her foot.

"Oh my God, Doug," she moaned dramatically. "What the hell is taking you so long? You're slower than the postal service. Slower than dial-up. If you were a Pokémon, you'd be Munchlax or Shuckle."

Doug clenched his fist and ground his teeth. He could be the bigger man and bear Beka's taunts in silence, but it was getting progressively more difficult. She clucked her tongue impatiently.

"Let's go, let's go," she said. "This should be done by now. You're as slow as a hockey player in algebra class."

Doug snapped and punched the door. "Enough, Rebecca!" he shouted. "Knock it off, okay? I'm trying to work here." He let out an annoyed grunt, paused a moment, and then continued ranting. "You're so damn opinionated, you know that? That's why I left! You criticize everything. It's insufferable."

Beka did not react well to the outburst. Her eyes bulged out, her nostrils flared, and her face turned bright red. She looked like she was about to turn into the Incredible Hulk. Doug immediately regretted what he'd said, but it was too late to take it back. He braced himself, hoping she wouldn't hit him.

"'Why you left'?!" she screamed, louder than a banshee, stomping her feet like a toddler. "You stupid, selfish son of a bitch! I don't care why you left! Not since you decided to go out on a cliffhanger. You left me with nothing, you prick! I never did anything to you to justify abandoning me like that, Doug."

He thought she was being melodramatic. "It's not like I left you stranded at a bus stop!" he whined, defensively. "I just walked away. I left you all the electronics, all the money in the joint account, everything in the fridge..."

"You took off with saying a word, asshole! No letter, no phone call, no text message. Nothing. That really sucked, Douglas. That was a real pitchfork in the balls." She shook her head, doubting he comprehended the pain he'd caused. "I called hospitals looking for you, Doug. We had plans that weekend. I'd made enough spaghetti for both of us and had all this sauce I couldn't get rid of..." She got wistful and her voice trailed off, but she kept shaking her head.

Doug put his tools down on the floor and stood up. "Listen, Rebecca," he said, softly, approaching her with open arms, "when I did what I did..."

"Oh, shut up, Doug!" she snapped, interrupting him. "I can't stand you. I don't want to talk to you, at all. Ever."

"Then why do you keep trying to pick a fight with me? Why do you rip on everything I say?"

Her answer was sharp and direct. "For fun. Because I hate you. I want to hurt you, Doug. Because I want you to know how much you hurt me."

The two of them stared at each other for a long time, with only the gentle hum of the electrical room as a soundtrack. Beka saw something in Doug's expression, something she hadn't seen since they reunited at that restaurant the night before. It was shame.

She turned away before she started feeling pity for the jerk.

Doug's pride kicked in again, and he resumed talking without thinking. "You know what?" he asked rhetorically. "It wasn't the greatest time of my life, either."

Beka groaned loudly, disgruntled. "Ugh, shut up! Don't talk to me. Just open the damn door!"

If Doug were a character in a comic strip, there would have been three big black squiggle marks over his head. He got back down on his knees, grabbed his lock-picking tool and shoved it into the lock, grumbling loudly all the while.

A loud click, and the door swung open.

Doug theatrically extended his arm into the room. "Your majesty!" he sang, in his most condescending voice.

If Beka were a cartoon character, she would have produced an anvil from behind her back and smashed it over Doug's head.

"I hate you so much," she seethed, slinking past him. Doug scooped up his equipment and began repeating the procedure on the electrical room's door locks.

The server room looked like the inside of a robot's stomach. It was warm and dark, the only real light coming from the hundreds of blinking, twinkling green and red power lights. Rows and rows of black computer towers were stacked on top of each other like bricks. An array of routers, splitters, signal boosters and other computer networking equipment was neatly rack-mounted on a shelf, with all of the appropriate cables dangled out the back like a frayed sweater. The walls were lined with bundles of yellow CAT-6 network cable, some a few feet thick, and tied together with plastic wraps. They snaked up to the ceiling and out into the rest of the building. The floor was littered with a dozen buzzing power bars, each plugged tight.

In the centre of the room, locked onto the equipment shelf, was a single computer monitor. Beka flicked it on, providing a cold blue glow to an otherwise dark room.

She glanced briefly at the clock on her phone. Time to get to work.

Grabbing the keyboard, her fingers began quickly dancing across the keys like a concert pianist at Carnegie Hall. The clattering of her breakneck typing echoed down the hallway.

In less than two minutes, she'd accessed all of the building's main systems. She found everything on the server neatly organized into different folders, making it incredibly easy to break into the areas she needed to.

"Only one password," she said to herself. "These noobers deserve to be cracked."

Before shutting anything down, she was careful to set up a feedback signal. If anyone were monitoring the network, they wouldn't see that it'd been disconnected. Once that was established, she shut down the building's alarm system and security cameras.

Another loud click, and the door to the electrical room unlocked. Doug pushed it open and got back on his feet.

The room was sparse and totally dark, but seemed to vibrate and pulse with unseen energy. It was empty except for a wall of twelve electrical circuit breakers, which droned endlessly at levels barely audible to human ears.

He pulled out a flashlight and clicked it on. He began searching the circuit panels, one switch at a time. Lucky for him they were clearly labelled. It only took a minute to find the power for the passenger elevators and shut it off. It took even less time to cut the phone lines.

When he was done, he pulled one last tool out of his duffle bag. It was a large, hand-held electromagnet, a little bigger than a standard power drill, with a power cable hanging off one end.

He slung it under his arm and walked over to the server room. When Beka was finished, he would demagnetize all of the servers, rendering them inoperable and useless. That would ensure every trace of the heist and their involvement in it, even the video footage, would be wiped out.

He stood right behind her, close enough to breathe down her neck. He crossed his arms and tapped his foot, mocking her earlier impatience.

Beka ignored him. She was too focused on the text flying past her on the screen. With just a few keystrokes, she'd locked down every exit in the building, including the front and side doors. She also locked every door leading into the main stairwell. She wanted to do the same with the doors to the emergency stairwell, but because of fire code regulations, they had no locks on them.

With the building completely secured, she paused a moment to crack her knuckles and recheck the clock on her phone. It had taken her four and a half minutes to lock everything down. Not her best time, especially considering how poorly protected this server was, but still faster than most people who call themselves "network crackers."

She shrugged and went back to work. Now all she had to do was get the building's rear shipping door open, and her work in the server room would be over.

***

Tucked away in the building's rear corner, the shipping and receiving area was only slightly less welcoming than a prison cell. The room was the usual small, cold, concrete box found in loading docks everywhere. It was a part of the building only visited by burly truck drivers and deliverymen. The floor was covered in scuffs and scrapes, a remnant of the hundreds of heavy packages dragged across its surface over the years.

Marcus and Kane were there, waiting patiently.

Eventually the giant steel garage door started to rise. A loud whirring sound resonated throughout the room as a motor pulled the door up to the ceiling. It rattled until it was all the way open, and then the noise stopped as suddenly as it began. A warm breeze from outside swept in through the open door.

Buff was on the other side, standing next to Surly Shirley's big truck. He jumped up into the shipping area and stood next to Marcus.

"We good?" he asked.

The old man nodded.

Without waiting, Buff bent down and opened the latch on the truck's back door. It slid aside with a sharp clank, and the door rolled up into the truck like a pull-down blind.

Light poured into the darkened trailer, revealing Dwayne, Big Frank, and Fou standing there. Dwayne and Fou both threw their hands up over their sensitive eyes. They'd been sitting in the dark for nearly thirty minutes, huddled around that enormous industrial drill.

The three of them anxiously jumped out of the truck.

Buff gave them a moment to stretch their legs while he examined the path to the service elevator. It was only twenty feet, maybe a little more, and completely unobstructed, but it would still take a Herculean effort to move the almost half-ton drill. They'd been smart enough to load it onto a wheeled dolly, which would make things slightly easier. Tied to the bottom of the dolly were four polyester ratchet straps, each with handles on the end.

After a signal from Buff, they all gathered around the drill. Kane got behind the dolly to push, while everyone else grabbed one of the straps. Once ready, they all heaved in unison, and the drill slid a few feet forward. They repeated the move twice more, and managed to pull the drill out of the truck and into the building. The back of the truck bounced up as all the weight shifted off the rear axles.

Buff shut both the truck's rear door and the garage door. He wiped the sweat from his brow and exhaled deeply.

Kane stepped up behind him and tugged on his arm. Buff leaned down to hear him.

"Seventh floor," Kane whispered. "Suite 704."

A malevolent grin spread across Buff's face like when the Grinch came up with his plan to steal Christmas. His mind reeled at the possibility of revenge against his old prosecutor.

"Thank you," he said to Kane, patting him on the back.

Marcus was watching this with a puzzled look on his face.

"What is it that ya two girlies is gossipin' 'bout?" he demanded.

"It's nothing, Marcus," Buff replied, calmly. "Don't worry about it."

Marcus silently fumed. He really didn't like secrets between team members. He wanted to know everything about the heist and the people pulling it. There was less chance of any unfortunate "surprises" popping up that way. He put his hands on his hips and stared Buff down, like an angry wife.

"Come on, Marcus," Buff whined. "We don't have time for this. Grab the other side. We need to get this thing upstairs now."

The old man bit his lip and resumed helping move the huge drill. He wanted nothing more to argue with Buff about his secretive behavior, but he wouldn't do it here in front of the rest of the team. He would wait and do it privately, when he could really unload on his old partner.

Everyone had to work together to move the mammoth machinery across the room. The strain was all over their faces, as they each turned bright red, grunting and wheezing. They were like Egyptian slaves building the pyramids, pushing an enormous limestone slab up to the peak.

It took a full five minutes, but they finally got the thing in front of the service elevator. Dwayne and Kane looked utterly exhausted. Big Frank hadn't even broken a sweat. Buff was also weary and drained, but a quick peek at his watch proved he didn't have time to rest. They needed to keep moving.

Marcus smacked the call button and the elevator doors slid open. There were a few resigned groans, but everyone got behind the dolly and pushed the drill inside. Once it was in place, the five men piled in around it. They were packed in tighter than a subway car at rush hour.

The doors slid close. Buff hit the button for the top floor, where the vault sat waiting for them, and the elevator started to rise.

# 7:15pm

Up in the accounting office, Harry was pounding his fists against his keyboard. He was right in the middle of his illegal money transfer when the network suddenly went down. He couldn't access the files he needed, and whenever he tried, the computer would chirp and freeze on an error message that read "ACCESSING NETWORK..." No matter what he did, no matter what keys he pressed, the tiny hourglass on the computer screen kept spinning, mocking his impotence.

Harry had only been able to secure a fraction of the fortune he intended to steal. He screamed, equal parts frustration and exasperation, and threw a tantrum worthy of a cranky toddler. With no one there to see him, he felt no need to inhibit his rage. Embittered and defeated, he stood up and kicked the hell out of his chair.

This scheme of his was a limited time offer. He was relying on the banks being closed today to cover his tracks. He couldn't just come back later and try again. If he didn't get back online and reinstate the transfer right away, his transgression would be discovered first thing in the morning.

He began pacing around the room, huffing loudly. He knew absolutely nothing about computers or how to fix them. Worse, he couldn't call the 24-hour tech support guys from the firm's IT department, because he'd have to explain what he was doing there.

The only solution he could come up with was to call down to the security guard at the front desk. Hopefully he'd know more about computers than Harry did. He'd give the guard a fake name, and pretend he was from the accounting department. With a little smooth talking, he could probably convince him to come up and look at his machine without asking too many questions. Once there, he could reconnect, or reboot, or restart, or whatever it was the nerds did to make the computers work.

Harry picked up the phone and held the receiver to his ear. There was no dial tone. He pounded the hook switch and pressed every button there was, but still nothing. He grumbled and slammed the phone back down in its cradle.

Now he'd have to go downstairs and talk to the guard in person.

Dammit, he thought, this couldn't be going worse.

He pushed his chair away from his desk and stood up. He grabbed his phone from under a stack of paper and shoved it into his pocket without looking at it. Thinking he'd be right back, he left his jacket and briefcase where they were.

He kicked the chair on his way out, venting a minor fraction of his stress.

Harry wandered down the hall to the passenger elevators, angrily muttering to himself. He occasionally kicked a filing cabinet along the way.

He pushed the elevator's call button. Normally, it lit up, but when Harry pressed it, nothing happened.

Even on the firm's busiest days, there was never a wait for a passenger elevator. They were state-of-the-art Otis Gen2 elevators, which used polyurethane belts instead of woven steel cables. It was a costly but energy-efficient system the firm had installed four years ago to take advantage of "eco-friendly" tax credits. Since then, it had been working perfectly every day, more reliably than any employee, until today.

Harry smacked the elevator door with his palm as hard as he could. Why now, of all times, would this thing choose to break down? It had been working just an hour earlier. He'd used it to get up here in the first place.

He really didn't want to walk down six floors of stairs, but it looked like he didn't have much of a choice. He thought his day couldn't get any worse. Cursing his foul luck, he turned to the stairwell door and tried pushing it open.

It didn't budge. He jiggled the door handle back and forth violently, and it still wouldn't move. He slammed into it with his shoulder, leaning all his weight against the door. Still nothing.

Harry was beginning to wonder if he'd stumbled into the middle of an episode of *The Twilight Zone*. It felt like someone was screwing with him. What the hell was going on here?

He exhaled loudly, frustrated. Now the only way to get down to the lobby would be by using the emergency stairs, which were all the way on the other side of the building. Using them would probably set off an alarm, but at least he knew those doors would be unlocked.

He kicked a few more filing cabinets as he double-backed down the hallway. Harry was not a man who handled anger well. He had a notoriously bad temper, and when he lost his cool, he became belligerent and physically violent. Over the years it cost him friends and kept most of his romantic relationships from lasting more than a few weeks. It almost got him disbarred once when he became enraged in the middle of a trial, threatened to kick the teeth out of the accused, and had to be held back by two corrections officers.

Whether aimed at tiny offences like an elevator not working, or massive schemes like the Norwegian-Canadian mob taking money he earned, Harry's untamed anger always came out like a powerful storm. Every perceived slight against him was a grave injustice, always intentional and always someone else's fault. For all his law degrees, nice suits, and fancy cars, Harry was still like a toddler when he didn't get his way.

He marched to the emergency stairwell like a grouchy elephant, grunting, and loudly stomping his feet.

There was a sign on the door, which read "EMERGENCY EXIT ONLY - ALARM WILL SOUND." Harry snickered as he pushed it open.

A shrill, piercing siren began to blare. Harry threw his hands up over his ears, his profane curses inaudible under the alarm's relentless clamor. The sound seemed to be coming from all directions.

I hate working here, he thought.

He started walking down the stairs. Six more floors until the lobby.

***

Very few people ever got to see the top floor of the building. Other than a cavernous boardroom, there were only five offices up there, one for each of the firm's partners: Bennett, Olsen, Nygärd, Jørgensen, and Holm. Their offices were spacious and lavishly decorated, but rarely ever used. Most cases were handed down to other associates in the firm, so the partners only came in for very special clients.

It was also the floor where the heads of the Norwegian-Canadian mob would meet once a month to discuss future business plans.

For that reason, it was designed to impress. The entire floor looked like an old library, all earth tones and elegant wood trim.The carpets had ornately detailed gold patterns on them. Elaborate sculptures by Henrik Hagtvedt and Brynjulf Bergslien sat atop pedestals shaped like Greek columns.

At the far end of the hallway, in a barren corner of the top floor, was the vault room. It was locked behind a door of tempered steel five inches thick, and secured with a card reader and passcode entered via numeric keypad.

Beka and Doug were already there. Doug was using his RFID scanning tool to open the door.

The others were some fifteen feet behind them, dragging the industrial drill. The enormous thing made a loud groan with every incremental push forward, and left the carpet in its wake decimated, tattered and torn beyond repair.

The men looked equally ragged. They were all sopping with sweat and visibly sore. Fou had thrown off his tie and suit jacket, and had his sleeves rolled up to the elbow.

Dwayne turned to Buff, looking like he was going to throw up.

"Hey, bud, we're not carrying this thing back down when we're done, are we?" he asked.

Kane and Marcus both laughed.

That's when they heard the alarm go off.

It startled them all, and they froze. For an instant, everyone thought they were caught. Some of them looked panicked. Big Frank didn't react at all. There was a second of confusion between them all, and everyone turned to Buff looking for guidance.

"What the hell is that screechin', b'y?!" Marcus screamed, furious.

"I don't know!" Buff shouted back. He turned to Beka. "I told you to turn off all the alarms!"

"I did!" she yelled angrily. "I shut the whole damn network off!"

Buff pointed up to the ceiling. "Then what the hell is that!?"

"I don't know! This doesn't make sense! The phone lines were cut, the server's powered down. There's no way to send a signal out!" She was fervent enough that Buff believed her.

"It must be a closed-circuit system," Doug said. "Probably some kind of internal alarm or something."

A lightbulb went off above Beka's head, and she snapped her fingers. "The emergency stairs!" she cried. "It's the alarm for the emergency stairs!"

Marcus's face went white.

"Lard t'underin'! There's somebody else in the building!" he shouted, agitated. "We should have swept them offices first, b'y, before tryin' to flux that damn drill-thing up the stairs! I tolds ya! I tolds ya a hundred times, me cocky!"

Dwayne and Kane started yelling out their own concerns. Soon, it was impossible to discern anyone's voice from the din. Between the alarm and the shouting, the noise in the hallway was unbearable.

Buff held out both his arms and silenced them.

"Stop it!" he yelled. "Everybody, calm down! It could be anything. Just because the alarm went off doesn't mean there's someone in the building, okay?"

"Ya want to take that chance, b'y?" Marcus scoffed, incredulous.

Buff shot him a dirty look. The old man wasn't helping the situation.

"All the building's exits are locked, right?" Buff asked Beka, giving her a quizzical look.

"Yes, of course they are," she said, resentful of being doubted.

"Okay, then even if there is someone loose in the building, they're locked inside and can't call out for help. That's good."

He took a moment to reflect before he started barking out more orders. He really excelled at this sort of thing, thinking on his feet and improvising a plan. He pointed at people as he spoke to them, sounding confident and commanding.

"Kane, you and your brother go down to the main floor and find out what tripped the alarm. If you do find somebody, tie them up and throw them into one of the bathrooms. Rough them up if you have to make them keep quiet, but do not hurt them. Make sure you keep your masks on. Take Big Frank with you, too. Call me on the radio and let me know what you find."

"Eh? Why the main floor?" Kane asked.

"If somebody set off the emergency stairwell alarm, then they're trying to leave the building, right?" Buff answered, confidently. "They'll try the front door first and spread out from there. That's where you'll find them."

Kane nodded. Buff's plan made sense. Dwayne and Big Frank signalled their agreement.

"Good," Buff said. "Doug, you stay here and get us into that vault room."

"No problem," he replied.

The alarm kept wailing incessantly in the background.

"And Beka," Buff continued, "please get back down to the server room, turn off that goddamn noise and disable the alarm permanently."

"Okay," she replied.

"Good. Thank you," he said with a nod.

"Anything I can help with?" Fou asked.

Buff let out a frustrated grunt. "I told you to keep quiet, Fou!" he shouted. "Just shut up, help us get that drill into place, and then stay out of our goddamn way."

Fou slunk back behind the drill, away from Buff.

"Now, are there any other questions?"

There were none.

"Good." Buff clapped his hands together. "Go."

With that, everyone scattered. Beka, Big Frank, and the Fodders ran back down the hallway and climbed into the open service elevator. The doors slid close behind them.

Doug turned his attention back to the lock on the vault room door.

Fou just stood there, uncomfortable and out of place, like a fly in a sugar bowl.

Marcus leaned back and crossed his arm, smiling broadly. He couldn't help but be impressed by Buff's leadership. The man exuded confidence, and inspired the same in his team. They didn't always agree, but the old man had to admit, Buff was a damn good thief.

Their task had just gotten a whole lot harder. Now the heavy, bulky drill would have to be pulled fifteen feet by just three men, one of whom was well past his strongest days. Considering how hard it was for six men to move it, this was probably going to take a while.

Buff cursed under his breath. He had originally planned to take this time to slip down to the seventh floor, find Harry Bockner's office and trash it. While it would accomplish nothing, Buff personally felt as though it was the most important goal of the heist. It would provide him with a sense of vengeance against the man who ruined the last two years of his life. Unfortunately, that would have to wait until after they got the drill into place.

He joined Marcus and Fou in grabbing one end of a strap with each hand. They started pulling in unison, and it felt like trying to pull a parked car.

***

Harry hated using the stairs. He was the kind of guy who would take the elevator just to go down a single floor. He wasn't lazy, but at his age, he took every chance he could to avoid walking. Having to hike down six flights of stairs took his foul mood and worsened it.

His head was throbbing. The alarm echoed relentlessly against the stairwell's concrete walls, like being stuck inside a church bell on Sunday morning. It was excruciating.

When Harry finally reached the door for the main lobby, he slammed into it, thrusting it open as if he were escaping from prison.

He walked out to find the floor completely deserted. There was no one behind the desk.

Harry wandered around for a bit, looking for some clue as to the security guard's whereabouts. He peered around every corner and checked every hallway. He always found the same thing: nothing.

"Hello?" he cried out. "Anybody here?"

There was no answer. It was unlikely that anyone could hear him over the alarm anyway.

He wondered where that stupid guard could be. That idiot wasn't supposed to leave the front desk unattended, ever. Maybe he had to go and turn off the alarm. If so, then what's taking him so long? Harry couldn't tell how long the alarm had been ringing, but it felt like hours. His temples were pounding like conga drums.

By this point, Harry just wanted to talk to someone - anyone - who could tell him what was going on. He concluded his best bet was to sit tight and wait for the guard to come back.

He couldn't stay here, though. That noise was just intolerable.

His car was just outside the front door. He could wait there. He was pretty sure he even had some aspirin in the glove compartment. He could sit comfortably, turn on the air conditioning, and listen to some classic rock. It would be perfect.

He walked over to the front door and tried pushing it open. It was locked.

Now he really felt like someone was screwing with him.

He tried again but it wouldn't budge. What the hell was going on here?

Through the door's glass window, he could see a battered old Ford Focus sitting in the parking lot. He tried to remember if it had been there when he first got to the office, but couldn't recall. Looking closer, he noticed there appeared to be a young man sitting in the driver's seat, watching traffic drive past the building.

Suddenly, an ominous feeling of dread overwhelmed him. Something about the guy in the car didn't sit right.

Harry quickly backed away from the door and ducked out of sight. He sat on the floor with his back against the wall, trying to make sense of the situation.

Who the hell was that kid in the parking lot?

This was like a horrible nightmare. He was trapped at work, alone, while a piercing siren screamed ceaselessly. There was too much going on at once for the old man to process. Harry started to panic. Things couldn't get any worse.

Down the hallway, where the elevators were located, he finally saw some movement. Above each elevator door was a row of lights that indicated what floor the elevator was currently on. As Harry watched, the lights above the far door were slowly clicking down. The service elevator was moving, and it was coming down to the ground floor!

Relax, Harry told himself. It might just be the security guard coming back to the desk. He probably has to do some kind of sweep of the building every time an alarm goes off. No reason to panic like a girl.

On the other hand, there was this intensely bad feeling growing in the pit of his stomach that couldn't be ignored.

He quickly decided there was no harm in trusting his gut, and found a place to hide. He ran to the other side of the lobby and crawled into the space between the wall and one of the large planters, just in case.

***

The service elevator shuddered to a stop at the second floor. It had been an uncomfortable ride down seven floors, as no one said a word. The only sound the entire trip was that of the droning, whining alarm.

As soon as the doors opened, Beka jumped out and dashed down the hall to the server room. The doors slid close behind her, and the elevator resumed its descent.

The three men put their masks back on, which made them look even more formidable and scary. Big Frank turned around so that he was facing both the Fodder brothers.

They held their breath, startled. In the two days they'd known Big Frank, they'd never once spoken to the man. The truth was that he scared them. They'd heard that he was violent and unstable, maybe even a psychopath, and he hadn't yet done anything to dissuade them from that idea.

As big as the Fodders were, Big Frank still towered over them like an oak tree. He glared down at them through squinted eyes. The expression on his face was blank and emotionless.

The Fodders glanced at each other and gulped.

Big Frank reached into his coat with both hands, one in each pocket, and produced two small handguns. They were black and silver Kahr PM40s, a fifteen-ounce, .40-caliber weapon that held six bullets. They looked almost futuristic, with textured polymer grips and matte-finished, stainless steel slides. He held them out like an offering.

The Fodders were genuinely surprised, and breathed a small sigh of relief.

Dwayne suddenly got very excited, like a kid on Christmas morning.

"Sweet!" he exclaimed, grabbing one of the guns from Big Frank's hand. The tiny weapon made him feel like a badass action star. He started posing with it, waving it around like James Bond and practicing his quick draw.

Kane leaned over, put his hand on Dwayne's gun and pushed the muzzle aside.

"It's not a toy," he said, gravely. He turned back to Big Frank. "I thought Buff said no guns."

Big Frank shrugged, giving the boys a look that said "who cares?" Dwayne laughed.

Kane thought about it for a moment, and took the weapon. It felt good in his hands. The longer he held it, the more it seemed like a good idea to carry it. If there really was a security guard loose in the building, he figured he probably should be armed, if only for his own safety.

"Is it loaded?" he asked.

Big Frank nodded.

"Wouldn't be much use if it weren't, eh?" Dwayne added, nudging his brother with his elbow. Kane punched him right back, just beneath his shoulder.

Big Frank reached into the front pocket of his coat and pulled out an enormous .50-caliber Desert Eagle handgun. Developed by the Israeli military, the Desert Eagle brand was synonymous with explosive power. It was a stunning work of engineering, equal parts alluring and terrifying. Its silver plating shimmered under the elevator's fluorescent lights.

Dwayne gawked at it in awe, as though he were seeing a woman's naked breasts for the very first time.

"She's a beauty!" he said, giggling like a smitten schoolgirl.

Big Frank gave him a knowing smile.

The three men prepared themselves as the elevator settled onto the ground floor. They huddled together, taking cover in an inside corner.

A tiny bell chimed, and the doors slid apart.

Kane poked his head around the corner. He saw nothing.

"Clear," he shouted.

One by one all three men scuttled out of the elevator with guns drawn.

Quickly, they each scanned the room, looking for any signs of movement. The alarm continued to blare, which meant they couldn't rely on their ears for help.

Kane gave a hand motion signalling the others to make their way down the hallway. They moved like soldiers during a raid, crouched down and shuffling from one cover point to the next. It was obvious they'd done this kind of thing before. Harry poked his head out from behind the planter half an inch. It was enough for him to catch a glimpse of the three men, and more importantly, their handguns. He retreated faster than a heartbeat, closing his eyes and hugging the floor.

Oh shit, he thought. This is a robbery!

His knees went weak and his stomach leapt up into his throat. Fear coiled around his body like a giant snake, paralyzing him. He was suddenly grateful for the earsplitting siren, because he was sure the armed men would've heard his heavy, panicked breathing. He tried not to move, and prayed the thieves wouldn't see him.

With a wave from Kane, the three men fanned out into the lobby. It was a huge, open space without much cover, and a cursory glance showed no obvious signs of anyone hiding. As far they could tell, the room was empty.

They slowly circled around the front of the desk. Big Frank swung around behind it, and even checked the space underneath, but found nothing. He lowered his gun and shook his head.

"Nobody here," Dwayne said. "Guess it was, like, a false alarm, eh?"

"Or the goof just hasn't made it down the stairs yet," Kane added. "We need to flush him out. Same way we get the damn raccoons out of the barn, eh? We split up. I stay here, and you guys get behind him and push him down to me. Right?"

There was no argument from the other two.

"Beauty. Dwayne, you go up to the fourth floor. Big Frank, you go to seven. Take the elevator up and work your way back down here. Check every room, every office, floor by floor. Use the emergency stairs coming down. I'll wait by the door."

A quick nod of agreement from Dwayne and Big Frank, and then they both ran back to the service elevator and dashed inside.

Once they were gone, Kane casually walked over to the door leading to the emergency stairwell. He put his back against the wall directly beside it, so that when whoever set off the alarm came running out the door, they'd run face first into the muzzle of Kane's handgun.

Harry's mind was racing. He didn't know what to do, so he started to focus on the few facts he was sure of: there were at least three armed thieves, they knew he was somewhere in the building and they seemed determined to find him. He was trapped in the lobby, and that goon down the hall wasn't going anywhere. He was going to be here a while.

His leg was starting to cramp up. He cursed himself for not hiding in the utility closet instead.

He knew he wouldn't be able to get out the front door, and there was a good chance the side doors were locked too. He realized it was unlikely he'd be able to get out of the building. If he stayed where he was, those thugs would surely find him. However, if he could get off the ground floor, he could probably find a place he could hide all night. But how was he going to get past the masked man with a gun?

Maybe he could use the alarm to his advantage, sneak up on the goon and knock him out... but Harry didn't have anything to hit him with, and he wasn't about to try using brute strength against a handgun. Maybe he could lure him away from the door, and then make a break for stairs... but the distance between Harry and the door seemed daunting, as wide as the ocean, especially since he couldn't run faster than a bullet.

Those were his options: fight or flight. Neither was very appealing.

Harry wiggled his arm against his side, sliding his hand into his pocket. He fished around for something, anything that might prove useful. His fingers brushed past his phone and some spare change, which were no help at all. Then, at the very bottom of his pocket, he found his car keys.

A plan began to formulate in his head. He would throw the keys to the other side of the lobby, away from the hallway where the stairwell was. Hopefully, the armed man would walk over to see what the noise was, and Harry could run to the stairwells. It was a terrible plan and he knew it, but he couldn't stay put. He had to do something. He had to try.

He began pulling his keys out of his pocket, fumbling in this prostrate position...

Without warning, the alarm went silent. The lobby was suddenly as quiet as a church, with every tiny sound reverberating against its high ceilings.

The car keys slipped from Harry's fingers and clattered against the granite floor. He hurriedly tried to snatch them up.

It was too late. Kane's head snapped towards the sound like a dog hearing someone at the door. Holding his gun out in front of him, he ran to the middle of the lobby and stood firm. He moved his gun from side to side, scrutinizing the room through his gun sights.

Harry held his breath. Beads of sweat were forming on his brow and trickling down the sides of his face. His wrapped his hand around his keys, making a fist so that their tips poked out between his fingers like claws.

"I know you're here, eh?" Kane shouted out. "Come on out, bud."

Tightening his grip on the gun, he slowly and silently shuffled two feet to the side. Peering around the corner of the largest planter, he saw Harry cowering on the floor.

Kane relaxed for a moment. It was just an old man! He was worried it would be some hotheaded security guard, amped up on coffee and Red Bull, thinking he could retake the building as though this were a bad action movie. This poor old guy didn't pose any threat. He was probably scared out of his wrinkly skin.

"I see you, you old fart," Kane said with a laugh.

Harry's heart sank. He kept his eyes shut tight as his bottom lip began to quiver. He was sure he was going to die.

"Get out of there, bud!" Kane continued, creeping towards him slowly. "I'm not going to hurt you, as long as you do what I say. Just let us do our thing, and then we're gone."

Kane's slinking footsteps echoed through the quiet lobby. Harry heard this, and his eyes started to fill with warm tears. He knew the armed gunman was only a few feet away, and getting closer.

Kane saw the old man's fear and tried to make his voice sound more soothing. With a little luck, he might be able to get him to willingly cooperate.

"Relax, bud," he said. "Everything's going to be fine, eh?" He crouched down and set his weapon on the floor. "Look, I'm putting down my gun. Nobody's going to get shot, right?"

He kept his hands held up at his chest with his palms out. He took another few steps forward, so that he was standing directly above Harry.

"Come on, bud. Let's go. Come with me, before things turn ugly."

Harry rolled over and started to stand up. It looked like he was surrendering.

Suddenly, acting on pure animal instincts, the old man shot his arm up into Kane's neck like a striking cobra, jabbing the tips of the keys into his throat.

Instantly Kane stumbled backwards. He threw his hands up around his neck, cradling the wound. Blood gushed forth like a broken water pipe, pouring out in cascades, spurting through Kane's fingers and spilling onto the polished floor. He gasped for breath, gurgling and choking like a dying fish.

Harry had shocked himself with what he'd done, and recoiled back behind the planter.

Kane continued to stagger around erratically, his eyes bulging. He was dizzy and turning pale. It wasn't a fatal blow, but it would knock him out if he lost much more blood, and he could feel himself fading. He had to take care of this old man while he was still conscious. Frantic, he searched for where he'd set down his gun.

Spotting it on the floor, he turned to pick it up. He took an unsteady step forward and slipped in a puddle of his own blood. His feet shot up from under him, and he fell backwards into the massive stone desk.

His head smashed against the edge and cracked in half, making a sound like a rotten turnip slamming against a street curb. Blood exploded from the wound like a geyser. Bits of skull and brain showered out in all directions. Kane's dead body collapsed onto the ground like a bag of dirt, cold and lifeless.

It took a few moments before Harry willed himself out from behind the planter. His body shook uncontrollably, but his breathing slowly calmed as the fear dissipated.

He couldn't take his eyes off Kane's body. He walked up next to it, examining it closely. He'd never seen a dead body before, let alone one that he'd killed. Surprisingly, he didn't feel anything like horror or revulsion. He didn't even feel any guilt; after all, he was only defending himself. What he felt was actually closer to pride. He liked to win.

Harry couldn't afford a moment of reflection. There were still at least two armed thieves loose in the building, and since he killed their comrade, it was unlikely they'd show him any mercy. He needed to arm himself, and then he needed to find a way to get out of the building.

He crouched down next to Kane's body and started going through his pockets.

The first thing he found was the expensive eXRS radio. It was spattered with warm blood. Harry shoved it into his pocket without a second thought, and continued searching the body.

He found Kane's collapsible baton and smiled, beaming as though he'd found gold. He'd seen these things on the news, used by police to quell riots and violent protests. He knew it could inflict a staggering amount of damage, and it felt good in his hand.

The small Kahr pistol lay on the floor a few feet away. Its shiny, silver plating was stained with sticky blood. Harry smiled smugly as he bent down and picked it up.

It was sleek, lightweight and still fully loaded. Handguns were a rare sight in this country, so Harry gazed at it in awe. He'd been target shooting a few times during his life, but always with a rifle, and always in a strictly monitored environment. Pistols were a new, exciting experience, and he liked it.

He wiped down the slide with the sleeve of his shirt. He checked to make sure the safety was on, and then stuffed it into his pants, tucking it under his belt.

He got back onto his feet and walked over to the front door, still holding the baton in his right hand. He flicked his wrist, and the baton extended out, snapping to its full length. He raised his arm and pounded the rod against the window.

It made a terrible crashing sound and shattered into a hundred pieces, spraying tiny bits of glass on either side of the door.

N-Dig heard the turbulent clatter from the parking lot. His mind had started to wander over the past hour, but the noise startled him back to attentiveness. He turned and saw Harry dragging his baton along the edges of the front door's window frame, scraping away as much broken glass as he could.

The driver jumped into action. He sat up straight and fumbled with his radio.

"Oh, uh, guys?" he said into it. "There's some dude down here breaking through the front door."

Harry heard the voice come from the radio in his pocket. He froze.

“What the hell are you waiting for?” Buff screamed back though the radio’s garbled speakers. “Get him! Stop him! Go!”

N-Dig seethed for a moment. He was the getaway driver and a lookout, not an enforcer. When this was over, he’d demand more money from Buff.

For now, though, he had a job to do. He shoved his radio into his pocket, reluctantly threw his car door open and jumped out. He sprinted towards the building, proving that he was as fast on his feet as he was behind the wheel.

Harry saw N-Dig charging straight for him like a rampaging elephant, a look of furious determination on his face. Caught off guard, he let the baton fall from his hand. It rattled and bounced away when it hit the ground.

Panicked, he raised the handgun he’d taken. Without thinking, he aimed it at N-Dig and squeezed the trigger.

There was an explosive clap, and the area filled with the pungent smell of nitroglycerin, sawdust, and graphite. The force of the blast pushed Harry back three feet.

The bullet whizzed past N-Dig’s head. Immediately, his thoughts snapped to self-preservation. He stopped running for the front door and dove to one side, trying to get out of the line of fire. He kept moving, knowing a target in motion is harder to hit than a stationary one.

Harry was learning that the hard way. He fired another shot wildly.

It missed N-Dig, striking the grass in front of him. A large chunk of turf burst out from the impact.

Running scared, N-Dig tripped over his own feet. When he fell to the ground, he tried to keep rolling.

Another booming, thunderous crack as Harry fired again. This time the bullet tore into N-Dig’s upper arm, just beneath the shoulder. The pain was sharp, sudden and searing. The young man stopped moving and let out a gut-wrenching scream.

For the second time tonight, Harry had shocked himself. He couldn’t believe what he’d done.

He watched as N-Dig wriggled in agony. Again, he felt no remorse, guilt or sorrow.

The wounded driver brought his radio up to his mouth.

“He shot me!” he screamed into it, screeching like a woman scorned.

“What? Who?” asked Buff.

“The guy’s got a gun! He fucking shot me! Get somebody down here!”

Harry shrank away from the door. He knew more people were on their way, probably with more guns. They likely wouldn’t be too happy seeing their friend with the bashed-in face lying on the floor, either. It was time to get out of there.

He flicked on his weapon's safety and stuffed it back into his pants. He turned around and ran straight into the emergency stairwell.

# 7:30pm

Up on the top floor, Buff had to strain to hear N-Dig's voice. It sounded soft and muddled coming out of his radio's tiny speakers.

"Uh, hey, there's some dude down here breaking through the front door," N-Dig said.

Everyone standing in front of the vault room stopped for a moment and looked at each other, a mix of shock and confusion on their faces.

Buff was neither. He was annoyed, and as he spoke into his radio, it showed.

"What the hell are you waiting for?" he screamed. "Get him! Stop him! Go!" He threw the radio down and shook his head in frustration.

Doug went back to work, progressing well with the vault room door. Things moved a lot faster once Beka had disabled that distracting alarm. Having already bypassed the card reader, he moved on to decrypting the six-digit numerical password. He had a small device that latched over the keypad. With the push of a few buttons, it scanned the individual keys to determine which six were pressed last. It took a while for the device to cycle through all possible permutations, but within a few minutes, he had the code for the door.

He shook his fist triumphantly, removed the device and punched the code into the keypad.

There was an electronic chime and the metallic sound of a latch sliding into place. The thick door swung to one side automatically, and the vault room was open. Everyone anxiously stepped forward to see what was inside.

The enormous Strongbox safe took up most of the room. It was larger than most of the offices in the building, and looked almost exactly like the pictures Buff had shown the group. It was all polished steel and smooth edges, like an exceptionally large freezer. One side of it was taken up by the vault door, which had a silver-plated, five-point spindle wheel on it, the kind you'd find in a bank.

Everyone stood in front of it, staring in awe. The sheer size of the thing was overwhelming. People don't use a vault this size unless they're protecting something worth a lot of money.

Marcus was positively giddy. He threw his arm around Buff's shoulder and squeezed.

"She's a thing of beauty, me b'y," he said.

"Do you need a moment alone with it?" Buff cracked, which made Marcus laugh.

"That's a big Twinkie," Doug said. Beka was the only one in the room who got the reference, but didn't laugh.

"We've got a lot to do," said Buff, in a commanding voice, "so let's get down to work. Doug, you bypass the sensors, and Beka, you disconnect the vault's network connection. We'll finish moving the drill."

He clapped his hand together, and everyone broke off to their respective jobs.

Both Beka and Doug walked over to the vault door and knelt down in front of it. Doug began pulling tools out of his duffle bag. Beka grabbed her tiny laptop, flicked it on and waited for it to boot up.

Buff, Marcus and Fou grabbed two straps each and continued dragging the hefty drill into the vault room.

Suddenly, their radios squawked and chirped again. The panicked, wailing voice of N-Dig came shrieking out.

"He shot me!" he screamed, in intense pain.

Again, everyone stopped, this time genuinely concerned.

Buff grabbed his radio. "What? Who?"

"The guy's got a gun! He fucking shot me! Get somebody down here!"

"N-Dig, slow down. Who's got a gun? Who shot you?"

"I don't know, man. Some old dude. The guy who was trying to break through the front door. He shot me, bro! Believe!" He let out another agonizing scream.

"Where is he? Is he still there?"

"I don't know, man. I think he went back upstairs."

"Where is everybody else? Where are the Fodders? Where's Big

Frank?"

"I don't know, dude. I'm just the lookout. Just get somebody down here now, bro!"

Dwayne's voice chimed in over the radio. "We're looking for the guy right now, eh?" he said. "I'm up on the fourth floor, Big Frank's on seven, and Kane should still be down in front lobby."

Buff cursed under his breath. His plan had barely begun to unfold, and it was already unraveling.

"N-Dig, where are you?" he asked into the radio. "Is Kane there with you?"

"I'm on the front lawn, bro, and I don't know where Kane is, but I'm hurt bad. I'm bleeding here, man. For real. Get somebody down here."

"Does anybody know where Kane is?"

There was no answer.

"Come in Kane. Do you read me?"

Again, no answer. Buff stomped his foot against the ground, clearly frustrated.

"Sit tight, N-Dig. I'm on my way down to you. Dwayne and Big Frank, you two keep checking the offices for our mystery guest. Don't let him leave the building."

"No problem, bud," Dwayne answered.

Buff shoved the radio into his pocket, taking a deep breath and rubbing his forehead. He could feel a headache starting to form.

"I'll be right back," he said, turning to Marcus. His voice was terse. "When I get back, I want to see that drill pressed up against the vault door. As soon as Beka and Doug are finished, we'll need Big Frank to blow the safe's outer shell. We have to move fast. We're already behind schedule."

"I knows the plan, b'y," Marcus said, indignant. "I helped ya plan the damn thing, me chummy, ya remember?"

Buff ignored him, and walked back towards the service elevator.

"I can help," Fou shouted down the hall. "I know first aid."

"Shut up, Fou," Buff replied, without turning around. He walked over to the elevator door, pressed the call button, and waited.

***

Harry was running up the stairs as fast as he could, taking them two and three at a time. He had no idea where he was going. He was simply moving without thinking, putting as much distance between himself and the thieves as he could. He could hear them talking to each other with his stolen radio, so he knew they were looking for him.

The stairs were a cement spiral, winding from the ground level up eight floors. They were cold, grey, and uniform. The only break in the monotony was a few insulated pipes and a bright red cabinet holding an emergency fire hose on the fifth floor. There was a concrete platform on every floor, another halfway between, and nine steps connecting them. With every platform, the stairs would turn at a sharp right angle. Harry had to be careful not to run up them too fast, or he'd get dizzy.

He was terribly out of shape. Barely up four floors, the old man was already winded. This was the most exercise he'd had in weeks, possibly months. The muscles in his legs strained with every stride, creaking like an old rocking chair.

But Harry felt no pain. Adrenaline was coursing through his veins like electricity in a circuit. The airways in his lungs opened up and his heart pumped faster, sending blood rushing to his quadriceps and hamstrings. His body was like a machine, moving on instinct, independent of rational thought. He was single-minded in his focus, intent on one goal: run. But he couldn't keep this pace up for long.

***

Big Frank finished a thorough sweep of the seventh floor. This was where the executive offices were, one for each of the associate lawyers in the firm. There were more than a dozen of them, each roughly the same size, spread out along the edges of the building so that each one had a window looking outside. A single corridor connected them all, circling around the whole floor. Normally, these offices looked as slick and sophisticated as the inside of a bank, decorated with dark wood, glass, and brushed silver. However, this floor was in the midst of renovations, and in a state of disarray. Everything was draped with huge plastic tarps, and various pieces of construction equipment were littered about the floor. Paint trays, rollers, and half-empty cans of primer were stacked into little piles in the corner. Some offices had been stripped down to their skeletal wood frames, while others were cleared of furniture and had become storage for supplies.

The construction made it easy to search the offices. There was a fine layer of sawdust that had fallen over everything, in which Big Frank was leaving distinct footprints as he skulked through the corridor. In every room he checked, that dust remained undisturbed. As far as he could tell, no one had been on this floor for quite some time.

Finding nothing, he made his way around to the emergency stairs.

He leaned against the door without opening it, and pressed his ear against it.

He heard Harry's footsteps echoing in the stairwell. The old man's pace had slowed to a trot.

Harry had just passed the fifth floor, and was circling up around the next platform. Exhausted, he was wheezing loudly.

By the time he climbed to the sixth floor, he had to stop and rest. He bent forward, resting his hands on his knees.

Holding his Desert Eagle tightly in one hand, Big Frank eased the door open as quietly as he could. Still, the latch made a noticeable thunk.

He knew instantly that he'd lost the element of surprise.

The hairs on the back of Harry's neck stood on end. He held his breath a moment.

Energy instantly surged back into his weary body and his instincts took control. He dove to one side, threw open the door leading into the accounting offices, and tore down the hallway as fast as he could.

Big Frank rushed down the steps, his big coat flapping behind him. He was vaulting down the stairs four at time, reaching the sixth floor in eleven seconds.

He stopped outside the door, cocked his gun and took two quick breaths.

Using it as a shield, he slowly pulled the door aside. With his pistol in his right hand, he stretched that arm around the corner and aimed it in front of him.

He made a wide arc around the door with his weapon pointed right at the edge, so that he could see anyone hiding around the corner before they saw him. The military refers to this tactic as "slicing the pie."

Seeing the area was clear, he poked his head around the door and took a quick assessment of the sixth floor.

The offices looked deserted and lifeless. They were just row after row of flat, dull cubicles that all looked the same, broken up only by the walls of identical filing cabinets. It was like an uninspired level in some cheap first-person shooter video game.

There were no signs of Harry anywhere.

Big Frank listened carefully. It was dead quiet, except for the buzzing fluorescent lights. He quickly deduced that his target had stopped running and gone into hiding.

He crouched down and shuffled into the hallway with his gun drawn. He kept his muzzle aimed low, cradling the weapon with both hands, and silently crept forward. The four rules of breaching and clearing structures in combat -- cover all immediate danger areas, check your corners, eliminate all threats, and make no mistakes -- were carefully obeyed. He moved slowly and surely, his eyes darting around the hall like a cat stalking a bird.

As he moved further down the corridor, he was struck by how convoluted and labyrinthine the offices were. There were a million places to hide. There were sizable nooks and crannies hiding behind each desk, and there was a desk in every cubicle. There were cubbyholes for photocopiers and paper storage everywhere, not to mention the number of closets and storage rooms.

Stooping, he walked along the cubicles, peering into the space under all the desks. He searched each one methodically and found nothing, but it was only a matter of time. When it came to tracking, Big Frank was a master, better than any bloodhound. Best of all, it didn't feel like a chore to him. It felt like fun.

He spun around a corner, turning north, aiming his gun into an unusually large office, reserved for storing paper records. It was empty. The walls were lined with giant, ugly filing cabinets, even bigger than those out in the corridor. He did a quick sweep, enough to be sure no one was there, and went back to checking the cubicles.

He searched another dozen. None had been disturbed in over a day.

Turning a corner east, he spotted something out of the corner of his eye.

He immediately took cover behind a desk, butting his shoulder against the cubicle wall. His position secured, he poked his head up and scanned the area.

He saw it again. Sticking out of a small alcove in a far cubicle was a fragment of an expensive suit jacket. It looked as though someone was hiding under a desk, with their back facing outwards. For most people, it would blend right in, barely visible, but to Big Frank it couldn't be more obvious if it had a spotlight pointed at it.

He raised his gun to eye level, putting that jacket directly between his sights.

His muscles tensed, he held his breath, and then squeezed off three quick rounds.

A deafening boom followed each explosive burst. The jacket was shredded to ribbons, with charred buttons and small ragged bits of fabric shooting out in all directions.

Big Frank popped out from behind the wall. He waited for a moment, his gun trained on what remained of his target. It was motionless.

He ran up to it and examined further. It turned out to be nothing more than a simple suit jacket draped over the back of a desk chair.

Anger flitted across his face. Big Frank hated many things, chief among them wasting ammunition. He clenched his fist and gritted his teeth. He was more determined than ever. He was certain that the intruder he was looking for was still on this floor, and he wasn't leaving until he found him.

He turned back to the corridor and kept looking, doubling his efforts.

Little did he know, Harry was only a few metres away. He'd

managed to scramble into the records office before Big Frank burst through the stairwell door. Thinking on his feet, he noticed there was a large rectangular gap in the corner, where two file cabinets met at a 90-degree angle. It was just big enough for an average man to fit inside. Wasting no time, he climbed up into it as quietly as he could and slid down to the floor. He'd been patiently waiting there ever since.

Harry had to cover his mouth to keep from screaming when the bullets started to fly. His body quivered with fear like a blade of grass on a windy day. He may have been ruthless enough to coldly shoot an unarmed man, but that didn't mean he was brave. It simply meant he had a heightened sense of self-preservation, to the point where he had almost no feeling for the welfare of others. Some might say that made him a sociopath, but he preferred to think of himself as a pragmatist. It's what made him a good lawyer.

Holding his breath, he could faintly hear Big Frank in the hall walking away.

Harry relaxed a little. This was all too much for him. The last hour had been unlike anything else in his life. His mind was racing. He couldn't think properly. He had to call the police.

His brain defaulted to lawyer mode. He could easily claim self-defence for shooting N-Dig. The fact that Kane died might make the argument slightly more difficult, but given the circumstances, the worst he could be charged with was accidental manslaughter. With his connections, he could get that charge waived without much hassle, and would never have to spend a second behind bars.

The embezzlement would be much harder to explain away. It might slip by unnoticed for a few hours, as any police investigation would focus heavily on the thwarted robbery. However, the authorities are exceptionally thorough on cases like this, and Harry hadn't even begun to cover his tracks when the network went down. Eventually, one way or another, somebody would stumble onto his scheme.

It was a risk he was going to have to take. These guys were too heavily armed to take on alone. He needed to call the cops. Hopefully, they'd take care of the thieves, and he could catch a flight out of the country before the police got to the accounting files.

Contorting himself like a circus act, he managed to slip his hand into his pocket and pull out his phone. He instantly flicked the tab on its side, putting it in "silent" mode. He checked the screen as he prepared to dial 9-1-1, and his heart sank. In the top left-hand corner of the shiny screen were the words "NO SIGNAL."

Harry cursed to himself. He was horribly uncomfortable, his body bent like a length of rope in a wine bottle. His back was in searing pain. His knees were curled up around his ears and his shoulders were pressed together, as if he was in the middle seat on an airplane sitting between two obese passengers.

He wasn't getting out anytime soon, though. Based on the gunshots he heard, those armed thieves weren't going to take him hostage - they wanted him dead. He was going to stay right where he was until he came up with a plan.

***

When the elevator reached the ground floor, Buff darted out like a firefighter charging into a burning building. He ran into the lobby at full speed, nearly tripping over Kane's lifeless body.

He skidded to a halt and threw his hand up over his mouth. In all of his criminal endeavours, he'd never seen a dead body before, and this one was especially grotesque.

Kane's corpse was splayed out on the floor like a wet rag doll. His head was caved in, and his face bashed so badly that he was nearly unrecognizable. Most of his teeth had been knocked out. There was a gruesome, egg-shaped hole where his nose was supposed to be. The body rested in a pool of blood over a metre wide, and the black sweatshirt had soaked through with the wet, coagulating mess. It was horrific.

A tidal wave of conflicting emotions flooded Buff's mind. He had a visceral reaction to the disturbing gore, both repulsed and shocked by it. He felt a crushing sorrow over Kane's needless death, and a bubbling, powerful rage directed at the man who murdered him. Strongest of all, though, was the self-doubt gripping him tightly by the throat. For the first time, Buff had to consider the fact that the heist could fail. He rubbed his forehead with the palm of his hand. His headache was getting worse.

The introspection was interrupted suddenly by the mewling cries of N-Dig, which were coming from outside. Buff snapped back into the moment and dashed over to the door.

He paused to examine where the glass had been smashed out. It was a huge, gaping hole, the kind that could probably be seen by any car driving by. This was bad.

Through the door, he saw N-Dig sprawled out on the front lawn. He was moaning loudly and writhing around in pain.

"I'm coming to get you," Buff yelled to him, "just stop screaming!"

N-Dig gave a wave of acknowledgement and quieted down to a whimper.

There was broken glass everywhere. Little bits were stuck into the doorframe, and thousands of tiny shards scattered on the ground. They crunched under his shoes.

Buff pulled off his sweatshirt and laid it out over the open doorframe, covering the jagged edges. He carefully climbed out and ran to N-Dig's side.

The young driver was pale and sweaty, cradling his injured shoulder with his left hand. Blood was bubbling up between his fingers.

"Jesus," Buff said, aghast. "Are you okay?"

"Are you trying to be funny?" N-Dig replied.

"How bad is it?"

"It's a bullet in my shoulder, bro."

"Let me take a look."

N-Dig winced as he pulled his hand back, revealing the bloody wound. It was a grisly mess of twisted muscle and torn flesh. The bullet impact was pretty high on the shoulder, high enough that it appeared to miss any vital arteries.

"It doesn't look that bad," Buff said. Of course, he was basing this opinion on medical knowledge gleaned from old episodes of *E.R.* He was no doctor, knew nothing about medicine, and this was the first true gunshot wound he'd ever seen.

"Feels like my arm is on fire, man," N-Dig pleaded, between gritted teeth. "Believe."

Buff ripped the sleeve off his hooded shirt and stretched it out. He used it as an emergency tourniquet, wrapping it around N-Dig's shoulder.

The driver let out another agonizing scream as Buff pulled the fabric tight. As long as pressure on the wound was maintained and bleeding was minimized, N-Dig would be able to tough it out for a few hours. At least, that's what Buff assumed.

"We need to get you inside," he said.

He made one last check on the makeshift bandage, ensuring it was secure, and then moved his arm around the back of N-Dig's neck. The young man sat up slowly, and then threw his arm around Buff's neck. They interlocked fingers, and working together got N-Dig back up onto his feet, with most of his weight resting on Buff's shoulders.

One laborious step at a time, he carried N-Dig back to the front door. It took several long, agonizing minutes. Buff did not like being exposed like this, but luckily not a single car drove past the building.

He helped N-Dig climb over the frame and into the lobby. He was halfway there when the young man saw Kane's body and shrieked in horror. His body went tense. He would have tumbled knees first into the broken glass if Buff hadn't caught him.

His injury was suddenly and completely forgotten. N-Dig wriggled himself loose and ran to one side, leaning against the wall with his left hand.

He bent forward and puked.

A few deep breaths and it was done. He had to turn around and press his back against the wall to keep from passing out.

"I guess you didn't know," Buff said. "Did you see anything?"

"Bro, this old guy was smashing through the front door. I got out of the car and ran after him, and he shot me."

"Did you get a good look at him?"

N-Dig nodded. "Old, grey hair, nice shirt. Harmless. Looked like a damn banker, bro. No way he beat down Kane like that himself. That's some chainsaw massacre level evil, man. For real."

"He looked like a banker, but he had a gun?"

"Believe."

Buff thought about his next move carefully. He was in damage control mode. He had to get Kane's corpse out of sight, so he decided to drag it into the elevator. They'd keep it on the seventh floor, where everything was already covered with tarps. He'd have to discuss with Dwayne what he wanted to do with the body.

He originally planned on having two people guarding the front lobby, but now his muscle and his getaway driver were both out of commission. The massive hole in the front door had to be dealt with as well. It was too visible to ignore, and there wasn't time to cover it up.

Buff got on his radio and called Big Frank. He told him to abandon his search for now, and to come back down to the lobby and take over for N-Dig as lookout. Besides, if the intruder tried to escape again, the front door was his only way out.

He was starting to feel a little better. They weren't beaten, just sidetracked. The plan still had every chance of succeeding.

There was only one more thing to do, and for Buff, it was going to be infinitely harder than breaking into a Strongbox vault.

He brought his radio back up to his lips. "Dwayne?"

"Yeah boss?" came the reply.

"Meet me up on seven right away. Take the stairs."

"No problem, bud."

Buff clicked the radio off and shook his head. He was not looking forward to telling that young man his brother was dead.

He helped N-Dig steady himself, and they walked back to the elevator. The two bloodstained men rode it all the way to the seventh floor with Kane's twisted, battered corpse.

# 8:00pm

Dwayne let out a primal scream that was long, loud and full of rage. He kicked over two big pails of paint primer, spilling gallons of the white slop all over the hardwood floor. He picked up a desk lamp and flung it against the wall, punching a hole in the plaster. He was a destructive force of nature, spinning around the room like the Tasmanian Devil.

Buff didn't bother trying to calm him down. He let Dwayne throw his little tantrum, if only to get the fury out of his system. He understood the young man's anger – if he'd just been told his only brother was dead, he'd probably react the same way.

He leaned against the far wall, standing over Kane's body. After bringing it up here to the seventh floor, he dragged it out of the elevator and rolled it onto a big white painter's tarp. The bloody remains were wrapped up like an Egyptian mummy.

N-Dig sat on the floor back by the elevator, as far away from the corpse as possible.

There was a booming crash as Dwayne overturned a large desk. A flurry of papers flew up into the air and floated to the floor.

"I'll kill him!" he screamed. "I'm going to murder the bastard!"

"I know," Buff replied, calmly. "I'm going to let you."

Those words gave Dwayne pause, and he stopped his rampage momentarily. He was audibly panting, his barrel chest heaving up and down.

"You can do whatever you want to him," Buff continued, "just keep him out of our way. He's going to ruin the plan."

He walked over to Dwayne and put a sympathetic hand on the young man's shoulder, whose eyes were welling up with tears.

"Just be careful," he said. "N-Dig said this guy has a gun."

Dwayne snickered and shook off Buff's hand. He arched his back and lifted the bottom of his shirt. Neatly tucked into the waist of his pants was the small black and silver handgun Big Frank had given him. The sleek, polished barrel shimmered in the fluorescent light.

"So do I," he said, pulling it out and twirling it around his index finger like an old gunslinger. The look in his eye indicated that he wasn't afraid of using it.

"You've got a gun," Buff said, dumbstruck. He looked unhappily surprised.

"No guff," scoffed Dwayne.

"Where the hell did you get a gun?"

"Big Frank gave it to me, eh?"

"What?! Why? I said no guns."

He reached forward and tried to take the gun from Dwayne's hand, but the young man pulled away. He seemed offended.

"I don't care what you said, bud," he spat. "I'm keeping the gun. If you've got a problem with that, you take it up with Kane."

Buff knew he was beat. There were few things more futile than trying to talk a man out of his vengeance.

He was not happy about leading a team of armed men. He knew from experience that if they were caught, the mere fact that they had firearms with them would more than double their sentence. That's why he explicitly demanded no one carry any guns on this heist. He wanted to tear a strip off Big Frank for bringing weapons after he'd promised he wouldn't, but Buff was too scared of the menacing brute to challenge him. At this point, it was best to just let the boys have their dangerous toys and hope for the best.

He held up his hands and backed a few feet away from Dwayne.

"Okay, okay," he soothed, "that's fine. You keep the gun. I just don't want you to get hurt. We can't afford to lose anyone else."

Dwayne snorted dismissively and slid his weapon back into his belt.

Buff's gaze drifted down to the floor, falling on Kane's lifeless body. He felt a horrible pain in the pit of his stomach. Whatever the outcome tonight, this heist was already a failure.

"Do you want me to tell the others?" he asked.

"Do whatever you want," Dwayne replied. "I don't care. I've got an old man to kill."

He gave the overturned desk one last kick and stormed off to the emergency stairwell.

Buff spent a solemn moment alone in the hallway, staring pensively at Kane's body. The guilt tore away at him. Nothing like this had ever happened to him before. For all of Buff's meticulous planning, he was responsible for a young man's death.

He thought about one of the last things Kane told him. It was the location of Harry Bockner's office on the seventh floor. Suite 704.

Buff spun around and paced up the hall, checking the office doors for numbers. He found Harry's office right away.

Not that it was hard to find. It was a corner office, one of the biggest on the floor. Of course, it was in a state of complete disarray because of the renovations. All of the furniture had been pulled into the center of the room and covered with protective plastic. The walls were bare, except for long strips of green paper tape lining the edges of the windows. Harry had pulled down his law degree, his school diplomas, and all his fancy artwork. The only personal item remaining was a framed picture resting on the desk, which had a translucent tarp draped over it.

Noticing it instantly, Buff ripped aside the plastic and picked up the photograph.

It was a picture of Harry leaning against a black Lamborghini Aventador LP 700-4. It was a gorgeous car, highly coveted amongst celebrities. Both Kanye West and Justin Bieber had one, as did athletes Kobe Bryant and Floyd Mayweather. It looked like Harry owned one, too: the car in the photo had a vanity licence plate that read "NVRLOSE."

In the picture, Harry was smiling like a fat man after a hearty meal. He looked exactly as Buff remembered him in the courtroom those few years ago: overpaid, smugly pompous and self-satisfied. This was the man that ruined him.

Buff threw the photo to the ground and stomped on it.

He left out a defeated sigh. He wouldn't be able to get back at the lawyer by trashing his office. The state it was in now, the old man would never even notice.

Buff backed out of the office. He had other, more important things to deal with right now, but he wasn't through with Harry Bockner. Somehow he would find a way to get back at the man who stole two years of his life.

In the meantime, he had to inform the rest of the team of Kane's unfortunate death. He pulled out his radio and brought it to his mouth, but had trouble finding the words.

***

Harry was getting a bad cramp in his right leg. He felt like he'd been stuffed inside a suitcase. He had no idea how long he'd been hiding behind these filing cabinets, but it seemed like hours. In all that time, he was careful not to move a muscle, but the fatigue was starting to catch up with him.

Still, he wasn't willing to make a move until he was absolutely sure there was no one out in the hallway waiting for him. He would wait patiently for a few more minutes, listening carefully for any sign that he wasn't alone.

When he was finally satisfied that the coast was clear, he grabbed the top of the filing cabinets with both hands. They groaned under his weight as he threw his legs over them, climbing out and landing on his feet like a cat.

He pulled out his gun and held it out in front of him. The barrel shook wildly as his hands trembled uncontrollably. He moved slowly and silently, tiptoeing out of the room like a kid sneaking out of bed early Christmas morning.

He snuck down the hallway one steady pace at a time, keeping his body crouched low. His heart was pounding like a racehorse on its final lap. Creeping along the wall, he found the office he'd been working in earlier and darted inside.

It was every bit as messy and cluttered as when he left it, but now there were a few bullet holes in the desk as well. The computer's 19-inch LCD screen was scattered in a thousand pieces around the office. A bullet had blasted right through the middle, leaving a massive hole the size of a golf ball.

Harry pounded his fists against the desk. Now that this workstation was out of commission, his whole embezzlement scheme was in jeopardy. He was right in the midst of transferring money into the Jamaican alias account when his computer went offline. The way the program worked was similar to the way a large video file is downloaded from the internet: if it's interrupted early, instead of getting half of the video, you're left with a single corrupted, unusable file. Unless Harry could finish the transfer and break up the alias account, he wouldn't be able to touch a dime of that money. All his hard work would have been for nothing.

Not too mention there was still a significant paper trail that traced back to him. Unless he could somehow get another computer working, finish the transfer and cover his tracks, the authorities would be able to connect him to the crime without much effort. Even if Harry survived the night, avoided the armed gunmen, and made it out of the building alive, he would likely go to jail.

He kicked the desk, and then leaned down to examine what remained of his jacket. It was in tatters, the victim of Big Frank's merciless marksmanship. Charred and torn pieces of Italian silk were strewn across the floor. Harry tried to pick it up, but it fell to pieces in his fingers.

He bit his lip. He loved that jacket – it was tailor-made. As his belly filled with frustration, his hands began to shake with rage.

Furious, he violently swept the broken monitor and everything else off the desk and let it smash against the floor. It sent a flurry of paper shooting up into the air.

He took a moment to regain his composure, and then slunk back into the hallway. He darted past the small kitchenette, turned a corner and dashed into another office. It looked similar to the one he was using earlier, except that its computer wasn't filled with shrapnel.

Keeping his body low to the ground, he flicked the computer on and waited for it to power up. It made a low hum as it slowly booted through the operating system.

After a few moments, it chirped loudly and the monitor flashed a warning message: "UNABLE TO ACCESS NETWORK."

Harry let out a frustrated groan. It wasn't just the computer terminal he was using earlier; it was the entire network that was offline. Without knowing much about computers or how they worked, he surmised the intruders had somehow shut it down.

He flicked the monitor off. Looking around the desk, he tossed a few loose papers aside, revealing the office phone. He picked up the receiver and put it to his ear. There was no dial tone. He pounded on every key, but nothing happened. The phone was dead. Angry, he threw it back down on the desk.

"Can I get everyone's attention for a second?"

Harry looked back down at the phone, dumbfounded.

"Please, just stop what you're doing for a second. It's important."

The voice was distorted, but definitely belonged to Buff. It wasn't coming from the office phone, but from the radio Harry had swiped from one of the thieves. He unclipped it from his waist and brought it up to his ear.

"I'm not really sure how to say this," Buff said, his voice breaking, "but I've got some bad news. Kane's dead. I'm sorry. I'm so sorry."

There was a long pause before he continued.

"Someone killed him. Somebody who I'm pretty sure is still in the building. A security guard we missed or something."

Harry smirked.

***

Dwayne was on the emergency stairwell, halfway between the sixth and seventh floor, when Buff's voice began blaring over his radio.

The young man immediately shut it off. He'd already been told about his brother's murder, and didn't want to hear about it again.

He shoved the radio back into his pocket and fought back tears. He clenched his fists, taking a moment to steady himself.

Between deep breaths, he could still hear Buff droning on.

"This someone won't be a problem for long," his voice said, far off in the distance. "I'm dealing with it. Everyone just stay calm and stay put."

Dwayne's ears immediately perked up. Someone close by had a radio on. It was coming from the sixth floor!

He ran down the steps, four at a time, until he got to the door to the sixth floor. He threw it open, suddenly and violently, and burst through in a rage.

"Stick to the plan and everything will be fine," said Buff over the radio. "I'm on my way upstairs."

The young man could tell by the voice that he was close. He raised his gun, pointing the barrel down a long empty hallway, and fired twice, blindly.

He waited a moment, and then heard exactly what he was hoping for: a soft thud, as if someone were diving into a cover position. That murderous old son of a bitch was definitely on this floor!

He took three quick, sharp breaths and ran down the hallway. He shot forward like a pouncing lion, letting nothing stand in his way. He flipped desks on their side and kicked over chairs. He was on a rampage, fuelled by vengeance. He was out for blood.

Dwayne tore down the main hall, stopping briefly at the office Harry was using earlier. He noted the abundance of bullet holes and scattered papers. It looked like a tornado had blown through.

His muscles tensed, and for a moment he felt genuine fear. He assumed that the armed gunman who killed his brother had also trashed this office. Given the ferocity with which this room was torn apart, he knew he was dealing with a madman.

There was suddenly a loud clatter behind him, like someone knocking over a shelf of tin cans. Dwayne thought the gunman was shooting at him.

He instantly flopped down onto his stomach and rolled to one side, tucking himself up against the wall as close as he could. As badly as he wanted to, he couldn't run out with guns blazing. He had to take his next steps cautiously, or he'd end up like poor Kane.

The young man's hand tightly wrung the grip on his handgun. He held it in front of him and poked his head out the door, looking down the hallway. It appeared empty.

Another loud crash.

Dwayne darted back into the office.

He tried to take a few deep breaths and psych himself up. He couldn't see anything from this position. If he wanted any chance of taking this guy down, he'd need to get out into the hallway.

Directly across from the office was a small nook in the hallway. It was designed for a photocopier that was never installed. Now it was just extra storage for blank paper, but there was just enough empty space to fit a grown man.

Wasting no time, Dwayne leapt towards it, slamming shoulder-first into the tiny alcove. His body crumpled backwards, and he braced himself with both hands to keep from rolling out into the hall.

He managed to quickly turn himself around and peek out from the recessed compartment.

The coast was clear.

Dwayne crawled out, slowly, and inched down the hallway, staying as low to the ground as he could. He'd now completely lost track of the intruder. He cupped one hand behind his ear, hoping to hear the gunman shuffling around and determine where he was hiding. Unfortunately, the only noise he could make out was a soft electronic tone, beeping rhythmically in the distance. It seemed to be coming from around the corner.

He got to the end of the hall and rolled against the closest wall for cover. He went into a crouched position and craned his head around the edge of the corner.

There was nothing there. He was looking into a handful of empty offices. They were all lifeless. The beeping sound was louder in this spot, so Dwayne knew that whatever it was, it was close by. There was no sign of the gunman, though.

Relieved, Dwayne got to his feet. To one side he noticed a kitchenette. It was small and untidy, with a sink in one corner, a refrigerator in the other, and a wooden counter between them. Sitting next to a silver toaster was the source of the mysterious beeps: a microwave oven, counting down from 27 seconds.

There was something inside, rotating slowly. It was hard to tell what that something was through the microwave's dirty front window, so Dwayne walked towards it to get a better look.

By the time he realized what it was, he was too late. Harry had thrown three aerosol cans of air freshener into the microwave before hitting the "COOK" button and running away. The cans were sparking wildly, expanding in all directions and glowing brightly. A half-second later, they exploded.

The burst rocked the walls of the sixth floor. Red hot shrapnel blasted out thirty feet in all direction. A small fireball shot up, flew past Dwayne's face and roared across the ceiling.

Before he could react to the searing pain, the oven's rigid metal handle struck the young man in the head. The impact crushed the bridge of his nose and tore open his right brow.

He fell backwards, wailing like an injured cat, and crashed against a filing cabinet. It fell into another, and an entire row toppled over like dominos with a booming metal racket. Dwayne collapsed on the ground.

The pain the young man felt was sharp, severe, and overwhelming. He threw his hands up over his face and curled into a ball. Blood gushed out his nose in awful spurts, choking his anguished screams.

He was badly hurt and he knew it, but he wouldn't let that stop him. The pain would subside eventually. Before this night was over, he would have his vengeance and kill that old bastard.

Dwayne covered his nose with the sleeve of his sweatshirt. The lightest touch felt like a sledgehammer pounding against his nasal bone. He could feel the burns on one side of his face beginning to blister. The pain was horrendous.

The old man would have to wait. He needed a few minutes to recover.

He let out another howling scream of rage.

***

By the time the microwave exploded, Harry had already circled around the far hallway back to the emergency stairwell. After the blast, he briefly heard Dwayne cry out in pain, moaning like a bleating lamb. It sounded like the thief was in real pain, which filled the old lawyer with a tremendous sense of pride.

Harry slowly and carefully pushed the door open just a crack, enough for him to poke his head into the stairwell. It appeared empty. He crept out one tentative step at a time, holding the door with both hands to keep it from making a sound, and then closed it behind him with equal caution.

He moved with confidence. For the first time since he encountered these intruders, he had a plan.

He was about to run down to the second floor, but stopped himself. His black, polished leather shoes would make a cacophonous clatter if he ran down the stairs, alerting anyone listening of his presence. If he was going to survive this ordeal, he'd have to be slicker than that. He'd have to move in stealth, silently in the shadows, like a ninja or a cat burglar.

That could be difficult for an old man like Harry, whose body wheezed and creaked like an old rusty wheelbarrow when he moved. He was terribly out of shape. The most exercise he'd had in months was playing eighteen holes with a client at Glen Abbey. If his plan was going to work, he was going to have to rethink how he moved, because normally he was about as stealthy as a bulldozer at the ballet.

Harry slipped off his shoes and tucked them under his arm. He carefully checked above and below him, ensuring the stairwell was empty. As quietly as he could, he tiptoed down the steps, creeping slowly towards the second floor.

***

Up on the top floor, the news of Kane's death did not go over well. Everyone carried on with the job at hand, but the mood in the vault room was tense and grim, to say the least.

Doug and Beka stood on opposite ends of the safe. They were each holding a small plastic voltmeter, slightly larger than a television remote. By running these devices along the edges of the vault, they were able to determine where the electric connections for the tremor sensors were and disable them. It was slow, tedious work, but it was the only way to get inside a Strongbox.

Fou was well behind them, leaning against the massive industrial drill. His face was red and his brow was sopping with sweat. After Buff went downstairs to take care of N-Dig, Marcus had left it to him alone to move the drill into place. It was a tough job, but Fou had managed to drag it a few feet beside the safe, ready to be deployed. Now he was just trying to stay out of the way.

Beneath his quiet exterior, Fou's mind was racing. He could feel his blood pressure rising. A lump began to form in his throat. In the years he'd spent working as an undercover officer, he'd never felt anxiety this strong before.

His orders had been to lay low and blend in, acting like a fly on the wall and gathering information without actually engaging in any illegal behaviour. Now that people were dying, the situation had changed and he didn't know what he was supposed to do.

The right answer was to do nothing. If he reacted in the wrong way, his cover would be blown and nearly a year's worth of investigative work would be wasted. His handlers had a plan to get him out that night; he just had to wait for their signal. All he could do right now was sit tight and stay quiet. Just keep a low profile, go with the flow and hope the cavalry comes charging in soon.

He took several long, deep breaths and tried to calm himself, but he had trouble concentrating. He couldn't think over the sound of Buff and Marcus arguing out in the hallway.

"I told ya that we ought to search the building and clear 'er out before we brings the drill in, b'y!" Marcus yelled. "I told ya three times, me son! Ya gots a head thicker than an anchor!"

"This isn't helping!" Buff shouted back.

He was on the floor, kneeling over N-Dig's prostrate body. Marcus was on the other side, standing over them both. He was still angry, but bit his tongue and stepped aside. He started pacing back and forth like an expectant father in a waiting room.

Buff slowly peeled back the torn, blood-soaked shirt he'd used to bandage the young man's arm and examined the wound. It was already looking much better, but still required medical attention.

He turned back to Marcus.

"Find me some clean towels," he ordered. "Quickly."

The old man grumbled, but obeyed. He ran off to the executive washroom, pulled two freshly laundered white towels off the rack, and then dashed back as fast as he could.

"Eh, how bad is she, b'y?" Marcus asked, handing the towels to Buff.

"The bleeding's stopped," he answered. "I think he's going to be fine. It will hurt like hell, and he'll need to get stitches at some point, but he should make it through the night in one piece."

He rolled the towels together and gently wrapped them around the wound. N-Dig let out a tiny moan as Buff applied more pressure.

Marcus started rubbing the back of his neck and resumed pacing around the room.

"This ain't good by a bunch, me son," he said. "The poor b'y looks like he's been hauled through a knot hole. Lard t'underin', me b'y, we gots the devil to pay and no pitch hot! This is as bad as a boot without a bottom, b'y. What the hell was gettin' on down there, me chummy? Who was this frigger with a gun?"

"I don't know," Buff answered with a shrug.

"It was some random old man, bro," N-Dig said, weakly.

"Huh? What do ya mean 'an old man'?"

"He looked like a banker, bro. For real."

"That don't make a lick of sense, b'y!" Marcus was getting louder and more animated with each sentence. "There ain't no bankers workin' here today! Must be a guard or janitor or something, eh? Right, b'y?"

Buff shrugged again.

Marcus slammed his fist against the wall.

"Dammit, b'y! We had us three whole days to case this office building, Buffy me chum! How comes ya didn't know a thing about this fella?!"

"I'm not Kreskin, Marcus," Buff replied, calmly and coolly.

The old man threw his hands up in the air, exasperated.

Suddenly, their radios came alive with the sound of Dwayne's voice.

"I had him," he said. It sounded as though he were speaking through gritted teeth. "He was on six, but he got away. Son of a bitch pulled some MacGyver shit up here, and turned a microwave into a damn bomb."

"I told ya," Marcus said. "You think a damn banker could do that?"

Buff waved the old man off with one hand, using the other to bring his radio up to his mouth.

"Dwayne, are you okay?"

"I'm pretty tore up," he answered, "but I've had worse. I'll live, at least long enough to kill that bastard."

"Do you know where he is?"

"I think he ran down to the fifth floor. Don't worry. I'll get him."

"Good. Be careful."

"Oh, by the way, I think this guy's got Kane's radio on him."

"What?!" Buff threw his head back and screamed in frustration. "You idiot!! Why didn't you say so?! Don't give away your position! Radio silence from now on, except in absolute emergencies. That goes for everyone. Stay off the air. Understand?"

Buff waited a few moments. There was no response.

"Good," he said. "Now find this guy!"

"So then, wise ol' fearless leader of ours," Marcus said loudly, instigating an argument, "what do ya want us to do now?"

Buff walked right up to Marcus and looked him in the eye. They looked like they were seconds away from brawling right then and there.

"We finish the job," Buff said assertively, puffing out his chest. "That's why we're here, right? We stick to the plan. Doug and Beka break through the sensors, Big Frank blows the outer shell, and then we drill through the lock. Nothing changes. As long as we keep this old man with a gun from leaving the building or calling the cops, he won't be a problem."

"'No problem?!' Yar duff, b'y, and ya gots me nerves rubbed right raw. Kane is dead, me b'y! That's a problem! What if this cracky arse kills another one of us, huh?"

"Calm down. He's trapped in here. Dwayne's scouring every floor looking for him, and Big Frank's guarding the front door so he can't get out. They'll find him and put him down, okay? Now let's get back to work. We can't afford to waste any more time on a distraction. We've got a job to do."

"Two fellas? That's it? That's yar big plan? Come on, b'y." Marcus shook his head and pointed over towards the vault room. "Send old Fou there to go look for him. He's not doin' nothing, b'y."

"No," Buff answered emphatically, his voice booming. "Fou stays right here. If you're so anxious to find this guy, Marcus, then you go look for him."

Marcus rolled his eyes and snickered. Before he could deliver a snappy comeback, Doug suddenly poked his head out the vault room door.

"Hey, you dudes mind keeping it down out here?" he asked, annoyed. His hair was mussed, and sweat was beading on his forehead. "This is delicate work, and it's tough to concentrate with you two yelling like women at a shoe sale."

"Sorry to disturb ya, me b'y," Marcus said, sarcastically, "but there's a wee bit of a situation brewin' out here, princess."

"Yeah, I heard. There's a guy running around the office with a gun. It's just like that *Under Siege* movie, except we're in a building instead of on a boat."

The old man looked at him as though he just laid an egg. "What's that ya talking about?" he asked.

"Dude, you know that Steven Seagal movie? The one with Tommy Lee Jones and Gary Busey?"

Marcus looked at him blankly. He'd obviously never heard of it.

"You should see it," Doug continued. "It's awesome. Seagal's this badass cook who has to stop a bunch of terrorists who highjack a boat."

"I don't get 'er, b'y. Which one of us is the badass?"

"No, no. He's the badass. We're the terrorists."

"We're no terrorists, b'y."

"That wasn't *Under Siege*," N-Dig said. "That was *Speed 2*, bro."

"No, no, no," Doug replied, emphatically. "*Speed 2* was terrorists on a cruise ship. *Under Siege* was on a Navy battleship. Those two movies aren't even in the same league, dude. Seagal would beat Keanu Reeves like a rented mule."

"Keanu Reeves wasn't in *Speed 2*, man," N-Dig said. "That was Robert Patrick."

"You mean Jason Patric," Fou corrected him. "Robert Patrick was the bad guy in *Terminator 2*."

"I thought *Speed* was on a bus," interjected Buff.

"The first *Speed* was about a bus," Doug replied, "but the second one was on a boat. There was another *Under Siege* movie, too, but I can't remember if it was terrorists on a plane or a train."

"It was a train," said N-Dig.

"Didn't he do a movie about terrorists on a plane?"

"That was *Passenger 57* with Wesley Snipes."

"No, I remember that one. I thought Steven Seagal made one about a plane too. I think Kurt Russell was in it."

"I don't know. I remember the movie he made about terrorists at a hockey game."

"*Sudden Death.* Awesome movie, but that was Jean-Claude Van

Damme. That's the one where he beats up a bad guy dressed as a penguin."

Fou began to laugh. "I remember that one! Van Damme played a French Canadian. They shot that during an NHL lockout. Luc Robitaille was in it."

"Shut up, Fou," Buff said dismissively. He pinched the bridge of his nose and hung his head. "Seriously, how many movies can there be with terrorists taking something over?"

"Oh, dude, there's so many," Doug said. "Everybody made one in the '90s. Stallone had *Cliffhanger*. Nicholas Cage had *Con Air*. Sean Connery had *The Rock*. Even Harrison Ford had that badass movie about Air Force One, but I forget what it was called. Bruce Campbell was in one where terrorists take over a ski resort. A ski resort! Who the hell wants to take over a ski resort?"

"I don't know," Buff replied. "Who the hell would want to watch a movie about it?"

"Good point."

"Hey, Siskel and Ebert," Marcus shouted, exasperated. "Thumbs up, thumbs down, nobody cares about yar damn movie reviews! What does this have to do with anything?"

"You really need to see *Under Siege*, dude," Doug said, with all seriousness. "Do you know how the bad guys in that movie figured out Steven Seagal was the one trying to kill them?"

"We're not the bad guys here, me chum!"

"They talked to him on the radio. You don't know anything about this guy! Maybe all you have to do is pay him off. I mean, isn't that what you did with that security guard? Even if he turns out to be some asshole who thinks he's Chuck Norris, at least you'd know who you're dealing with."

Buff got quiet and contemplative.

Marcus wasn't convinced, and he was tired of wasting time.

"I don't want to hear another word about action movies, Dougie b'y!" He marched over to the young man and gently pushed him back into the vault room. "Do ya not have some sensors ya ought to be takin' care of? Quit yar blearin' and get back to work, ya blabber tongue!"

Doug didn't bother fighting. He went back to the safe and continued disarming the sensors. As abusive as Marcus could be, he was still nicer than most of the assistant directors Doug dealt with on set.

The thought of trying to contact the gunman struck a chord with Buff. The more he stewed on it, the more sense it made. He grabbed Marcus by the arm and pulled him aside.

"That's not a bad idea," he said. "We should try to talk to that guy on the radio."

"No, me son," Marcus replied, decisively. "That's inviting all kinds of trouble that we don't needs. Yar the one who just said we stick to the plan, b'y!"

"Just consider it."

"I says 'no,' b'y."

Buff grabbed his old friend by the shoulders and squeezed.

"Why are you fighting me, Marcus?"

Just as the argument was about to get heated, the service elevator chimed and the doors slid open. Out walked Surly Shirley, wearing a mean, sour-faced look that could turn men to stone. She marched right up to Marcus, like a frustrated mother about to scold her child, and angrily poked at his chest with her finger.

"Is it true?" she demanded.

"Eh, love? What's this that's got y'all biniky, me girlie?"

"You know damn well what, cocksucker! Kane. Is he fucking dead?"

Marcus lowered his head. He couldn't bear to look her in the eyes as he answered.

"Yes," he said, gravely.

Shirley raised her hand to hit him, but stopped herself. Instead, she stuck out her finger and waved it in the old man's face.

"You bastard. Fuck you. Fuck this. Fuck all this. I'm out."

Suddenly she had Buff's attention as well.

"What?" he shouted, running over to her side. "Why?"

"Don't do this, me girlie," Marcus pleaded. "We needs ya on the team."

"Fuck it," she said, waving them off. "I'm gone. I'm fucking leaving. I just thought I should tell you in person."

She turned and charged back into the elevator like Clark Kent running into a phone booth. She hit the button for the ground floor.

Buff and Marcus chased after her, holding the elevator door open.

"No, please," Buff said, "we need you. You can't leave."

"I can do whatever I fucking want, asshole! You knew my rules! No guns, no hostages, and no fucking dead bodies! Now get out of my fucking way!"

"Please, please, we can't do this without a truck. We have no other way of getting this drill out of here. We need your truck."

"I don't give a fuck."

"Shirley, me love," Marcus said, trying to sound charming, "please don't go."

She looked up, and her face softened. She leaned forward and gave Marcus a hug.

"I'm sorry, Uncle Marcus," she said, softly, "but this job's fucked. I'm jumping ship before anyone else gets hurt. So long, cocksuckers."

Lunging forward, Surly Shirley pushed the two men out of the elevator.

They regained their balance just in time to see her give a meek little wave as the doors slid shut.

Buff and Marcus looked at each other for a moment. The old man stifled a nervous laugh, shook his head and walked away.

He went to one of the executive offices and kicked open the door. He marched in and stood by the window, fuming. After a minute or so, he saw Shirley's truck pull out of the parking lot and drive away.

Buff stood in front of the elevator for a long time, contemplating his situation. This heist was in a nosedive. That truck was crucial to their plan. Now there was no way to get everyone out of there - N-Dig's car would barely fit half the team. The drill needed to be hauled away when they left, too. It could be traced directly back to him.

Maybe if Big Frank brought extra explosives, he could blow up the drill when they were finished with it. As long as it was destroyed beyond recognition, Buff should be safe. But he'd still have to find another getaway car somewhere.

He pounded his fist against the wall in frustration. He didn't have time for this. He was supposed to use this time to ransack the building, and see if there was anything else of value that he could steal. Now he was going to have to scramble and find some kind of replacement for the truck.

Surly Shirley was right. This job was fucked.

***

Harry sat outside the door to the server room, putting his shoes back on. He'd safely made it down to the second floor without being detected.

He thought he'd have to kick through the door, but to his surprise, it was unlocked when he found it. That wasn't a good sign. He carefully swung the door open and walked inside.

Instantly he knew something was wrong. Although his profession never brought him down to this part of the building, he correctly assumed the dozens of computer servers in here would normally be buzzing and humming loudly. Now, it was dead silent. None of the machines were turned on. It was a tomb for dead electronics.

He tried flicking a few of the power buttons, but it was futile. Nothing happened. Nothing worked.

Whoever those thieves were, they were really good, he thought. Somehow they'd disabled every electronic device in the room, and he wasn't smart enough to fix any of it. The clock on his microwave at home was perpetually blinking "12:00."

So much for his big plan to get the network back online. He had hoped that the servers were just powered down, and all he had to do was turn them back on. That's what he did at home when his internet went down.

This was turning out to be the worst Canada Day of his life. He kicked the door in a burst of frustration.

Harry walked out of the server room and wandered down the hallway, unsure of what to do next. He stopped in front of a closet door, with a small sign on it that read "SUPPLIES." Curious, he tried the doorknob.

It was locked.

Something on the far wall suddenly caught his attention. It was a fire axe, hanging in a small cabinet behind a pane of glass. The head of axe was painted bright red, and there was thick black rubber around the handle for added grip. For a few moments, Harry considered reaching for the axe and using it to knock down the door to the supply closet.

Instead, he pushed at the door with his shoulder, and it gave way without much effort. Harry walked into the custodial closet and flicked on the light switch.

The room was bigger than a single-car garage. The walls were cinder block, and metal pipes of various diameters snaked along the ceiling. It was lined with rows of shelves, all filled with cleaning supplies. There was a plastic sink in one corner, next to a pair of blue metal lockers, the kind you'd find in a gym. The other corner was cluttered with brooms, mops, buckets, a vacuum and a large floor buffer.

If Harry were the kind of man who cleaned his own home, this place would have been a veritable treasure trove. In his present situation, however, he doubted there would be anything of use to him.

He started examining the various products lining the shelves. There were over a dozen boxes of toilet paper, another dozen of paper towels. Eight big plastic bottles of hand soap, two and a half gallons each. Thirty rolls of duct tape. Several large jugs of bleach and ammonia. There were products he recognized, like Drano, Goo Gone, CLR, and Armor All. There were lots more he'd never heard of before, most of them industrial-strength chemicals in gallon-sized bottles -- things like floor polishes, dish soaps, window cleaners, disinfectants, and degreasers.

His eyes flitted over the warning labels on the bottles. Almost all of them had a bold red triangle on the side, highlighting a creepy monochromatic skull and crossbones. Some featured the silhouette of a flame inside a black diamond. All were marked with words like flammable, combustible, caustic, corrosive, explosive, and highly poisonous. These chemicals could be extremely dangerous. They could even be used as weapons.

Harry looked down at the handgun he was carrying. He knew almost nothing about it, or any kind of gun, really. He knew how to fire it, and figured out how to engage the safety, but that was it. He couldn't get the clip to slide out, so he couldn't even check how many shots he had left. He definitely couldn't remember how many he'd fired. As powerful as the firearm was, he was now realizing he would need a few more weapons in his arsenal.

He started pulling things off the shelf, starting with the large jugs of ammonia. He examined each carefully, thoroughly reading through the list of ingredients. He was no chemist, but he did play with fire a lot as a child, even dabbling in making his own small explosives. It was just a phase, which quickly ended after setting a neighbour's bed on fire, but he retained a lot of that knowledge. He learned at a young age how much firepower was in the household chemicals most people kept in the cupboard under the sink. When mixed in the proper ratios, they could be combined to create some lethal substances.

Looking closer, he saw that there were actually a lot of useful items here. He could probably build some pretty deadly booby traps with this stuff, like trip-wires, deadfall traps, or incendiary devices. He chuckled to himself, excited by the possibilities.

He checked inside one of the lockers. There he found a canvas grocery bag and a Zippo windproof lighter full of fuel. He pocketed the lighter, and then took the canvas bag, went back to the shelves and started tossing things into it.

Within minutes it was stuffed full.

Harry slung it over his shoulder and walked out of the room, turning off the lights and closing the door behind him. He guessed he'd be returning to this closet at some point soon for more supplies.

He made his way back to the stairwell door, and smirked as he pushed it open. He felt a renewed sense of purpose. This old dog still had a few tricks up his sleeve.

# 8:30pm

Dwayne had some pretty severe burns along the side of his face. The skin was pink and blistered, slathered in blood. He looked positively ghoulish, like an extra in a gory zombie movie. The pain was tremendous, but the young man didn't show it. He fought it back. He didn't have time for pain. He needed to find this guy.

For him, the fight was personal. He was going to find the creep who murdered his brother, and he was going to reach down his throat and rip out his stomach. Literally. As furious as he looked now, fuelled by vengeance and adrenaline, he could probably do it.

He'd rampaged through most of the fifth floor, leaving a terrible swath of destruction in his wake. The offices there looked as though a wild bull had charged through them.

Canadian farm boys have a reputation as being sweet, well-meaning hosers who are generally pretty harmless. Dwayne was proving just how wrong that stereotype was. He was more like one of the jacked-up, fist-swinging brutes that filled the rowdy Sudbury bars on Saturday nights.

***

Upstairs, Buff wandered into the vault room to check on Beka and Doug. They were standing on either side of the Strongbox safe, working furiously on the security system. Doug's tools were strewn about the floor. They were clearly nowhere near finished.

"How are things going?" Buff asked, masking his impatience.

Doug turned towards him and stood up.

"Smooth as frozen silk, dude," he replied. "We just need another five, maybe ten minutes."

"Good. Keep me posted."

He gave them both a nod and went back out into the hallway. Doug returned to work.

Buff walked back into the executive office Marcus had kicked open. It had since become the team's unofficial base of operations.

It belonged to one of the firm's main partners, and looked like the inside of an old Norwegian stave church. Everything was made of wood - from the polished floors to the high ceilings, to the big desk in the middle of the room. Each piece of furniture was ornately carved, and appeared hand made. There were two spacious leather couches on one side of the room, and two more chairs on the other. There was a small window looking out over the west end of Toronto, but most of the light came in through a massive skylight above.

N-Dig was resting on one of the leather couches, and Marcus was watching over him. Both of them looked ragged and exhausted. Fou was there as well. He was standing in the corner, looking down at the parking lot through the window. No one gave Buff as much as a passing glance when he came in.

One look at his crew and he knew they were all losing faith in his ability to pull off this heist. He wanted to give a rousing speech to inspire the troops, but he didn't have it in him. At this point, he was just as pessimistic as the others.

It had been a while since he'd heard anything from either Dwayne or Big Frank, and he was starting to worry. These were the two strongest men he had on the team. If this armed old man could take them out, they were in serious danger.

He looked down at his radio. He was going to have to try and talk to this guy. He knew it would piss off Marcus, but he had to take the chance.

He clicked the transmit button and cleared his throat.

"I would like to speak to whoever has been running around the building with a gun," he said.

Marcus's jaw dropped. He came charging over and tried to pull the radio from his friend's hands.

"What are ya doing, b'y?!"

Buff pushed him back.

"Relax," he commanded, throwing his hand up in the old man's face. "I might be able to buy us some time."

"Ya don't go poking an animal once ya got 'er in a cage!" Marcus yelled, shaking his head. He threw his arms up in the air, and then skulked off to the corner where he crossed his arms and pouted.

"I think there's been a misunderstanding," Buff continued into the radio. "I think we got off on the wrong foot. I just want to talk."

He waited for a long time. There was no reply.

Buff pressed on. "We don't want anyone to get hurt. We never did. I don't think you did, either. I think we can find a way to put this whole messy incident behind us, no questions asked. Think of it as an opportunity. How much do you think an agreement like that might cost?"

Another long pause. No answer.

Buff was about to give up and put his radio away when it suddenly crackled to life. Harry's angry, irritated voice came barking out of it.

"You've got some balls on you, pal," he said. "You're guilty of robbery, break and enter, assault, possession of illegal firearms, and at least a dozen other charges, not to mention the property damage. You're going to be spending the rest of your natural life locked in a cage, you son of a bitch. I don't think you're in any position to bargain."

Buff paused for a moment before he answered. He thought the voice sounded familiar, but he couldn't place where he'd heard it before.

"Maybe," he replied, calmly, "but you killed one of my men. You're a murderer."

"Self-defence, pal. Look it up. I'd be charged with aggravated assault, maybe. Involuntary manslaughter at worst, but I can promise you I wouldn't spend a minute behind bars."

Things suddenly clicked into place inside Buff's head.

How had he not recognized that voice right away? If he lived for a thousand years he'd never forget it. He had to throw his hand over his mouth to keep from blurting it out. It was Harry Bockner!

He couldn't believe his ears. Harry Bockner, prosecutor, the man who stole two years of Buff's life. He couldn't fathom what kind of cosmic coincidence had brought them together like this, but he wasn't going to squander his good fortune.

Before the night was through, Buff promised himself, he would make that soulless lawyer suffer.

"Do you work at Bennett, Olsen, Nygärd, Jørgensen, and Holm?" Buff asked, coyly. "I assume you're a lawyer, given your extensive knowledge of the criminal code."

"I'm an exotic dancer," Harry snapped back.

Buff forced a laugh. "You're funny, too."

"Listen to me, shithead," the old man said, trying to sound threatening, "you're about to have the worst night of your life. Either you let me walk out that front door, or prepare for the storm."

"I'm afraid that's not an option."

"Then things are going to get real ugly, pal. I will find you, I will crush you, and I will scrape what's left of you off my goddamn shoe, you understand? You have no idea who you're dealing with."

"Oh yes I do," Buff replied, confident. "You're an old piece-of-shit lawyer named Harry Bockner, and you're an asshole."

Marcus spun his head around so fast his neck nearly snapped. His eyes looked as though they were about to pop out of his head. He was astonished. Buff had never given any indication that he might actually know that madman with a gun.

"What the hell is this?" he shouted. "Ya know this figger, b'y?"

Buff waved him off again, like a librarian shushing a noisy child. He was anxious to hear what Harry had to say next. He waited, but there was no reply.

"No pithy comeback?" he mocked. "No vulgar one-liner?"

"How the hell do you know my name?" demanded Harry, the fury in his voice palpable.

Buff's answers were calm and cool. "We know quite a bit about you, Harry. May I can you Harry?"

"You can call me Mr. Bockner, you little prick."

"Okay then, as you wish, Mr. Bockner. I suggest you listen to what I have to say."

"Who the hell are you? Somebody I put away? Somebody I pissed off?"

"Well, you are starting to piss me off, but this has nothing to do with you. It's just a matter of inconvenient timing. All you need to know is I'm the one who's trying to get you out of this building alive. I don't want you, sir, or anyone else getting hurt, understand? Now, how much will it cost to make you play nice?"

"Do you have any idea how much I charge an hour, dickhead? Money is nothing to me. I already have more than Oprah. Not to mention you're a damn criminal. Why should I listen to you instead of hanging up and calling the police?"

"Well, sir, because we're well-armed and we outnumber you. All the exits have been sealed, and all the communication systems have been cut off. You can't call the police. If you don't get out of our way, we can make this very difficult for you, Mr. Bockner."

"I think you're underestimating how difficult I can make the next few hours of your life, asshole. I've worked here a long time, and I know this building inside and out. You could have a team of twenty men chase me around for days without finding me. I can be anywhere."

The office filled with silence.

"I told ya not to provoke him," Marcus said, shaking his head.

"But I'm not unreasonable," Harry continued. "I don't want a war. You stay out of my way, I'll stay out of yours."

Buff breathed a sigh of relief.

"Just get the computer network back on," Harry added, "and I'll leave you alone."

"Uh, wait. What was that? I don't understand."

"The computer network. Turn it back on or there's no deal."

The caveat hit like a punch to the gut. Buff had asked Beka and Doug to shut the network down, and they were usually pretty thorough. He was sure that it was impossible to do what Harry was asking.

"You mean the building's internal network?" he asked. "That's not easy. That might take some time."

"You've got fifteen minutes."

"I'll need more than that."

"That's all you get."

"Listen, it just can't be brought back up that fast..."

"Try," Harry barked, cutting him off. "Try really hard. Oh, and one more thing. I want to know your name."

"What? Why?"

"I want to know who I'm talking to. You know who I am."

"No."

"Tell me your goddamn name or there's no deal."

"Fine. It's Buff."

"No, no. No code names. Your real name."

"Everybody calls me Buff."

"'Buff?' That's not a name, it's what you do to a car's hood. I want to know your name. The one your parents gave you."

Buff exhaled loudly. He was confident that Harry wouldn't remember him, but hated giving the old man any power over him. Everyone in the room was looking at him expectantly. He had no choice.

"Bryan," he said, begrudgingly.

"Well, Bryan, if you don't get that computer network back online, I'm going to kill you and every single member of your team. You've got fifteen minutes."

The radio let out a quick burst of static and then turned off.

Buff turned and looked to his old mentor, expectantly.

"Do you think he could really do it?" he asked.

"I don't know, b'y," Marcus said with a scoff. "Maybe ya should ask Kane."

"Well, what do you think we should do?"

The old man laughed scornfully. "Don't look to me, b'y! Yar the one that's fuckin' the chicken, me chum, alls I'm doin' is holding 'er for ya."

***

Meanwhile, in the vault room, Beka and Doug had been working side-by-side for the better part of an hour. There was still a lot of tension between them. They hadn't traded blows, and things never devolved into a screaming match, but they'd been needling each other every chance they got.

They still had a job to do, and were civil enough to stay out of each other's way. They kept their insults mild and tame.

Their invective was also incredibly nerdy. She called him a "smeghead," a "scruffy-looking nerf herder," and most hurtful of all, "Milhouse." He made fun of her hair, saying it made her look like a 12 year-old Katy Perry fan. She listed things she thought he was dumber than, like a houseplant, a tribble, curling, old people on Twitter and the *Dumb & Dumber* sequel *Dumb & Dumberer*. He mumbled a Klingon insult under his breath, which roughly translated to "your mother has a smooth forehead."

As the night wore on, it slowly became rather playful and sweet. In a strange sort of way, they seemed to be rekindling their friendship, bonding over a common task through good-natured ribbing.

They were progressing well. Beka only had a few more encrypted codes to crack before the vault's network connection was broken. Doug had already finished checking three sides of the vault for tremor sensors, and was well into the fourth and final wall.

He dragged his small sensor-detecting device along the edge of the safe. He couldn't reach the bottom corner, because Beka was standing in his way. He gently nudged her, and for the first time that night, she didn't react as though he had leprosy.

"I'm sorry," he said softly.

"No problem," she replied. "My fault."

It was the first moment of real tenderness between them. All of the hard feelings, bad memories, and awful things said seemed to evaporate. This was the kind of spark that got them together in the first place.

Beka got a wistful look in her eyes as she recalled some of the good times they had together. She spent several months trying to shut those memories away, but spending time with Doug brought them flooding back.

She smiled, reflecting on better days and wondering what could have made them drift so far apart.

"Doug, can I ask you something?"

"You just did."

"Why did you leave without saying anything?"

Doug thought carefully before answering.

"I was tired," he said. "I knew if I tried to talk to you about things, it would lead to another big fight. I couldn't take another fight. I was tired of fighting."

"Yeah, okay, but you could have just left a note or sent a text or something. Anything."

"I didn't know what to say. There was nothing I could write down that would make it easier, and I didn't want to hurt you. It was just easier for me to run away."

She said nothing and considered his words. They seemed heartfelt, but the logic just didn't add up.

"That's bullshit," she blurted, matter-of-factly. "Leaving without a word just hurt me more. You knew it would, Doug."

"I know, I know," he stammered, holding his hands up in defence. "You're right." He paused to take a deep breath. "The truth is, well... I wanted to break up in person, but I couldn't do it. I knew I'd look at you and I wouldn't be able to do it. I had to walk away, suddenly and without warning, otherwise I'd never leave you."

If Beka had been a more vulnerable woman, this would have been the moment where she swooned and fell into his arms, reigniting a passionate relationship that ends happily ever after. Unfortunately, that's not what happened.

Beka realized he was pandering to her. It made her sick to her stomach. All her disgust towards Doug came rushing back. She scoffed and rolled her eyes.

"Ugh, you're the worst," she said with a sneer. "I hate you so much. You can cram it with walnuts, ugly!"

Doug shook his head. This girl was more difficult now than when they were dating. He'd never understand her, and would certainly never please her. It was probably best if he just went back to work, he thought.

"Whatever you say, Rebecca."

Doug turned his attention back to the sensor-detector and resumed scanning the vault wall.

"Stop doing that," she replied, angry.

"Doing what?"

"Stop calling me 'Rebecca.' My name is Beka. Beka Byte."

Doug groaned. "No, it's not. It's Rebecca. I mean, what are you, a hacker in the '90s? Do you hang out with 'Acid Burn' and 'Crash Override'? Do you listen to Prodigy and drink Jolt Cola? Stop acting like a child. Beka Byte sounds like something from a bad William Gibson novel."

Beka let out an annoyed, exasperated grunt. "What is your problem, huh? Acting like a dick won't make yours any bigger. And for the record, Doug isn't a name either. It's a verb."

"Thanks," he said, laying the sarcasm on thick. "I can always count on you to point out my faults."

"Well, there's no shortage of them. Go back to working your stupid $1.99 TV movies about two-headed sharks. You're good at stuff nobody watches."

Now the gloves had come off. Monsters weren't just Doug's livelihood, they were his passion. Attacking that was, in his opinion, a low blow. He decided to hit back below the belt.

"You know what, Rebecca? I think you were a lot funnier about fifteen pounds ago."

It was as if a hydrogen bomb went off in the room. Beka turned bright red and started shaking with rage. She turned around and punched Doug right in the nose, which started to bleed. He staggered backwards.

"Fuck you!" she screamed. "I hate you! I hope you die, slowly and painfully and violently. I hope you get cancer! Ass cancer! I hope you develop a giant, bulbous black tumour inside your ass, and it grows to the size of a pumpkin, and hangs out the back of your pants like a wet, leathery beehive that all the neighbourhood kids take turns poking with a stick! I hate you! I hate you!"

Doug was speechless. There was no comeback for that. His mouth hung open like the hole in a birdhouse. Blood dripped down the tip of his nose, splattering all over his shirt.

Buff came running into the room. He'd heard Beka screaming, and assumed that all hell had broken loose. He half expected to see them wrestling in a pool of blood, a knife at each other's throats.

"What the hell's going on in here?" he shouted.

"Nothing," Doug said in a nasal voice, waving off Buff. He had one hand cupped over his nose. "Everything's fine. We're almost done."

Beka scoffed. "He's almost done," she said with an air of superiority. "I am done. The network's disconnected, and now I'm leaving. I don't want to be in the same room with this asshole anymore."

Without waiting for a reply, she pushed Buff aside and stormed out of the vault room. No one tried to stop her.

Buff looked back to Doug. He knew working together would be tough for the two former lovers, but he didn't expect this level of dysfunction.

Not that it mattered. Getting that safe open was the only thing that was important. He seriously hoped the fight these two were having didn't do anything to jeopardize that.

"What happened?" he asked, calmly.

Doug just shrugged.

"Women," he said dismissively, shaking his head.

Buff didn't have time for these petty squabbles.

"Are you finished?" he asked, firmly and directly.

"No," Doug answered, sheepishly.

"How much more time do you need?"

"Five minutes, maybe ten."

"That's what you said last time."

"What do you want me to say? You can't rush art."

Buff raised his wrist, checked his watch and grumbled. They were behind schedule. He'd hoped that Big Frank would have already started setting the explosives by now. It was imperative to the plan that they go off at precisely 9:15 p.m.

"Fine. Go. Do it right, but do it quickly," he said. "We're running out of time. Big Frank still has to do his thing with the Strongbox."

"Whatever you say, boss," Doug said. "I hope you know what you're doing. I've worked on a lot of movies with pyrotechnics, and I promise you that blast is going to make a hell of a lot of noise, dude. Somebody's going to hear it."

Buff gave a coy smile. "Don't worry about that," he said, with a voice as soothing as a late-night announcer on public radio. "I have a plan. Oh, that reminds me. Do you think you would be able to get the computer network back online?"

"I thought you wanted the network shut off."

"I know, I'm just asking. Could you turn it back on, if you had to?"

"No way, dude. That's impossible. After Rebecca did her thing, I went over those servers with an electromagnet. They are permanently inoperable."

"Nothing's impossible, Doug. There must be something you can do."

"Dude, it can't be undone. You can't take the eggs out of a cake once you bake it."

Buff sighed loudly.

"Are you sure?" he asked.

"Almost positive," Doug said, "but you're asking the wrong guy. Computer networks are Rebecca's world. That's what she does all day. She's the one you should talk to."

Buff nodded. "Thanks," he said, "now hurry up and get that vault finished."

The young man went back to work without another word.

Walking back out to the hallway, Buff found Beka in a corner, sitting in a leather chair. She had it balanced so that the back of the chair rested on one wall while she sat sideways and propped her feet up against the other wall. She had her phone out, and was quietly playing Tetris.

Buff walked over beside her.

"That was great work on taking down the network," he said.

"It's what I do," she replied, without taking her eyes off her game. "Your cheque cleared, so here I am. I would have preferred to work without Doug, though."

"I understand. I appreciate that. I'm sorry. You did great work, though."

"It was easy. Their network was pretty unsecure. Anyone could have done it, but nobody would have been as fast."

"I appreciate that. Thank you."

There was an awkward pause.

Buff had hoped to broach the subject through small talk, but that wasn't going to happen. He'd have to be more direct.

"I have a question," he stated. "Do you think you would be able to get the computer network back online?"

"Nope," she said, bluntly. "I shut it down hard, like you paid me to. It's unfixable. You can't get it back online. You can't unbake a cake, you know."

"Yeah, I've heard that before. I get it, but this is important. There's an idiot with a gun running around and I'm trying to keep him calm. Please. Is there anything you could do to get the network back up and running?"

"Ugh, really?" she whined. She threw her phone down and turned her attention directly to Buff. "It would be really hard, like level 8-3 hard. Doug zapped all the servers, so they're toast. The only way you could get the network back up now would be to do some kind of dirty hard-wire. That might work."

"Could you do it?"

"Could I? I don't know. Maybe. But will I? Not a chance."

"What? Why not?"

"You just said there's an insani-maniac running around with a gun! I'm not getting into the middle of this! Don't ask me to go collect the honey after you've kicked the beehive. I'm not down with this death-match crap. I signed up to take down a couple of networks, and I did a pretty kick-ass job, if I do say so myself."

She put her phone back in front of her face and resumed her game, ignoring him.

Buff was speechless. He didn't know how to react.

He knew he didn't have time to argue. He needed to get Big Frank setting those explosives. He would deal with Beka's little outburst later.

He ran back to the executive office. N-Dig was still laying prone on one of the big couches. He looked pale, with his clammy skin covered in a thin layer of dampness. Marcus stood over him, wiping the sweat away with a white towel.

Buff felt his heart sink. He was about to do something he really didn't want to.

N-Dig did look better than he did twenty minutes ago, but he still needed more rest, and at some point he'd need to see a doctor. Right now, though, Buff needed him to guard the front door.

He pushed his way beside Marcus and sat down next to the wounded driver.

"How are you feeling?" he asked, sincerely.

"I'm good, bro, considering," N-Dig replied, with his chin up. "I'll be fine. For real."

"Do you feel up to standing guard in the front lobby?"

"What?!" shouted Marcus, outraged. He grabbed Buff's shoulder and pushed, almost knocking both of them off the couch. "He's no going anywhere, b'y. He's been shot in the arm, me son!"

"I know, but we need Big Frank to set the explosives. Someone's got to watch the front door."

He turned to N-Dig, the only man whose opinion mattered.

The young driver sat with an expressionless face for some time. He was not hired on as muscle, and hated being told what to do. If he was going to go above and beyond the call of duty, it was going to be on his terms.

"It's all good, bro," N-Dig said, struggling to stand up. "I'll do it."

"Like hell ya will!" Marcus screamed. "Buff, ya bastard, this b'y is in no shape to be guarding a damn parkin' lot! Yar no sendin' the b'y downstairs!"

Buff got right into his old friend's face. "Somebody has to!" he yelled.

"Send yar b'y Fou there. There's nothing wrong with him, eh?"

"No!" Buff shouted defiantly, like Charlton Heston in *The Ten Commandments.* He was making a stand. "He stays right there. He's not going anywhere. N-Dig says he can do it, so he's going to do it. And I don't care what you have to say about it, Marcus. Understood?"

Marcus muttered something unintelligible under his breath. It was directed at Buff, and it wasn't a compliment.

"Are you sure you're up for this, N-Dig?" Buff asked.

N-Dig answered with a question. "Big Frank is giving me a gun, right?"

Marcus smiled.

Buff was caught off guard. He didn't have an answer, and started stammering. "I, uh, I don't know. I was, well, there weren't supposed to be any guns on this, uh..."

"Bro, I'm not going in without heat," he answered. "Not when there's some nutbar running around shooting holes in people. You get me a piece, and I'll guard your front door, man. But not before. Believe."

N-Dig was defiant. Buff wanted to argue with him, but knew he couldn't. There was no way to dispute the kid with a bullet in his shoulder without looking like a complete jerk.

"Fine," he said. "I'll see what I can do."

He gave a curt nod to both Marcus and N-Dig, and then left. He walked down the hallway to the service elevator and got inside.

As the doors slid closed, he started rubbing his temples. His head was throbbing. There were too many complications piling on top of each other. He had to get a gun for N-Dig, somehow convince Beka to try and turn the network back on, find a replacement for Surly Shirley's truck and make sure Big Frank got those explosives placed in time.

The stress-free job his sister got him right out of jail, where he filled boxes with Styrofoam packing peanuts, was starting to look really good in hindsight.

***

It had been years since Harry had this much energy. He was running up and down the emergency stairwell at a frantic pace, setting up booby traps wherever he could, and wasn't the least bit tired. He hadn't even broken a sweat. He was working harder than a bartender on New Year's Eve, but was excited, eager and enthused. In fact, he was actually having fun.

He'd already constructed some pretty ingenious traps. He covered the stairs between the second and third floors with slippery liquid hand soap, leaving a tiny bare gap on every third step so that he could run through quickly if necessary. He emptied the rest of the hand soap into two buckets, which he left on the fourth and fifth floor, in convenient locations where they could be scooped up by a running man and thrown onto the path behind him. He strung up a few strands of heavy telephone cable like tripwires across the top step of every flight. He blanketed two platforms, one on the third floor and one on the fourth, with paper towels and toilet paper, and kept an open bottle of flammable cleanser next to each. In every other corner of the stairwell, he placed a large pile of powdered dish soap, which could be kicked up into a blinding white fog in seconds. And he was just getting started. He had a few other big ideas that he hadn't had time to set up yet.

Harry hoped to eventually have similar booby traps all over the building, not just in the stairwell, but this was the easiest place to start.

He didn't know anything about hunting or setting traps, but he had a natural knack for it, and was moving along with quiet efficiency. He was improvising, using whatever he had on hand as a weapon. Some of these ideas were based on things he vaguely recalled from his time in the Boy Scouts, but most were culled from the numerous late-night *MacGyver* marathons he watched while in college.

However, it's highly unlikely that the titular hero of that old TV show would approve of Harry's tactics. Richard Dean Anderson's one-named secret agent hero always preferred non-violent resolutions, even refusing to carry a firearm. Well, Harry kept his gun close, and he sincerely hoped that the traps he was laying would cause serious physical injury. He was more like the eight year-old protagonist in the *Home Alone* movies -- intentionally and sadistically maiming and beating those two hapless burglars with bricks, paint cans, nails, and irons.

He doubted all his traps would be effective. Some of them would never be tripped at all, but those that were would hopefully cause a lot of damage - puncturing flesh or breaking a few bones. None of them were lethal, they were merely inconvenient obstacles, intended to slow down and wound the intruders.

This was by design. Harry's plan was to incapacitate one of the thieves so he could take them hostage. With his gun to their head, he'd get on the radio and force Buff to get the computer network turned back on. Hopefully that would leave him enough time to finish his money transfer and cover-up the embezzlement before the thieves could find him.

He made his way up to the fifth floor landing and tied another tripwire across the top step.

The canvas bag he was using to carry supplies was feeling pretty light. He needed to replenish. Harry decided to turn around and head back down to the custodial closet.

That's when he noticed the bright red cabinet affixed to the wall. Curious, he pried it open. In it was an indoor fire hose, fifty feet in length, with a heavy brass nozzle on one end.

A deliciously malevolent idea popped into Harry's head.

He grabbed one end of the hose and began unwinding it from the spool. Holding it under his arm, he walked back down two floors, stretching the tan hose down the stairwell as far as it would go.

He'd almost reached the third floor when he was caught by one of his own tripwires. He managed to keep his balance, but he dropped the fire hose. The heavy nozzle landed with a loud clang against the concrete steps, and continued to let out a ringing clatter as it bounced down the stairs. It sounded like someone had thrown a full can of paint into a clothes dryer.

Harry knew somebody had to have heard that. He needed to hide, and fast. Without hesitation, he turned and ran back up the stairs.

***

Down in the main lobby, Big Frank sighed loudly. He'd been dutifully guarding the front door for almost an hour. He was a vigilant sentry, but this was hardly the best use of his talents. He was a man of action, and being told to stay in one place was tedium.

It was incredibly frustrating. There was a madman on the loose, and Big Frank hadn't even wounded him yet. He should be out there, stalking him throughout the building, not watching over a broken door. If people found out, he thought to himself, his reputation would be ruined.

At one point, he was so bored he went looking in the closet for a broom and swept up all the broken glass. He respected Buff enough to obey his orders, but his trigger finger was getting itchy, especially when there was some scum punk lurking the halls with a loaded weapon.

Suddenly, there was a loud, resounding crash in the emergency stairwell.

Instantly, Big Frank whipped his handgun out. He threw his back up against the wall and darted over to the stairwell door, moving with blinding speed.

His heart swelled and his pulse quickened. Finally, he was going to get to have a little fun.

With his left shoulder pressed against the door, he leaned back and opened it just a crack, enough to poke out the muzzle of his gun. He paused a moment and listened.

Hearing nothing, he pushed against the door with full force and it flew open. He swung his body around, took three steps into the stairwell, and flattened himself against the wall closest to the stairs. He kept his weapon aimed above him at the space between the stairs, a massive abyss that plunged eight storeys from the roof to the bottom floor.

In his peripheral vision, he saw something dash away two floors above him. It was Harry, scurrying up the stairs.

Big Frank squeezed off three quick rounds in his direction. The bullets whizzed through the air and punched holes in the wall, blasting out hard bits of shrapnel only a few metres behind Harry's scampering feet.

One of these sizable chunks of concrete exploded out and bounced off the old lawyer's right leg. It stung worse than a snakebite. Harry let out a whimper of pain and tried to keep running, but his stride slowed to a hobble.

He dove to the ground, out of Big Frank's sight. It didn't dissuade the juggernaut in the black coat one bit. The giant man just smiled coyly and holstered his handgun.

Reaching behind him, he pulled out the two Uzi submachine guns he had strapped to the back of his shirt. He pointed them up towards Harry and fired wildly.

One side of the stairwell was instantly shredded, as dozens of bullets perforated the wall. Huge clouds of concrete dust billowed out, hanging in the air like falling snow. The heavy remnants of walls around Harry rained down on him in pebble-sized chunks. He kept his arms over his head, while the staccato blasts of the two Uzis drowned out his harrowed screams.

When high-powered weapons like these are used in action movies, people seem to have an endless supply of bullets, firing non-stop for minutes on end. The Israeli-made Uzis are especially popular in this regard, namely because when fired they spit out a blast of flame up to a foot long. On film, this looks absolutely spectacular.

In reality, however, an Uzi like Big Frank's has a rate of fire of 600 rounds per minutes. While aftermarket drums could offer capacity of up to 100 rounds, Big Frank found he couldn't conveniently stuff those into his pants, and stuck with the 50 round extenders. That meant that exactly five seconds after he squeezed the trigger, it was all over. He was out of ammo.

The clattering noise ceased. Big Frank waited for the smoke to clear.

Harry took the brief silence as his cue. He pulled out his gun, flipped the safety off and rolled away from the wall, sticking his pistol out past the edge of the steps. He blindly fired two shots.

They didn't impact anywhere near Big Frank. They ricocheted around a bit, and then two hot, flattened bullets fell to the ground on the bottom floor.

The hulking giant sighed. His barrage of Uzi fire had accomplished nothing.

He threw his useless submachine guns to the ground, and grabbed the handgun from his waist. He looked up and blasted another four shots in Harry's direction.

Big Frank started thundering up the stairs, firing as he ran. Each gunshot made a rattling, cracking, booming sound like fireworks set off inside a dumpster. The stairwell shook and quaked with every blast.

Big Frank was charging harder and faster with every stride, taking two or three steps at a time. He quickly dashed up to the second floor landing, grabbed the metal railing and swung himself up onto the next flight of stairs, all while spraying a barrage of shots above him. He was speeding up the stairwell like a chimpanzee that just drank a gallon of coffee.

Harry crawled up the stairs to the next platform and rolled into the corner, covering his head with his arms. He was just eleven short steps away from the fourth floor landing, but the blazing hail of gunfire had him trapped. Bullets were smashing into the cement all around him.

Big Frank was closing in. He was one flight of stairs above the second floor when he obliviously ran into a huge puddle of hand soap.

It was like hitting a patch of ice. His foot skidded on the slick surface and darted off at a weird angle, causing his whole body to jerk to one side.

He held out his arms to steady himself. His body shuddered backwards as he struggled to find his balance, staggering like a drunk, when his foot snagged one of Harry's tripwires. He collapsed down onto one knee, toppled to one side and tumbled painfully down the stairs.

The shooting stopped briefly. Harry triumphantly shook his fist, ecstatic that his trap worked. He seized the moment and jumped to his feet, dashing up a flight of steps before Big Frank rolled to a stop.

Harry was moving fast, but every step felt like agony. His bruised calf was starting to swell and throb. He stumbled around the corner, grabbed the railing and pulled himself up the next flight.

Big Frank landed flat on his ass, dazed and bruised but not badly hurt. He rolled onto his back, raised his gun and fired again.

The shot hissed past Harry's ear. It was close enough that he felt the warm blast against his face. That was too close.

The old lawyer doubled his efforts. He sprinted with all his might up to the fourth floor landing.

Horrible sharp pain shot from the back of his right leg up to his spine. Harry gritted his teeth, trying to ignore it. He was moving with purpose. He hoped to lure his attacker into another one of his booby traps.

Big Frank held one hand against the wall, pressed his weight against it and got back onto his feet. Now he was angry.

He made another attempt at getting up the slippery stairs. To make it, he'd need both hands, so he reluctantly holstered his gun.

He tightly grabbed hold of the railing and wedged his feet into the groove where the step met the wall. One step at a time he pulled himself up past the soapy mess.

It was slow going, but it didn't discourage Big Frank. As long as he was able to keep one eye on Harry, he knew the old man wouldn't be able to get very far. No matter how fast he could run, Big Frank's bullets ran much faster.

Rather than run into the fourth floor offices and hide, Harry ran right past the door and charged up the stairs. He was wheezing loudly.

Glancing up, he noted the emergency fire hose he'd laid out on the steps, long and flat, stretched all the way down beyond the third floor. Big Frank ran right past its heavy brass end, completely ignoring it in his rush to get through the spilt soap.

That fire hose was heavier than it looked. Harry had found it surprisingly difficult to unwind and drag down the stairs. He grinned, excited that he might actually get to use it. He'd been worried all that hard work was for nothing.

He pushed himself forward and finally ascended onto the fifth floor platform. He dove straight for the red cabinet and grabbed the water release valve with both hands.

He tried to turn it. It wouldn't budge.

He gave it another panicked jerk, but it was stuck.

No, no, no, he thought, not now. He tried tightening his grip on the valve, but it kept slipping away beneath his sweaty palms.

He could hear Big Frank's boots slapping against the concrete. He was bounding up around the third floor landing, and gaining fast.

Harry held his breath and concentrated. He quickly wiped his hands on his pants, spread his feet apart and tried again.

He strained against the valve. It creaked and moaned in resistance for a moment, and then finally moved. The pipes hissed and gurgled as water began to flow.

The valve was spinning freely now, and Harry let out a sigh of relief. He cranked it open as far as it would go, and the hissing turned to a rumble as the water rushed through. The hose quickly inflated, swayed from side to side, and then rose up off the ground like a cobra hypnotized by a snake charmer.

Three floors down from where Harry stood, a torrent of water gushed out the end of the hose with enormous pressure, almost 150 pounds per square inch. It was strong enough to knock the sturdiest man off his feet. The bulky, seven-pound metal nozzle was an even greater threat, whipping about in a rapid motion, erratically and uncontrollably. It made a resounding clang as it battered against the walls, like a hammer striking a bell.

The relentless blast of water swooped around and pushed Big Frank backwards. He reached out for the railing, but it was just out of reach.

His fingers brushed past it and he fell down. Hard.

His head bounced off the first step.

His arm twisted unnaturally against the second.

Before collapsing awkwardly at the bottom, his foot caught the edge of the railing. His ankle was pulled to the left, his body fell to the right, and his leg snapped in two.

Big Frank screamed in agony. It was a loud, shrill, piercing wail.

A big jagged piece of his fibula was poking out through his pants, sputtering blood like a garden sprinkler. His leg was twisted around backwards. It dangled limply like a piece of cooked spaghetti.

The hose continued to swing about wildly, like a massive, thrashing anaconda. A torrent of water surged out its mouth, blasting Big Frank right in the face. The sudden, immense pressure smashed in his eardrum.

A sharp, blinding pain exploded inside his skull, as though someone drove an iron stake through his ear. He instantly lost the ability to maintain equilibrium, and rolled onto his side like an infant in a crib. He cried out, but his voice couldn't be heard over the hose's deafening roar.

The world was starting to go dark for Big Frank. He was losing consciousness.

He tried to look up, but his vision was fading. The last thing he saw was the big brass nozzle at the end of the hose rise up, bounce off the wall with incredible force, and soar upwards through the space between the stairs like a horse rearing back.

Then Big Frank passed out.

He always thought he would die on his feet in a hail of bullets. He was a vigilante who chased after bad people. It was only a matter of time before he went up against someone who was bigger, stronger, and faster. Someone who shot straighter and hit harder. He would face that person head on and fight until he had nothing left. Though Big Frank would lose, he would go out like a man.

Not like this. Not beaten by an old man with a garden hose.

The hose's nozzle smacked into one railing, ricocheted off the underside of a flight of stairs, and dove straight down, crashing against Big Frank's chest.

His breastplate caved in, his ribs were crushed, and his heart stopped instantly. He was dead.

Harry poked his head over the edge of the railing. His view from that angle was pretty limited. He couldn't see the body, but he did see an arm jutting out from the edge of the stairs. It was motionless.

Maybe that was too much, he thought. The guy could still be alive. He hoped he was still alive. He'd only wanted to injure him. It's pretty hard to hold a dead man hostage.

He turned around and shut the water off. The blaring rush was quickly silenced. The hose deflated slowly, collapsing against the wet steps. The stairwell echoed with the sound of water dripping down to an enormous puddle on the bottom floor.

He swung around and looked over the railing again. Big Frank wasn't moving.

Dammit, thought Harry. The guy was probably dead. He didn't feel any guilt, just frustration. If he wanted the computers back online, he was going to have to find somebody else.

# 8:45pm

The elevator made a tiny ding as it reached the main floor. The doors opened, and Buff walked out into the empty lobby.

It was eerily quiet. A warm, gentle breeze wafted in through the hole in the front door. The mess of broken glass had been neatly swept up. There was no sign of Big Frank anywhere.

Buff called out his name a few times, but there was no answer.

He checked his watch and cursed under his breath. This was the last thing he needed right now. He was running out of time and patience. He had to find Big Frank and get those explosives planted right away.

He unclipped the radio from his belt and thumbed the transmit button.

"Hey, Big Frank," he said. "Where are you?"

There was a long pause before the reply, but the voice that answered didn't belong to Big Frank. It was Harry's.

"Hey there buddy!" the old lawyer said, with the inflection of a taunt. "How are things going? Having trouble keeping track of your team?"

Buff's heart sank. He'd rather have invasive rectal surgery than deal with this asshole.

"Well, Bryan, maybe I can help," the lawyer continued. "Which one is Big Frank? Is he the big guy in the trench coat? The one who's built like a Clydesdale? I wouldn't expect him to answer. It's tough to talk with your head caved in."

"No, no, no," shouted Buff. "Don't do that. There's no need for that. Please. We'll get the network back up and running. We're working on it right now."

"Too late, pal. You had your chance."

"You don't understand," Buff pleaded. "The servers were wiped out with an electromagnet. It's going to take a while to get them back online. I need more time, Mr. Bockner. Please."

"Tough luck. Time's up, dickhead."

Buff clenched his fists. The muscles beneath his left eye began to twitch. Something inside him snapped. He'd had just about all he was willing to take from this old man, and he wasn't going to be ordered around anymore.

"You know what, you son of a bitch?" he said, growling. "I don't care. I tried being nice. I tried reasoning with you. You want to play hardball? Fine. Do your worst. You're no threat. You're a sad, weak, pathetic old man who couldn't beat up a fourth grader. You probably can't even get a hard-on without a blue pill. You're locked in here with guys who are bigger, stronger, and better armed than you. My boys are going to find you, and then they will kill you, Mr. Bockner. I never wanted to hurt anyone, but you've forced my hand. If you want to stay alive, I suggest you find a good hiding spot, stay there and leave us the hell alone. This will all be over soon."

Harry's responded with a hearty, carefree laugh.

"Last time I checked, I was still here and you were down at least two men," he said. "Have it your way, pal. Come and get me. You're right. This will be over soon, for all of you. You fucked with the wrong lawyer. And Bryan, I want you to know that I'm going to kill you last."

"Big words from a small man. You really think you stand a chance against us, asshole?"

"We'll see. By the way, you might want to send somebody over to the stairs and mop what's left of your friend Frank off the floor. Happy Canada Day."

The radio clicked off.

Buff was furious. He screamed with so much fury that his throat hurt. He ran over to one of the planters and kicked it in frustration. Unsatisfied, he grabbed one of the ferns by the stem, ripped it out of the dirt and smashed the roots against the floor. He utterly destroyed the leafy plant. It accomplished very little, but it made him feel better.

When he was finished, he was panting heavily. He sat down on the planter and buried his head in his hands. His headache was getting worse.

***

In 1989, Jeff Cooper wrote *The Principles of Personal Defence*, a modern classic on mental conditioning and survival in the face of unprovoked violence. Cooper was a veteran of both World War II and Korea, and one of the 20th century's foremost experts on the use of firearms. In the book, Cooper states that the most important tool for surviving a lethal confrontation is neither a weapon nor martial skill, but rather having the proper mindset for combat.

To illustrate his point, he introduced the Cooper Colour Code comprised of four colours. These do not relate to alertness or tactical advantage but to one's state of mind. Cooper wrote that each colour represents "the degree of peril you are willing to do something about."

The first stage is white, or a relaxed and unprepared state. If attacked in this condition, the only thing that will save a victim is the inadequacy or ineptitude of the attacker.

The second stage is yellow, or relaxed alertness. This is when there is no specific threat, but someone finds themself in an unfamiliar setting or among people they don't know. When in condition yellow, one is prepared to defend themselves if necessary, but not looking for a fight.

The third stage is orange, or focused alertness. In this state, the focus is on a specific target that has caused the escalation. This is when someone sets themselves a mental trigger - meaning, "if the target does this, I will need to stop them." In this condition, one is prepared to fight - hanging right on the precipice before striking, ready to react. It is an exhausting state, and remaining in it can cause mental strain.

The final stage is red, which is engagement. The mental trigger established in the orange stage has been tripped, and one is ready to take action. The only concern on one's mind is what's on the other end of their sidearm's front-sight.

The Colour Code was developed to help soldiers think during a fight. As the level of danger increases, so does one's willingness to take more serious action. If someone has to defend themselves while in the red stage, the decision to use lethal force has already been made, and they will be able to react without panic or hesitation.

Dwayne was deep into the red stage, and he hadn't even found Harry yet.

The younger Fodder brother had thoroughly demolished the fifth floor looking for the man who killed his kin. It looked as though a giant bulldozer had driven through it. He'd smashed holes in walls, knocked over shelves, and broke everything he could find. He was unhinged and rampaging, like a mother bear after someone dared get between her and her cubs.

He stopped throwing furniture long enough to hear Buff and Harry over the radio. While they screamed at each other, Dwayne ran over to the emergency stairwell, stopping just outside the door.

He flipped his handgun on its side and slid out the magazine.

Six shots left. More than enough.

He popped the ammo back into his gun, took a breath and burst out the door. He gave no thought to stealth or cover, waving his weapon around as though he were swatting flies.

There was a puddle of water at his feet. He noticed the damp, limp fire hose stretched out down the stairs. There were little flakes of wet paper stuck to the wall, and a pile of damp powder in the corner. It looked like a frat house after a particularly raucous house party.

Dwayne moved cautiously. He could hear heavy footsteps smacking against the steps below him. He craned his neck over the side to get a better look.

There was Harry, hustling down the stairs with both hands on the railing. The steps were slick with water from the hose, so he was moving carefully. He was one flight away from the fourth floor landing.

Two shots rang out as Dwayne fired in his direction.

The bullets missed Harry's head by several feet. Golf ball-sized holes blasted out of the wall, erupting in tiny puffs of crushed cement.

Dwayne saw Harry spin around, and their eyes met.

The young man adjusted his aim, but before he could squeeze the trigger, the old lawyer dove into the corner and rolled out of view.

If the young Fodder hadn't been so enraged, he would have been impressed. He couldn't believe how spry the old-timer was. He ran after him.

Around the first corner, he saw Harry get into a kneeling position, grab his gun and hold it out with both hands. He rested his elbow on his knee to steady it.

Dwayne darted out of the way just before a thunderous gunshot rang out. The bullet whizzed past his neck, and he narrowly avoided having the back of his head blown off.

Adrenaline surged through his body, and his muscles reached peak efficiency. He ran towards the old man at full speed, jumping steps three at a time. He was right behind Harry.

The old lawyer was frozen in place. The muscles in his finger tensed around the trigger again, but the gun clicked empty. Nothing happened.

He was now unarmed.

In a desperate move, he threw his useless pistol at Dwayne as hard as he could. The young man had to dodge to one side to avoid being hit in the chin.

It was just enough of a distraction for Harry to jump up, grab the railing and sail around the steps like a gymnast on the pommel horse.

Dwayne never stopped moving. He fired another three times, shooting wildly like Yosemite Sam. None of the bullets came close to their target. He wasn't a very good shot when standing still, and while running, he couldn't hit the ground beneath his feet.

Harry tumbled onto the fourth floor landing and scrambled to the door. He slammed his shoulder against it and ran through.

Right on his tail, Dwayne charged down to the fourth floor just as the stairwell door shut with a loud clack.

He stopped beside it and put his back to the wall, taking a quick breath. Dwayne could afford a quick rest. The old man was cornered.

He was about to smash through the door when something in the distance caught his attention. At first he thought it was just the nozzle of the fire hose hanging over the edge of the steps. He leaned forward to get a better look.

It was Big Frank's arm. Blood was trickling down his fingertips.

Rage boiled inside Dwayne hotter than a thousand nuclear reactors. His muscles went tense, his eyes bulged and his body shook.

He turned to the door, raised his foot up to his waist and kicked the handle like an angry mule. It flew off the hinges like cardboard and flopped against the floor with a thud.

Dwayne stormed through the open door.

The fourth floor was ominously dark. The lights were out and the office doors were all closed.

There was a white panel of eight switches on the wall. Dwayne flicked them all on, and the entire floor lit up with buzzing fluorescent lights.

This part of the building was reserved for both paralegals and the less successful associates. Everything was slick and sleek, with a clean, modern design that left no room for clutter. The office walls were constructed of frosted glass and accented with varnished wood, with the associate's name etched on one side. There were about thirty associate offices, each around 600 square feet. More than half of them had a front office for an administrative assistant as well. The paralegal's offices were significantly larger, and located in the northwest corner of the building.

It was as lifeless as a tavern on a Sunday morning.

Dwayne pulled the radio from his pocket and thumbed the transmit button.

"I've got him," he said. "The old goof with a gun. He's on four."

There was a pause before Buff's voice answered. "Is he dead?"

"Not yet, but I think Big Frank is. The old guy wasn't lying, eh? You better get down to the emergency stairs on the second floor."

"Alright, thanks," Buff said, wearily. "Good luck."

Dwayne snickered. "Don't need it, bud."

He stuffed his radio back into his pocket, held out his gun and crept forward.

The place was as quiet as a crypt. Dwayne knew the old man was hiding here, somewhere, and he was going to find him.

But he wasn't going to do it by sneaking around like a ninja in black pajamas. Stealth wasn't part of his skill set. He thought back to his childhood, when he'd play hide-and-seek with his brother. He was never able find Kane, and would inevitably lose his patience and throw a tantrum.

"Where the hell are you, you old prick?" he shouted down the hall. "Get out here. You think you're some badass tough guy, eh? I am going kick your teeth out! I'm going to beat eighteen pounds of shit out of you, and then rip all your goddamn hair out and force-feed it up your asshole! Get out here now!"

He ran over to a desk and flipped it onto its side, sending everything on it crashing to the ground. A jar of flowers that were resting atop it fell to the carpet and smashed into fifty pieces. A porcelain mug with a photo of a kitten on its side landed unscathed and rolled to Dwayne's feet.

He picked it up and flung it against the wall. The mug shattered, leaving a sizeable dent in the plaster.

"Come on, bud!" he screamed. "You wanna go? Show me what you've got!"

There was a sudden noise coming from the other end of the hall. It sounded like heavy footsteps, muffled by the carpet.

Dwayne didn't waste a second. He took off running, chasing after the sound. He got all the way to other side of the building without seeing anything.

When he reached the corner, he stopped. Three separate offices all met at this point, each with their own small receptionist's desk in front of them. They all had a panel in the front that went down to the floor, so there was no way to tell what was behind them. All the office doors were closed.

He guessed that the old man was cowering behind one of those desks. Lucky for Dwayne, he'd already had a lot of practice flipping over office furniture.

With his gun aimed in front of him, he crept over to the closest one. He grabbed the corner of the desk with one hand, crouched down and heaved. It toppled backwards with a shattering racket, as the phone, computer monitor, stapler, and everything else crashed to the floor.

There was no one behind it.

Bobbing his head as though it were on a swivel, Dwayne swung around the other side of the next closest desk.

There was no one there, either.

Behind him, Harry leapt out of a small alcove, holding a metal letter opener in his hand like a knife. He darted towards Dwayne like an angry tiger.

The young man was caught off guard, but his reaction was instinctive. He knelt down and charged at Harry like a defensive lineman after the snap.

The old man was knocked off his feet. He dropped the letter opener, letting out a hard groan as his body crumpled in a heap.

Dwayne pounced on him.

Harry tried squirming away, but the hulking hillbilly had all his weight resting on the old man's legs.

They struggled briefly. Before Dwayne could get in a good punch, Harry twisted his body and he rolled sideways, pounding his elbow into the young man's nose.

He let out a sharp yelp, jumped off Harry and stumbled backwards.

The old man didn't miss a beat. He reared his leg back so his knee touched his chest, and kicked Dwayne in the balls with all the force his could muster.

Dwayne bent forward, buckling in on himself, and moaned like a lost cat. His face went crooked and he wheezed loudly.

Harry scrambled back onto his feet, grabbing his blade in the process.

As Dwayne caught his breath, he took a quick step forward, clenched his fists and swung at Harry with a left hook.

The punch connected with full force. Harry felt as though a dump truck ran into his face. He saw stars float above his head like a Looney Tunes cartoon. His nose started to bleed and he staggered backwards, out of Dwayne's reach.

The two men stood a few feet apart from each other, taking half a second to regain their bearings. Dwayne had his fists raised like a fighter in a cage match, while Harry held his blade out in front of him, wildly slashing at the air back and forth.

Each of them had a look of desperate resolve in their eyes.

Harry blinked first. He charged at Dwayne holding out his letter opener like a rhino with its head down.

The young man smiled.

He darted right, sidestepping Harry's attack. In a single, sweeping motion, he pivoted backwards, grabbed the old man's wrist with one hand, his elbow with the other, and twisted.

The muscles in Harry's arm twitched involuntarily, and the letter opener fell from his grasp.

Before he could yell out in pain, Dwayne kneed Harry hard in the gut. He then threw his arm around the old man's body and slammed him against the floor.

When Dwayne jumped off, the old lawyer tried to roll away.

Harry got six inches before he was kicked twice in the stomach, hard enough to feel organs contract. He tried to scream, but couldn't. It felt as if all the oxygen was suddenly sucked out of him. Tears streamed down the side of his face.

Dwayne kicked him again.

The Colour Code that Jeff Cooper developed was an adaptation of one the United States Marine Corps uses to differentiate states of readiness. The main variant between the two systems is that the Marines include a fifth stage: condition black. It represents the catastrophic breakdown of mental and physical performance. This occurs when one has not adequately prepared, and the mind is overwhelmed with stress.

While beating on this old man, Dwayne fell right into the black stage.

He still had the upper hand, but he was no longer thinking straight. He'd let his rage and anger get the better of him. He kept kicking repeatedly, without looking, as hard as he could, with the intent to cause the maximum amount of suffering.

"This is for Kane!" he screamed, over and over again.

Eventually Dwayne got winded, and stopped to catch his breath. He was panting like a dog in the sun, looking over the old man with disgust. Harry's eyelids were flitting rapidly as he struggled to stay awake.

Dwayne knelt down beside him and lightly slapped the side of Harry's face to revive him.

"You still with me, bud?" he asked, menacingly. "Don't you go dying on me now!"

Harry's eyes went wide and focused on Dwayne. The old man's face was bloodied and bruised, but he was still conscious.

"I've got big plans for you, eh?" the young man continued to scream. "Nobody fucks with the Fodders, you stupid son of a bitch!"

The old man wasn't quite as dazed as Dwayne thought. While the surviving Fodder brother dramatically lectured him, Harry inched his outstretched arm towards the fallen letter opener. It was less than a foot from his fingertips, but with Dwayne right in his face, it might as well have been a mile.

"I'm going to kill you, very slowly. I'm going to gut you like a salmon before I stomp on your face."

With nothing left to lose, Harry lunged forward and wrapped his fingers around the blade's handle.

Dwayne noticed instantly. He went to pull out his gun, but he was half a second too late.

Harry jabbed the sharp end of the letter opener into Dwayne's foot.

The young man threw his head back and let out a piercing shriek of anguish.

Three seconds later, Harry had rolled away to safety and was back up on his feet. He was hobbling, moving no faster than a running toddler, but made it around the corner and out of sight.

Dwayne was in intense pain. It was a crushing, searing agony that shot straight up his leg. His knees went weak. Every move he made only twisted the blade in the wound, sharpening the sting.

He took three quick breaths, clenched his teeth and pulled the letter opener out with one stroke, like ripping off a bandage. It only exacerbated the pain. He screamed again, louder this time. A glob of warm blood spurted up out of the wound.

The rage inside him boiled hotter.

He grabbed his gun and limped off after Harry, lurching as fast as he could. Every step felt like he was dragging his foot through a bonfire. He made his way around the corner without looking first.

He was smacked in the face with a huge cloud of thick, black powder, like a wall of soot. Harry had taken one of the photocopier's extra cartridges of toner ink and ripped one side of it open before throwing it in Dwayne's face. The billow of dark grit burned the young man's eyes. It got in his nose, in his mouth, even down his throat.

Dwayne threw his hands over his face.

Harry turned and ran in the opposite direction, as fast as his crippled body would allow. Now he had the upper hand.

The young man stumbled back against the wall, his eyes watering as though he'd just seen Bambi's mother get shot. His face and hands were stained black with a fine layer of inky dust. His mouth tasted like motor oil. He was coughing, gagging and spitting like a thirty-year smoker.

It took him quite some time to regain his composure. In between his own gasps, he could hear the old man shuffling around the floor, opening drawers and rattling things around on desks. He was up to something.

Dwayne's vision regained focus, and he saw the top of the old man's head sticking up from behind a desk. There was a ripping sound, like cloth being torn, coming from his direction.

Whatever he was working on, Dwayne wasn't going to give him the chance to finish. He raised his weapon and fired.

The bullet missed Harry by a few inches and tore apart one corner of the desk, leaving a jagged, splintered hole. The old man dropped to the floor, pressed his body against it and threw his arms over his head.

Dwayne took a few steps forward and fired again.

Click. Out of ammo.

He angrily threw his gun aside and shambled forward. He moved with tenacious persistence, growling through every step like an angry dog. His injured foot left a trail of bloody smears behind it.

Harry poked his head up and saw the young man was unarmed.

Sensing an opportunity, he dove out and ran across the open hallway into an office on the other side, where Dwayne couldn't see him.

This only angered the young man, fuelling him to push his body harder and move faster. In his head, the loudest song Slayer ever recorded was playing at maximum volume.

He was closing in fast, maybe ten feet away from the office Harry ran into. Another few steps, and he'd be within spitting distance of the open door.

He turned to face it, ready to pounce.

Before he could act, Harry came charging out towards him, shielded behind a large leather office chair on casters.

It looked ridiculous, but it worked. Dwayne was pushed backwards. At sixty pounds, the chair was too heavy to easily tip over. The young man tried fighting back, but couldn't reach behind the chair's high, ergonomically designed back.

Harry shoved it harder and refused to stop moving, pushing the young man towards a specific spot. Once he had Dwayne right where he wanted him, he jerked the chair to a stop.

Dwayne stumbled and fell backwards. His body twirled as he fell, and a half second before he landed, he realized exactly what Harry had been up to.

The old man had scooped up several sharp, pointy letter openers off the different receptionists' desks. He used duct tape to hold them upright in a cluster of spikes on the floor. They were like the devastating Punji sticks the Viet Cong used in the Vietnam War.

Dwayne fell chest-first onto the deadly, silver-plated prongs. The blades pierced through his skin and buried themselves in his heart and lungs. Blood poured out of him in crimson waves, pooling around him.

He gasped once, lost consciousness, and died.

Harry spun the chair around and collapsed into it.

He looked like hell. He felt even worse. His body ached all over. Every part of him was tender and swollen. His breathing was heavy and laboured. He was pretty sure a couple of his teeth were knocked loose in the fight. He'd need time to recoup.

The old man looked down at Dwayne's body, and his mouth stretched into a wide, malevolent smile. He wasn't sure if that was the third or fourth man he'd killed that night, but either way he didn't feel the least bit guilty about any of them. If anything, he felt pride. He was actually pretty good at this.

He reached for Dwayne's radio and turned it on.

"One more dead asshole," he bragged. "I bet if you take them all to the same funeral home you can get a group discount. Your move, Bryan."

He started to laugh. He waited anxiously for Buff to respond, eager to taunt him some more, but he never did.

Harry grumbled and let the radio fall to the floor.

Then he passed out.

***

Buff found himself standing over Big Frank's corpse. He'd carefully made his way up the emergency stairwell to the third floor, and was baffled by the state of the place. It was a horrible mess. Everything was soaking wet, and the fire hose was inexplicably stretched out as far it could reach.

Worst of all, the strongest, toughest, meanest man on his team was now a twisted, gory carcass, sprawled across a flight of stairs. He was barely recognizable, save for the big black coat. His head was just a shapeless, pulpy, spongy pile.

Big Frank was dead. Kane was dead. Harry claimed Dwayne was dead, too.

Buff shook his head and started feeling sorry for himself. He couldn't understand how everything had gone so wrong. He was renowned for meticulously planning every heist he pulled. He'd done all the right research, assembled a team of experts, paid off the right people, everything.

None of it seemed to matter now. Part of him wanted to just give up and go home, but he knew that wasn't an option. Between the FBI and his parole officer, he had too much invested in this operation. There was also the fact that if he didn't retrieve what was in that safe, the French-Canadian mob would find him and bury a .22-caliber bullet in the back of his brain.

Buff wasn't sure if he could salvage this situation. Losing Big Frank was a huge blow, and not just because of the extra muscle he provided. He was their munitions man. Without his explosives, they wouldn't be able to get through the vault.

Buff knelt down beside Big Frank and sighed. He'd seen too many dead bodies this evening.

He started rooting through his pockets. He quickly found two semi-automatic pistols - a Beretta PX4 and a Springfield Armory XD-S, four fully-loaded magazines for each, a five-shot .38 Special revolver, and a handful of loose bullets of various calibers. That was just in his coat.

There were even deadlier weapons hiding in his pants. Buff found an eight-ounce M84 stun grenade, two lipstick-sized electric detonators, and most importantly, a thirty-gram brick of white powder wrapped in plastic, about the size of a pack of gum.

That powder was exactly what Buff was looking for. It was cyclotrimethylene-trinitramine, better known as cyclonite, or RDX. "Research Department Explosive" was recognized as one of the world's most powerful high-explosives, with one and a half times the destructive power of TNT. It was widely used by both sides during World War II. The compound known as C-4, the favourite explosive of bad guys in action movies, contains 91% RDX. It was also a major component in Semtex, which is used in controlled demolition projects to raze structures.

Buff knew exactly what it was, but he didn't know what to do with it. He had no idea how volatile the stuff was. He didn't have a clue as to what quantity to use, how to properly apply it, or how to avoid blowback after detonation. The only one who knew any of that information was now dead at his feet.

All Buff knew was that they needed it. That RDX was the only way they were getting inside the Strongbox vault. He'd figure it out somehow.

He packed the Beretta and as much of the ammunition as he could into his pockets. He lifted his pant leg and tucked the revolver into his sock. Finally, he slid the other automatic into the waistband of his pants. He looked like a low-rent Rambo.

The last thing he grabbed was the small stick of explosives. He held his hand out with his palm facing up, and carried the RDX like a waiter delivering foie gras on a silver platter. He was worried it could go off at any moment, and treated it as such.

He nervously made his way back up the stairs.

# 9:00pm

Buff was exhausted by the time he got the brick of RDX up to the top floor. Six floors was a lot to climb, especially with the creeping fear that what he was carrying could explode at any moment. His hair was mussed and his shirt was soaked through with sweat.

He opened the stairwell door to find Beka sitting in a leather chair, still playing Tetris. It looked as though she hadn't moved since he last spoke to her.

Her eyes lifted from her game for a moment, long enough to see it was just Buff, and then returned to her phone's tiny screen.

He nodded in her direction. She ignored him.

Buff marched past her and into the executive office where the rest of the team was waiting. N-Dig and Marcus were each stretched out on leather couches, listening to Doug. The tattooed young man was sitting on top of the big desk, telling stories about some of the film sets he'd worked on. Fou stood in the corner, away from the others but listening intently. Everyone seemed relaxed and jovial, as though they were lounging around a campfire.

"Tell me, b'y," said Marcus, "did ya ever work on a movie with Stallone?"

"No, not with Stallone," Doug said, "but I've got a great story about him. I heard it from the sound guy on this Lorezno Lamas movie I worked on."

"Which one?" N-Dig asked.

"*Snake Eater 5: Die, Dyson, Die,*" he answered.

"Ah, yes! A classic," N-Dig said with a laugh.

"Where was I?" Doug asked. "Oh right. The sound guy knew a guy who worked on that Stallone movie where he played a cop. I can't remember which one. It doesn't matter. Anyway, they're on set, right? While the crew is setting up for the next shot, Stallone takes some girl he found into his trailer. She starts, you know, going down on him, and he keeps saying 'cup da balls, cup da balls' in that weird, deep, punch-drunk voice he has. Thing is, he still has his wireless mic on."

The room erupted in uproarious laughter.

"The sound guy heard it, and recorded it. He played it for the whole crew."

The team's laughs got louder and more raucous.

Buff stood behind them all, stone-faced, carefully laying the RDX safely on the ground.

"Wait, it gets better," Doug continued. "One of the grips actually makes up shirts that say 'cup da balls' on them. So, that movie ends, and then months later, the sound guy gets a phone call at six in the morning. Some other sound guy got sick, and they want him to come in last minute. It's all a big rush, so they don't tell him anything about the show other than its name and where the location is. The 'cup da balls' shirt is the only clean thing he has, so he throws it on and drives to set."

"When he gets there, he finds out it's another Stallone movie! He knows he has to change his shirt, but before he can, he bumps into Stallone as he's coming out of his trailer. Like, they literally collide into each other."

"So, Stallone looks down, sees the guy's shirt, and goes, 'I say that,' and then kept walking. 'I say that!' Like it was a 'No Fear' shirt, right? Dude has absolutely no self-awareness at all."

Everyone except Buff laughed again.

The frazzled leader of this team had heard enough.

Without saying a word, he walked into the centre of the room, pulled the Beretta out of his pocket, held it above his head, aimed at the ceiling, and fired.

The thunderous boom startled them all. Marcus jumped out of his seat, and Beka came running in from the hallway. Everyone turned to Buff, and they could see from the expression on his face how outraged he was.

"Glad to see you're all having such a good time," he said, sarcastically, "but this isn't summer camp, boys. It's a heist. I've tried to be nice, tried to keep everyone happy and let you all do your own thing. Well, the party is over!"

He slammed his fist against the desk for emphasis.

"No more democracy!" he continued. "This is a coup d'état, and I'm the new dictator. I've got a job to do, and I would appreciate it if you guys would get up off your asses and help me. I don't care if you want more money. I don't care if it's not why you were hired. If this fails and one of us goes to jail, we all go to jail, understand? We're all in this together now, so you will all do exactly as I tell you to. I don't want to hear any whining. I don't want to hear any complaining. In fact, I don't want to hear anything from any of you except 'yes Buff.' Is that understood?"

They all nodded obediently. The room was deadly silent, with everyone in quiet shock. Buff's outburst had both scared and shamed them. He didn't lose his temper like that often, but when he did, it was truly terrifying.

Even Marcus was surprised. In all the years they'd known each other, he'd never seen his friend so upset.

"Look, Buff, I'm sorry," Doug said, sincerely. "I didn't mean to upset..."

"Shut up," Buff interrupted loudly, snapping at him like an angry cop. "Didn't you hear what I just said?"

"I know, but I wanted to..."

Buff got right in Doug's face and screamed the words.

"Didn't you hear what I just said?" He was in an unhinged rage, shaking his fists and stomping his feet. He looked like an angry Gary Busey, ranting and raving hysterically.

Everyone took a subtle step backwards.

"Yes, Buff," Doug said, quietly.

"Thank you," Buff replied sternly. He knew he was making everyone tense, and he relished it. He paused a few moments, letting them all sweat it out a little more. He held his hands together behind his back and paced back and forth, like a drill instructor in front of a row of new recruits.

He quietly walked over to N-Dig and examined his wounded arm. It still looked rough, but now that it'd been cleaned and tended to, it was clear the young man would easily survive.

"You feeling better?" Buff asked him.

"Yeah, bro," N-Dig answered. "I'm good. For real."

"Good."

Buff handed his gun over to N-Dig.

"Now get downstairs and guard the front door," he ordered, flatly.

The young man bristled. He hated being told what to do, but figured this probably wasn't the best time to fight that battle.

He looked over the Springfield XD handgun he'd been given. The young man was proficient with firearms, but had never seen a pistol so beautiful. It was slick, compact, and unbelievably aggressive. The palm had a moulded checkered pattern. There was even a rail under the barrel for a laser-sight. Just holding it made N-Dig feel tougher.

He stuffed it into his pants and gave Buff a nod. Without delay, he walked out of the office and took the elevator down to the main lobby.

Buff turned to Beka.

"We need to try and get that network back online," he said. "I know it's not easy, but I don't care. We need to give this old fart what he wants. He's already fucked up too much of the plan."

"I don't think she can, dude," said Doug, cautiously. "Those servers are fried. I wiped them out myself."

Buff started getting angry again. He didn't look at Doug as he answered him, talking through clenched teeth. "I don't care how it gets done, just do it!"

Doug sighed.

"I can try," Beka said, unsure, "but I don't want to do it. I really don't want to get shot."

"Doug will go with you," Buff said.

That didn't fill her with confidence. Her lip curled and she put her hands on her hips. She clearly didn't like the idea. Doug wasn't too keen on it either.

However, one look at Buff and they both realized this was a fight they couldn't win.

"Ugh, fine," Beka said, with an air of resignation. She held out her hand. "Give me a gun."

Buff reached down into his sock and pulled out the revolver. He paused for a few moments of consideration, and then handed it to Doug.

"Hey!" Beka shouted, stamping her foot. "Why are you giving it to him? That's sexist, you asshole!"

"If I give it to you," he answered calmly, "you'll probably shoot Doug."

That caught her off guard. She thought about it for a second.

"You're probably right," she conceded.

Doug cradled his new weapon as though it were a precious jewel.

"Thank you," he said with a gracious bow.

"Be careful," Buff warned him. "It's loaded. If you shoot your eye out, I'm not taking you to the hospital."

Part of Buff still hated the idea of everyone running around the building with guns, but that train had already left the station. The best he could hope for now was that they wouldn't blow their own feet off.

"Now, please, hurry," he said. "Go."

Both Beka and Doug turned and walked out of the office.

"Anything you want me to do?" Fou asked.

"No," Buff said sharply. "Just shut up."

Fou slumped down onto one of the leather couches.

With the room emptied, Marcus walked up to Buff and stood beside him, gently putting his arm around his old friend's neck.

"What's wrong with ya, me chum?" Marcus asked him, softly. "Handguns and temper tantrums? That's not yar style, b'y. Ya blowed up worse than a kitten with a gaffer in 'er gob, chum. I ain't never seen ya like this. Yar givin' me the bivers. Yar supposed to be a professional, me son."

"I know," Buff said, repentant. "I'm sorry I lost my temper, but we've been here two hours and we don't seem to be any closer to getting inside that vault. This heist is turning into the biggest disaster since, well, since the last one I tried to pull, when I got arrested."

"No reason to blear. The bottom ain't fell out of 'er yet, me chum. Ya can no change the direction of the wind, but ya can adjust yar sails. So, if ya tells me what ya want, we'll do 'er directly, b'y."

"Come with me to the vault room."

"Sure thing, b'y," Marcus replied, "but I don't know what ya expect to do in there. We can't start the drilling 'til Big ol' Frank gets back with the explosives, proper thing, me son. The shell on 'er is too thick, b'y."

"Big Frank is dead."

"No he ain't, b'y." Marcus waved a dismissive hand in Buff's face. "That fellar on the radio's just tryin' to gets a rise out of ya. Some cod-liver drinkin' ol' geezer couldn't take down Big Frank. The b'y is made of rock."

"No, he's dead. I saw the body myself."

Marcus's mouth dropped.

"Go on with ya!" he exclaimed, shocked. "Lard t'underin'! I can't believe it, b'y. How in hell's blazes did anyone get the jump on that mean ol' cracky? The guy was as big as the side of a barn! Well, I suppose that's the end of 'er, me chum. She's all screwed up now, b'y, and we is on a slab. We can't pull this heist without Big Frank."

Buff carefully picked the small brick of RDX up off the ground. He carried it over to Marcus and held it in front of the old man's face.

"What's that?" the old man asked.

"The explosives Big Frank was going to use."

"No foolin'? Ya sure ya should be tossin' it around like that, chum? That's some squish, b'y, and dangerous to boot. Big Frank was the only one who knew how that piece-a-stuff works! I sure don't know anything about 'er!"

"Me neither, but it's got to be done." He checked his watch. "We've got less than fifteen minutes before they have to go off, or this robbery isn't going to happen."

"Buff, me chum..."

"There's no time for debate. I'm doing this with or without your help."

Marcus threw his arms up in defeat.

"If this thing blows up and I lose a hand, then yar buyin' me a hook to replace 'er!"

He laughed heartily as he walked with Buff out of the office.

***

Things were quiet on the fourth floor. Harry was slumped in an office chair, drained and weary, slowly drifting back to consciousness. His body was bruised, tender, and bathed in sweat. He looked like Rocky Balboa after ten rounds with Apollo Creed. He needed time to recover, at least a few days, but had no such luck. Those thieves were after him. He had to keep moving.

After killing so many of their men, he must have put a serious dent in their plans by now. He had no idea how long he'd been passed out, but was sure he didn't have more than a few minutes before they found him.

He got up from his chair and hobbled around. Everything ached, but he could move without much trouble. He saw Dwayne's gun lying in the middle of the hallway, picked it up and stuffed it into his pants.

Exhausted and beaten, Harry was rethinking his plan to take a hostage. He didn't have the strength to fight anyone else.

He considered his next move, and realized he didn't have many left. As soon as he began transferring money from those Norwegian accounts without authorization, he'd effectively ended his career. There was no way of putting that genie back in the bottle. Tomorrow this place would be crawling with cops and extra security. The whole building would probably be labelled a crime scene and closed down for days. All of the computer networks would be scrutinized. The theft would be discovered sooner or later, and Harry would go to jail.

He wished he could just run away, sneak out of the building and grab the next flight to Jamaica, leaving the law offices of Bennett, Olsen, Nygärd, Jørgensen, and Holm behind.

Unfortunately, that wasn't an option. This illegal money transfer was an "all or nothing" deal, and he couldn't leave until it was complete. If he didn't get the money soon, he'd lose it all. The accounts would freeze and the money would vanish. He needed to finish that transfer tonight, because he certainly didn't have the personal savings to bankroll a retirement in the Caribbean. Not to mention the difficulty of living as a fugitive for the rest of his life.

He couldn't leave until he was absolutely sure he had his money, and that his ass was good and covered.

He wondered what time it was. It felt as though it were after midnight. He had no idea how long he'd been running around the building, but it was probably more hours than he put in on a regular workday.

Over by the main hallway, he heard the gentle hum of one of the elevators slowly descending. From the indicator lights above its doors, he could see that it was going down to the ground floor.

He suddenly realized that by locking off everything but the service elevator and the emergency stairs, Buff's team had inadvertently limited their ability to move through the building. If Harry were to somehow cut off their access to the elevator, they'd be forced to use the stairwell. If he blocked off the stairs, then the thieves would be trapped inside like rats.

It wouldn't be easy. Taking out an elevator was no simple task. The building's service elevator was an older model than the regular passenger cars. It was held up by six redundant, steel hoist cables, each one over six inches in diameter and capable of supporting one and a half times the elevator's maximum capacity. In addition, there were numerous other safety devices to keep it functioning properly, like emergency tethers, hydraulic buffers to cushion sudden impacts, and a device called a "governor," which can detect whether the elevator's moving too fast and apply brakes to stop it.

He'd never be able to cut the support cables, and he didn't know enough about electrical systems to shut the elevator off.

But he did know how to start very large fires.

Retracing his steps, he had to go back down the hallway to find his precious bag of supplies. He'd accidentally dropped it during his chase with Dwayne.

He looked through it, making sure he didn't lose anything important. There were a number of bottles in the bag, most of which had warning labels on the side that read "FLAMMABLE."

Any one of those chemicals would work well, but Harry was unsure if they would burn hot enough to actually take the elevator out of service.

For that, he would require something a little stronger. At the bottom of the bag he found the two things he was going to need: a jug of ammonia, and a small vial of iodine tablets he pulled out of a first aid kit. Both are relatively safe substances, but when mixed in the proper proportions, the ammonia reacts with the iodine to form tiny crystals of nitrogen triiodide - one of the most world's most destructive contact explosives.

Harry had discovered this unique substance at nine years old, back when lighting fires gave him the sense of power he now felt from wielding the law. He spent many summer afternoons mixing together random chemicals he found under the kitchen sink. The first time he made nitrogen triiodide, it took almost two months for his eyebrows to grow back.

When dried, the inorganic compound is highly shock sensitive and can be detonated with even the lightest touch of a feather. This sensitivity means that nitrogen triiodide is impossible to store or transport, and has no practical commercial value. For what Harry had planned, though, it was just perfect.

It would make a very big, very powerful boom.

***

A big explosion was exactly what Buff and Marcus were worried about. They were carefully, painstakingly applying the RDX along the seams of the vault door. They used small coffee stir-sticks to gently nudge the explosive powder into the crevices, and then worked it in softly with a cloth, similar to the way one would use baking soda to clean grout in the shower.

It was a slow process, taking almost ten minutes to outline the whole vault door with explosive powder. That was twice as long as Buff had anticipated. He had less than five minutes before the explosion needed to happen. He seriously doubted whether he had enough time to finish.

The two thieves were sweating like old men in a sauna. Neither had any idea what they were doing. Buff had a vague idea how powerful RDX was, in the same way the average person knows that a shark has sharp teeth. He hoped they were properly applying it to the vault, but knew they were just guessing. They were both terrified of the explosives being set off accidentally, and wished Big Frank was still here to do this job.

Buff pulled the two detonators out of his pocket. They looked homemade and harmless. They were small tubes of polished aluminum, about three inches long, with a single thin wire sticking out of the bottom. On the top was a tiny red button, which triggered a ten-second timer when pushed. There was adhesive along one side so they could stick it to any surface.

Buff took one and placed it on the right side of the vault. He straightened out the wire and carefully slid it into the sticky white powder. He repeated the process on the left side with the other detonator.

When he was finished, he wiped his brow and breathed a sigh of relief.

"I think that should do it," he said.

"I hope so, b'y," Marcus replied, "but I suppose we'll find out soon enough, eh?"

Buff checked his watch again. "Sooner than you think. Just over four minutes, I think."

"Cutting 'er close, b'y. Do ya think we used enough?"

"We used all of it, Marcus."

"Oh. Well, do ya think maybe we used too much? Ya don't want anybody to hears 'er."

"Nobody's going to hear it. Trust me. I have a plan." Again, Buff looked down at his watch. "And it looks like we're going to just barely make it."

"Lard t'underin'! I dies at ya, b'y. Is ya taking a rise out of me? All night long ya've been blabberin' on and on, with more tongue than a logan and more lip than a coal bucket, about how these explosive things had to be in by a certain time. That don't make a lick of sense, b'y. We gots all night, me chum!"

"No, we don't. We've got just over four minutes."

Buff walked over to Marcus and patted him on the shoulder reassuringly.

"Everything's going to be fine, Marcus. We're in the home stretch now, okay? I'm going to go wait in the office by the window. When I give the signal, you press the trigger buttons on the detonators and run out of the room. Got it?"

"Sure thing, b'y," Marcus said with a shrug. He wasn't confident, but had given up arguing with Buff. They needed that vault open, and this was the only way to do it. If they'd done anything wrong, the whole thing was going to literally blow up in his face. At least he'd go out with a bang.

***

Beka and Doug found all the computers in the server room were beyond repair, just as they suspected. It would be impossible to bring the network back online without bringing in all new equipment.

Doug tried flicking the power switch a few times. When it failed to do anything, he kicked it.

"I don't know what they expect you to connect to. The servers are totally bonked. They all need to have their hard drives replaced. This is all just scrap metal now. We're screwed."

Beka wasn't ready to give up just yet. On the bottom shelf in a dark corner of the room she saw something that might be able to help them. It was an ancient Dell computer, unplugged and covered with a fine layer of dust. The machine was at least ten years old, probably more. There was a sticker on the side proudly noting the Intel Pentium III chip inside, a microprocessor that ceased production around 2004.

She correctly surmised that the law firm used this antique as their fail-safe system. Every few months, someone would backup all crucial system files onto the old computer, and then unplug it and stick it in a corner. That way, even if there were a catastrophic power surge, they would still be able to recover some information.

"Did you fry this one?" she asked, pointing to the old Dell.

Doug shook his head. "Nope. I didn't even see that one."

"Good. I have an idea. Maybe all we need to do is make it seem like the network is back online. I can hook up this old jalopy to the router, partition the thing into as many separate drives as I can, say the magic words, and 'poof!' Instant fake network."

"But the router's fried, too."

"No problem. We've got the service hub for the phone system. That still works. We just have to patch everything in manually."

Doug groaned, knowing how difficult that would be. They were going to have to dig into the cabling in the wall and patch lines together by hand. It would be hard, tedious work.

"Are you insane, woman? Do you have any idea how long that's going to take?"

"Grow a pair, Poochie," Beka answered, "or you'll always be a failure."

She spun around and kicked a sizable hole into the drywall. She reached inside and began pulling out telephone cables by the armload.

Within minutes, both Beka and Doug were on their hands and knees, grabbing strands out of the wall and ripping them apart. Next, they'd strip away the plastic shielding, revealing four tiny wires, each slightly more than a millimetre thick. The ends of those wires would have to be individually threaded into the corresponding plate on the telephone patch bay.

It was taxing work, and they were both getting terrible cramps in their fingers like old seamstresses with arthritis. The room was unbearably humid. It was also small and cramped, so the two of them were working right on top of each other. They were shoulder to shoulder, like two scorpions in a bottle fighting for space.

They scoffed and huffed every time their hands accidentally touched. It was awkward and uncomfortable. Even though they weren't speaking, the tension between them was unmistakable.

At one point, they both reached down for the same wire at the same time, and their heads collided. It made an audible clunk, and they both cried out.

Neither of them apologized. They looked at each other and grimaced, incensed that they had to work together.

Beka rolled her eyes and went back to unspooling the network cables.

Doug gritted his teeth and tried to do the same.

He followed one wire from the hole in the wall to the floor. It snaked around behind him. He couldn't easily reach it without turning around, so he tried to shift his weight and spin in place.

It didn't work. As he moved, his left foot came down hard on Beka's right hand.

She yelped in pain.

"Watch it, asshole!" she cried, recoiling.

Doug had his back to her and couldn't see what was going on. He tried to crane his head around to see her, but in doing so he accidentally elbowed her in the nose.

Again, she yelped in pain, louder this time. She cupped her nose with one hand, and punched Doug in the shoulder with the other.

"You stupid son of a bitch!" she screamed, smacking him as hard as she could. "What the hell is wrong with you?"

"I'm sorry," Doug said. "It was an accident."

"You were a fucking accident. I wish you were dead. I hate you so much."

"Well, this isn't exactly fun for me either."

Beka let out another frustrated moan.

"You know what? Get out. I can't work with you."

She grabbed him by the arm and forcibly dragged him to the door.

"What?" he asked, dumbfounded. "Beka, come on. You can't do this all by yourself."

"Just watch me."

He tried wrenching his arm from her grip, but she was latched on tighter than a pneumatic vise. She pushed him out the door and slammed it behind him.

Doug stood out in the hallway, still not exactly sure what just happened. He heard the door lock shut.

He waited a second, and tried the doorknob. It wouldn't budge.

"Rebecca, open the damn door!" he demanded.

She ignored him.

He yelled her name and pounded on the door, screaming until he was hoarse. He looked like Fred Flintstone bellowing for Wilma. Beka just ignored him.

Furious, Doug knew exactly how to get his retributition. He reached into his shirt pocket, pulled out his RFID scanner, and flipped open a tiny compartment on its side. With a few simple tweaks he was able to alter the device so that it could permanently lock the door to the server room.

He got down on one knee and proceeded to run the scanner over the door's security panel, chuckling to himself maliciously.

Beka was oblivious, but probably wouldn't have cared. She was just grateful to be rid of the pest. Now that she had a little more space, she was free to stretch her arms and take a deep breath. She cracked her knuckles and got back to work.

***

Harry was in the fourth floor hallway, kneeling in front of the service elevator. He had everything he needed neatly laid out in front of him. Three paper coffee filters were set to one side, on which he'd mixed ammonia with iodine. It was drying into a layer of slushy orange paste. Beside those were stacks of blank paper, an empty cardboard box, several bottles of highly flammable cleaning products, a screwdriver, and the Zippo lighter he'd found.

He pressed the elevator's call button.

When the doors slid open, he darted away, waiting a good ten seconds before looking inside. He wanted to make absolutely sure the elevator was empty.

Once he saw the coast was clear, he held the door open with his foot. Leaning over, he reached down and grabbed the screwdriver. In one elegant motion he wedged it into the bottom of the door and stepped back.

Harry was starting to feel pretty confident about his plan.

He began by taking the blank sheets of papers, crumpling them up, and tossing them onto the elevator floor. Before long he had it carpeted with loose pages, the same way people start campfires with old newspaper.

There was a small spot in the middle of the elevator that he tried to keep clear. That's where he placed the empty cardboard box.

He grabbed the cleaning bottles and furiously unscrewed the caps, letting them fall to floor and bounce away. He poured every last drop of the flammable solvents onto the elevator floor, letting the paper soak in as much as it could. When he was finished, the place reeked of chemicals, the way public pools stink of chlorine.

The last thing he did was the most dangerous. He held his breath as he grabbed the coffee filters one at a time and gently placed them onto the cardboard box. As long as the nitrogen triiodide was still damp, the chances of Harry accidentally blowing himself up were marginal.

At least, that's what he hoped. He treated those coffee filters as lightly as a baby kitten, setting them down as though they were made of brittle porcelain. They smelled horrible, like a combination of soiled diapers and a sweaty locker room.

Once all three coffee filters had been laid without exploding, Harry stepped back and exhaled slowly, relieved.

When he picked up the lighter, he paused for a moment to consider how much damage he was doing to his employer's building. It made him smile.

Holding the Zippo between two fingers, he spun the flint-wheel and ignited a small flame. He watched it burn a few seconds, bright and consistent.

He gently set the lighter down onto the cardboard box, as though building a house of cards. It was resting on its base, so that the slightest nudge would knock it over and touch off a massive blaze.

Without stepping into the passenger car, he leaned into the elevator and hit the button for the ground floor. He pulled the screwdriver out of the door and ran away.

The doors slowly slid closed, and the elevator began to descend. Next stop, *kaboom!*

# 9:15pm

Beka found it much easier to work without Doug's constant distraction. All he ever did was aggravate her and get in the way. She had no idea what she ever saw in the boy, and knowing that she'd once shared a bed with him made her skin crawl.

She tried to put him out of her mind, and focus on connecting the backup server to the phone system's service hub. The room was a complete mess, as all the cables that were pulled from the wall were stripped and left in a tangled jumble on the floor. Beka had to wade through them just to get from one corner to the other. She eventually moved the old computer closer to the wall so she wouldn't have to walk so much.

Before long, she had everything wired up. As she threaded the last strand of cable into the hub and twisted it into place, the computer lit up and its hard drive whirred to life. She grabbed a monitor and keyboard off the shelf and connected them.

Once it had booted up, Beka started partitioning the hard drive as many times as she could. She was essentially dividing the computer's memory up into increasingly smaller chunks. This meant that to anyone connecting to the computer remotely, it would appear as though there were multiple hard drives, instead of just one. She hastily renamed each new partition, giving it the impression of a genuine computer network.

Beka took all the files from the main hard drive and copied most of them to the new partitions. When she'd finished, she quickly looked over the layout of the files. It didn't match the old network exactly, but it was a close enough approximation to fool a computer novice.

She was pretty proud of the work she'd done, but wished she knew precisely what the gunman was looking for on the network. It would have made it easier to tailor the subterfuge to his needs. Regardless, she was confident this plan would slow the madman down for a bit.

Trembling, she grabbed her radio and flicked it on.

"Okay, guys, I did it," she said.

"Beka, I'm sorry, but now's not a good time," Buff replied, impatiently. "We're right in the middle of something."

"The network's back up."

That got Buff's attention. "Really? Oh, that's great!" He sounded relieved. "In the whole building?"

"Everywhere but the top floor."

"Nice work, Beka. Thank you."

Their conversation was suddenly interrupted by Harry's coarse voice, warbling out through the radio.

"You've got a woman on the team?" he said in a mocking tone. "I'm impressed. That's very progressive."

"Suck my dick," Beka said, flatly.

"Well, well, aren't you a feisty one?" Harry said, derisively. "You know, women like you are what kept me out of family law."

"I bet women kept you out of a lot of things," she answered.

"Don't taunt him, Beka," pleaded Buff. "Look, Mr. Bockner, you got what you wanted. The computer network is working again. Now, please, just leave us alone."

There was a long pause before Harry responded.

"That bitch better not be lying," he said, deadly serious. "If I find anything wrong, she's the first one I'm going to kill."

The radio clicked off.

Beka hated letting the old man have the last word, but realized it was best for him to feel as though he had the upper hand. The intention had been to slow him down, and so far, it was working. Now, she had to get back upstairs before he found out the network was a fake.

She went to the door, unlocked the latch and tried to open it.

It wouldn't budge.

Grabbing the handle with both hands, she tried pulling the door open. Again, it wouldn't move.

She checked the latch again. It was unlocked, but the door still refused to open.

Beka felt her throat close up. She was trapped in here, and worse, she was unarmed.

***

Buff was inside the executive office with his face pressed against the window. Through the glass he could see a stunning array of vivid, dynamic colours showering the sky, right on schedule. Every year on Canada Day, the local Kiwanis club would spare no expense in staging the most elaborate, most impressive fireworks display in Toronto. It was a highlight of the summer that drew in people from all around the city, and it always started an hour after sunset, at precisely 9:15 p.m. The cracking booms made by the show resonated for miles like thunder. It would be more than loud enough to mask any noise Buff's team made.

He watched as another tiny cluster of bright stars burst in a dense sphere and expanded outwards, like a giant chrysanthemum, with each pinpoint of light leaving a trail of burning particles behind it. It was truly spectacular.

Buff turned and ran to the door of the office.

"Now!" he shouted, through cupped hands.

Marcus was in the vault room, but he heard him loud and clear.

"See ya on the other side, me chum!" he yelled back to Buff.

The old man reached for the detonators. There was a tiny button on top of each one, a little smaller than the crown on a wristwatch. He clicked them both.

They made an intermittent beeping sound and the lights on them began to flash.

Six seconds later, and Marcus was outside the vault room and around the corner. Over the years he'd heard stories of safe-crackers dying after getting hit with shrapnel while trying to blow open a vault, and so he took cover to avoid the same fate. No matter how good a burglar you are, if you accidentally blow yourself up in the end, it's the only part people remember, and becomes your legacy.

Four more seconds of total stillness followed.

Suddenly, the vault room erupted in an ear-smashing, bone-shaking explosion.

The sound was louder than two steam trains smashing into each other. The explosion tore across the floor, rocking the building. Huge, blinding walls of flame soared in all directions, consuming office furniture and leaving black scorch marks on the wall. The concussion wave sent a powerful blast of searing hot air shooting down the corridor, shattering windows. Desks and chairs were sent flying, along with big, jagged chunks of the vault's heavy metal door.

For a few moments, Marcus felt as if he was trapped inside a Michael Bay movie.

The fire receded and the hallway filled with wispy white smoke, like a thick fog. The stench of sulphur and burnt paper came with it.

The old man got up off the floor and dusted himself off. The blast had rattled him. He waved his hands in front of his face, coughing loudly. He couldn't see anything. His ears were ringing like he'd been sitting front row at a heavy metal concert. The smoke stung his eyes, and they began to water.

"Marcus?" Buff's voice rang out through the haze. "Are you okay?"

"Fine, b'y," he answered, between bouts of choked hacking. "I think we used a tad too much of those explosives, eh?"

Buff laughed.

As the smoke slowly dissipated, the two men could see each other again. Buff went over and put a hand on his old friend's shoulder.

"Need a minute?"

"No, b'y. I'm good. That was something, eh? Lard t'undering! If that won't knock the outer shell off, b'y, then nothing will, me chum. That was louder than the horn on a cargo freighter. I hope there's still something worth stealing left in there, b'y!"

Buff held out his hand and helped Marcus get to his feet. They nodded to each other and went into the vault room.

They found the air inside a murky, smoky soup. The walls of the room looked like the inside of a fireplace. The floor was littered with pieces of the vault door, which had blown out into small, mangled shards. The industrial drill had been blown back into the corner of the room, and much of the metal had been tarnished and blackened.

The room began to clear. The two men could finally see what the explosives had done to the Strongbox.

Their mouths dropped.

Amazingly, the safe itself was still standing, completely intact, but the door was little more than scrap metal now. There was a large, concave imprint in the middle of it, like an apple with a bite out of it. The explosion had collapsed the door inwards, like a frat boy crushing an empty beer can.

Neither one of them could believe it. Fully half of the door was missing. This was supposed to be their biggest obstacle of the night, and now, it was nearly obliterated.

"Oh me good Lard!" exclaimed Marcus. "Would ya takes a gock at that! I'd say we done used just enough, b'y! There ain't enough there to pray over, me chum."

He walked over to the vault door and pressed his hand against the imprint. It was still warm. Marcus giggled and clapped his hands, as excited as a kid on a trampoline. Buff just looked confused.

"Things might have just slew 'round for us, me b'y."

"What do you mean?"

"I mean that big bada-boom did not just take out the outer shell, me chum. She took out half of the door with 'er! That's just some nish metal there we got to deal with, maybe only a couple of inches. We only needs an hour to drill through 'er, b'y! Maybe even half of that!"

Buff smiled, bigger and wider than he had all night. At last, a little good luck.

"It's about time we caught a break," he said.

"Wait a fair wind, me son, and you'll get one," Marcus replied.

Too bad they didn't have time to dwell on their good fortune. They couldn't celebrate until that vault door finally swung open and they got what was inside.

"Let's get to work. Help me get this drill back into place."

The two of them got behind the huge piece of equipment and began pushing it back to its spot in front of the vault door.

***

Down in the front lobby, N-Dig was largely oblivious to the pyrotechnics going on seven floors above him. He was too distracted by the handgun Buff had given him. Sitting on the desk, he was twirling the weapon on his finger like a gunslinger in an old cowboy movie. It was a lot more difficult than he expected, mainly because the Springfield XD was such a big, bulky gun.

He was just starting to get the hang of it when he heard a loud pop coming from down the hallway. A half-second later, he felt the building around him shudder slightly.

N-Dig grabbed the desk with both hands to brace himself, and then froze until the shaking subsided. He had no idea what just happened. He knew Buff and Marcus were doing something with explosives, but thought it was just to break the vault door open. That shouldn't have been powerful enough to make the whole office tremble. It's not like earthquakes were a common problem in Toronto, either.

Suddenly, there was a loud, calamitous crashing sound, like metal grinding and scraping against itself. It came from the service elevator. A huge puff of dense purple smoke billowed out through the elevator doors, followed by a blast of heat and an unspeakably pungent odour.

N-Dig's hand tensed around his gun's grip, squeezing so hard the frame was digging into his skin. He pulled back the hammer until it clicked.

He swallowed once and held his breath, and then ran over to look inside the elevator car.

The shock of the blast in the vault room had been enough to set off Harry's homemade explosives a little early. They'd actually knocked the elevator off its guardrails, and the passenger car was now wedged on the bottom floor at a lopsided angle. At the same time, the lit Zippo was knocked onto the floor, igniting the combustible cleansers Harry had spread everywhere.

The service elevator was engulfed in flames. The floor was gone, replaced by a vigorous pyre, with giant columns of fire stretching up the walls and devouring everything they touched. It was growing bigger right before N-Dig's eyes.

He watched helplessly as the inferno began spilling out into the hallway like water from an overturned glass. The blaze was spreading quickly.

N-Dig didn't know what to do. In a panic, he grabbed his radio, fumbled with the transmit button and tried calling up to Buff.

"We've got a fire down here, bro. For real." he said.

"What are you talking about?" Buff asked.

"The elevator. It's on fire, bro. Believe. It's roasting."

"What happened? What'd you do?"

"It wasn't me, man! I didn't do anything. I wasn't anywhere near it, bro. Believe. It just came down and a bonfire fell out. I think it was probably that old guy who did it. For real, bro."

There was no reply over the radio. Upstairs, Buff was letting out an aggravated stream of profanity, so foul and obscene it would offend sailors.

It was a long time before he finally responded.

"Just stay there," he said, out of breath. "We can't let this guy leave the building."

"Fine. What do you want me to do about the fire?"

"Do you have any marshmallows?"

"No."

"Then put it out."

"How?"

"Do I sound like Smokey the Bear? I have no idea. Try water."

"Where am I supposed to get that, bro?"

"You can scoop it out of the toilet for all I care. I'm a little busy up here, N-Dig. Figure it out for yourself. Find a fire extinguisher. Smother the fire. Buy it dinner and say it's pretty. Just deal with it."

N-Dig shoved his radio back into his pocket, muttering under his breath. Now he was expected to put out fires, too? He hated being told what to do.

He began furiously searching around the lobby for a fire extinguisher. By law, every commercial building is required to have at least one portable canister on every floor. He could see where one was supposed to be: there was a red hook on one of the marble pillars, but it was empty.

There was nothing under the desk, in the closet, or anywhere else, as far as N-Dig could tell.

The fire from the elevator was spreading. The granite floor wouldn't burn, but the flames were finding a path along the wood trim lining the hallway and up the expensive wallpaper. If something wasn't done soon, the fire was going to eat through the walls and grow out of control.

N-Dig was coming apart. He didn't know what to do. Behind the wheel, he was a racing phenomenon, but when faced with a real problem on his feet, he was as hapless as a Hawaiian hockey player.

There was no way he was going to put out the blaze.

Another loud crash, this time from further down the hallway. One of the smaller planters had toppled onto its side as fire consumed the thick foliage. It created a wall of flame between the young man and the front door, blocking him in.

The fire was already taller than him, and rising faster than a magic beanstalk. The heat was unlike anything he'd ever felt.

N-Dig's thoughts immediately turned to self-preservation. He spun around, kicked open the stairwell door and ran through it.

***

Harry was charging through the hallways of the fourth floor, desperately searching for an open office and a computer. He'd also felt the building shudder, so he knew he didn't have much time. If he couldn't complete the money transfer now, it was never going to happen.

He quickly found what he needed. He turned the computer on, and then grabbed a chair and took a seat while he waited for it to boot up. His foot tapped impatiently as the machine cycled through its various start-up files, displaying the results as a scroll of text on the monitor. The wait was interminable.

Finally, the operating system finished loading, and the main window came up. Shaking with anticipation, he gently nudged the mouse to one side, moving his cursor over the icon that connected to the building's network. He clicked it.

For a moment, nothing happened. Harry slammed his fist against the desk, furious. He thought he'd been lied to.

After a beat, the computer whirred to life, and his cursor switched from an arrow to an hourglass. A few seconds later, the window for the main network flashed on the screen. It looked exactly as Harry remembered it. He sighed in relief.

Time to get to work. His original plan had been to carefully and thoroughly hide his crime by breaking up the stolen money into smaller accounts and covering his tracks with fraudulent paperwork. There was no time for that anymore. He had to transfer all the money into his Jamaican account as fast as he could.

It was a risky move that put a big target on his back. There was a chance someone would notice it was missing before he was out of the country. The account would be frozen, the transaction cancelled, and he'd never get any of that money. However, if he could get to his bank in Kingston before they found out, he was confident he could launder the money properly. It wasn't a great plan, but it was his only chance.

Harry accessed the files for the firm's accounting department and opened them. He searched through the list until he found the application that connected him to the international bank accounts.

He smiled deviously as the program loaded. Within moments the screen displayed a listing of accounts in bank branches around the world. He scrolled through the numbers, looking for the three-digit code that represented Norway.

He quickly found the one he was looking for and clicked on it.

The computer lagged for some time before the financial information appeared. When it finally did, Harry's heart sank.

These numbers were all wrong. The account balance was over thirty thousand dollars off from what it had been just two hours previous. Something didn't add up.

Harry clicked over to the account history. According to these figures, there hadn't been a transaction in almost six weeks, something he knew to be inaccurate. He felt his blood pressure rise as he opened a new window and checked a different account. Same thing - no activity for two months. He began grinding his teeth, seething.

Scrolling back to the main window, Harry right-clicked his mouse and chose the "SEARCH" option from the drop-down menu. He looked through the preference pane until he found the icon marked "MOST RECENT." He clicked it, and a huge list of files was displayed on the screen. The newest was modified over a month ago.

He realized he'd been duped. This network had to be a fake, some kind of old backup system or something.

It was over for Harry Bockner. His embezzlement scheme had collapsed like a tower of Jenga blocks, and couldn't be salvaged. The old lawyer was never going to get his hands on that money. Worse, since he hadn't falsified any paperwork, it was inevitable that the authorities would discover his crime. He would soon be a fugitive, and would have to flee the country with whatever money he could secure that night. It might last him a month or two, if he budgeted conservatively.

Harry felt a spark of anger flash into being. It quickly grew within him until he thought he was going to burst from the sheer agony of it. His face turned a dark shade of red as that anger turned to rage.

Furious, he grabbed the computer monitor with both hands, pulled it off the desk and flung it against the wall. It fell to the ground with a thunk, twisting the screen's bezel but otherwise remaining intact. He ran over and smashed his heel against it, cracking the LCD panel like a thin sheet of ice.

He was apoplectic. Harry had never felt outrage this extreme before. There was only one word for it: hatred. Those who ruined his plans would soon feel his wrath.

He ripped the radio from his belt and turned it on. He took a deep breath before he spoke.

"You must think I'm pretty stupid, Bryan," he said flatly. "You thought I wouldn't notice, right? Well, let me tell you something, you son of a bitch, I didn't get to be the top lawyer in this firm by letting assholes like you scam me. I warned you, I am not a man to be fucked with. If I were you, I'd find a place to hide."

"What the hell are you talking about?" Buff answered, confused.

"You know exactly what I'm talking about! The network is a fake!"

"No, no, no. That's impossible. Mr. Bockner, my people are the best. If they say it's working, then it's working. You must be doing it wrong. Did you try restarting your computer?" There was a tinge of contempt in Buff's voice.

Harry fumed. "I'm coming for you, Bryan," he said with enmity. "I'm coming for your whole goddamn team. None of you are getting out of here alive, but I'm taking out that mouthy little bitch first." The way he said the words was chilling.

"No, please, Mr. Bockner, don't..." pleaded Buff, stuttering. Harry heard the fear in Buff's voice. It was genuine, and made the old lawyer smile.

"You had your chance, asshole," Harry continued, coldly. "Before the night is over, I'll make you beg for your life... and I'll say, 'no.' You picked the wrong day to rob from the wrong goddamn law firm."

The radio made a rude squawk and clicked off.

***

The tiny bit of elation Buff got from the team's progress through the vault door was quickly deflated by Harry's threats. It was taking a physical toll on him. He had a pounding headache, and after moving the drill into place, his arms were sore and his back ached. He needed to rest, but there was no time for such luxury.

He was worried about the rest of his team, and turned to Marcus.

The old man and Fou were hovering around the industrial drill like moths around a lightbulb.

"What should we do?" Buff asked him.

"Eh, b'y?" Marcus said. "Ya get this massive thing into position, and then ya power through what's left of the door. Ya should know this, me chum. It was yar plan."

"No, Marcus, I mean about this guy with the gun."

"That figger? Toss that catch overboard, me son. He's not worth the trouble. Now get over here and get through that colliwoggin' vault!"

"Marcus, he's going to kill them," Buff pleaded. "He already took out Big Frank and the Fodder brothers. We have to do something."

The old man rolled his eyes, annoyed. "She's not me problem, bud. Ya seems to be the only one who even knows anything about him." He turned away and knelt beside the drill, tightening the diamond-tipped bit into place. He hummed contently as he did it, unconcerned with the safety of the others on the team.

Buff sighed loudly and walked out into the hallway. He paused a moment, searching for the right words, and then addressed everyone over the radio.

"I assume everyone heard what that madman said," he said, a tinge of anger in his voice. "We can handle this. I want everybody to get back upstairs. Doug, is Beka still with you?"

There was a pause before he answered.

"Uh, no," Doug said hesitantly. "No she's not."

"What?" Buff yelled. "Why not? Where is she?"

"I'm stuck in the server room," she said.

"Stuck? What do you mean? How'd you get stuck?"

"I locked her in," Doug said sheepishly.

"You what?" Buff roared, incredulous. "Why the hell did you do that? What's wrong with you?"

"I knew it was you, you son of a bitch!" Beka screamed.

"Hey, she kicked me out first!" Doug protested.

"I don't care!" Buff spoke with authority. "Get her out of there! Now!"

"I know, I know," said Doug. "I'm on it."

"That was very unprofessional, the both of you," Buff said. "If we make it out of here alive, I'm never hiring either one of you again. Look, everybody, get your asses up here as soon as you can. If we have to take him out, we'll take him out as a team. Keep your guns out and the safeties off. If you run into him on your way back up, shoot to kill."

After a beat, the sound of Harry laughing cackled out the radio.

"I won't be hard to find," he said with an aggressive tone, "but I promise that I'll be the last thing you see before you die. And make no mistake, every one of you will die tonight."

***

Doug didn't like Beka. He used to, but tonight verified those feelings evaporated a long time ago. She could be so insistent, so pushy, so opinionated it drove him mad. He couldn't imagine what he ever saw in her. Still, he didn't want to see her hurt by some crazy old man with a gun.

He fumbled with the RFID scanner in his hands, trying to unlock the server room. The device made a low hum, like a subwoofer hitting a deep bass note. It was having trouble getting a reading, because Beka was pounding on the other side of the door like a hurricane. The whole thing shook and rattled wildly, and Doug could hear her shouting obscenities at him.

"Goddammit, you son of a bitch!" she yelled. "When I get out of here I'm going to rip your balls off with my bare hands!"

Doug tried to ignore her. He'd already pleaded with her to be quiet and stand back from the door, but that just made her scream louder. It was enfuriating, but he had to admit he deserved it. He shouldn't have locked her in.

For an instant, he thought he'd successfully unlocked the door, because he heard a loud thump. He quickly realized the noise was behind him, coming from the emergency stairs.

Without a second thought he dropped his tools and ran over to the stairwell door.

"Hey! I can hear you running away, you bastard!" Beka screamed, muffled behind the server room door. "Where the hell are you going? Get back here!"

Her voice faded away as he pushed the door open and cautiously walked into the stairwell.

Right away, Doug heard N-Dig beneath him. The getaway driver was rushing upwards, sloshing through deep puddles as he climbed the stairs.

Thinking it was Harry, Doug immediately whipped out his gun.

He glanced over the railing, but couldn't see who was running up towards him. He wasn't willing to wait and find out.

He flicked off the safety and started shooting, firing two blasts down the stairs. Unprepared for the weapon's powerful kick, Doug was knocked back three feet. He stumbled to keep his footing.

Both shots bounced off the walls, creating clouds of dust and leaving giant round pockets in the concrete.

The bullets whizzed past N-Dig, missing him by several feet. He jumped back down the stairwell and dove into the corner.

N-Dig couldn't see anything above the stairs in front of him, but he was convinced it was Harry that was shooting at him.

Without hesitation he pulled out his gun and aimed it up the stairs. He fired three shots without looking.

Doug and N-Dig entrenched themselves into safe positions and continued to blast away blindly. Neither had the slightest idea who they were actually shooting at.

The area filled with the sharp, tumultuous sound of intense, rapid gunfire like popcorn popping, but exponentially louder. Blazing metal pellets sliced through the air at unimaginable speed, ricocheting off the walls and dancing around the stairwell. The smell of gunpowder was thick.

Doug fired another three rounds in N-Dig's direction.

He responded by shooting back four times.

Neither of them hit anything but concrete.

Feeling lucky, N-Dig jumped up one set of stairs with two strides and rolled into the corner.

Another shot rang out. N-Dig felt the warmth of the bullet's wake dart past his ear.

Instinctively, he spun around, raised his gun and fired twice.

The bullet connected, striking Doug in the fleshy part of his thigh, just above the knee.

The boy let out a piercing, high-pitched shriek as his lower limb ruptured open, causing searing pain. Muscles snapped, skin was torn and bones cracked. Blood was bubbling out like a broken drinking fountain.

He threw the gun down and clamped his hands over the gushing wound, moaning like a toddler stung by a bee.

N-Dig heard his cries, instantly realized his mistake and lowered his weapon.

"Doug?" he shouted up.

"N-Dig?!" Doug cried back, between guttural screams. "Is that you? I'm hit."

"I'm coming up."

Wasting no time, N-Dig ran up to the second floor landing.

There he found Doug hunched in a ball, with his leg sticking out at a sharp angle as if he were doing some strange yoga position. He was cradling his wound and crying in horrible pain.

N-Dig was overcome with grief. He quickly put his gun away and knelt down beside the man he shot.

"Oh Jesus!" he said, full of sincere regret. "I'm sorry, bro. For real."

"You stupid bastard!" Doug cried through gritted teeth. "You shot me!"

"Bro, I'm sorry. I thought you were the guy."

"Do I look like the guy, dickhead?"

"I couldn't see you, bro, I just heard the shots. It was friendly fire. Believe."

"'Friendly fire?!'" Doug raved. "Shooting at someone is inherently unfriendly, N-Dig! What do you do with people you don't like, huh? You stupid prick!"

"Hey, you were shooting at me, bro!"

"I wasn't aiming for you!"

Doug's eyes were wet and his voice was cracking, as though trying not to cry. Sprawled out on the floor, he looked and sounded like a child who fell off his bike. He was wincing and moaning.

"Ah Christ, it hurts, it hurts. It hurts!"

The pain was unbearable. It felt like he had a red-hot billiard ball inside his thigh, pushing its way out. He couldn't hold back the tears anymore, and started to sob.

N-Dig felt horrible about what he'd done, but seeing Doug in this helpless state, he had to stifle a laugh. The men he usually hung around were made of sterner stuff.

"Come on, man," he said. "You'll be fine, bro. We'll patch you up good, for real. Let me take a look."

Doug hesitantly moved his shaking hands away from his leg, revealing a squishy, pulpy crevice covered by a ragged flap of skin. It was grisly and nasty, a mess of wet flesh and sinew, as if he'd spilled a meaty pasta sauce on his leg. For a second, N-Dig thought he saw bone.

Gobs of blood spurted out in wound. It was definitely bad.

The only experience N-Dig had with gunshot wounds was the one he'd received earlier that evening. As far as he could tell, Doug's was much, much worse.

N-Dig ripped the arm off his hooded sweatshirt. He wrapped it like a tourniquet around Doug's leg, just as Buff and Marcus had done with his shoulder. He tried to tie a knot in the fabric, which is extremely difficult with only one healthy arm.

Doug screamed loudly when N-Dig tightened it.

"Careful!" he cried.

"Relax, bro," N-Dig said. "This will stop the bleeding. I know exactly how you feel, man. Believe." He nodded to his own wounded arm. "It'll be better soon, bro. It won't stop hurting, but after a while it won't kill so bad. For real."

Doug was growing pale and sweating heavily. He grabbed N-Dig's good arm and pulled him in closer.

"Sorry I was shooting at you, dude," he said, softly.

"It's alright, bro. I'm sorry I shot you. Believe. I'm really sorry. I've never shot anyone before."

"No worries, dude. I've never been shot before."

N-Dig looked back down at Doug's injury. It was bleeding like an oil tanker with a hole in the side, and he quickly realized that a single tourniquet wouldn't be enough.

He grabbed his pants and ripped off the bottom of the right leg.

He was wrapping it around Doug's wound when both of them heard a loud metallic clatter coming from the landing above them.

It was deep and resonant, like a metal trashcan dragged along a cement floor. It sounded like something big and heavy was being pushed out into the stairwell. The racket was impossible to ignore, and getting louder.

"What the hell is that?" Doug said, worried.

N-Dig put his finger over his lips and turned towards the noise. He stood up, carefully took three steps, and craned his neck upwards.

Even standing on the tips of his toes, he couldn't see anything.

One second later, the terrible noise suddenly stopped.

Thinking he'd been spotted, N-Dig ran back down beside Doug. The two men looked at each other, holding their breath. They waited for a tense moment, expecting the stairwell to erupt in gunfire.

Those blasts never came. Instead, if they listened very carefully, they could just barely make out a soft, high-pitched whine, the kind that metal makes as it is stretched to its breaking point.

There was a snap, and then suddenly a roaring clatter. It sounded like dozens of paint cans being thrown from a moving car, and it seemed to be coming towards them.

N-Dig stood up again and finally saw the source of the commotion: there was an enormous Xerox photocopier barrelling down the stairs. Harry was behind it, gleefully pushing the thing like a battering ram.

Propelled by its own weight, it was racing downhill as fast as a stone sinking in water. The photocopier was just the right size to slide between the railings and swing around the corners without losing much momentum.

N-Dig's mouth dropped.

Moving without thinking, he raised his arm and fired at it three times.

The first bullet buried itself deep in the machine's belly, ripping apart its plastic shell. The other two bounced off its metal frame and flew off like sparking embers. Harry was well shielded from gunfire behind the chunky photocopier.

It collided with the wall, rebounded back and careened around the corner faster than ever. Ten more steps and the heavy machine would be on top of the two young men.

In a flash, N-Dig leapt down and wrapped his arms around Doug's chest. The injured man screamed in horrible pain.

N-Dig didn't have the patience to reason with him.

"Come on, bro! Let's go! Move!" he yelled.

Doug wasn't moving fast enough. Without waiting for his help, N-Dig lifted him up off the ground and violently carried him backwards, out of the photocopier's path.

Doug's wounded leg was dangling limply, dragging along the ground like tin cans behind a newlywed couple's car. It was dead weight, anchoring him in place and slowing them both down.

The photocopier bounced around the last corner. It was hurtling down the last set of stairs at tremendous speed when the front caster snagged the edge of the top step.

Harry jumped back. The machine shuddered in place for a second, and then bounced up over the stairs. The huge, heavy thing was flipped upside-down and soared through the air.

For an instant, time slowed to a crawl. The two men watched helplessly as the bulky photocopier floated above them.

N-Dig dropped Doug and dove out of the way.

Doug fell to the floor and gasped, as he suddenly realized his time was up.

A heartbeat later, time resumed to normal, and all five hundred pounds of the photocopier came tumbling down onto him, crushing his legs.

He let out a shrill, piercing howl, with the ferocity of a teething baby.

Just as the photocopier came to rest, N-Dig jumped back onto his feet and brandished his gun. He swung his body around the crumpled machine, giving him a clear shot of Harry.

He pulled back the hammer and prepared to fire.

In a flash, Harry leapt at N-Dig with his arms out. He flicked his wrist, and the collapsible baton he'd stolen from Kane telescoped out to its full length with a loud snap.

He swung the baton in front of him, and it connected with N-Dig's hand.

The pistol was knocked to the floor, and then slid over the edge of the landing and dropped to the bottom of the stairwell.

The blow opened a stinging gash in N-Dig's hand, but before he could react, Harry battered him again. He smacked his baton against the young man's wounded shoulder three times in quick succession, and followed that up with a vicious belt across his jaw.

N-Dig fell to the ground like a bag of dirty laundry. Blood gushed from his mouth and nose, drowning out his harrowing screams.

Harry took a step back and pulled out the Kahr PM40 handgun he'd taken from Dwayne. He took a shooter's stance and aimed it at the young man.

"Freeze, asshole!" he roared. "One move and I park a quarter ounce of lead in your forehead!"

N-Dig weakly held up his hands in surrender.

Harry glanced over at Doug, who was clearly unconscious. He didn't appear to be breathing.

Another one down. Harry's ego swelled. He smirked and puffed out his chest.

"Where's the girl?" he demanded, pushing his gun into N-Dig's face. His voice was quivering with anger.

"I don't know," N-Dig said, meekly.

"Wrong answer, pal."

The old man cocked his weapon.

N-Dig began waving his arms wildly. "No! No, bro, please!" he pleaded. "Don't shoot me, man. She should still be in the server room. I think she was locked in, but I don't know. Honest. Believe!"

"And the others? How many are there?"

"I have no idea, bro! I don't know any of these people! For real! I don't know who's alive and who's dead. I don't know what the plan is. I don't know anything! I'm just the driver, bro! Believe!"

Harry took a few steps forward and shoved the barrel of his gun against N-Dig's nose. The young man closed his eyes, swallowed hard and held his breath.

"Where are they?" he asked menacingly.

"I don't know!" the young man screamed. "I think they're on the top floor, okay? I mean, they're supposed to be. For real, bro, I'm telling you. That's all I know. Just please don't shoot me, man."

A mischievious smile formed on Harry's face, and he started to laugh maniacally. He pulled the radio from his belt and clicked it on, all while keeping his gun on N-Dig.

"Hey, Big Bryan, my buddy!" he said into it, with swaggering condescension. "I'm making friends down here! You should come and join the party! Bring some beer, though. Your pal with the dreadlocks is looking mighty thirsty. The other one, though, that dorky looking guy with tattoos, he won't be able to make it. Ever again."

"Dammit, Harry, let him go!" Buff's voice screamed, distorting through the radio's tiny speaker. The frustration in his voice was palpable. "He's just a kid!"

"Well, thanks to you, this kid is never reaching manhood. Any last words for him?"

"For Christ's sake, Harry! What the hell is wrong with you? He's got nothing to do with this! If you've got a problem, you come and face me, man to man."

"Soon enough, asshole. And unlike your friend here, I'm going to kill you very slowly."

Harry clicked off his radio and shoved it back onto his belt.

"Get up," he told N-Dig, waving the gun in his face.

The young man cringed. He hated being told what to do.

"What for?" he asked.

The response was a swift bash to the face with the butt of Harry's weapon.

"I said 'get up!'" the old man screamed.

N-Dig shook his head and spat out a wad of blood. Anger rose up inside him like seasickness on rough waters. He was through being bossed around. He was no longer afraid, and looked right into Harry's face.

"No," he replied, firmly.

"What did you say to me?" Harry's eyes went wide and his nostrils flared.

"I said no, bro."

Harry pushed the barrel of his gun into N-Dig's forehead, with enough force to leave an imprint.

"You're taking me to that server room," he growled, "and you're getting that bitch to open the door. Your life depends on it."

"No," N-Dig growled back.

As quick as a frog catching a fly, his left hand shot up and grabbed Harry's wrist, twisting the gun towards the stairs. The old man gasped in shock.

"I have had enough!" N-Dig shouted, spraying spittle in Harry's face. "I was just supposed to be the getaway man, bro. For real. I wasn't even supposed to come into the building. Now I've got a damn bullet in my shoulder! All night long I've been taking orders, been told what to do, but now I'm sick of it, man! Believe! If you have to shoot me, then you go ahead and you shoot me! Otherwise, I'm leaving."

He pushed Harry away, hard. The trigger on the old man's gun snapped, and the pistol made a hollow click.

The lawyer had been bluffing. He was out of bullets!

N-Dig shot up off the ground as though he'd been struck by lightning. He blasted two quick jabs into Harry's ribs before delivering a decisive upper cut.

The old man's knees buckled and he collapsed.

As he fell, he flailed out and caught hold of N-Dig's pant leg.

He wrapped both arms around the young man's calves in a bear hug, and clung on as tightly as he could. N-Dig tried shaking him off, batting at the top of Harry's head with his fists.

The old man rolled onto his side like an alligator caught in a snare, and N-Dig fell on top of him.

Despite their age difference, the two were pretty evenly matched. They traded several blows, rolling and wrestling violently on the floor.

It was nearly a stalemate, until Harry managed to get on top of the young man. He had his hand up under N-Dig's chin, and was pushing against his windpipe.

Gagging loudly, the young man wrapped his hands around Harry's head and dug his thumbs into the old man's eye sockets. He squealed, gnashing his teeth.

They were both straining as hard as they could, hoping the other would submit first.

Seconds away from losing consciousness, Harry forced himself to raise his arm, and jammed his elbow into N-Dig's wounded shoulder as hard as he could.

Instantly, all the muscles in the young man's body tensed and seized. The pain was strong and severe. It felt as if hot lava was shooting through his veins, and he was burning alive from the inside. His face turned bright red, and he screamed so loud his teeth shook.

Harry grabbed the side of N-Dig's head, clutching a handful of dreadlocks by their base. He pounded the young man's head against the ground, smashing it into the concrete until his scalp split open.

Groggy and dazed, N-Dig felt more of his senses slip away with each blow. His face was covered in blood, pouring out the wound in his head and gushing from his nose, mouth and ears. He tried to fight back, but was too weak to strike a connecting hit.

Harry pulled back, raised his fist and threw a punch hard enough to bruise his knuckles.

The young man stopped resisting. His body went limp.

Exhausted but determined, Harry grabbed N-Dig by the legs and slowly dragged him to the edge of the steps.

N-Dig tried to scream, but all that came out were a few murmurs. His dreadlocks were draped over his face, a matted mess of blood and sweat. Darkness was enveloping and swallowing him, like a landslide devouring a mountain road.

The last thing he saw was Harry's boot smash against his cheek as the old man kicked him over the edge.

The beaten young man's body dropped through the empty space between the stairs. He soared for just a moment, before his head collided with a metal railing. It made a thunk and bounced off with a tiny burst of blood and pulp. His body twirled backwards, spun in midair and landed on the ground floor with a chilling squish. N-Dig was dead.

Harry took a second to lean over the railing and make sure the kid was dead.

Satisfied, he swivelled around and focused on Doug.

The poor young man looked like a cartoon character, with his bloody torso sticking out from under the battered photocopier. His eyes were closed and his skin was pale. His chest didn't appear to be moving. He looked dead.

Harry smiled. That was another two dead bad guys. He was losing count of how many he'd killed, and feeling really satisfied with himself. He was seriously considering putting out an ad in *Soldier of Fortune* when this was finished, and taking on a second career as mercenary. He obviously had the skills.

He was exhausted, panting like a threatened animal. He took a few moments to catch his breath and bask in his victory, and then turned his attention to the server room.

He grabbed the empty gun off the ground, kicked open the door and ran down the hall. He was going to get into that room or tear it down trying.

Beka was still inside, and she was terrified.

She wasn't exactly sure what was going on, but she knew it wasn't good. When she heard gunshots and the jarring noise the photocopier made, she started barricading the door. She jammed a chair under the handle, and stacked everything that wasn't nailed down in front of it.

When she was finished, she grabbed a heavy piece of shelving that she could wield like a club, if necessary. She held it tightly and cowered in the corner, like Jamie Lee Curtis at the end of *Halloween*.

She grabbed the radio from her pocket and frantically pushed the button to transmit.

"Hey, uh, guys?" she said, nervously. "There's something going on down here. It sounds like somebody's fighting Mechagodzilla out there!"

"Just stay in the server room, Beka," Buff yelled, although she could barely hear him. His voice was drowned out by the horribly loud, crunching squeal of the industrial drill.

"I can't hear you," she cried.

"I said 'stay in the server room.' That door is three inches thick. As long as you keep it locked, nobody's getting in. There's a reason we had to bring Doug along. Just stay put. We're almost finished up here."

"What?!" she yelled, incredulous. "'Listen, you don't understand. I think that guy killed Doug, or least took him out back behind the woodshed and stomped on him. Either way, not good, and I'm pretty sure he's coming for me next! You guys have got to help me!"

She waited a moment, but no response came.

"Hello?" she pleaded. "Buff? Anyone? Hello?"

Again, no answer.

"Screw you guys!"

Frustrated, Beka threw her radio against the opposite wall. She shuffled back deeper into her corner, holding the makeshift club close to her chest.

She watched the door jitter and shake as someone pounded against it from the other side.

It was Harry, who was battering it with his fists. He tried kicking the door handle with the heel of his shoe, but it slipped away harmlessly. He was thrashing like a dog that needed to be let outside. He screamed until his voice went hoarse.

"Open the door!" he yelled. "I know you're in there! Do you hear me? Open the damn door right now!"

There was no answer, which just made his anger boil hotter.

"If you don't open this door right now, I'm going to break it down and kill you, asshole!"

He kept punching it until his hands were bright red. The door made a hollow thud with every hard smack of his fist, and he wasn't making so much as a dent in it.

He couldn't get the thing to budge. Doors like this were built to withstand earthquakes. Harry realized trying to punch his way through like The Incredible Hulk was a pretty futile move.

He looked around the hallway, and suddenly remembered something he'd seen while raiding the janitor's closet. There was a bright red fire axe in a glass case hanging on the wall.

He turned and ran towards it like a kitten to catnip.

He smashed out the glass with his elbow and pulled out the axe. It was slick and shiny, lightweight and easy to swing, weighing less than the typical axe you'd use to chop firewood.

Harry twirled it once in the air. It felt good in his hands.

He marched back to the server room door, limping slightly and grunting the whole way. He looked like the serial killer in a bad slasher movie, dragging the axe's blade along the floor behind him.

When he reached the door, he took a lumberjack's stance in front of it, holding the axe with two hands.

"Last chance, pal!" he screamed, stomping his foot. "Little pig, little pig, let me come in, or I'll huff, and I'll puff..."

Without finishing his rhyme, he furiously swung the axe against the door.

It connected with a resounding clang, leaving an impressive gouge in the metal frame.

Harry laughed maniacally, reared back and swung again. All his rage was poured into tearing down this door. He was beyond reasoning with.

Inside, Beka could feel his intensity. The door was quaking as though hit by a wrecking ball. She knew her barricade wouldn't hold up for long.

She held her wooden club tighter.

Harry took another swing, but this time it went wide and got caught in the doorframe. The metal caved in, and the door cracked as it broke away from one of the hinges. The whole thing heaved outwards slightly, as all the weight of Beka's barricade pushed against the other side.

Inside the server room, Beka let out a piercing scream. She threw her hand over her mouth to muffle it.

The hinges were the door's weakness. A combination of regular usage and poor maintenance had caused the metal to soften slightly, enough to crumble under a few sharp hacks from a strong axe. Harry grinned maliciously.

"I'm coming!" he yelled. "In just a few minutes you'll be just as dead as your friends out here!" He laughed again.

A few more hearty swings of his axe at the base of the doorframe, and the second hinge snapped.

The door heaved a few inches more.

Beka was really freaking out now. She began to shake uncontrollably. Tears were streaming down her cheeks.

The door was creaking and moaning as the last hinge struggled to hold Harry back.

He swung the axe in just the right spot three times, and finally the hinge shot off faster than a bullet. The door collapsed to the ground with a loud thump, like a drawbridge being lowered. All the furniture and shelves Beka had used to block the door tumbled out into the hall with a noisy crash.

Harry kicked the junk aside, using the axe to clear a path like an explorer chopping through jungle brush.

Beka screamed again. She jumped to her feet, wielding the flimsy piece of shelving in front of her.

"Get away from me!" she cried.

Harry whipped out his unloaded handgun and aimed it at her.

"Drop it!" he yelled.

She hesitated.

"I said 'drop it!'" he yelled again, louder this time. He followed up by pulling back the hammer on the gun.

Beka threw the piece of wood to the floor and raised her arms.

"Well, well," Harry said, lasciviously, "You're cuter than you sound on the radio. What's with the hair, sweetheart? Do you do magic tricks at birthday parties?"

"Kiss my ass," she said, defiant.

"Not a good idea to piss off the man with the gun, lady. If I were you, I'd be trying to think of a reason why I shouldn't kill you. You lied to me about the computer network." His face curled into a devilish smile. "I don't like it when people lie to me."

With a gun aimed at Beka in one hand and an axe in the other, he started slowly walking towards her. He raised the axe and wiggled it in her face.

"Get away from me, you psycho!" she yelled, pushing herself as far back into the corner as she could go. "I'm not lying to you. The servers are fried! Look at the wires everywhere, dude. I tried to fix it!"

"I bet you'd work a lot harder if I hacked off your foot, you bitch!"

He lunged forward and pushed her to floor, hard. She screamed as she collapsed. Harry pinned her to the ground with his foot.

"Hold still," he said, raising the axe up over his head. "This will only sting for a minute!"

Just as he was about to slam the fire axe down on her leg, a thunderous gunshot rang out. A blistering hot bullet whizzed through the air and struck Harry in the left cheek of his buttocks.

He cried out in pain and dropped the axe.

Both he and Beka turned to see a half-dead Doug, sprawled out on his belly in the hallway, with a smoking pistol in his hands.

His legs dangled lifelessly behind him. He looked like a piece of roadkill, bruised, bloodied, barely breathing and covered in open wounds. Somehow Doug had pushed the oppressive photocopier off of himself, crawled to the server room, and used his last ounce of strength to shoot Harry.

"Go! Run!" he tried yelling to Beka, but it came out as a grumble.

Doug's eyes fluttered long enough for him to see Harry wailing in agony, clutching his ass with both hands. He smiled and let his head fall to the ground, exhaling loudly. The gun fell from his limp fingers.

The old man was down, but not out. The shot had only grazed him. While he was overcome with pain for the moment, he'd soon be back up on his feet with a bad limp and a worse attitude.

Beka seized the moment and darted past him, running out of the server room.

She went to Doug and crouched beside him.

His breathing was shallow. He probably had only a few minutes left.

"Doug?" she asked, softly.

His right eye batted open and glanced at her. He smirked.

"I still hate you," she said, smiling.

"I know," he replied.

They looked at each other one last time. A thousand conflicting emotions swirled together inside both of them.

Beka gave him an appreciative nod.

Doug smiled, and then his eyelid flittered and closed.

She got to her feet and glanced quickly to Harry. He was already trying to stand up again.

Without looking back, she ran down the hall as fast as she could and slammed through the door to the stairwell.

Harry was woozy, drunkenly lumbering back and forth as he tried to find his balance. He groaned loudly and deeply, like an injured sea lion. His backside prickled painfully, as though he'd sat on a barbecue grill.

After a few minutes, his head stopped spinning and he regained his senses.

He looked over to Doug and clenched his teeth together. Now he had someone to focus his fury on.

"Nice shootin', Tex!" he yelled, taunting the young man.

Harry reached down, picked the axe up off the ground, and shuffled over to Doug's inert, prostate body. The young man looked cold and lifeless. Harry kicked the gun out of Doug's reach and then squatted down beside him.

"Look at you, big man!" he said, mocking. "The piece of shit that refused to be flushed. You're like that damn Energizer bunny. You've got some big lead balls, kid, but shit in your brain."

Doug didn't move.

"Hey! You still with me, pal?"

Harry nudged the young man's body with his foot, and a strained gurgle escaped Doug's lips. His eyes opened like slits, and he groaned. He wasn't dead yet.

"There you are!" the old man said, smiling. He waved the blade in front of Doug's face, causing him to recoil in terror. "Good morning, sunshine! Not so tough with an axe in your face, huh?"

He put his foot on the dying boy's chest and pushed down, hard. Doug squealed, which made the old man laugh.

"I have to tell you, kid, I'm a damn good lawyer. They used to call me 'Harry the Hammer.' I'm mean and meticulous, ruthless and thorough. I don't just prosecute people, I destroy and devastate them. When I'm through, they are ruined, both financially and mentally. But, I don't take any pleasure from it. Ever. Maybe a little professional pride, sure, but never any pleasure. It's just business."

He leaned down closer, getting right in Doug's battered face.

"With you, though, kid, this is personal." He flashed a venomous smile and got back to his feet. "You can scream if you want, but it won't help. If it's any consolation, though, from now on I'll probably think of you every time I try to sit down."

Harry raised the axe up over his head. Doug shut his eyes and winced.

"Say goodnight, asshole!" the old man screamed as he brought the heavy blade down against Doug's shoulder. The young man's neck split apart like a melon, and a burst of wet red pulp sprayed out in all directions.

***

Beka was running down the stairs at full speed, with one hand on the railing to guide her to the ground floor. Her feet slapped against the concrete steps as quickly and loudly as a Neil Peart drum solo. Her heart was racing even faster, threatening to burst right out of her chest.

She got to the bottom of the steps and stopped suddenly, nearly tripping over N-Dig's twisted, mangled corpse. The young man's body was bent around itself like a pretzel, and his neck jutted out at an unnatural angle. Half of his head had caved in and spilled out all over the floor.

Beka threw her hand up over her mouth. She was too shocked to scream.

She closed her eyes, steadied herself, exhaled deeply, and calmly walked over to the door.

After she grabbed the metal doorknob, her hand instinctively pulled back. It was hot.

She paused a moment, confused, and then pressed her palm against the door. It was like touching one of those cast iron radiators found in old apartment buildings.

Beka took a few steps back. She took a breath, and then ran into the door at full speed, shoulder-first.

It burst open to reveal a towering wall of flame engulfed the entire lobby, stretching from the floor to the ceiling. It was all burning -- the furniture, the plants, the artwork, everything. Plumes of black smoke billowed into the stairwell, stinging her nostrils.

Beka glanced back up the stairwell. In a blink she made her decision. She would rather face the fire and risk burning alive than retreat one foot closer to that armed madman.

She dropped to her knees and crawled out into the lobby, carefully keeping under the acrid smoke. In grade school, a local fireman visited her class and explained what to do in case of a fire. All these years later, those lessons were finally coming into play.

The fire was hungry, angry, and uncontrollable. Beka was doing her best to avoid the flames, which roared like a hungry lion. The blaze flickered and danced wildly around her, constantly moving hues of deep reds, glowing copper, and molten gold. She felt her skin roasting under the intense heat, as though she were crawling through a potter's kiln. Her clothes were quickly soaked through with sweat.

Sparks crackled and popped around her. She scuttled across the floor like an infant, shuffling on all fours through the inferno. Flames were darting out and reaching for her from every angle, but she managed to dodge the most severe by moving quickly.

Her head darted around looking for the front door. Everywhere she looked, the only thing she could see was fire, raging intensely and growing larger by the second.

Beka panicked. She was lost.

She lurched forward blindly, and her hand stumbled over something round and metal. It was blistering hot with sharp edges.

She jerked her hand back. There was a nasty burn at the base of her hand, and her palm had been sliced open. Blood trickled out and ran down her arm.

Looking down, she saw the source of her injury: it was the umlaut from the law firm's name, the one that hung on the wall in shiny silver letters. The fire had caused it to pop off the wall, and then tarnish and blacken in the scalding heat.

Beka didn't have time to treat the wound. She needed to get out of there fast, and she needed to keep moving.

Since the title on the wall was located at the far side of the lobby, she made a split-second deduction. The front door was likely behind her. Based on that hunch, Beka turned herself around one hundred eighty degrees and bounded forward like an unleashed dog.

Every time her wounded hand touched the ground was agony, like sharp iron spikes driven up her wrist and into her arm. The poor girl was living inside a nightmare, but it would not slow her down.

The hellfire threatened to swallow her with every step, but she was just too fast. She was like the hero at the end of every action movie ever made, outrunning a massive fireball in slow motion.

Before she realized it, she slammed up against the front door. Her knees skidded to a halt, sliding through countless tiny shards of broken, shattered glass. They dug into her skin, and she cried out.

The roaring inferno drowned out her screams.

Summoning incredible inner strength, she fought through the pain and found the hole in the door. She wearily stood up, her knees buckling and straining. Blood poured down her calves from dozens of punctures, many of which still had hunks of glass protruding from them. The pain was overwhelming, unlike anything she'd ever felt before.

She steadied herself, inhaled once and shut her eyes.

This is going to hurt, she thought.

In one smooth, acrobatic motion, Beka leapt up, dove through the hole in the door and rolled in midair. She landed on the hard cement path with her upper back, avoiding the worst of the broken glass, and kept rolling.

When she came to a stop, she started coughing and couldn't stop. Between the smoke inhalation, the exhaustion, the terror, and having the wind knocked out of her from the tumble, it took her quite some time to regain her breath.

Beka looked like she'd just lost a fight with a cougar. Her face was covered in cuts and scrapes, and her limbs were littered with horrible bruises, wounds and gouges. Her hair was singed and matted to her forehead, while her clothes were tattered, charred and dripping wet with perspiration. She was the girl at the end of a horror movie, the one who survives the ordeal and is victorious over the masked killer.

She slowly, painfully got back up onto her feet. She tried to stand straight, but her tense, seizing muscles forced her to hunch over at an uncomfortable angle. She looked back, watching as enormous flames leapt out from the front door and licked the side of the building. It produced a warm orange glow that lit up the night sky. This fire was now raging out of control, like something out of an Irwin Allen movie.

Beka thought for sure the building would be destroyed. She doubted there was any way the others on the top floor could safely get out now. As awful as this evening had been, she wasn't so cold as to leave the others stranded. She had to warn them.

She reached down for her radio. It wasn't there, and suddenly she remembered tossing it against a wall in anger. She kept searching her pockets until she found her phone.

It wasn't getting a signal. Beka couldn't believe that Doug's cell blocker could still be functioning. She smacked the side of it with her palm. When that didn't work, she tried hoisting it into the air for better reception. She looked like Prince Adam with his sword over his head, transforming into He-Man. Unfortunately, the phone still refused to work.

Beka stuffed the phone back into her pants. She would call 9-1-1 as soon as she could get a signal, but first she'd have to find a way out of here. There were no buses out this far west, and she certainly couldn't walk back downtown.

She turned towards the parking lot, where she saw N-Dig's rusty old Ford Focus sitting idle. She feebly limped over to it, shaky but resolute, with a glint of hope in her eyes. That beaten down old car was her salvation, her light at the end of the tunnel.

Throwing herself against it, she peered down through the driver's side window. The keys were still in the ignition.

Beka smiled and sighed in relief.

With her good hand, she opened the car door and sunk into the seat the way an overworked farmer climbs into bed. She turned the engine on and listened to it purr.

She turned her head and took a final glimpse of the law offices of Bennett, Olsen, Nygärd, Jørgensen, and Holm. Her smile grew wider, feeling a twinge of glee as the building burned like Chicago in 1871. If she'd had a fiddle with her, she would have played it.

Instead, she threw the car into first gear and slammed her gas pedal down to the floorboard. Her tires squealed loudly as she tore out of the parking lot.

***

The noise from the industrial drill was deafening, making an unbearable whining, scraping, crunching commotion. It sounded like giant nails were being dragged across the world's largest chalkboard. The tip of the diamond drillbit chewed through the vault's metal plating at a steady pace, spitting out tiny bits of alloy no bigger than a grain of sand.

Marcus stood directly behind the drill, carefully guiding it into place. He wore big plastic safety goggles over his eyes and a look of assurance on his face. He looked like a grandmaster chess player, lost in concentration and focusing deeply on the next move.

Buff stood with Fou in the corner of the room. They were both covering their ears, wincing at the terrible racket.

The floor around the drill was littered with big piles of metal shavings. Some were almost three inches high, which they all took as a clear indication that things were progressing along nicely.

Buff was starting to get anxious. He palms were sweating, and his heart was racing a little faster. It had been a long time since he'd cracked a safe. He had no doubt he could still do it; safe-cracking is one of those skills you never forget, like riding a bike. If anything, the idea excited him. His own eagerness scared him a little.

Buff waited as long as he could, but eventually the anticipation was too much for him. Like an impatient child during a long car ride, he felt the need to ask "are we there yet?"

He walked up behind Marcus and tapped the old man on the shoulder.

Marcus stopped the drill's motor. He turned to Buff, slipping off his goggles and pulling an orange foam earplug out of his ear.

"She's a real beauty, eh b'y?" he said proudly, motioning to hole as though he were marrying it. "Look how clean that bore is, me son! This thing's a true marvel of engineering, chum. She's cutting through 'er like a breaker through nish ice."

"How much longer do you think it'll be?" Buff asked.

"Tough to say, b'y, but she won't be long. Things are goin' faster than I thought they would, me chum. A quick drash ought to do it, and we'll be through 'er directly. Maybe another ten, fifteen minutes, b'y."

"Good."

Buff smiled and patted Marcus on the back. It had been a horrible night, but there was a chance they'd get through this thing unscathed.

Marcus nodded and turned back to the drill, putting his eye and ear protection back on. He powered the motor back up, and within seconds the room filled with the enormous machine's ear-splitting howl.

The blaring clatter was rattling Buff's teeth. He felt another pounding headache creeping up on him. After fifteen seconds, he couldn't stand it anymore, and turned to leave.

He walked over to Fou.

"Stay here," he said. He had to yell in his ear to be heard over the drill's drumming. "Don't talk. Don't move. Don't touch anything."

Fou smiled and nodded, stifling a yawn.

Buff walked out the vault room and down the hallway, rubbing his temples. The horrible drilling sound faded the further he went.

He was like an expectant father in the waiting room, restlessly pacing back and forth. Anxious and jittery, he twiddled his fingers and ran them through his hair to busy himself. The anticipation was killing him. He wanted to get into that vault and get this job over with.

Suddenly, his radio chimed on.

"Hey Bryan! Better hire more bad guys!" It was Harry's voice, but not the calculating, persuasive lawyer he'd spoken with most of the night. This man sounded deranged and unhinged.

Buff stopped dead in his tracks.

He was incensed, but hid it well. He unclipped his radio and brought it up to his mouth.

"What did you do?" he asked.

"Exactly what I said I would, pal. I warned you not to mess with me. I told you to get that computer network working again. I told you to stay out of my way. You didn't listen. Now, they're going to be cleaning your friend with the glasses off the wall with a sponge for months. His buddy with the dreadlocks doesn't look much better."

Buff exploded in rage, kicking the wall as hard as he could.

"What the hell is wrong with you?!" he screamed. "Those people didn't do a thing to you. The only reason they were even down there was to try and get that damn computer network turned back on for you. We tried to help. I did everything you asked me to do, you son of a bitch!"

"Well, you did a shitty job!" He cackled loudly. "Look, I'm the hero here, pal. You're the gang of thieves breaking into our vault. I'm just a concerned citizen trying to make a difference."

Buff took a long, deep breath before replying.

"I'm going to kill you, Harry," he said, coldly.

"What was that, Bryan?"

"I said I'm going to kill you. This is your last night in this world. You will not live to see tomorrow. I will find you, I will break and twist things inside you, and then I will be the last living thing you ever see. You are going to die screaming. Soon."

"Oh, I didn't realize I was dealing with Charlie Bronson here! Tell you what, tough guy. Let's see what you've got. I'm on my way to the top floor right now, and I'm looking for you, Bryan, but I'm not going to kill you, at least right away. No, I'm just going to hurt you as severely as I can while keeping you conscious. I will beat you so bad you won't believe it, even while it's happening. You'll wish your father had pulled out early. You'll be picking up your teeth with broken fingers, and when it's over, I will knock you down and beat you again."

"I'm waiting, asshole. Just say when," Buff replied, flicking his radio off.

# 9:30pm

About a kilometre away from the office building, Beka pulled into the parking lot of a small gas station and parked the car. She was still in shock, quivering as if taking a cold shower. Her hands were gripped tightly around the steering wheel. It took her a few moments to compose herself.

She pulled her phone out of her pocket and tried dialling 9-1-1. Her hand shook uncontrollably, and her fingers fumbled over the keypad. She was in such a panic that she could barely dial the right numbers.

She put the phone to her ear and listened to it ring. She tapped her foot anxiously.

"Come on, come on..." she mumbled impatiently.

Finally, a pleasant young man answered.

"9-1-1," he said, flat and direct. "What is your emergency?"

"I need a fire truck on Matheson Boulevard," Beka yelled, clearly agitated. "There's a building on fire! You have to hurry!"

"Which building is that, ma'am?"

"The big one. The law offices of Bennett, Olsen, and... and, I don't know, a bunch of random Swiss guys. You can't miss it. It's the tall building with flames coming out of it."

The last remark made the clerk chortle.

"Okay, ma'am," the man continued, "emergency vehicles have been dispatched to the scene. They should be there right away." Beka could hear him typing away madly at a keyboard as he spoke.

Beka leaned forward, resting her forehead against the steering wheel, and breathed a sigh of relief. She felt as though a huge weight had suddenly been lifted from her shoulders.

She clicked her phone off, quickly wiped away any fingerprints, and then tossed it out the window. Since it could connect her back to the heist, she didn't dare keep it on her anymore. She felt a twinge of regret, since she had an impressive high score in Tetris saved on that phone.

The car grumbled loudly as Beka started the engine. She took a deep breath and smiled. It was finally over.

She drove away and never looked back. This night had been the single worst experience of her entire life. She vowed to herself from that moment on she would never take a job she couldn't do from bed in her pyjamas.

***

Marcus was standing behind the drill, pushing all his weight against it and forcing the diamond-plated tip deeper into the steel door. The vault was starting to show some resistance, making the heavy piece of machinery shudder and squeal. The drill bit was shaking like an epileptic on the dance floor, shooting out grey, acrid smoke.

The old man eased the machine back, and then gently poured coolant along the edge of the bit. It made a soft hissing sound as the liquid splashed onto the hot metal.

He knew he was really close. Most safes are constructed with several layers of composite materials to hamper any attempts to break into them. This particular Strongbox model included a layer of tar to fill the room with smoke if someone tried to cut into it with a torch. Marcus had already breached that, as well as the layer of copper plating intended to dissipate heat. He was almost all the way through the safe door.

The drill had pierced through to the vault's penultimate layer: the "hard plates" barrier. These were composed of high-density metals, stitched together in a manner designed to eat boxes of drillbits. Luckily, that huge explosion had burned most of it away. There was less than an inch left, and years of experience had taught Marcus the proper techniques to chew through these hard plates without much difficulty.

He pushed the end of the drill back into position and slid the bit into the hole he'd bored. The machine whirred and grinded for a minute or two, and then jerked back suddenly. It had finally pushed through the hard plate.

Marcus flicked the drill off and peeled off his goggles, letting them dangle around his neck. He took a quick inspection of the vault door, and then clapped his hands and cheered, excited.

He turned to Fou. The young man was still standing in the corner, expressionless.

Marcus ran up to him and slapped him on the shoulder. Fou flinched. For a second, he thought the old man was going to really hit him.

"Show us a smile, me b'y!" Marcus laughed. "This ain't no funeral. We're almost there!"

Fou stared at him with an incredulous, confused expression. He watched the old man dance out the door and down the hall.

Marcus found Buff dragging heavy pieces of furniture out of the executive office and pushing them to the emergency stairs. He already had a big couch and two high-backed leather chairs stacked in front of the door.

"Lard t'underin'!" the old man exclaimed. "What in the hell? Why is ya redecorating this place, me chum?"

"I'm blocking the door," Buff replied. "He's coming up here."

"Who's that now?"

"Have you not been paying attention? Remember Harry Bockner, the lawyer who's been systematically killing off everyone on our team? Yeah, he's on his way up."

"That ol' dog ain't mucked off yet? He's some cracky, eh b'y? He's got yar nerves rubbed right raw, me cocky! Ya ain't scared of that ol' fart, is ya? We can gives him a crack, b'y!"

"Tell that to Big Frank and the Fodders."

"Aye. Point taken, b'y."

"I'm not afraid of him, but I sure as hell don't want to get dragged into some stupid fight with him. I'm not going to let this asshole ruin my life a second time. I just want us to get into the vault and then get out of here."

"Well then, me son, yar in luck! That's exactly why I comes to see ya. We drilled through all the metal plates, chum, and we just hit the glass re-lockers. She's been cleared out, b'y. I done all that I can. The rest of 'er is on yar shoulders, me b'y."

"Already?" Buff sounded surprised and excited. "Why didn't you say so? Let's go!"

He jumped up and ran down the hall, with more energy than he'd shown all night long. Marcus followed closely behind him.

They ran back into the vault room and got on either side of the drill. Buff waved Fou over. The three of them grabbed a corner each and dragged the enormous machine away from the safe. It groaned as it moved.

With the space clear, Buff bent his knees and put his eye next to the bored-out hole in the door. He pulled a small flashlight from his pocket and began examining it.

Marcus and Fou both stepped back to let the master work his magic.

Looking down the small tunnel, roughly an inch and a half wide,

Buff could see the vault's glass re-lockers on the other side. This is a device common in all high-end safes. It's a simple pane of glass behind the hard plate barrier, with four heavy, spring-loaded re-locking bars attached to it by a cable. In theory, when the drill bit strikes the glass sheet, it shatters. This starts a chain reaction, causing the re-lockers to shoot out, blocking the vault's bolts and making it four times harder to break open.

As Buff examined the glass re-lockers on this Strongbox, he found that, miraculously, the glass hadn't even been scratched. He had to admire Marcus's work. Truly, nobody handled a drill better than him.

Buff reached into his bag of supplies and began pulling out his safe-cracking tools. After slipping on a pair of latex gloves, the first thing he grabbed was a can of compressed air, which he aimed into the hole in the door. He gave it a few squirts, blowing out the excess metal shavings and ensuring that he had an unobstructed view of the glass re-lockers.

The next piece of equipment he used was a long, thin aluminum tube, about ten inches long. It was hollow, with one end encircled by a black plastic suction mount. There was a thin rod along the outside of the tube that would tighten the mount and lock it into place.

Buff carefully inserted it into the hole so that the end with the suction mount pressed up against the glass. Shoving it in as far as it would go, he held it steady with one hand, and then pulled back on the thin rod with the other. He felt the metal tool securely brace against the glass pane. He pulled both hands away slowly and cautiously, and the tube held firm.

Reaching into his bag, Buff pulled out another aerosol can. It was filled with compressed tetrafluoroethane, an inert gas most commonly used as a refrigerant in air conditioners. Upon vaporization, it absorbs a considerable amount of thermal energy, meaning it significantly lowers the temperature of any object it contacts as it evaporates. It gets cold enough to inflict frostbite on exposed skin.

Buff slid the can's nozzle into the free end of the metal tube and squeezed the trigger. A powerful blast of frosty, frigid air shot out the end and filled the hole in the vault.

The glass fogged up and instantly froze through to the other side.

After a quick inspection, Buff set the can aside and pulled out a smooth, thick metal rod. It had been machined to fit inside the aluminum tube perfectly, like an electrical plug into a socket. He wiped it down with his sleeve, and then delicately slid it into place.

Once he was confident he had it aligned just right, he took a deep breath. He only had one shot at this next step, so he had to get it right. Closing his eyes, he wished for the best. He cupped the rod's exposed end with his palm and slammed it forward with as much force as he could muster.

It made a soft, empty crack. Buff pulled the rod out of the tube, and blew out the hole with compressed air. A shower of cold shattered glass shot out. He knelt down, examined his work, and smiled.

The operation had been a complete success. He'd made a perfect hole, slightly bigger than a penny, right through the glass while still holding the pane intact. It went straight through to the lock's tumblers.

Marcus and Fou looked at each other, smiling. They were suitably impressed.

Buff reached into his bag and pulled out a specialized, expensive-looking borescope. It was long and thin, and looked like a kitchen utensil. There was a flexible black tube with an eyepiece on one end and an objective lens on the other, with a bundle of relay optical fibers linking them. It was originally designed for inspecting aircraft engines and industrial turbines, which meant that the tube was small enough to fit into the most inaccessible spaces.

He slid the end with the lens into the bored-out hole. Through the eyepiece, he had a clear, intimate view of the safe's locking mechanism.

Buff grabbed a set of metal pliers from his bag. They were smaller than the kind found in an ordinary hardware store. The tongs on them were almost two feet long, and as thin as a yo-yo string. The ends came to a sharp point.

He carefully slid those into the hole in the vault, jamming them under the borescope.

This was the moment of truth. Everything had been leading up to this.

Buff cracked his knuckles and got to work.

Leaning down, he peered into the eyepiece and kept his attention focused on the locks. Wedging the pliers against the top of the tumblers, he was able to spin them clockwise. Through the borescope he could see exactly where to position the lock's tumblers so they would align and click into place.

He felt an overwhelming wave of excitement wash over him. The tips of his fingers tingled as he gently nudged the locks into place, one micrometre at a time. His heart started racing, as though he were kissing a girl for the very first time.

This is what Buff was best at, and he'd missed it. It filled him with indescribable satisfaction. Nothing could compare to it. It had been a long time since he felt this sensation, but he recognized it instantly.

The first three tumblers popped into position with little effort. The fourth and last proved a little more difficult, as it was set further back in the lock. Buff had to really strain to get the pliers in deep enough to guide the flat metal disc into place. After some struggle, he was able to finally get it aligned with the others.

The lock made a deep, loud click. Buff felt it shake in his hands.

He pulled out the borescope and stepped back. The immense metal door slowly swung open.

Marcus threw his fist into the air and cheered. He turned to Buff and smiled, giving his old protege an appreciative slap on the back.

"That's some fine work ya done there, me son," he said.

Buff felt a swell of pride in his chest.

Together they stepped through the door and walked into the vault. Fou casually jogged over and followed suspiciously close behind them.

The inside of the huge metal Strongbox was larger than an apartment in Tokyo. The walls were lined from floor to ceiling with shelves of varying sizes. Unfortunately, they were mostly empty.

As the three men looked around, their hearts sank. The vault was way too big, considering what had been locked inside. There were no jewels or gems, no cash, and no bars of gold. Other than some original, unframed Norwegian artwork, it looked like the only things in there were stacks of legal files.

Buff pulled a few pages out of a pile, passing a couple over to Marcus. He looked them over.

Fou sidled up behind him and leaned over his shoulder, reading the paperwork with great interest. Buff ignored him.

It appeared to be accounting ledgers, but neither Buff nor Marcus could understand any of it. Not only was the math too complicated, but all the pertinent information was written in a foreign language as well.

Buff flipped through a few more pages. It was all gibberish.

"What the hell is this? Swedish?" he yelled.

"Norwegian," Marcus replied. "These are bank records, b'y. This is all financial paperwork. Looks like what we gots here is a copy of every transaction the Norwegian mob's made over the past three years, me son."

"Bank records!?" Buff exclaimed, dumbfounded. "What the hell do the French want with a bunch of Norwegian bank records?"

"Gots me some vexed, b'y. If I had to flice a guess, I'd say that ol' goat Jacques wants a gock at what the Norwegian mob's been haulin' in."

"Corporate espionage? Really?" Buff let out a snort of disgust and threw his handful of papers into the air. They slowly fluttered to the floor like huge snowflakes.

Fou reached down and scooped a few of them up, scanning through them as quickly as he could.

"I can't believe this!" Buff continued to rant. "Jacques lied to me! He told me we were looking for evidence the Norwegians had that could get him put behind bars for life! All he wanted to know was how much fucking money they have!"

"Well, me b'y, I think there's a lot of things Jacques didn't tell ya."

Out of nowhere, Marcus whipped a handgun out of his pocket and aimed it at Fou. He fired without hesitating.

The undercover officer was shot square in the throat, severing vital arteries and shattering the spinal cord just beneath the skull. The wall behind him was instantly repainted with his blood. He was dead before his hefty corpse hit the ground.

Buff nearly jumped out of his skin.

Before he could react, Marcus had the weapon trained on him, aimed right between the eyes.

"Don't move, me son," he said, coldly.

Buff's mouth hung agape. He was speechless. He couldn't think. His brain refused to consider that Marcus would betray him like that. He looked like a deer caught in the headlights.

"Surprised, eh?" the old man said with a sinister laugh. "I tells ya, b'y, the look on yar face right now almost makes it worth all the malarkey ya put me through tonight."

"Marcus," Buff stammered, helpless, "what the hell have you done?"

"Hey, ya did this to yar own self, b'y! Ya got the devil to pay and no pitch hot, me cocky, so I be taking advantage of 'er. As they say, it's not everyday that Morris kills a cow, eh?"

Buff was even more confused now.

"Huh?"

"I had me a meeting with yar ol' pal Jacques last night, me son, and I told him everything. I told him about Fou, I told him about the FBI, and I told him about all the other deals ya got wrapped up around this heist without telling anybody. He was not too happy with ya after that, b'y, but he was pretty happy with me. Loyalty's important to the man. He agreed to pay me a hundred grand to finish the job, so long as once the safe was cracked I put a bullet in Fou's head... and then another one in yar head, b'y."

Buff held up his hands and took a slow step backwards.

"Marcus, please, don't..."

The old man had zero sympathy.

"Sorry, Buff," he said with a smirk, raising his gun. "Take care."

Before he could fire, Buff did the only thing he could and threw the borescope in Marcus' face.

The old man instinctively jerked to one side to avoid it. His finger inadvertently tensed around the trigger, and a powerful blast rang out.

The shot went wide, burying itself in the wall behind Buff's head.

Buff dove to the ground and scuttled behind the drill. He used the massive industrial machine to shield himself, pressing himself against it tightly. He desperately wanted the pistol in his pocket, but couldn't reach for it without exposing himself.

Marcus took another shot. It caught the top corner of the machine and ricocheted off into the ceiling.

He ran forward three short strides and tried swinging around the other side of the drill.

Anticipating this, Buff shoved his leg out into the old man's path. It snagged his foot, and Marcus fell forward.

The old man let out a loud groan as he collapsed.

Buff instantly reared up with his other leg and kicked Marcus square in the face.

A fat spurt of blood flew out the side of his mouth as his head was knocked backwards. The gun flew out of the old man's hand, slid across the floor and came to rest in the far corner.

Before Marcus could recover, Buff got to his feet, pulled out his handgun, and aimed it at his old friend.

His finger danced along the edge of the trigger, eager to squeeze.

Looking down his gun sight, he watched the whimpering old man struggle for breath. Marcus had been his mentor for over thirteen years. He was closer to him than his own parents. He'd learned from him, trusted him, and considered him a close friend. Even though Marcus had just tried to kill him, Buff couldn't bring himself to fire.

He flicked the safety on and stuffed the gun back into his pocket. Fighting back an army of conflicting emotions, he took a final look at his former companion and then sprinted out of the vault room without looking back.

Buff quickly realized he was trapped on the top floor. All of the elevators were out of service, the stairwells were locked down, and he'd blocked the emergency stairs with office furniture. He had nowhere to go.

In a panic, he ran into the executive office and slammed the door shut.

He got behind the massive wooden desk in the middle of the room and pushed. It groaned loudly, sliding at an awkward angle. The thing was unspeakably heavy. Buff's muscles strained to move it.

He managed to get it within five feet of the door when it shuddered to a halt. The front corner snagged on the carpet.

Buff pushed harder, shaking the desk. It wouldn't budge.

No, not now, he thought. Not now!

He ran around to other side, grabbing the bottom edge of the desk. Flexing like an Olympic weightlifter, he pulled up with all his might and nudged it up over the lip in the carpet. He let go, and the desk came crashing down like a tree falling in the forest.

He dashed across the top and got behind the other side, pushing it flush against the door.

Buff was out of energy, but he forced himself to continue. He knew Marcus well enough to know that a single desk wouldn't stop him.

Summoning reserves of strength he didn't know were there, Buff ran around the room, grabbing furniture and throwing it in front of the door. Three chairs, a computer, a small end table, and a large bookshelf all became part of the barricade.

He finished just in time. As he threw one last chair onto the pile, he heard Marcus come barrelling down the hallway and smash against the office door.

"Open the door, Buff, me chummy!" the old man screamed. "I wasn't really going to shoot ya. Let's talk about this, b'y!"

Buff was trapped inside. Worse, for the first time that night, he was scared. He couldn't believe Marcus had actually fired at him. When it happened, there was a deranged look in the old man's eyes that he'd never seen before. He was no longer the same man Buff had respected and looked up to for so many years.

He glanced around the office. It was a single room with no closet. There was nowhere to hide. They were eight floors up and there were no balconies, so he couldn't go out the window.

He looked up and saw a large air vent above the desk, just big enough to fit through.

The very thought of climbing through it made his already-swollen muscles throb with pain, but he had no choice. It was his only exit.

Marcus kept pounding against the door with his fists.

"Come on, Buff!" he yelled. "Let me in, b'y! This ain't what ya think!"

Buff climbed onto the desk and jumped up. He managed to grab the vent on his first attempt and rip it from the ceiling. He threw it aside.

He felt the desk shimmy beneath his feet. Marcus was now ramming a large coffee table into the door, over and over again. With a little time and effort, he would breach the office.

With no time to lose, Buff spit into each hand and rubbed them together. He placed his feet shoulder-width apart, anchored them firmly, bent his knees, and jumped.

He soared up and caught the bottom ledge of the opening with both hands. He dangled for a second, grunting, and then pulled himself up into the vent like a groundhog climbing into its burrow.

It was tight and cramped. The air vent was only about three feet wide and less than two feet tall, which meant there was barely any room to maneuver inside. The darkness didn't help things, either. The ventilation system was lit as well as the inside of a cow's gut.

Regardless, Buff carried on, squeezing himself through the narrow vent as fast as he could. He wriggled his shoulders from side to side, and pushed himself forward with his feet. It was slow moving, but he was steadfast. The vent's walls were cold, unfinished sheet metal, which scraped against Buff's arms and knees as he moved. The flashbang grenade in his pocket, the one he'd taken off Big Frank's corpse, was digging into his hip.

A strong breeze of cold air blasted him in the face. Instantly his skin constricted, and a rash of goosebumps broke out over his arms. It was just one more discomfort that Buff didn't need.

He didn't know where he was going, and didn't have a plan. All he knew was that if he wanted to stay alive, he had to get out of this building.

He put his head down and kept moving.

***

After several minutes of struggle, Marcus got the office door to open just a crack. He continued battering it, making the hole bigger, and then wedged a table leg into the gap and tried to pry it open. Even then it wasn't wide enough to climb through, and he had to push against the door to shove the desk aside.

It was a squeeze, but he was eventually able to wiggle his way into the empty office.

There was no sign of Buff anywhere.

Marcus saw the cover for the air vent lying on the floor. It was misshapen and broken, as though it had been ripped from the wall.

He looked up, saw the hole in the ceiling and realized how Buff escaped.

He cursed loudly. The old man knew he wasn't strong enough to climb up into the vents himself. Those days were long past him. If he was going to take out his old friend, he was going to have to find another way.

Marcus was very angry, but he didn't scream, kick furniture or throw a tantrum. Instead, he leaned back against the big wooden desk and carefully considered his next move.

He thought about it for a few minutes, and then grabbed his radio.

"Hello?" he said into it, cautiously. "Mr. Bockner? Are ya there? I want to speak with ya, me chum."

"Who the hell is this?" Harry answered, confused and angry.

"Sir, my name is Marcus, and I gots an offer I want to make ya."

"Either you're making fun of me, Marcus, or you've got one hell of a speech impediment. Where the hell is Bryan?"

"There's been a change in leadership, Mr. Bockner. I'm the b'y who's calling the shots from now on, me chum."

"That's funny, because it looks to me like you're not calling jack shit. You think you can smooth talk your way out of this, pal? I've got five dead assholes here who think differently."

"Mr. Bockner, I ain't the uptight figger ya been gabbin' with all night. I ain't trying to talk ya into nothing, b'y. Our goals are the same, me chum. I don't want ya to change a single thing yar doing. What I want to do is offer ya ten thousand dollars, and all ya gots to do is kill Buff, which ya says ya were already goin' to do, eh b'y?"

"Excuse me?" Harry said, stunned. "Let me make sure I understand you, buddy, because most of what you just said sounds like gibberish. You want me to kill your partner? Why?"

"Don't ya worry about that, b'y. I gots me reasons. So, me cracky, do we have us a deal or not?"

There was a long pause as Harry considered the offer.

"Well?" Marcus asked, impatiently.

"Give me a second to think," Harry said defiantly. "You're not exactly winning me over by rushing me, pal."

"I don't care, b'y," Marcus snapped, "because I don't have the time. Right now ya have three options. Ya can leave the building and get nothing, kill me and get nothing, or kill me ol' buddy Buff and get ten thousand dollars. The choice is yars, me son."

Another long pause. Marcus worried that Harry wouldn't cooperate.

"Have you got that money in cash?" Harry asked.

Marcus smiled.

"Of course, me chum," he answered. "More than enough."

"Good. Where is he?"

"He was up here on the top floor, but he just crawled up into the air vents, so the li'l figger could be anywhere in the building by now."

"I'll find him. Have the money ready."

Marcus heard the radio click off at the other end.

As he walked back to the vault room, a warm feeling of satisfaction came over him. He was going to come away from this heist the big winner. He imagined Jacques would be very proud of him, and would offer him a regular job. Maybe even make him a made-man.

He wore a joyous grin as he resumed picking up the banking paperwork off the floor.

***

The air vents were no place for a claustrophobic. Luckily, Buff had no such fear, but it didn't take long before he started to feel the walls constrict around him. It was nothing but a very long, very narrow, very dark corridor that seemed to stretch to infinity. He couldn't see the far end, or even a few feet in front of his own face. It was pitch black.

Buff crawled through the ducts at an agonizing pace, inching along like an earthworm in a drinking straw. It was gruelling work. His shoulders were sore, his back ached, and the skin on his knees was rubbed raw. Despite the constant breeze, sweat was pouring down from his brow, and he could barely twist his arm enough to wipe his face.

After a few minutes, he collided with a metal panel, head first.

He'd reached a fork in the road. The air duct branched off to the left and the right.

Buff had no idea where he was or where he should be going. He assumed he'd been dragging himself eastward. He knew the vents all dumped out into a maintenance room on that same floor, and he was fairly certain it was in the southeast corner.

Following that logic, he went right.

By the time Buff realized what a horrible mistake he'd made, it was too late.

There was a sudden, eight-foot vertical drop in the shaft, and he unknowingly pushed himself right into it. He screamed as he fell.

He hit the bottom of the air duct with a heavy thud. He heard plaster wheeze and crack, and then suddenly crashed through the seventh floor ceiling.

Buff landed on a pile of old painter's trays with a violent clatter. Shards of cheap, crumpled plastic shot out. Giant globs of thick, half-dried paint were sent flying in all directions, splattering against the floor and walls. An enormous cloud of drywall dust was kicked up, filling the air with a chalky white powder.

Pain shot through Buff's body like billiard balls after a break. The sting was bold and blinding, as though flaming charcoal were grinding into his spine. He rolled over onto his back and splayed out on the ground, loudly groaning in torment. He stayed there for several minutes, trying not to move, waiting for the throbbing misery to subside.

He was in the middle of a dark and lifeless hallway. This part of the building was under serious renovations, so everything was covered in plastic sheets and canvas tarps. Several walls were missing, with just the bare wood frames showing. Almost every corner had some stationary power tool tucked into it, from table saws and drill presses to grinders and sanders. There was also a variety of hand tools and building supplies strewn about the floor.

Once the pulsating, stabbing pain receded, Buff grabbed a stray desk chair and used it to pull himself onto his feet. He still ached all over, but he was pretty sure he hadn't broken any bones. His only concern was his need to keep moving, and to get himself out of this building.

He reached for his handgun and slid out the magazine. He still had plenty of ammo.

At that moment, Buff suddenly heard something in the distance. It was a crunchy, whirring sound.

With his weapon drawn, he silently crept as quickly as he could down the hallway, chasing the noise. Sensing a trap, he moved carefully, checking each office until he reached the doorway of the last one. The sound was coming from just around the corner.

Buff tensed, and then spun towards it.

He found a lonely 12-inch mitre saw spinning noisily. It was sitting in the corner of a big open room, partitioned into three sections with wood framing. This was clearly intended to be three separate offices once all the construction was finished.

Buff relaxed for a moment, grinning at his own nervousness. He was about to go and turn it off, but he stopped himself.

Someone had to turn that thing on, he thought to himself. Harry was on this floor! The old man was probably trying to lure him into an ambush. Well, Buff wasn't going to fall for it. He may not have been much of a Kenny Rogers fan, but he did know when to walk away and when to run.

He took two big, slow steps backwards.

Suddenly, another loud buzzing noise started up behind him. He turned and saw an industrial disc sander whirring vigorously. One by one, machinery around the room was turned on, adding to the grating, jarring mechanical orchestra. The noise was deafening. The old man was using the noise of the heavy machinery to cover the sound of his movements.

Buff swallowed nervously, feeling surrounded. The gun trembled in his hand as he held his position, darting his eyes from side to side. He knew Harry was in here somewhere. He strained his eyes, desperately looking for some sign of movement, but couldn't see anything through the darkness.

He couldn't think straight, either. The coarse rattling of all the heavy tools was too distracting. His heart was racing.

It suddenly hit him: the circuit breaker panel! It was the only place Harry could possibly get all those machines turned on. He wasn't exactly sure where it was located, but figured it was in the maintenance room

Instantly he darted around and scampered down the hallway.

He was within a few feet of the maintenance room when Harry suddenly burst through the door. Buff narrowly avoided colliding into him.

The old man looked like a walking Jack Davis cartoon. His hair was matted, his clothes were torn, and he was spattered with blood from head to toe. He was hunched over and standing awkwardly. In one hand he held the gun he'd stolen from Doug, and in the other was his trusty fire axe, dripping gore. He had a crazed, homicidal glint in his eyes, and wore a terrifying smirk.

"Where do you think you're going, pal?" Harry barked.

Without waiting for an answer, aimed his weapon at Buff and fired.

Harry was a half-second too late. Buff dove to one side and rolled into an empty office, while the shot ricocheted off a support beam and sailed off into the ceiling.

The office was missing two of its walls, and had no furniture in it. There was nowhere for Buff to hide. He jumped through the empty frame and scrambled into the next room.

Harry followed closely behind him, firing another two shots. They both went wide. The sound of the blasts was muffled slightly by all the machine noise.

Buff charged towards the only cover he could see – a stack of drywall, piled over four feet high. He clumsily leapt behind it to safety.

The old man skidded to a halt a few feet away and unloaded his clip. A half-dozen shots of blistering hot metal plunged deep into the gypsum board, sending chunks of plaster flying. Buff felt every impact, but was unharmed.

Harry squeezed the trigger again, but it clicked empty.

He angrily threw the gun aside, and then grabbed the axe handle with both hands and raised it over his head.

"Hold still now," he growled. "This won't hurt a bit!"

Screaming loudly, he rushed straight at Buff.

The younger man jumped up, held out his gun and fired, striking the old man square in the belly.

Harry was knocked backwards several metres. He fell into a pile of construction supplies, screeching in pain as he collapsed. Boxes of screws were knocked over, spilling hundreds of tiny metal pieces across the floor. Spools of electrical tubing crashed to the ground and rolled away.

Blood spewed out of Harry's wound in thick spurts. He clamped down on it with both hands, dropping the axe at his feet.

Buff calmly walked towards him, with the firearm aimed squarely at his chest. The old man was trapped.

As he watched Harry squirm and cower at the end of his gun barrel, he savoured every second. It filled him with a sense of supreme satisfaction. He'd been waiting years for this moment.

"One move and you're a stain on the carpet," he threatened, pulling the hammer back on his pistol. "You have no idea how long I've been looking forward to this, Mr. Bockner."

Harry spat out a mouthful of blood.

"Why?" he asked angrily, with a raspy voice. "Because I killed your friends? You stupid son of a bitch. That was self-defence, pal. I didn't take down anyone who wasn't coming at me. If you don't like it, you need to find a new line of work."

"Oh, no. You don't understand. I've wanted to kill you for years." He took a step forward and waved the gun in Harry's face, taunting him.

The old man didn't look scared; he just looked confused and befuddled.

"Huh? You did all this just to get back at me?"

"Don't flatter yourself," Buff snorted. "It was just a happy coincidence."

Harry shook his head in disbelief.

"Who the hell are you?" he asked. "What did I ever do to you?"

Buff walked right up to Harry and smacked him in the face with the butt of his gun.

The old lawyer's head was knocked back with a powerful force. He grunted loudly.

"You stole two years of my life, you son a bitch!" Buff cried, spraying spittle as he shouted. "I only had one charge! One stupid, insignificant break-and-enter charge. I should have been in and out of jail in a couple of months, at the worst. But you, you ugly piece of puke, you had to insist on a harsh sentence! You took everything from me!"

Buff had screamed himself hoarse. Without taking the gun off Harry, he put his free hand on his knee and slumped down. He was exhausted, and his head was pounding.

He could see the old man was racking his brain, trying to recollect where they'd met before. It was obviously in a courtroom, but Harry worked on so many cases over the years, they all seemed to bleed together. He tried, but couldn't come up with anything.

"Hey, I was just doing my job, pal," Harry said with a shrug.

Enraged, Buff marched over and hit him again, harder this time. Harry's head rocked back and bounced off the hardwood floor.

"That's what pisses me off the most!" Buff snarled. "You don't even care! You don't remember me. You have no idea who I am. I was just another billable hour to you. You've probably ruined the lives of hundreds of people over the years and never given any of them a second thought, because you thought you were 'just doing your job.'"

Harry tried to laugh, but choked on some of his own blood.

"You're right," he said, wheezing. "I don't remember you, and you know what? I don't care. It was your fault you got arrested. I'm supposed to feel bad for you because you went to jail? You're a damn criminal, you asshole. You're the bad guy! Don't do the crime if you can't do the time, pal. I'm glad I ruined your life, you whiny son of bitch. I'd do it again for free."

Buff was in an enraged fury, ready to end Harry's life, when something the old lawyer said struck a chord with him.

Wait a minute, he thought to himself. I'm the bad guy?

In that instant, Buff suddenly realized what kind of a person he wanted to be. He'd come out of prison determined to turn his life around. However, if he killed Harry, there would be no going back to a normal existence. He would be committing to being a criminal for the rest of his life.

Harry hadn't ruined Buff's life, but instead shown him the value of his freedom. If anything, the old man ruined his own life by being a miserable, unsympathetic jerk.

Buff no longer wanted to hurt him. He didn't feel any ire towards Harry at all, only pity. This horrible, wrinkled old fart was a man without empathy, and so full of anger and animosity and self-righteousness that he couldn't let anyone else have an inch. In his mind, if he didn't get the biggest slice of the pie, nobody got to eat any. Mr. Bockner wasn't worth wasting a bullet on.

Buff lowered his gun and clicked the safety on.

"You know, Mr. Bockner," he said, calmly, "I've never killed anyone. Even after everything you've done tonight, I don't see a reason to start with you. I'm leaving."

Unlike Buff, Harry wasn't the type to show mercy. He saw an opportunity and seized it.

In one swift motion, he grabbed an open box of nails and flung it at Buff as hard as he could.

Hundreds of small, thin rods of sharp galvanized steel rained down on him. He reacted instinctively, dropping the gun and throwing his hands up over his face.

Harry grabbed the fire axe and jumped to his feet, taking a stance like a baseball player ready for the pitch.

"Now you die!" he screamed, and charged full speed at Buff.

With no time to react, Buff dropped to the floor and reached for his gun...

*Clang!* Harry brought the axe crashing down between Buff and the handgun, just inches from young man's fingertips. He used the edge of the blade to slap the pistol away like a hockey puck after the face off.

Harry reared back for another swing.

Buff rolled to one side, feeling dozens of loose nails and screws dig into his skin. He didn't stop moving until he was well out of the old man's reach.

When he got to his feet, he saw a large sledgehammer with a black steel head resting against a wall frame. He scooped it up and wielded it in front of him like a sword.

Harry ran straight towards him, waving his axe from side to side as though conducting an orchestra. He thrust the blade at Buff, who swung the sledge like an Olympic hammer thrower, smashing it against the axe head and deflecting the attack.

The two men stood in place, assuming the en garde position. They began slowly circling around each other. Harry would shuffle in one direction, and Buff would take a step in the other, maintaining the distance between them.

The two men readied their weapons, steadied themselves and then lunged at each other like fighting dogs.

Harry attacked first, forcefully jabbing his axe towards the young man's throat.

Buff flinched, jumping backwards, and struck back with equal force.

They traded feints, thrusts and parries with the lightning speed of two swordsmen in an Errol Flynn swashbuckler. The room filled with the echoing jangle of tempered steel colliding. The battle was positively ferocious, as the two men bucked, jostled, shoved, pushed, and punched with brutal savagery.

Harry faked left, and then twirled in place, ramming the edge of his axe into Buff's shoulder. The top of the young man's arm was sliced open.

Buff recoiled, wincing.

The old man smirked.

"I'm going to chop you up into a thousand little pieces, you son a bitch!" he taunted.

That half-second he took to gloat gave Buff the advantage he needed. He choked up on his hammer's handle, swung back and roughly poked the butt into the wound in Harry's gut.

The old lawyer doubled over and moaned painfully.

Buff didn't waste a second. He came at Harry with a flurry of hits, battering the old man with everything he had. Harry tried to retreat, but Buff just kept coming, backing him into a corner.

With the old man on the ropes, Buff got ready to deliver the decisive blow. He raised the sledgehammer up over his head as though swinging a golf club, and then brought it right back down as hard as he could, aiming straight for Harry's face.

The old man dodged out of the way the last second.

The hammer's head smashed into a stack of eight windowpanes leaning against a wall frame. They shattered in an epic, teeth-rattling explosion of glass. Shards of all shapes and sizes burst out like water from a broken dam.

Harry grabbed Buff by the wrists and pushed him back. The younger man tried to hold his ground, but they were both knocked into a load-bearing beam, dropping their weapons. Harry took his free hand and wrapped it around Buff. With a tight bear hug around him, he threw his weight back and they both collapsed onto the ground.

The floor was carpeted with nails, screws, and broken windows. It was a dangerous meadow of sharp, thorny fragments of metal and glass, anxious to pierce, poke and stab. Harry and Buff were rolling around atop it like children on a gym mat, punching at each other blindly.

They wrestled like two old grizzlies, grunting and clawing while the ground crunched beneath them. It felt like being stung from head to toe by dozens of bees all at once. They spiralled across the floor from one side of the room to other, occasionally crashing against one of the many chugging, whirring stationary tools.

The fight was taking its toll, as both men were nearing exhaustion. They exchanged half-thrown punches and quick jabs between laboured gasps.

Harry managed to get one hand behind Buff's head. He tightly grabbed a clump of hair and pulled back, hard. When his adversary wailed, Harry socked him right in the nose.

Blood began to pour out Buff's nose. He couldn't breathe, and started to choke.

Reflexively, Buff loosened his grip on Harry. The lawyer climbed on top of him and pounced, pummelling him mercilessly. He dug his fingers into the side of the younger man's head and proceeded to pound it against the floor repeatedly.

Buff flailed his arms out and ruthlessly clapped his hands against Harry's ears. The old man felt them pop loudly. He shot up, arching his back, and threw his arms over his head, screaming. He felt nauseous and dizzy, like being on a boat during an intense storm.

It was enough for Buff to shift his weight, free his leg, and kick Harry in the stomach as hard as he could. The old man flew backwards.

It didn't knock Harry off his feet, but it did put enough distance between them that Buff could scramble to one side and pick up a nail gun off the floor.

An industrial nail gun uses 120 pounds per square inch of force, so that nails come shooting out at over 500 feet per second. The injuries they can cause are often more devastating than a gunshot.

Buff pointed it at Harry and fired wildly.

The first few shots pinged against the floor and flew away harmlessly. However, once he learned how to compensate for the nail gun's recoil, he became as accurate a sharpshooter as Annie Oakley. The old lawyer tried to scramble out of the way, but it was futile.

Buff buried an 18-gauge steel nail into Harry's arm, just above the elbow. The old man screamed so loud the walls shook. Blood dribbled out in thick spurts.

"That one's for Doug!" Buff cried.

He squeezed the trigger a few more times, and another nail shot into Harry's thigh.

"And that's for Big Frank!"

Two more struck the old man in the ankle.

"And those are for the Fodders!"

He fired six more shots, right in the middle of Harry's chest.

"And these are for me!!"

The nails penetrated deep through the old lawyer's breastplate, snapping ribs and tearing flesh. They ripped apart his lungs and heart, shredding them to ribbons. With so many nails poking out of him, Harry looked like a voodoo doll.

The old man screamed like a banshee.

Gravity carried his body backwards, and it collapsed on top of a running table saw. The diamond-cut teeth on the 12-inch blade hooked into the old man's skin and tore through it like wet snow. It chewed him up almost instantly. Bits of bone, muscle, fat, and guts sprayed out in a bloody geyser.

What was left of the old lawyer's body went limp. Harry Bockner was dead, and he died screaming.

It was a horrific scene, more ghastly than any horror film. Harry's corpse looked like roadkill that'd been run over with a lawnmower. The floor was covered in a thick, pulpy slop of gore, as though someone was making a strawberry smoothie and forgot to put the lid on the blender.

It took Buff a minute to catch his breath. He was still reeling from what just happened. He was shaken by Harry's gruesome demise, but wasn't going to dwell on it. It wasn't intentional, and the old lawyer would have done the same to him if he'd had the chance. Buff was just happy to get out alive.

He threw the nail gun aside and brushed himself off. There were little screws and bits of glass all over his body, embedded in his skin. He was weak and weary, aching all over, and looked as though he'd been pushed through a garbage disposal. Every step he took was agony.

The young man walked over to Harry's body and reached into the corpse's pockets. It was a macabre, repulsive task that Buff did not enjoy.

He fished through and found a set of keys for a BMW. He smiled brightly and shoved them into his own pocket.

Satisfied he wasn't going to find anything else, Buff got back on his feet. He hobbled to the emergency stairwell as fast as his ragged, beaten legs would carry him.

# 9:45pm

Things were surprisingly serene outside the law offices of Bennett, Olsen, Nygärd, Jørgensen, and Holm. The bottom half of the building was almost entirely engulfed in flames. Waves of bright orange, yellow, and magenta poured out the windows and lapped at the side of the office, charring it black. Black smoke rose up into the night sky, choking out the stars.

The concrete tower burned silently, except for the sound of sirens approaching from the distance. It sounded like there were a lot of them.

***

Halfway between the sixth and seventh floors, Buff was weakly limping down the stairs. His movements were slow and stiff, as though his joints were rusted. He tried not to think about everything he'd just been through, so he could focus on getting out of the building.

No matter how hard he tried, however, he couldn't shake the image of Marcus pointing a gun in his face. It was something that would haunt him forever. He needed to know why his old friend did it. He needed closure.

When he reached the first landing, he pulled the radio out of his pocket and flicked it on.

"Anybody still out there?" he asked.

There were a few moments of static before Marcus finally answered.

"Oh my Lard, Buff!" he said, in his most innocuous voice. "It's some good to hear yar voice, b'y! What are ya at? How's ya gettin' on? I been worried sick about ya, me cracky!"

"Bullshit," Buff sneered. "You tried to shoot me, you son of a bitch!"

"Easy there, me son. Mind yar tongue. No need for such harsh words, b'y. Yar still alive, ain't ya?"

"Watch yourself, Marcus. Don't get cheeky. I've already killed one old man tonight."

"Ah, so ya did kill that other figger, eh?"

"I did indeed."

"Is ya killin' me next, b'y?"

Buff held his tongue for a moment. In many ways, the betrayal he felt was so strong that he really did want to kill his old friend. However, he knew he would never actually go through with it. There was simply too much history between them. He was also way, way too exhausted and bruised to survive another vicious brawl.

"I was considering it," he said gravely, "but no. I'm walking out the front door, and I'm going to put as much distance between myself and this place as I can. But before I do, I want to know why you did what you did."

"What do ya mean, me cocky?"

"You know what I mean, you old bastard. Why did you stab me in the back? Why did you throw away the thirteen years we've known each other?"

"That's a bit overdramatic there, b'y."

"You tried to kill me, Marcus. I think I'm being the perfect amount of dramatic."

The old man sighed loudly.

"It weren't nothing personal, me son," he said, apologetic. "This was pure business. This was my chance to finally get some regular work, to make a name for meself with a group of real professionals. I'm living in a van, me son! I is as broke as a head with nare tooth, b'y! I'm gutfoundered, Buff me chum. All in, and then some. Maybe you want to break free of the crime life, but she's all I got, b'y."

"I'm not an idiot," Buff said, defiantly. "This wasn't about business. You hate the French and you hate the mob. You wouldn't talk to Jacques if his voice made your dick longer. This was absolutely personal. I saw that look in your eyes. You wanted to kill me."

"Ya let me down, me son," the old man admitted, his anger clearly building. "I just could not trust ya no more. Ya told me we was in this together, b'y, and then ya go and make all these other plans behind me back. Ya told me nothing! Nothing! I taught ya everything ya know, ya ungrateful, cracky bastard!" Marcus screamed the words until his voice cracked. He dropped his tone to a hoarse whisper and continued. "That hurt, b'y. Ya have not ever let me down before."

"Marcus, you could have just talked to me about it."

"That's a load of horseshit. Ya wouldn't listen to me, b'y. Ya would have just told me to 'relax' and then shut me down like ya always do. I tried, me son. I told ya many times that things weren't right. Ya weren't like this before ya went in, neither, b'y. Ya used to take the advice I gave ya. Ya changed. Ya did this to yar self."

Buff laughed derisively.

"Fine," he scoffed. "Whatever helps you sleep at night."

"Hey, ya can think what ya want, b'y. Ya were plenty keen to sell out me and the others for a chance at a regular life. Don't wag yar finger at me just because I was willing to do the same to have the life yar giving up."

The young man shook his head, disappointed. He regretted starting this conversation.

"I think you made a big mistake," he said.

"Well, b'y, that's too bad. I'm sorry ya see 'er that way."

Buff continued walking down the stairs, one agonizing step at a time. When he reached the sixth floor landing, he started feeling intense heat. It was rising up from beneath him in strong, fervent waves. The smell of acrid smoke wafted in the air.

He was halfway down the next flight when he saw the tips of bright glowing flames, dancing and swaying up all the way from the bottom floor. The blaze was destructively climbing up the stairs, chewing through whatever stood in its way, and it was growing. Any steps beyond the next landing were engulfed in fire.

Buff stood there helplessly, with his mouth hanging open in shock.

A literal wall of flames shot up beside the young man, blocking his path. He couldn't continue down the stairs. He was trapped.

The steps beneath him rumbled and heaved. He needed to get out of there, fast.

As he slunk back up the way he came, his thoughts turned back to Marcus. The old man likely knew nothing about the inferno raging beneath his feet. With the fire spreading, the old man had no hope of escaping the top floor unless he took action immediately.

A lot of opposing ideas swirled around inside Buff's head. He knew turning back and rescuing Marcus was the right thing to do, despite his misgivings and furious anger. However, he couldn't forget that the old man had tried to kill him once already. There was no guarantee he wouldn't turn around and try to finish what he started.

Buff got an idea. He picked the radio back up and held it to his face.

"Hey, old friend," he said calmly. "We both had a pretty rough night. Maybe said and did some things we're not proud of. Is there any chance we could just shake hands and put this whole thing behind us?"

"Ya serious there, me cocky?" Marcus replied, laughing. "Lard t'underin'! I think that ship has sailed, b'y. Ya had yar chance and ya blew it. Jacques was pretty adamant that he did not want ya coming back alive, chum."

"Really, Marcus? You'd choose that old fart over me?"

"That's the way it is, me b'y."

Buff slumped his shoulders in disappointment. His old friend truly was gone.

"Goodbye Marcus," he said sincerely.

"Goodbye, Buff me ol' chum," the old man replied.

It was the last the two men would ever speak to each other.

With that, Buff flicked off his radio and tossed it over his shoulder. It smacked against the concrete steps, split into three pieces, and bounced off into the flames.

He trudged back up to sixth floor with a heavy heart, but didn't have time for reflection. He'd lament what happened to Marcus later.

Panting heavily and drenched in sweat, Buff's main concern at the moment was exactly how he was going to get out of the building. It seemed as though he'd inadvertently cornered himself when he asked Doug and Beka to electronically seal off all the exits. With the fire burning out of control, it was a very real possibility that Buff might not get out of this alive.

He reached for the door, laying his palm against it. It was still cool.

Leaning against it with his shoulder, he slammed through the door and staggered into the main hallway of the sixth floor.

Buff darted his head from side to side, looking desperately for the nearest window. He scurried through the accounting offices like a lost pet looking for its owner.

Finally, he spotted one at the far end of the hall and ran towards it.

It was an enormous pane of glass, five feet tall and over seven feet wide. Through it Buff could see out into the parking lot, which looked positively serene in the moonlight. Off in the distance, he saw flashing red and blue lights, and they were headed in his direction.

Immediately Buff grabbed a heavy wooden office chair, lifted it as high as he could and threw it against the window.

The chair bounced off and splintered into several pieces. It didn't even dent the glass. The window was made of structural laminated and tempered glass, almost an inch thick and able to withstand a tremendous deal of horizontal force without breaking.

Frustrated, Buff stomped his foot like a petulant child.

There had to be another way out. He tapped his forehead with his knuckles, racking his brain. He started pacing back and forth anxiously.

He stopped suddenly and snapped his fingers.

Reaching into his pocket, he pulled out the M84 flashbang he'd been carrying around. It was the standard-issue stun grenade for the United States Army. Just over five inches long, the device contained a magnesium-based charge inside a perforated steel body. When detonated, the outer casing absorbs most of the blast, emitting only a blinding flash and a bang that's louder than a jet engine.

Buff placed it in front of the window, hoping the explosion would be concussive enough to blow it out. He pulled the pin and ran away, diving behind a cubicle wall.

He shut his eyes and stuck his fingers in his ears.

*Ka-boom!!*

It was like being inside a lightning strike. The stun grenade made a pounding, thunderous clap that violently shook the walls. It was a quick, eruptive pop, but it sounded as loud as an ocean liner crashing into a mountain. It was matched with a sharp, piercing blast of luminescence as bright as a dozen lighthouses. The room suddenly smelled like a burning tire. Tiny shards of shattered glass sprayed out across the room. Dirt and loose papers were kicked up.

After a few moments, the dust settled and the air cleared. The office window had been replaced by a massive, gaping hole. A warm breeze wafted in through it.

Buff tried to stand, but felt confused and disoriented. The flashbang had been a little too effective.

Lumbering from side to side like a drunken sailor, he shuffled over to the smashed window. His ears were still ringing.

He put his hands down on the windowsill and stuck out his head. The calm night air helped steady him, clearing his head and soothing his nausea. At least, until he looked down.

Six storeys don't seem like much, but it was enough to make Buff's knees weak and his palms sweaty. He wasn't really afraid of heights, but he was afraid of falling, breaking half the bones in his body and dying of internal hemorrhaging. Not to mention the flames he saw shooting out the windows of the first three floors.

He didn't have any other choice. He was just going to have to be careful. That window was his only way out, and considering how much smoke he could smell, he needed to hurry.

Buff went back to frantically scurrying around the office, except this time he was ripping open closet doors, looking for some kind of rope. He found tins of instant coffee, boxes of stationery supplies, old umbrellas, small appliances, and lots of other useless junk.

He almost gave up hope until he found a small spool of computer cable tucked under a desk. There were no markings to indicate how long it was, but it looked to be at least a hundred feet. Not that it mattered. Buff had no choice. It was all he could find, so he would have to make it work.

He scooped up the cables and carried them over to the window.

Taking the free end in one hand, he tied it to the leg of the heavy wooden desk as tightly as he could. Considering his life depended on this cable holding, he tied another two knots into it, and then tugged on the other end, making sure it was secure.

Buff threw the rest of the spool out the window. It clattered against the side of the building as it fell.

Holding the dangling cable in his hands, he proceeded to carefully thread it around both thighs. That way it would squeeze taut if he lost his grip, and hopefully he wouldn't fall to his death.

One thought kept repeating itself in Buff's mind: this is a bad idea.

He took a deep breath and said a silent prayer. It was now or never.

Buff climbed out the window and over the ledge. Hanging six storeys up from the side of the building, he had serious regrets about taking this job. There were hundreds of ways it could have played out, but never had Buff considered he might close out the night by dangling from a tiny plastic cable above a raging inferno.

Don't look down, he thought.

He slowly shimmied to the bottom. It was an arduous, painful process that took its physical toll. The cable was digging into his skin. It had sliced up his palms and bruised his inner thighs. His back ached like never before.

As he inched his way down, it was becoming clear to him that the cable was too short.

He reached the end of it, but was still suspended over twenty feet above the ground. There was no way he'd be able to climb back up, and his sweaty hands were losing their grip on the cable. There were flames right beneath him and rising quickly, licking the bottom of his feet and searing his calves. He felt like a marshmallow roasting above a campfire.

Exhausted, Buff decided to give in to gravity and go the only direction he could - down. He closed his eyes, let go of the cable and dropped into the fire, screaming.

He landed on his side with a hard thud, and kept rolling to diffuse the impact.

His body crunched and his muscles snapped. The pain was as strong as it was severe. It instantly took hold of Buff's entire body, like the poison from a venomous snake. He could barely breathe, his vision was fading, and he was pretty sure he'd broken a few bones.

Enormous, roaring walls of flame towered around him. It

encroached on him immediately, igniting his clothes and burning his skin.

Buff fought to stay alive. His body's defences kicked in, and a huge surge of adrenaline shot through his veins.

Seconds later, he jumped up off the ground like a runner after the starter's pistol goes off. He hobbled urgently through the blaze, moving fast. Every step felt like wading through a pit of hot coals, but he resisted the pain and ran towards the parking lot.

Buff collapsed on the hood of Harry's beloved BMW M5, groaning and gasping. He was coughing like a sixty-year smoker. His mouth and nose were bleeding profusely. His skin was blistered and sensitive to the touch. His hair was singed. At that moment, he wanted nothing more than to roll over and die.

The sirens in the distance were getting closer. It sounded like there were a hundred police cars approaching.

Buff slapped the side of his face, shocking himself back to alertness.

He fished into his pocket and found Harry's keys. They felt like iron barbs on his scorched hands.

Struggling, he forced them into the car door and unlocked it.

Buff climbed in, woozy and shaken. His eyelids felt as though they weighed a thousand pounds. His head started to droop...

He smacked himself again, harder than last time. He had to stay conscious.

Buff threw the key into the ignition. The engine let out a thunderous roar as it screamed to life.

The shiny red car tore out of the parking lot at warp speed.

Buff glanced up into the rearview mirror and saw the law office engulfed in flames. It was a hellish sight. A row of six emergency vehicles crested up over the hill behind him and sped towards the blaze.

He put the gas pedal to the floor and didn't look back.

***

Back on the top floor, Marcus was collecting the last of the paperwork in the vault. He wouldn't be able to get a dime from Jacques without them. There were reams and reams of sheets, enough to fill two hefty bankers boxes. The old man would need to use both arms to carry them downstairs. He wished those damned lawyers had put their giant vault in the basement.

Marcus carted the heavy boxes down the hallway.

When he got to the stairwell door, he realized he was going to have to move the furniture Buff had piled up in front of it. His back was already sore.

He resigned himself to more heavy lifting. The old man put the boxes aside and began by pulling down the leather chairs.

That's when he noticed the room was getting hotter.

Figuring he was just overworked, Marcus ignored it. He wiped the sweat from his forehead and pushed the couch away from the door.

He reached for the doorknob. It was warm to the touch.

The old man flinched.

This can't be good, he thought.

He opened the door, curious but cautious.

On the other side, Marcus was met with a wall of torrid, glowing, roaring flames. It was aggressively charging up through the emergency stairs like an invading army.

He jumped back. He was trapped.

Panicked, he retraced his steps, rushing back to the vault. He grabbed the crow bar off the ground, and then doubled back into the hallway and around the corner.

There was another door that led to another maintenance stairwell. Marcus knew that Doug and Beka had electronically sealed off these exits, but he hoped to be able to force his way through. He thrust the crowbar into the doorframe and pushed against it.

It didn't work. The door wheezed and buckled, but refused to pop open.

Black smoke began filling the hallway, seeping up through the air vents. Marcus could feel the temperature rising steadily.

Suddenly, a flash of fire darted up from under a door and caught one of the framed paintings. It burst into hot flames and snaked upwards. Within seconds, the entire wall was ablaze.

Marcus dropped the crowbar and ran.

Above him, the fire spread across the ceiling like milk from an overturned pitcher. It was consuming the building at a staggering rate.

The old man looked up.

"Lard t'underin'," he said to himself. "I is tits up in the rhubarb."

Fire overtook the roof, and it caved in on top of Marcus. He was instantly crushed under a pile of molten plastic, burning wood, and jagged chunks of concrete.

# July 2

Buff had driven for several hours, headed north. He had no predetermined destination; he just wanted to put as much space between himself and Toronto as he could. Once outside the city, he stuck to the side roads, driving past sleepy farms and untended woodland. He didn't speed, drive recklessly, or anything else that would attract attention. It was bad enough he was in such a flashy car.

It was a constant struggle to remain conscious. Every part of him ached. He'd broken several bones and lost a lot of blood.

Shortly after midnight, he simply couldn't drive anymore. He found a secluded park and pulled into it, hiding the BMW behind a large, leafy bush. Wounded and sweaty, Buff turned the car off, slid his chair back and fell asleep.

He awoke a few hours later, as the sun rose over the surrounding trees. The rest had done very little to heal his broken body. It was just as sore as it had been the night before.

He continued to ignore it. He still had work to do.

Buff drove down the road until he found a closed roadside diner with a pay phone in the parking lot. The red sports car skidded to a halt beside it. Buff jumped out, climbed into the phone booth and called up his contact at the FBI.

It started ringing. The handset trembled as Buff's arm shook uncontrollably.

"Agent Johnson's office," a familiar man's voice answered. "How may I help you?"

"I'd like to speak to Ronald Johnson, please," Buff said.

"This is he. Who is this?"

"It's Buff."

"Buff?!" he screamed, exploding in rage. "Goddammit, where are you?"

"I'd rather not say."

"You stupid son of a bitch! You've got some balls calling me after the shit you pulled last night! When you fuck up, you fuck up big. Do you have any idea how big you fucked up last night? Really big, Buff. It's bad. You just knocked up the ugliest girl in town."

"It wasn't my fault!" Buff protested. "It was my partner. I was double-crossed."

"A double-cross? Who are you, James Cagney? A good man died last night. A man you were contracted to protect. And yet you made it out and he didn't. If anyone was double-crossed, Buff, I'd say it was me."

"Hey, the only reason I was there at all was because of you, asshole. A lot of good men died last night, not just your agent. I tried to save him. I didn't want anyone to die. There was this lawyer in the building who thought he was Chuck Norris..."

"What?" the agent interrupted. "Who the hell is Chuck Norris?"

"You can't be serious," Buff scoffed, incredulous. "You really don't know who Chuck Norris is?"

"I don't care who Chuck Norris is! I don't want to hear any more excuses, Buff. You fucked up, and you've got one chance to redeem yourself. Tell me my officer didn't die for nothing. Tell me you recovered some of that paperwork. Tell me you brought back some shred of evidence."

Buff sighed loudly.

"Nope," he said, defeated.

"Nothing? You came back with nothing?"

"Hey, you don't understand..."

"Oh, I understand, alright. I understand that a year-long investigation got flushed down the toilet, one of my best was killed, and all the evidence went up in flames. It's also my understanding that this is entirely your fault."

"I barely got out of there alive!"

There was a pause. Agent Johnson didn't want to talk to him anymore. As far as he was concerned, Buff was working for the Montagne family.

"Why are you even calling me?" he asked, exasperated.

"I wanted to talk about getting paid..."

"Money!?" The agent was screaming so loud his voice was distorting through the telephone receiver. "You audacious son of a bitch! You're not getting a single damn dime, you bastard! You are going to jail for murdering a federal officer! If you hadn't left such a mess here, I'd be hunting you down myself, right now!"

Buff hung up the phone.

He went back to his car, sat in the driver's seat and sulked for a long time. It seemed as though he'd blown his one shot at redemption, and would never have a "normal" life. He was branded a criminal, again. Everything he'd worked so hard for over the past week was gone forever.

***

Being a coroner is a tough job, especially in a city as large as Toronto. The hours are long, the pay is small, and the work isn't just challenging, it's often unsettling. They play a crucial role in police forensics, and yet most feel unappreciated by cops.

Mainly, though, they hate having their lunch interrupted.

Dr. Scully was the chief coroner for the city, and she was in the midst of an unexpectedly frantic day. Seven bodies were recovered in the early morning hours from the massive blaze at the law offices of Bennett, Olsen, Nygärd, Jørgensen, and Holm. They all needed to be identified as soon as possible, so she came in before dawn to start the autopsies. She'd spent the morning cleaning and examining the corpses, looking for tattoos or birthmarks, as well as taking blood samples and dental impressions. It took hours.

When she finally got a break, she sat down to enjoy a delicious smoked-beef sandwich. She'd barely chewed her first bite when five uniformed police officers stormed into her office. They surrounded her, shouting questions like reporters in a media scrum.

"One at a time, please," Dr. Scully said quietly, putting down her sandwich.

She could tell immediately from their uniforms that these officers weren't all from the same department. Two of them were from the narcotics squad, and another was a member of the Guns and Gangs division. One of them was even from the provincial police.

"Are you sure you brought enough cops?" she joked.

They didn't laugh.

The tall man who'd led the officers in stepped forward, waving the others back. He was the sergeant in charge of the investigation into the fire at the law office. He explained that it was now a criminal case, and that they suspected the bodies recovered belonged to men who had been trying to rob the firm. He asked if they could see them.

She led them all into the morgue. The room was cold and lifeless, constructed of cold steel, and refrigerated to keep the cadavers from decomposing. It had a sterile, chemical smell like a hospital operating room. A series of fifteen cold chambers were stacked along one wall. Seven of them were open with the trays slid all the way out. On each tray rested a severely charred corpse in a body bag.

They looked like chicken that had been left on the barbeque too long. Their faces were twisted and unrecognizable. The skin had shriveled up and blackened, all hair had been singed off, and some of their extremities had burned away to ash. It was a gruesome scene, but Dr. Scully treated it as casually as a mechanic would a disassembled motor.

"They were all badly burned in the fire," she said, "which has made it difficult to obtain a positive identification. Fingerprinting is impossible. I took some teeth impressions, but I'm still waiting to hear back on dental records. The only person I've been able to identify with any certainty is this man."

She walked over to the body on the far table and glanced at the toe tag.

"His name is Harry Bockner, age fifty-seven."

"He was lawyer at the firm," the sergeant explained.

"Jesus Christ," one of the narcotics cops said with disgust, looking over the body as though it were a sideshow attraction. "What a mess. It looks like someone tore through him with a chainsaw."

"It's worse than you think," Dr. Scully replied, opening the body bag further. "See these lacerations along the arm? That's where I pulled out two carpenter's nails. There were a few embedded in his leg, too. Whatever happened, it was vicious. Someone went medieval on this man."

"I think it's safe to assume he was a hostage," the sergeant said.

"Not necessarily," the coroner argued, pointing to open wounds on Harry's seared hands. "Look at these marks on the knuckles. See how the skin folds backwards? That indicates forward thrust and impact. These are not defensive scars."

"He could be working with them, sir," theorized the officer from the gang unit. "This could be an inside job."

"I appreciate the enthusiasm, gentlemen," the sergeant stated with authority, "but with all due respect, let's keep the speculation to a minimum. We've got a team of our best men on the case, and I'm confident in their diligence. You were brought in to identify the bodies only."

The other cops grumbled their submission.

The sergeant turned back to the coroner.

"What about the rest of them?" he asked her.

"Those two are definitely related," she replied, pointing to the bodies of the Fodder brothers. "The blood tests were conclusive. There was massive head trauma on the first body. The second has multiple puncture wounds through the lungs and heart."

The sergeant pulled the provincial police officer closer.

"It has to be them," he said.

The officer bent down and examined both corpses closely. They were so mangled and scorched that he could barely discern whether the remains were even human.

After a cursory inspection, he looked unconvinced.

"It can't be them, sir," he said, shaking his head. "I've been following these knuckleheads for months now. They never leave that farm, sir. They're growers. They're hillbillies. This wasn't their work. They're not the type to break into vaults. They couldn't break into a cold sweat."

"Did you not hear what I just said about conjecture?" the sergeant said tersely. "We don't have time! Officer, can you identify these two men as Kane and Dwayne Fodder?"

"I'm sorry, sir, but I can't. They're too burnt up, and I don't think it's them."

The sergeant gritted his teeth.

"Where are you from, anyway?" one of the gang unit cops asked.

"Wellington County," the officer said.

"You guys get a lot of big cases out that way?" one of the narcotics cop snickered.

The other men chuckled derisively. The OPP officer looked hurt.

"Settle down, boys," Dr. Scully said. "We're all on the same team here."

"What about him?" the sergeant asked, pointing to N-Dig's body.

The coroner looked back down at her notes.

"He has massive trauma to the head and shoulders," she said, "consistent with a fall from a great height. It's pretty safe to say that was the cause of death, but look at this." She pointed to the body's shoulder. "There's a bullet wound right here. A fresh one, too. Someone obviously tried to clean and treat it, but it appears as though the cartridge is still embedded in the tissue."

The two cops from the drug squad stood over the body. They barely glanced at it, but had no doubt that it was the man they were looking for.

"That's him," one of the said. "That's definitely him."

"We've been trailing this guy for weeks," added the other. "Staking out the pizza place where he works. He goes by the street-name 'N-Dig'."

"Can you connect him to the Fodders?" the sergeant asked.

"Those two bodies do not belong to the Fodders," the OPP officer shouted. “Listen to me, I know these guys. I just saw them on their farm the other day!”

“You’re sure about that?”

“Absolutely. This kind of job was way out of their league.”

The sergeant sighed loudly, and then walked over to Big Frank’s body.

“What about this guy?”

“Smashed skull,” the coroner began, reading from her notes, “some blunt force trauma, as well as impact wounds on the face, neck, and chest. It looks like the impact was the cause of death, but there is one thing I haven’t been able to explain. His eardrums are ruptured. It could be caused by standing too close to the explosion that sparked the fire, maybe? I’m not sure yet.”

The officer from the Guns and Gangs unit examined Big Frank’s body closely.

“Is it him?” the sergeant asked.

“Tough to say,” the cop replied. “It doesn’t really look like him, but he’s built just as big. I have to tell you, though, I know for a fact the guy I’m looking for would never work with a two-bit gang-banger like this Dig-Dug idiot...”

“N-Dig,” the drug squad cop corrected him.

“Whatever,” he continued. “He wouldn’t be seen with him or two small-time dope peddlers like the Fodders.” He turned and looked to the provincial officer. “No offence.”

“Hey, none taken,” he replied. “Those two bodies do not belong to the Fodders.”

The sergeant ignored him, turning to the coroner and pointing to the last two bodies. They belonged to Marcus and Doug.

“What about them?” he asked.

“I’ve got more questions than answers regarding these two,” she said, walking over to the old man’s corpse. “I haven’t been able to determine a cause of death on this one. Blunt force trauma to the head, crushed vertebrae along the neck, and lungs that suggest he suffered serious smoke inhalation. I can’t be exactly sure what killed him. Otherwise, no distinguishing marks, but early blood tests show he’s in his fifties or sixties.”

“Probably a hostage,” the sergeant mused.

The coroner moved over to Doug’s body.

“I haven’t had a chance to do a thorough examination on this body yet,” she said, “but the probable cause of death was the deep, severe laceration to his face and neck. There’s probably some blunt force trauma there, too.”

“Any leads on who either of these two might be?”

"Not yet, but it looks like this young man had tattoos on his arms. Once we reconstruct those it should make finding out who he is easier."

"So, can we get a positive ID on any of these guys? As soon as we can identify one, we can piece together who the others are."

"Oh, that's definitely N-Dig," one of the drug squad cops said assuredly.

"If it is, then that's definitely not Big Frank," the Guns and Gangs officer said.

"Those aren't the Fodder brothers, either," said the OPP officer, confidently crossing his arms.

All of the police officers continued to argue loudly. The sergeant in charge tried to take command, but everyone kept shouting over each other. They all had a different theory on how the big heist went down, and how everyone was killed. They jabbered on like politicians on an unproductive day in the House of Commons.

Dr. Scully rubbed her forehead. She couldn't take it anymore.

"If you need anything else from me," she said, walking out of the morgue, "I'll be in my office finishing my sandwich."

***

It was a busy day at Pearson International Airport. As the largest airport in Canada, it was always bustling, but during the summer's first long weekend, things got especially hectic. With children fresh out of school, thousands of families chose this time to start their vacation.

The airport's main terminal was the most congested. Reserved for domestic flights, it was as crowded as the parking lot outside the Super Bowl.

Beka was among the horde, waiting at the end of a very long, winding line. She was almost unrecognizable. She'd quickly dyed her hair black, and wore the plainest, most modest outfit she owned.

In her hand she held a one-way ticket to Vancouver. She had a few friends out west, and figured it would be a good place to lay low for a few months. Maybe she would find an apartment and live there permanently. Beka didn't really have a firm plan in place, but was determined to leave Toronto as quickly as possible.

Despite her worries, she had no problems getting through security and her plane left as scheduled. Police were never going to be able to link her to the attempted heist at the law firm.

Coincidentally, Donald Thorp - the security guard at the law firm that the team paid off -- was at the airport at the exact same time, although he was in the terminal for international flights. With no luggage and only a small carry-on bag, he had a one-way ticket bound for Jamaica. He had a younger brother who lived down there, and had arranged to stay with him for a while.

His brother had a good job at a small bank branch in Montego Bay, servicing international accounts. One of his biggest clients happened to be a Canadian lawyer by the name of Harry Bockner.

Together the Thorp brothers would be able to drain a significant amount from Harry's account without raising suspicions. They would split the profits amongst themselves equally, each walking away with over $80,000. It would be enough for them to each buy their own small place and retire on a peaceful, secluded beach.

As he boarded the plane, he flashed the flight attendant the biggest, happiest smile he'd ever worn in his life.

***

Surly Shirley sat in her trailer at the Ontario Food Terminal, thumbing through a thick stack of newspapers. They were all afternoon editions; the morning papers lay in tattered piles at her feet. In the background a police scanner chattered endlessly. She'd spent the morning listening to it, but was unable to cull much good information from the garbled transmissions.

She was looking for any information she could find on the heist, and what the police knew about it. The only articles she could find were vague and brief, hidden in tiny corners of the local news section. Most barely mentioned the robbery, and focused instead on the massive fire that took down the building. There was no comment from the building owner, and the police praised the valiant attempts of the brave firefighters, but said little else.

This could only mean one thing. The cops were puffing up the role of the first responders to distract from their own failures. The building couldn't be saved, all the suspects died, and they didn't have a clue what actually happened in that building. They couldn't even ascertain who was a thief, who was a hostage, who inflicted the carnage, and what – if anything – they were trying to steal. There were too many loose threads to string together after the fact, and Shirley knew from experience that the case would quickly go cold.

She stretched and yawned loudly, exhausted. She hadn't slept in almost thirty-six hours. After leaving the law office, she spent the night diligently covering her tracks by ditching the truck at a friendly auto-wrecking yard, and then having the tires shredded and burned so the treads could never be matched. There was nothing left for authorities to connect her to the crime.

I deserve a fucking vacation, she thought.

She flipped the newspaper to the travel section, and began perusing the airline ads. There was a sale on flights to France. It was supposed to be lovely there this time of year.

***

Later in the afternoon, Buff found himself inside a private office at the Canada Revenue Agency. It was drab, beige, and sparsely furnished, exactly the sort of thing you'd expect to find in a federal bureau that spared every expense.

Buff sat alone at a large wooden table. Clearly nervous, his palms were sweating and one of his legs was shaking uncontrollably. All of his instincts kept telling him to run, but he knew if he wanted to avoid jail, he had to stay. This was his last gamble, and it was a long shot.

Eventually a small, balding gentleman in a suit and tie came into the room carrying a notepad. He looked fastidious and conservative, the way most accountants do.

He held his hand out to Buff.

"Good afternoon, sir," the agent said. "I'm afraid I didn't catch your name."

"It's Buff," he replied, shaking the man's hand.

"I'm sorry. What's your name?"

"You know what? Never mind. It's not important. We can go over that later."

The agent raised a single eyebrow inquisitively, paused for a moment, and then sat down.

"My colleague outside said you wanted to speak with me," he said, pulling a blue pen from his pocket. "I'm a very busy man who usually insists on appointments, but apparently you were adamant that I needed to hear what you have to say. So, sir, let's hear it."

Buff cleared his throat.

"Do you like sports?" he asked, completely serious.

The agent was stunned, and a little irritated.

"Is this supposed to be a joke, sir?"

"No, it's not," Buff said sincerely. "Please, humour me. Do you know anything about sports?"

"I think it's Huey Lewis's best album."

"Funny. What about hockey? Have you ever been to a local junior game?"

The agent went from annoyed to infuriated. He put the pen back in his pocket, gathered his notepad and stood up.

"I don't have time for this nonsense," he said. "If you want somebody to talk to, call one of the phone numbers in the back of the classifieds."

As he went for the door, Buff grabbed him by the arm and pulled him closer.

"Wait," Buff pleaded. "This is important. Have you ever been to the Jean Béliveau Arena?"

The agent's eyes suddenly lit up. Buff noted the recognition and pounced on it.

"Good, it was you," he said, relieved. "I'm sorry for being so mysterious, but I had to make sure it was true that your agency was following Jacques Montagne and the French mob."

"I'm afraid I don't know what you're talking about, sir," the agent replied, guarded.

"Well, the FBI seems to think you've been watching him. They were pretty sure one of your agents was there when he offered me almost two-hundred grand to rob a law office. I came here on the small chance they were right."

"I'm not at liberty to discuss ongoing investigations."

"Are you at liberty to listen?"

The agent gave him a knowing smile and sat back down.

"I thought so," Buff said. "Look, I'm in a bit of a jam, and I need some help. If you like what you hear, maybe we can work out a deal."

"I can't promise anything," the agent said. He readied his pen and paper, and then looked to Buff expectantly. "Go ahead."

Buff looked at the notepad and scoffed.

"It's a lot," he said with a chuckle. "Your hand's going to get really cramped. I've got names, dates, and locations that go back years. You should probably get a camera. I think you'll want to record this."

# July 3

The raid happened just before dawn. Working under the direction of the Canada Revenue Agency, three heavily armed teams of local and provincial police officers swarmed the residence of Jacques Montagne. He was handcuffed and unceremoniously escorted into the back of a police cruiser wearing his slippers and silk pajamas. They arrested him and eight other members of the French-Canadian mob family, including Roche, and also gathered enough evidence to put the crime boss away for life. Organized crime, at least from the French-Canadian perspective, was effectively knocked out of business.

For his contribution to the investigation, Buff entered into the Federal Witness Protection Program. He was given personal security and a new identity, dependent on his testifying at trial. No charges were ever laid against him, and his previous criminal record was wiped clean, although he still had to regularly check-in with a parole officer.

Because the CRA considered the information he provided so significant, he was given preferential treatment in terms of compensation. Normally, budgets are calculated based on one's standard of living prior to entering the program, assuming they weren't living off the avails of crime. However, Buff was given a one-time payment of $6000, as well as a monthly stipend of $800 for as long as he stayed in the program. That was well above average.

He was wasting no time in putting that money to good use. His new bodyguard was under strict orders to get him out of the city, but Buff was able to convince him to make one brief stop first.

A shiny black Ford sedan pulled onto Mutual Street and found a parking spot. It was directly in front of the apartment building where Emily lived. The passenger door opened and Buff climbed out. His burly bodyguard, clad in a plain black suit, quickly followed him.

The young man tried waving his protector off. "It's okay," he said. "I'll only be a minute."

"I'm sorry, sir," the guard replied, gruffly, "but I'm not to leave your side until we reach our destination."

Buff groaned. "Fine," he grumbled. "Just be cool. Keep it clean, and don't get any ideas. She's my sister."

"I have no interest in your personal life, sir."

They walked up the front steps to the door. There was a small panel beside the entrance, which listed all the tenants in the building. Buff found his sister's name and pushed the corresponding button.

The panel buzzed loudly, and after a few moments, Emily's voice came through the scratchy speaker.

"Hello?" she said.

Buff swallowed hard. He had to choose his words carefully, or else his sister would dismiss him outright.

"Hey Emily," he said, hesitantly. "I think we need to talk. Can you spare a few minutes?"

His sister responded with an annoyed grunt. "You've got some balls coming back here," she grumbled. "There's nothing to talk about. I told you I didn't want to talk to you anymore."

"Please, Emily, it's important," he pleaded.

"Are you in trouble again?" she asked, accusatory. "Dammit, if you're looking for a place to hide out, I'll call the police myself..."

"No, no. It's nothing like that. Just give me two minutes, and I'll explain everything. After that, you'll never see me again, if that's what you want. I promise."

There was a long pause as she considered his words. As much as she wanted to deny him, he was family, and she couldn't turn her back on that fact. Part of her would always forgive him.

"Fine," she said, reluctantly, "but you're not coming upstairs. I'll be down there in a second."

Buff let out a sigh of relief. If she was willing to talk, that meant there was hope of salvaging the relationship.

The wait for her to get to the front door was interminable. When she finally arrived, she was wearing sweatpants, an oversized T-shirt, and pink slippers adorned with tiny bunny ears. Buff had obviously woken her up.

"Did I catch you on your day off?" he asked.

Emily shot him a sharp look. "My first one in a long time. Most of the world sleeps in when they get a day off work, Bryan. You'd know that if you tried living like a grown-up for more than a week." She gave the bodyguard a wary glance. "Who's this?"

The guard looked her up and down, and then nodded approvingly. Buff rolled his eyes and clucked his tongue.

"He's nobody," he replied. "Ignore him. Listen, Emily, I don't have a lot of time to explain..."

"I knew it! I knew you'd get yourself into trouble again."

She moved to shut the door, but Buff shoved his foot into the doorframe before she could close it all the way.

"No I didn't!" he shouted, pushing the door back open. He closed his eyes and took a second to regain his composure. He knew his sister had every reason to be suspicious. To get her to listen, he needed to calm down.

"I did the right thing, Emily," he continued, keeping his voice low. "I went to the police. I named names. I got bad people arrested, and I'm going to testify against them in court."

His sister stood there with an expressionless look on her face. Her eyebrows were arched, as though she were waiting for the rest of the story.

Buff persisted. "It's true. Did you read about all those Montagne crime family members getting hauled away to jail this morning?"

Emily shook her head, no.

"Oh." He was hurt a little, but tried not to show it. "Well, that was me. I did that."

He paused a moment, expecting more praise than he was getting. His sister just stared at him, a wave of doubt spreading across her face.

"I don't believe you," she said.

"It's true!" Buff was emphatic. "You can look it up! I'm not a criminal anymore, Emily. I'm the good guy!" He turned to his bodyguard and poked him. "Come on, buddy. Back me up here. Show her your badge."

The suited guard paused dramatically, shifting his gaze between the two siblings. He let out a sigh of defeat, and then reached into his pocket. He pulled out the leather wallet that housed his gold-plated CRA badge and handed it to Emily.

"It's true, ma'am," the guard said. "While I wouldn't downplay the role of the arresting officers, he did play an integral part in our investigation."

Emily looked over the guard's badge the way a jeweller examines an unfamiliar stone. It looked real enough, but she was still skeptical of her brother's intentions, and rightfully so. She handed it back with a shrug.

"That's nice," she said in a way that sounded condescending.

Buff chuckled wryly. He knew she wouldn't be easy to convince.

Not that it mattered. He didn't come here seeking adoration. He was trying to make amends.

He reached into his coat pocket and pulled out an unsealed white envelope. In it was exactly five grand in crisp, freshly printed hundred-dollar bills. He handed it to his sister and smiled.

"Hope this covers my share of the rent," he said.

Emily cocked her head, confused, and reluctantly took the envelope. "What's this?"

"It's for being the only one who believed in me," Buff said, sincerely. "No one else thought I was capable of making a change in my life. I'm sorry I couldn't tell you about this earlier, but I wasn't sure I was going to make it out in one piece."

His sister's eyes went as wide as dinner plates as she began to thumb through the cash. She was stunned. Her jaw dropped to her chest, but the only sound she made was a quizzical grunt.

"Is this legit?" she asked the bodyguard.

"Yes ma'am," he replied. "Just make sure you report the income on next year's taxes."

She was overjoyed, but worked hard not to show it. She didn't want to give her brother the satisfaction, at least not yet. Instead, she smiled politely and gave Buff a nod of thanks.

"You wouldn't believe what I had to go through to get that," he said.

"Why don't you guys come upstairs, have a cup of coffee and tell me all about it?" she offered.

"No," the guard interjected. "That is out of the question. We have a schedule to maintain, and we need to get going."

Buff looked at his sister and sighed. "One day, we'll sit down, and I'll tell you the whole story," he promised.

"Where are you going?" she asked.

Before Buff could answer, the bodyguard put his hand on the young man's chest to stop him.

"That's privileged information, ma'am," he said curtly.

Emily scoffed. "What are you, a secret agent?"

"I'm going into witness protection," Buff answered, flatly.

The guard hung his head. "You're not supposed to tell anyone that," he grumbled.

Astonished, Emily was at a loss for words. She brought her finger up, making a motion as though about to speak, but nothing came out.

Buff put a reassuring hand on her shoulder.

"I know, it sounds crazy, but it's for the best. I'm going up north.

Not too far from mom and dad's place, actually. I was thinking of giving them a call, and maybe offering to take them out to dinner."

Emily smiled. "I think that's a good idea."

She held out her arms, and the two siblings hugged for a long time.

The bodyguard eventually had to tear them apart, urging Buff to leave. The young man rushed through a goodbye as the guard pulled him back into the black sedan.

Emily stood at the door, tightly clutching the money in her hand. It was enough to cover almost five months rent. More than that, she'd noticed a change in her brother. It was something she noticed that first night he got out of prison, but hadn't reappeared until today - humility and guilt. She wasn't ready to say he'd completely reformed, but she was happy to admit there was hope he could.

The car pulled away, drove down the street and disappeared into traffic. She hoped she'd see her brother again soon.

www.ingramcontent.com/pod-product-compliance
Lightning Source LLC
Chambersburg PA
CBHW071136260626
47162CB00003B/815

* 9 7 8 0 9 9 1 9 0 8 7 2 1 *